THE SWISS FAMILY ROBINSON
BY JOHANN DAVID WYSS

JOHANN DAVID WYSS (1781–1830). Philosopher, pastor and educationalist, Wyss is now remembered only for his children's book, whose fame obscures his own.

Little is known about the author's life but he was born in Berne in Switzerland in 1781 and, after schooling, attended various German universities. When he was twenty-five, he was appointed Professor of Philosophy at the Academy of Berne. He was also Librarian in Chief and held both these posts until his death. His other books include *Du Souverain Bien*, a two-volume work of moral philosophy published in Germany in 1811, and three collections of Swiss folk tales. He died in Berne in 1830.

The Swiss Family Robinson was inspired by Defoe's *Robinson Crusoe* (1719). Wyss's father, impressed by Defoe's mixture of adventure, Protestant morality and natural history, suggested that Johann update the island adventure and apply it to the survival of a family. The result was written in German and first published in two parts in Zurich in the years 1812–13. There were more than twenty French editions in the following years; the first English translation appeared in 1814. The book was to be more popular in English and French than in its original language. Successive editors tended to alter the text radically, omitting some of the repetitive moralizing and gradually updating much of the information concerning the natural history of the castaway's island. In such forms the story has remained popular with parents and children alike for nearly two hundred years.

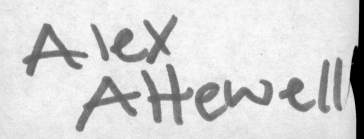

PENGUIN POPULAR CLASSICS

THE SWISS
FAMILY ROBINSON

J. D. WYSS

PENGUIN BOOKS
A PENGUIN/GODFREY CAVE EDITION

PENGUIN BOOKS

Published by the Penguin Group
Penguin Books Ltd, 27 Wrights Lane, London w8 5tz, England
Penguin Books USA Inc., 375 Hudson Street, New York, New York 10014, USA
Penguin Books Australia Ltd, Ringwood, Victoria, Australia
Penguin Books Canada Ltd, 10 Alcorn Avenue, Toronto, Ontario, Canada m4v 3b2
Penguin Books (NZ) Ltd, 182–190 Wairau Road, Auckland 10, New Zealand

Penguin Books Ltd, Registered Offices: Harmondsworth, Middlesex, England

First published 1812–13
Published in Penguin Popular Classics 1994
1 3 5 7 9 10 8 6 4 2

Printed in England by Clays Ltd, St Ives plc

Except in the United States of America, this book is sold subject
to the condition that it shall not, by way of trade or otherwise, be lent,
re-sold, hired out, or otherwise circulated without the publisher's
prior consent in any form of binding or cover other than that in
which it is published and without a similar condition including this
condition being imposed on the subsequent purchaser

CONTENTS

5

CHAPTER I

A Shipwreck, and Preparations for Deliverance

ALREADY the tempest had continued six days; on the seventh its fury seemed still increasing; and the morning dawned upon us without a prospect of hope, for we had wandered so far from the right track, and were so forcibly driven toward the southeast, that none on board knew where we were. The ship's company were exhausted by labour and watching, and the courage which had sustained them was now sinking. The shivered masts had been cast into the sea; several leaks appeared, and the ship began to fill. The sailors forbore from swearing; many were at prayer on their knees; while others offered miracles of future piety and goodness, as the condition of their release from danger. "My beloved children," said I to my four boys, who clung to me in their fright, "God can save us, for nothing is impossible to Him. We must however hold ourselves resigned, and, instead of murmuring at His decree, rely that what He sees fit to do is best, and that should He call us from this earthly scene, we shall be near Him in heaven, and united through eternity. Death may be well supported when it does not separate those who love."

My excellent wife wiped the tears which were falling on her cheeks, and from this moment became more tranquil: she encouraged the youngest children who were leaning on her knees; while I, who owed them an example of firmness, was scarcely able to resist my grief at the thought of what would most likely be the fate of beings so tenderly beloved. We all fell on our knees, and supplicated the God of Mercy to protect us; and the emotion and fervour of the innocent creatures are a convincing proof that even in childhood devotion may be felt and understood, and that tranquillity and consolation, its natural effects, may at that season be no less certainly experienced. Fritz, my eldest son, implored, in a loud voice, that God would deign to save his dear parents and his brothers, generously unmindful of himself: the boys rose from their posture with a state of mind so improved that they seemed forgetful of the impending danger. I myself began to feel my hopes increase, as I beheld the affecting group. Heaven will surely have pity on them, thought I, and will save their parents to guard their tender years!

At this moment a cry of "Land, land!" was heard through the roaring of the waves, and instantly the vessel struck against a rock with so violent a motion as to drive every one from his place; a tremendous cracking succeeded, as if the ship were going to pieces; the sea rushed in, in all directions; we perceived that the vessel had grounded, and could not long hold together. The captain called out that all was lost, and bade the men lose not a moment in putting out the boats. The sounds fell on my heart like a thrust from a dagger: "We are lost!" I exclaimed, and the children broke out into piercing cries. I then recollected myself, and, addressing them again, exhorted them to courage, by observing that the water had not yet reached us, that the ship was near land, and that Providence would assist the brave. "Keep where you are," added I, "while I go and examine what is best to be done."

I now went on the deck. A wave instantly threw me down, and wetted me to the skin; another followed, and then another. I sustained myself as steadily as I could; and looking around, a scene of terrific and complete disaster met my eyes: the ship was shattered in all directions, and on one side there was a complete breach. The ship's company crowded into the boats till they could contain not one man more, and the last who entered were now cutting the ropes to move off. I called to them with almost frantic entreaties to stop and receive us also, but in vain; for the roaring of the sea prevented my being heard, and the waves, which rose to the height of mountains, would have made it impossible to return. All hope from this source was over, for, while I spoke, the boats, and all they contained, were driving out of sight. My best consolation now was to observe that the slanting position the ship had taken would afford us present protection from the water; and that the stern, under which was the cabin that enclosed all that was dear to me on earth, had been driven upwards between two rocks, and seemed immovably fixed. At the same time, in the distance southward, I descried through clouds and rain, several nooks of land, which, though rude and savage in appearance, were the objects of every hope I could form in this distressing moment.

Sunk and desolate from the loss of all chance of human aid, it was yet my duty to appear serene before my family: "Courage, dear ones," cried I on entering their cabin, "let us not desert ourselves: I will not conceal from you that the ship is aground; but we are at least in greater safety than if she were beating upon the rocks; our cabin is above water; and should the sea be more calm to-morrow, we may yet find means to reach the land in safety."

What I had just said appeased their fears; for my family had the habit of confiding in my assurances. They now began to feel the advantage of the ship's remaining still; for its motion had been most distressing, by jostling them one against another, or whatever happened to be nearest. My wife, however, more accustomed than the children to read my inmost thoughts, perceived the anxiety which devoured me. I made her a sign which conveyed an idea of the hopelessness of our situation; and I had the consolation to see that she was resolved to support the trial with resignation. "Let us take some nourishment," said she; "our courage will strengthen with our bodies; we shall perhaps need this comfort to support a long and melancholy night."

Soon after night set in; the fury of the tempest had not abated; the planks and beams of the vessel separated in many parts with a horrible crash. We thought of the boats, and feared that all they contained must have sunk under the foaming surge.

My wife had prepared a slender meal, and the four boys partook of it with an appetite to which their parents were strangers. They went to bed, and, exhausted by fatigue, soon were snoring soundly. Fritz, the eldest, sat up with us. "I have been thinking," said he, after a long silence, "how it may be possible to save ourselves. If we had some bladders

or cork-jackets for my mother and my brothers, you and I,
father, would soon contrive to swim to land."

"That is a good thought," said I; "we will see what can be
done."

Fritz and I looked about for some small empty firkins;
these we tied two and two together with handkerchiefs or
towels, leaving about a foot distance between them, and
fastened them as swimming-jackets under the arms of each
child, my wife at the same time preparing one for herself.
We provided ourselves with knives, some string, some turfs,
and other necessaries which could be put into the pocket,
proceeding upon the hope, that if the ship went to pieces in
the night, we should either be able to swim to land, or be
driven thither by the waves.

Fritz, who had been up all night, and was fatigued with
his laborious occupations, now lay down near his brothers,
and was soon asleep; but their mother and I, too anxious to
close our eyes, kept watch, listening to every sound that
seemed to threaten a further change in our situation. We
passed this awful night in prayer, in agonizing apprehensions, and in forming various resolutions as to what we
should next attempt. We hailed with joy the first gleam of
light which shot through a small opening of the window. The
raging of the winds had begun to abate, the sky was become
serene, and hope throbbed in my bosom, as I beheld the sun
already tinging the horizon. Thus revived, I summoned my
wife and the boys to the deck to partake of the scene. The
youngest children, half forgetful of the past, asked with
surprise, why we were there alone, and what had become of
the ship's company? I led them to the recollection of our
misfortune, and then added, "Dearest children, a Being
more powerful than man has helped us, and will, no doubt,
continue to help us, if we do not abandon ourselves to a
fruitless despair. Observe, our companions, in whom we
had so much confidence, have deserted us, and that Divine
Providence, in its goodness, has given us protection! But,
my dear ones, let us show ourselves willing in our exertions,
and thus deserve support from heaven. Let us not forget this
useful maxim, and let each labour according to his strength."

Fritz advised that we should all throw ourselves into the
sea, while it was calm, and swim to land.—"Ah! that may
be well enough for you," said Ernest, "for you can swim;

but we others should soon be drowned. Would it not be better to make a float of rafts, and get to land all together upon it?"

"Vastly well," answered I, "if we had the means for contriving such a float, and if, after all, it were not a dangerous sort of conveyance. But come, my boys, look each of you about the ship, and see what can be done to enable us to reach the land."

They now all sprang from me with eager looks, to do as I desired. I, on my part, lost no time in examining what we had to depend upon as to provisions and fresh water. My wife and the youngest boy visited the animals, whom they found in a pitiable condition, nearly perishing with hunger and thirst. Fritz repaired to the ammunition room; Ernest to the carpenter's cabin; Jack to the apartment of the captain; but scarcely had he opened the door, when two large dogs sprang upon him, and saluted him with such rude affection that he roared for assistance, as if they had been killing him. Hunger, however, had rendered the poor creatures so gentle that they licked his hands and face, uttering all the time a low sort of moan, and continuing their caresses till he was almost suffocated. Poor Jack exerted all his strength in blows to drive them away: at last he began to understand, and to sympathize in their joyful movements, and put himself upon another footing. He got upon his legs, and gently taking the largest dog by the ears, sprang upon his back, and with great gravity presented himself thus mounted before me, as I came out of the ship's hold. I could not refrain from laughing, and I praised his courage; but I added a little exhortation to be cautious, and not go too far with animals of this species, who, in a state of hunger, might be dangerous.

By and by my little company were again assembled round me, and each boasted of what he had to contribute. Fritz had two fowling-pieces, some powder and small-shot, contained in horn flasks, and some bullets in bags.

Ernest produced his hat filled with nails, and held in his hands a hatchet and a hammer; in addition, a pair of pincers, a pair of large scissors, and an auger, peeped out at his pocket-hole.

Even the little Francis carried under his arm a box of no very small size, from which he eagerly produced what he called some little sharp-pointed hooks. His brothers smiled scornfully. "Vastly well, gentlemen," said I; "but let me tell you that the youngest has brought the most valuable prize, and this is often the case in the world; the person who least courts the smiles of Fortune, and in the calm of his heart is scarcely conscious of her existence, is often he to whom she most readily presents herself. These little sharp-pointed hooks, as Francis calls them, are fishing-hooks, and will probably be of more use in preserving our lives than all we may find besides in the ship. In justice, however, I must confess, that what Fritz and Ernest have contributed will also afford essential service."

"I, for my part," said my wife, "have brought nothing; but I have some tidings to communicate which I hope will secure my welcome: I have found on board a cow and an ass, two goats, six sheep, and a sow big with young: I have just supplied them with food and water, and I reckon on being able to preserve their lives."

"All this is admirable," said I to my young labourers; "and there is only master Jack, who, instead of thinking of something useful, has done us the favour to present us two personages, who, no doubt, will be principally distinguished by being willing to eat more than we shall have to give them."

"Ah!" replied Jack, "but if we can once get to land, you will see that they will assist us in hunting and shooting."

"True enough," said I, "but be so good as to tell us how we are to get to land, and whether you have contrived the means?"

"I am sure it cannot be very difficult," said Jack, with an arch motion of his head. "Look here at these large tubs. Why cannot each of us get into one of them, and float to the land? I remember I succeeded very well in this manner on the water, when I was visiting my godfather at S——"

"Every one's thought is good for something," cried I, "and I begin to believe that what Jack has suggested is worth a trial: quick, then, boy! give me the saw, the auger, and some nails; we will see what is to be done." I recollected having seen some empty casks in the ship's hold: we went down, and found them floating in the water which had got into the vessel; it cost us but little trouble to hoist them up, and place them on the lower deck, which was at this time scarcely above water. We saw, with joy, that they were all sound, well guarded by iron hoops, and in every respect in good condition; they were exactly suited for the object; and, with the assistance of my sons, I instantly began to saw them in two. In a short time I had produced eight tubs, of equal size, and of the proper height. We now allowed ourselves some refreshment of wine and biscuit. I viewed with delight my eight little tubs, ranged in a line. I was surprised to see that my wife did not partake our eagerness; she sighed deeply as she looked at them. "Never, never," cried she, "can I venture to get into one of these."

"Do not decide so hastily, my dear," said I; "my plan is not yet complete; and you will see presently that it is more worthy of our confidence than this shattered vessel, which cannot move from its place."

I then sought for a long pliant plank, and placed my eight tubs upon it, leaving a piece at each end reaching beyond the tubs, which, bent upward, would present an outline like the keel of a vessel; we next nailed all the tubs to the plank, and then the tubs to each other, as they stood, side by side, to make them the firmer, and afterwards two other planks, of the same length as the first, on each side of the tubs. When all this was finished, we found we had produced a kind of narrow boat, divided into eight compartments, which I had no doubt would be able to perform a short course in calm water.

But now we discovered that the machine we had contrived was so heavy, that, with the strength of all united, we were not able to move it an inch from its place. I bade Fritz fetch me a crow, who soon returned with it: in the meanwhile I sawed a thick round pole into several pieces, to make some rollers. I then, with the crow, easily raised the foremost part of my machine, while Fritz placed one of the rollers under it.

"How astonishing," cried Ernest, "that this engine, which is smaller than any of us, can do more than our united strength was able to effect! I wish I could know how it is constructed."

I explained to him as well as I could the power of Archimedes' lever, with which he said he could move the world, if you would give him a point from which his mechanism might act, and promised to explain the nature of the operation of the crow when we should be safe on land.

One of the points of my system of education for my sons was to awaken their curiosity by interesting observations, to leave time for the activity of the imagination, and then to correct any error they might fall into. I contented myself now, however, with this general remark, that God sufficiently compensated the natural weakness of man by the gifts of reason, of invention, and the adroitness of the hands; and that human meditation and skill had produced a science, called mechanics, the object of which was, to teach us how to make our own natural strength act to an incredible distance, and with extraordinary force, by the intervention of instruments.

Jack here remarked that the action of the crow was very slow.

"Better slow than never, Jack," replied I. "Experience has ever taught, and mechanical observations have established as a principle, that what is gained in speed is lost in strength: the purpose of the crow is not to enable us to raise anything rapidly, but to raise what is exceedingly heavy; and the heavier the thing we would move, the slower is the mechanical operation. But are you aware what we have at our command, to compensate for this slowness?"

"Yes, it is turning the handle quicker."

"Your guess is wrong; that would be no compensation: the true remedy, my boy, is to call in the assistance of patience and reason: with the aid of these two fairy powers I am in hopes to set my machine afloat." As I said this, I tied a long cord to its stern, and the other end of it to one of the timbers of the ship, which appeared to be still firm, so that the cord being left loose would serve to guide and restrain it when launched. We now put a second and a third roller under, and applying the crow, to our great joy our machine descended into the water with such a velocity that, if the rope had not been well fastened, it would have gone far out to sea. But now a new difficulty presented itself: the boat leaned so much on one side that the boys all exclaimed they could not venture to get into it. I was for some moments in the most painful perplexity; but it suddenly occurred to me that balast only was wanting to set it straight. I drew it near, and threw all the useless things I could find into the tubs, so as to make weight on the light side. By degrees the machine became quite straight and firm in the water, seeming to invite us to take refuge in its protection. All now would get into the tubs, and the boys began to dispute which should be first. I drew them back, and seeking a remedy for this kind of obstacle, I recollected that savage nations make use of a paddle for preventing their canoes from upsetting. I once more set to work to make one of these.

I took two poles of equal length, upon which the sails of the vessel had been stretched, and having descended into the machine, fixed one of them at the head, and the other at the stern, in such a manner as to enable us to turn them at pleasure to right or left, as should best answer the purpose of guiding and putting it out to sea. I stuck the end of each pole, or paddle, into the bunghole of an empty brandy-keg, which served to keep the paddles steady, and to prevent any interruption in the management of our future enterprise.

There remained nothing more to do, but to find in what way I could clear out from the incumbrance of the wreck. I got into the first tub, and steered the head of the machine so as to make it enter the cleft in the ship's side, where it could remain quiet. I then remounted the vessel, and sometimes with the saw, and sometimes with the hatchet, I cleared away, to right and left, everything that could obstruct our passage; and, that being effected, we next secured some oars for the voyage we resolved on attempting.

We had spent the day in laborious exertions; it was already late; and as it would not have been possible to reach the land that evening, we were obliged to pass a second night in the wrecked vessel, which at every instant threatened to fall to pieces. We next refreshed ourselves by a regular meal; for, during the day's work, we had scarcely allowed ourselves to take a bit of bread, or a glass of wine. Being now in a more tranquil and unapprehensive state of mind than the day before, we all abandoned ourselves to sleep; not, however, till I had taken the precaution of tying the swimming apparatus round my three youngest boys and my wife, in case the storm should again come on. I also advised my wife to dress herself in the clothes of one of the sailors which were so much more convenient for swimming, or any other exertions she might be compelled to engage in. She consented, but not without reluctance, and left us to look for some that might best suit her size. In a quarter of an hour she returned, dressed in clothes of a young man who had served as volunteer on board the ship, and I soon found means to reconcile her to the change, by representing the many advantages it gave her, till at length she joined in the merriment her dress occasioned, and one and all crept into our separate hammocks, where a delicious repose prepared us for the renewal of our labours.

CHAPTER II
A Landing, and Consequent Occupations

BY break of day we were all awake and alert, for hope as well as grief is unfriendly to lengthened slumbers. When we had finished our morning prayer, I said, "We now, my best beloved, with the assistance of Heaven, must enter upon the work of our deliverance. The first thing to be done is to give to each poor animal on board a hearty meal; we will then put food enough before them for several days; we cannot take them with us; but we will hope it may be possible, if our voyage succeeds, to return and fetch them. Are you now all ready? Bring together whatever is absolutely necessary for our wants. It is my wish that our first cargo should consist of a barrel of gunpowder, three fowling-pieces, and three carbines, with as much small-shot and lead, and as many bullets as our boat will carry; two pairs of pocket-pistols, and one of large ones, not forgetting a mould to cast balls in; each of the boys, and their mother also, should have a bag to carry game in; you will find plenty of these in the cabins of the officers." We added a chest containing cakes of portable soup, another full of hard biscuits, an iron pot, a fishing-rod, a chest of nails, and another of different utensils, such as hammers, saws, pincers, hatchets, augers, etc., and lastly, some sailcloth to make a tent. Indeed the boys brought so many things that we were obliged to reject some of them, though I had already exchanged the worthless ballast for articles of use in the question of our subsistence.

When all was ready we stepped bravely each into a tub. At the moment of our departure the cocks and hens began to cluck, as if conscious that we had deserted them, yet were willing to bid us a sorrowful adieu. This suggested to me the idea of taking the geese, ducks, fowls, and pigeons with us; observing to my wife that, if we could not find means to feed them, at least they would feed us.

We accordingly executed this plan. We put ten hens and an old and a young cock into one of the tubs, and covered it with planks; we set the rest of the poultry at liberty, in the hope that instinct would direct them towards the land, the geese and the ducks by water, and the pigeons by the air.

We were waiting for my wife, who had the care of this last part of our embarkation, when she joined us loaded with a large bag, which she threw into the tub that already contained her youngest son. I imagined that she intended it for him to sit upon, or perhaps to confine him so as to prevent his being tossed from side to side. I therefore asked no more questions concerning it. The order of our departure was as follows:

In the first tub, at the boat's head, my wife, the most tender and exemplary of her sex, placed herself. In the second, our little Francis, a lovely boy, six years old, remarkable for the sweetest and happiest temper, and for his affection to his parents. In the third, Fritz, our eldest boy, between fourteen and fifteen years of age, a handsome, curl-pated youth, full of intelligence and vivacity. In the fourth was the barrel of gunpowder, with the cocks and hens, and the sail-cloth. In the fifth, the provisions of every kind. In the sixth, our third son, Jack, a light-hearted, enterprising, audacious, generous lad, about ten years old. In the seventh, our second son, Ernest, a boy of twelve years old, of a rational, reflecting temper, well informed for his age, but somewhat disposed to indolence and pleasure. In the eighth, a father, to whose paternal care the task of guiding the machine for the safety of his beloved family was entrusted. Each of us had useful implements within reach; the hand of each held an oar, and near each was a swim-

ming apparatus, in readiness for what might happen. The
tide was already at half its height when we left the ship, and
I had counted on this circumstance as favourable to our
want of strength. We held the two paddles longways, and
thus we passed without accident through the cleft of the
vessel into the sea. The boys devoured with their eyes the
blue land they saw at a distance. We rowed with all our
strength, but long in vain, to reach it: the boat only turned
round and round. At length I had the good fortune to steer
in such a way that it proceeded in a straight line. The two
dogs, perceiving we had abandoned us, plunged into the
sea and swam to the boat; they were too large for us to
think of giving them admittance, and I dreaded lest they
should jump in and upset us. Turk was an English dog, and
Flora a bitch of the Danish breed. I was in great uneasiness
on their account, for I feared it would not be possible for
them to swim so far. The dogs, however, managed the affair
with perfect intelligence. When fatigued, they rested their
fore-paws on one of the paddles, and thus with little effort
proceeded.

Jack was disposed to refuse them this accommodation,
but he soon yielded to my argument that it was cruel and
unwise to neglect creatures thrown on our protection, and
who indeed might hereafter protect us in their turn, by
guarding us from harm, and assisting in our pursuit of animals for food. "Besides," added I, "God has given the dog
to man to be his faithful companion and friend."

Our voyage proceeded securely, though slowly; but the
nearer we approached the land, the more gloomy and un-
promising its aspect appeared. The coast was clothed with
barren rocks, which seemed to offer nothing but hunger and
distress. The sea was calm; the waves, gently agitated, washed
the shore, and the sky was serene in every direction; we
perceived casks, bales, chests, and other vestiges of ship-
wrecks, floating round us. In the hope of obtaining some
good provisions, I determined on endeavouring to secure
some of the casks. I bade Fritz have a rope, a hammer, and
some nails ready, and to try to seize them as we passed. He
succeeded in laying hold of two, and in such a way that we
could draw them after us to the shore. Now that we were
close on land, its rude outline was much softened; the rocks
no longer appeared one undivided chain; Fritz, with his

hawk's eye, already descried some trees, and exclaimed that they were palm trees. Ernest expressed his joy that he should now get much larger and better cocoanuts than he had ever seen before. I, for my part, was venting audibly my regret that I had not thought of bringing a telescope that I knew was in the captain's cabin, when Jack drew a small one from his pocket, and with a look of triumph presented it to me.

On applying it to my eye, I remarked that the shore before us had a desert and savage aspect; but that towards the left the scene was more agreeable; but when I attempted to steer in that direction, a current carried me irresistibly towards the coast that was rocky and barren. By and by we perceived a little opening between the rocks, near the mouth of a creek, towards which all our geese and ducks betook themselves; and I, relying on their sagacity, followed in the same course. This opening formed a little bay; the water was tranquil, and neither too deep nor too shallow to receive our boat. I entered it, and cautiously put on shore to a spot where the coast was about the same height above the water as our tubs, and where, at the same time, there was a quantity sufficient to keep us afloat.

All that had life in the boat jumped eagerly on land. The dogs, who had swum on shore, received us, as if appointed to do the honours of the place, jumping round us with every demonstration of joy; the geese kept up a loud cackling, to which the ducks, from their broad yellow beaks, contributed a perpetual thorough bass; the cocks and hens, which we had already set at liberty, clucked; the boys chattering all at once, produced altogether an overpowering confusion of sounds: to this was added the disagreeable scream of some penguins and flamingoes, which we now perceived; the latter flying over our heads, the others sitting on the points of the rocks at the entrance to the bay.

The first thing we did on finding ourselves safe on *terra firma,* was to fall on our knees, and return thanks to the Supreme Being, who had preserved our lives, and to recommend ourselves with entire resignation to the care of his paternal kindness.

We next employed our whole attention in unloading the boat. We looked about for a convenient place to set up a tent under the shade of the rocks; and having all consulted and agreed upon a place, we set to work. We drove one of our poles firmly into a fissure of the rock; this rested upon another pole, which was driven perpendicularly into the ground, and formed the ridge of our tent. A frame for a dwelling was thus made secure. We next threw some sail-cloth over the ridge, and stretching it to a convenient distance on each side, fastened its extremities to the ground with stakes. Lastly, I fixed some tenter-hooks along the edge of one side of the sail-cloth in front, that we might be able to enclose the entrance during night, by hooking in the opposite edge. The chests of provisions, and other heavy matters, we had left on the shore. The next thing was to desire my sons to look about for grass and moss, to be spread and dried in the sun, to serve us for beds. During this occupation, I erected near the tent a kind of little kitchen. A few flat stones I found in the bed of a fresh-water river, served for a hearth. I got a quantity of dry branches: with the largest I made a small enclosure round it; and with the little twigs, added to some of our turf, I made a brisk cheering fire. We put some of the soup-cakes, with water, into our iron pot, and placed it over the flame; and my wife, with my little Francis for a scullion, took charge of preparing the dinner.

In the meanwhile, Fritz had been reloading the guns, with one of which he had wandered along the side of the river. He had proposed to Ernest to accompany him; but Ernest replied that he did not like a rough, stony walk, and that he should go to the seashore. Jack took the road towards a chain of rocks which jutted out into the sea, with the intention of gathering some of the mussels which grew upon them.

My own occupation was now an endeavor to draw the two floating casks on shore, but in which I could not succeed; for our place of landing, though convenient enough for our machine, was too steep for the cask. While I was looking about to find a more favourable spot, I heard loud cries proceeding from a short distance, and recognized the voice of my son Jack. I snatched my hatchet, and ran anxiously to his assistance. I soon perceived him up to his knees in water in a shallow, and that a large lobster had fastened its claws in his leg. The poor boy screamed pitiably, and made useless efforts to disengage himself. I jumped instantly into the water; and the enemy was no sooner sensible of my approach, than he let go his hold, and would have scampered out to sea, but that I indulged the fancy of a little malice against him for the alarm he had caused us. I turned quickly upon him, and took him up by the body, and carried him off, followed by Jack, who shouted our triumph all the way. He begged me at last to let him hold the animal in his own hand, that he might himself present so fine a booty to his mother. Accordingly, having observed how I held it to avoid the gripe, he laid his own hand upon it in exactly the same manner; but scarcely had he grasped it, than he received a violent blow on the face from the lobster's tail, which made him loose his hold, and the animal fell to the ground. Jack again began to bawl out, while I could not refrain from laughing heartily. In his rage he took up a stone, and killed the lobster with a single blow.

Ernest, ever prompted by his savoury tooth, bawled out that the lobster had better be put into the soup, which would give it an excellent flavour: but this his mother opposed, observing, that we must be more economical of our provisions than that, for the lobster of itself would furnish a dinner for the whole family. I now left them, and walked again to the scene of this adventure, and examined the shallow: I then made another attempt upon my two casks, and at length succeeded in getting them into it, and in fixing them there securely on their bottoms.

On my return, I complimented Jack on his being the first to procure an animal that might serve for subsistence.

"Ah; but *I* have seen something too, that is good to eat," said Ernest; "and I should have got it if it had not been in the water, so that I must have wetted my feet——"

"Oh, that is a famous story," cried Jack: "I can tell you what he saw,—some nasty mussels: why, I would not eat one of them for the world.—Think of my lobster!"

"That is not true, Jack; for they were oysters, and not mussels, that I saw: I am sure of it, for they stuck to the rock, and I know they must be oysters."

"Fortunate enough, my dainty gentleman," interrupted I, addressing myself to Ernest; "since you are so well acquainted with the place where such food can be found, you will be so obliging as to return and procure us some. In such a situation as ours, every member of the family must be

actively employed for the common good; and, above all,
none must be afraid of so trifling an inconvenience as wet
feet."

"I will do my best, with all my heart," answered Ernest;
"and at the same time I will bring home some salt, of which
I have seen immense quantities in the holes of the rocks,
where I have reason to suppose it is dried by the sun. I
tasted some of it, and it was excellent."

He set off, and soon returned: what he brought had the
appearance of sea-salt, but was so mixed with earth and
sand, that I was on the point of throwing it away; but my
wife prevented me, and by dissolving, and afterwards filtering some of it through a piece of muslin, we found it
admirably fit for use.

"Why could we not have used some sea-water," asked
Jack, "instead of having all this trouble?"

"So we might," answered I, "if it had not a somewhat
sickly taste." While I was speaking, my wife tasted the soup
with a little stick with which she had been stirring it, and
pronounced that it was all the better for the salt, and now
quite ready. "But," said she, "Fritz is not come in. And
then, how shall we manage to eat our soup without spoons
or dishes? Why did we not remember to bring some from
the ship?"—"Because, my dear, one cannot think of everything at once. We shall be lucky if we have not forgotten
even more important things."—"But, indeed," said she,
"this is a matter which cannot easily be set to rights. How
will it be possible for each of us to raise this large boiling
pot to his lips?"

I soon saw that my wife was right. We all cast our eyes
upon the pot with a sort of stupid perplexity, and looked a
little like the fox in the fable, when the stork desires him to
help himself from a vessel with a long neck. Silence was at
length broken, by all bursting into a hearty laugh at our
want of every kind of utensil, and at the thought of our own
folly, in not recollecting that spoons and forks were things
of absolute necessity.

Ernest observed that if we could but get some of the nice
cocoa-nuts he often thought about, we might empty them,
and use the pieces of the shells for spoons.

"Yes, yes," replied I; "*if we could but get,*—but we have
them not; and if wishing were to any purpose, I had as soon

wish at once for a dozen silver spoons; but, alas! of what use is wishing?"

"But at least," said the boy, "we can use some oyster-shells for spoons."

"Why, this is well, Ernest," said I, "and is what I call a useful thought. Run then quickly for some of them."

Jack ran first, and was up to his knees in the water before Ernest could reach the place. Jack tore off the fish with eagerness, and threw them to slothful Ernest, who put them into his handkerchief.

Fritz not having yet returned, his mother was beginning to be uneasy, when we heard him shouting to us from a small distance, to which we answered by similar sounds. In a few minutes he was among us, his two hands behind him, and with a sort of would-be melancholy air, which none of us could well understand.—"What have you brought?" asked his brothers; "let us see your booty, and you shall see ours."—"Ah! I have unfortunately nothing."—"What! nothing at all?" said I.—"Nothing at all," answered he. But now, on fixing my eye upon him, I perceived a smile of proud success through his assumed dissatisfaction. At the same instant Jack, having stolen behind him, exclaimed, "A sucking pig! a sucking pig!" Fritz, finding his trick discovered, now proudly displayed his prize, which I immediately perceived, from the description I had read in different books of travels, was an agouti, an animal common in that country, and not a sucking pig, as the boys had supposed.

Fritz related that he had passed over to the other side of the river. "Ah!" continued he, "it is quite another thing from this place; the shore is low, and you can have no notion of the quantity of casks, chests, and planks, and different sorts of things washed there by the sea. Ought we not to go and try to obtain some of these treasures?"—"We will consider of it soon," answered I, "but first we have to make our voyage to the vessel, and fetch away the animals: at least you will all agree, that of the cow we are pretty much in want."—"If our biscuit were soaked in milk, it would not be so hard," observed our dainty Ernest.—"I must tell you too," continued Fritz, "that over on the other side there is as much grass for pasturage as we can desire: and besides, a wood, in the shade of which we could repose. Why then should we remain on this barren desert side?"— "Patience," replied I; "there is a time for everything, friend Fritz: we shall not be without something to undertake to-morrow, and even after to-morrow. But, above all, I am eager to know if you discovered, in your excursion, any traces of our ship companions?"—"Not the smallest trace of man, dead or alive, on land or water," replied Fritz.

Soon after we had taken our meal, the sun began to sink into the west. Our little flock of fowls assembled round us, pecking here and there what morsels of our biscuit had fallen on the ground.—Just at this moment my wife produced the bag she had so mysteriously huddled into the tub. Its mouth was now opened; it contained the various sorts of grain for feeding poultry—barley, peas, oats, etc., and also different kinds of seeds and roots of vegetables for the table. In the fulness of her kind heart she scattered several handfuls at once upon the ground, which the fowls began eagerly to seize. Our pigeons sought a roosting-place among the rocks; the hens, with the two cocks at their head, ranged themselves in a line along the ridge of the tent; and the geese and ducks betook themselves in a body, cackling and quacking as they proceeded, to a marshy bit of ground near the sea, where some thick bushes afforded them shelter.

A little later, we began to follow the example of our winged companions, by beginning our preparations for repose. First, we loaded our guns and pistols, and laid them carefully in the tent; next, we assembled together and joined in offering up our thanks to the Almighty for the succour afforded us, and supplicating his watchful care for our preservation. With the last ray of the sun we entered our tent, and, after drawing the sail-cloth over the hooks, to close the entrance, we laid ourselves down close to each other on the grass and moss we had collected in the morning.

CHAPTER III
Voyage of Discovery

I WAS roused at the dawn of day by the crowing of the cocks. I awoke my wife, and we consulted together as to the occupations we should engage in. We agreed that we should seek for traces of our late ship companions, and at the same time examine the nature of the soil on the other side of the river, before we determined on a fixed place of abode.—My wife easily perceived that such an excursion could not be undertaken by all the members of the family; and she courageously consented to my proposal of leaving her with the three youngest boys, and proceeding myself with Fritz on a journey of discovery.

The children were soon roused; even our slothful Ernest submitted to the hard fate of rising so early in the morning.

We now prepared for our departure: we took each a bag for game, and a hatchet: I put a pair of pistols in the leather band round Fritz's waist, in addition to the gun, and provided myself with the same articles, not forgetting a stock of biscuit and a flask of fresh river water. My wife now called us to breakfast, when all attacked the lobster; but its flesh proved so hard, that there was a great deal left when our meal was finished, and we packed it for our journey without further regret from any one.

In about an hour we had completed the preparations for our journey. I had loaded the guns we left behind, and I now enjoined my wife to keep by day as near the boat as possible, which in case of danger was the best and most speedy means of escape. My next concern was to shorten the moment of separation, judging by my own feelings those of my dear wife; for neither could be without painful apprehensions of what new misfortune might occur on either side during the interval. We all melted into tears:—I seized this instant for drawing Fritz away, and in a few moments the sobs and often repeated adieus of those we left behind died away in the noise of the waves which we now approached, and which turned our thoughts upon ourselves and the immediate object of our journey.

The banks of the river were everywhere steep and difficult, excepting at one narrow slip near the mouth on our side, where we had drawn our fresh water. The other side presented an unbroken line of sharp, high, perpendicular rocks. We therefore followed the course of the river till we arrived at a cluster of rocks at which the stream formed a cascade: a few paces beyond, we found some large fragments of rock which had fallen into the bed of the river: by stepping upon these, and making now and then some hazardous leaps, we contrived to reach the other side. We proceeded a short way along the rock we ascended in landing, forcing ourselves a passage through tall grass, which twined with other plants, and was rendered more capable of resistance by being half dried by the sun. Perceiving, however, that walking on this kind of surface in so hot a sun would exhaust our strength, we looked for a path to descend and proceed along the river, where we hoped to meet with fewer obstacles, and perhaps to discover traces of our ship companions.

When we had walked about a hundred paces, we heard a loud noise behind us, as if we were pursued, and perceived a rustling motion in the grass, which was almost as tall as ourselves. I was a good deal alarmed, thinking that it might be occasioned by some frightful serpent, a tiger, or other ferocious animal. Our alarm was, however, short; for what was our joy on seeing rush out, not an enemy, but our faithful Turk, whom in the distress of the parting scene we had forgotten, and whom no doubt our anxious relatives had sent on to us!

We again pursued our way. On our left was the sea, and on our right the continuation of the ridge of rocks which began at the place of our landing, and ran along the shore, the summit everywhere adorned with fresh verdure and a great variety of trees. We were careful to proceed in a course as near the shore as possible, casting our eyes alternately upon its smooth expanse and upon the land in all directions to discover our ship companions, or the boats which had conveyed them from us; but our endeavours were in vain.

When we had gone about two leagues, we entered a wood situated a little further from the sea: here we threw ourselves on the ground, under the shade of a tree, by the side of a clear running stream, and took out some provisions and refreshed ourselves. We heard the chirping, singing, and motion of birds in the trees, and observed, as they now and then came out to view, that they were more attractive by their splendid plumage than by any charm of note. Fritz assured me that he had caught a glimpse of some animals like apes among the bushes, and this was confirmed by the restless movements of Turk, who began to smell about him, and to bark so loud that the wood resounded with the noise. Fritz stole softly about to be sure, and presently stumbled on a small round body which lay on the ground: he brought it to me, observing that it must be the nest of some bird. —"What makes you of that opinion?" said I. "It is, I think, much more like a cocoa-nut."

"But I have read that there are some kinds of birds which build their nests quite round: and look, father, how the outside is crossed and twined."

"But do you not perceive that what you take for straws crossed and twined by the beak of a bird, is in fact a coat of fibres formed by the hand of Nature? Do you not remember to have read that the cocoa-nut is enclosed within a round, fibrous covering, which again is surrounded by a skin of a thin and fragile texture? I see that in the one you hold in your hand, this skin has been destroyed by time, which is the reason that the twisted fibres (or inner covering) are so apparent: but now let us break the shell, and you will see the nut inside."

We soon accomplished this; but the nut, alas! from lying on the ground, had perished, and appeared but little different from a bit of dried skin, and not the least inviting to the palate.

A little later we had the good luck to meet with another nut. We opened it, and finding it sound, we sat down and ate it for our dinner, by which means we were enabled to husband the provisions we had brought. The nut, it is true, was a little oily and rancid; yet, as this was not a time to be nice, we made a hearty meal, and then continued our route. We did not quit the wood, but pushed our way across it, being often obliged to cut a path through the bushes over-run by creeping plants, with our hatchet. At length we reached a plain, which afforded a more extensive prospect, and a path less perplexed and intricate.

We next entered a forest to the right, and soon observed that some of the trees were of a singular kind. Fritz, whose sharp eye was continually on a journey of discovery, went up to examine them closely. "Oh, heavens! father, what odd trees, with wens growing all about their trunks!" I had soon the surprise and satisfaction of assuring him that they were bottle gourds, the trunks of which bear fruit. Fritz, who had never heard of such a plant, could not conceive the meaning of what he saw, and asked me if the fruit was a sponge or a wen.—"We will see," I replied, "if I cannot unravel the mystery. Try to get down one of them, and we will examine it minutely."

"I have got one," cried Fritz, "and it is exactly like a gourd, only the rind is thicker and harder."

"It then, like the rind of that fruit, can be used for making various utensils," observed I; "plates, dishes, basins, flasks. We will give it the name of the gourd-tree."

Fritz jumped for joy.—"How happy my mother will be!" cried he in ecstasy; "she will no longer have the vexation of thinking, when she makes soup, that we shall all scald our fingers."

We accordingly proceeded to the manufacture of our plates and dishes. I taught my son how to divide the gourd with a bit of string, which would cut more equally than a knife; I tied the string round the middle of the gourd as tight as possible, striking it pretty hard with the handle of my knife, and I drew it tighter and tighter till the gourd fell apart, forming two regular-shaped bowls or vessels; while Fritz, who had used a knife for the same operation, had entirely spoiled his gourd by the irregular pressure of his instrument. I recommended his making some spoons with the spoiled rind, as it was good for no other purpose. I, on my part, had soon completed two dishes of convenient size, and some smaller ones to serve as plates.

Fritz was in the utmost astonishment at my success. "I cannot imagine, father," said he, "how this way of cutting the gourd could occur to you!"

"I have read the description of such a process," replied I, "in books of travels; and also that such of the savages as have no knives, and who make a sort of twine from the bark of trees, are accustomed to use it for this kind of purpose."

"And the flasks, father; in what manner are they made?"

"For this branch of their ingenuity they make preparation a long time beforehand. If a negro wishes to have a flask, or bottle with a neck, he binds a piece of string, linen, or bark of a tree, or anything he can get, round the part nearest the stalk of a very young gourd; he draws this bandage so tight that the part at liberty soon forms itself to a round shape, while the part which is confined contracts, and remains ever after narrow. By this method it is that they obtain flasks or bottles of a perfect form."

Our conversation and our labour thus went on together. Fritz had completed some plates, and was not a little proud of the achievement. "Ah, how delighted my mother will be to eat upon them!" cried he. "But how shall we convey them to her? They will not, I fear, bear travelling well."

"We must leave them here on the sand for the sun to dry them thoroughly; this will be accomplished by the time of our return this way, and we can then carry them with us; but care must be taken to fill them with sand, that they may not shrink or warp in so ardent a heat." My boy did not dislike this task; for he had no great fancy for the idea of carrying such a load on our journey of further discovery. Our sumptuous service of porcelain was accordingly spread upon the ground, and for the present abandoned to its fate.

We amused ourselves, as we proceeded, in endeavouring to fashion some spoons from the fragments of the gourd-rinds. I had the fancy to try my skill upon a piece of cocoa-nut; but I must needs confess that what we produced had not the least resemblance to those I had seen in the Museum at London, and which were shown there as the work of some of the islanders of the Southern Seas.

Meanwhile, we had not neglected the great object of our pursuit,—the making every practicable search for our ship companions. But our endeavours, alas! were all in vain.

After a walk of about four leagues in all, we arrived at a

spot where a slip of land reached far out into the sea, on
which we observed a rising piece of ground or hill. On a
moment's reflection we determined to ascend it, concluding
we should obtain a clear view of all adjacent parts, which
would save us the fatigue of further rambles. We accordingly accomplished the design.

We did not reach the top of the hill without many efforts
and a plentiful perspiration: but when there, we beheld a
scene of wild and solitary beauty, comprehending a vast
extent of land and water. It was however in vain that we
used our telescope in all directions; no trace of man appeared. A truly embellished nature presented herself; and
we were in the highest degree sensible of her thousand
charms. The shore, rounded by a bay of some extent, the
bank of which ended in a promontory on the farther side;
the agreeable blue tint of its surface; the sea, gently agitated
by waves in which the rays of the sun were reflected; the
woods, of variegated hues and verdure, formed altogether a
picture of such magnificence, of such new and exquisite
delight, that, if the recollection of our unfortunate companions, engulfed perhaps in this very ocean, had not intruded
to depress our spirits, we should have yielded to the ecstasy
the scene was calculated to inspire. In reality, from this
moment we began to lose even the feeble hope we had
entertained, and sadness stole involuntarily into our hearts.
We, however, became but the more sensible of the goodness of the Divine Being, in the special protection afforded
to ourselves, in conducting us to a home where there was no
present cause for fear of danger from without, where we
had not experienced the want of food, and where there was
a prospect of future safety for us all.

We descended the hill, and made our way to a wood of
palms: our path was clothed with reeds, entwined with other
plants, which greatly obstructed our march. We advanced
slowly and cautiously, fearing at every step to receive a
mortal bite from some serpent that might be concealed
among them. We made Turk go before, to give us timely
notice of anything dangerous. I also cut a reed-stalk of
uncommon length and thickness, for my defence against any
enemy. It was not without surprise that I perceived a gluti-
nous sap proceed from the divided end of the stalk. Prompted
by curiosity, I tasted this liquid, and found it sweet and of a

pleasant flavour, so that not a doubt remained that we were passing through a plantation of sugar-canes. I again applied the cane to my lips, and sucked it for some moments, and felt singularly refreshed and strengthened. I determined not to tell Fritz immediately of the fortunate discovery I had made, preferring that he should find it out for himself. As he was at some distance before me, I called out to him to cut a reed for his defence. This he did, and without any remark, used it simply for a stick, striking lustily with it on all sides to clear a passage. The motion occasioned the sap to run out abundantly upon his hand, and he stopped to examine so strange a circumstance. He lifted it up, and still a larger quantity escaped. He now tasted what was on his fingers. Oh! then for the exclamations—"Father, father, I have found some sugar!—some syrup! I have a sugar-cane in my hand! Run quickly, father!"—We were soon together, jointly partaking of the pleasure we had in store for his dear mother and the younger brothers.

Fritz cut at least a dozen of the largest canes, tore off their leaves, tied them together, and putting them under his arm, dragged them, as well as he was able, through thick and thin to the end of the plantation. We regained the wood of palms without accident; here we stretched our limbs in the shade, and finished our repast. We were scarcely settled, when a great number of large monkeys, terrified by the sight of us and the barking of Turk, stole so nimbly, and yet so quietly up the trees, that we scarcely perceived them till they had reached the topmost parts. From this height they fixed their eyes upon us, grinding their teeth, making horrible grimaces, and saluting us with screams of hostile import. —Being now satisfied that the trees were palms, bearing cocoa-nuts, I conceived the hope of obtaining some of this fruit in a milky state, through the monkeys. Fritz, on his part, prepared to shoot at them instantly. He threw his burdens on the ground, and it was with difficulty I, by pulling his arm, could prevent him from firing.

I now began to throw some stones at the monkeys; and though I could not make them reach to half the height at which they had taken refuge, they showed every mark of excessive anger. With their accustomed trick of imitation, they furiously tore off, nut by nut, all that grew upon the trunk near them, to hurl them down upon us; so that it was with difficulty we avoided the blows; and in a short time a great number of cocoa-nuts lay on the ground round us. Fritz laughed heartily at the excellent success of our stratagem; and as the shower of cocoa-nuts began to subside, we set about collecting them. We chose a place where we could repose at our ease, to feast on this rich harvest. We opened the shells with a hatchet, but first enjoyed the sucking of some of the milk through the three small holes, where we found it easy to insert the point of a knife. The milk of the cocoa-nut has not a pleasant flavour; but it is excellent for quenching thirst. What we liked best was a kind of solid cream which adheres to the shell, and which we scraped off with our spoons. We mixed with it a little of the sap of our sugar-canes, and it made a delicious repast.

Our meal being finished, we prepared to leave the wood of palms. I tied all the cocoa-nuts which had stalks together, and threw them across my shoulder. Fritz resumed his bundle of sugar-canes. We divided the rest of the things between us, and continued our way towards home.

CHAPTER IV

Return from the Voyage of Discovery—A Nocturnal Alarm

MY poor boy now began to complain of fatigue; the sugar-canes galled his shoulders, and he was obliged to shift them often. At last he stopped to take breath.—"No," cried he, "I never could have thought that a few sugar-canes could be so heavy. How sincerely I pity the poor negroes who carry heavy loads of them! Yet how glad I shall be when my mother and Ernest are tasting them!"

"I am not without my apprehensions, that of our acquisition we shall carry them only a few sticks for firewood; for the juice of the sugar-cane is apt to turn sour soon after cutting, and the more certainly in such heat as we now experience; we may suck them, therefore, without compunction at the diminution of their numbers."

When we reached the place where we had left our gourd utensils upon the sands, we found them perfectly dry, as hard as bone, and not the least misshapen. We now, therefore, could put them into our game-bags conveniently enough, and this done, we continued our way. Scarcely had we passed through the little wood in which we breakfasted, when Turk sprang away to seize upon a troop of monkeys, who were skipping about and amusing themselves without observing our approach. They were thus taken by surprise; and before we could get to the spot, our ferocious Turk had already seized one of them; it was a female who held a young one in her arms, which she was caressing almost to suffocation, and which incumbrance deprived her of the power of escaping. The poor creature was killed, and afterward devoured; the young one hid himself in the grass, and looked on, grinding his teeth. Fritz flew like lightning to make Turk let go his hold. He lost his hat, threw down his tin bottle, canes, etc., but all in vain; he was too late to prevent the death of the interesting mother.

The next scene that presented itself was of a different nature, and comical enough. The young monkey sprang nimbly on Fritz's shoulders, and fastened his feet in the stiff curls of his hair; nor could the squalls of Fritz, nor all the shaking he gave him, make him let go his hold. I ran to them, laughing heartily, for I saw that the animal was too young to do him any injury, while the panic visible in the features of the boy made a ludicrous contrast with the grimaces of the monkey, whom I endeavoured to disengage.

With a little gentleness and management I succeeded. I took the creature in my arms as one would an infant, nor could I help pitying and caressing him. He was not larger than a kitten, and quite unable to help himself; its mother was at least as tall as Fritz.

"What shall I do with thee, poor orphan?" cried I; "and how, in our condition, shall I be able to maintain thee? We have already more mouths to fill than food to put into them, and our workmen are too young to afford us much hope from their exertions."

"Father," cried Fritz, "do let me have this little animal to myself. I will take the greatest care of him; I will give him all my share of the milk of the cocoa-nuts, till we get our cows and goats; and who knows? his monkey instinct may one day assist us in discovering some wholesome fruits."

"I have not the least objection," answered I. "You have conducted yourself throughout this tragi-comic adventure like a lad of courage and sensibility, and I am well satisfied with every circumstance of your behaviour. It is therefore but just that the little protégé should be given up to your management and discretion."

We now thought of resuming our journey. The little orphan jumped again on the shoulders of his protector, while I on my part relieved my boy of the bundle of canes. Scarcely had we proceeded a quarter of a league when Turk overtook us full gallop. The young monkey appeared uneasy from seeing him so near, and passed round and fixed himself on his protector's bosom, who did not long bear so great an inconvenience without having recourse to his invention for a remedy. He tied some string round Turk's body in such a way, as to admit of the monkey's being fastened on his back with it, and then in a tone of genuine pity, he said, "Now, Mr. Turk, since you had the cruelty to destroy the mother, it is for you to take care of her child." At first the dog was restive, and resisted; but by degrees, partly by menaces, and partly by caresses, we succeeded in gaining his good-will, and he quietly consented to carry the little burden; and the young monkey, who also had made some difficulties, at length found himself perfectly accommodated. Fritz put another string round Turk's neck, by which he might lead him, a precaution he used to prevent him from going out of sight.

Thus proceeding, we soon found ourselves on the bank of the river, and near our family, before we were aware. Flora from the other side announced our approach by a violent barking, and Turk replied so heartily, that his motions unseated his little burden, who in his fright jumped the length of his string from his back to Fritz's shoulder, which he could not afterwards be prevailed upon to leave. Turk, who began to be acquainted with the country, ran off to meet his companion, and shortly after, our much-loved family appeared in sight, with demonstrations of unbounded joy at our safe return.

I gave my wife an account of our journey and our new acquisitions, which I exhibited one after the other for her inspection. No one of them afforded her more pleasure than the plates and dishes, because, to persons of decent habits, they were articles of indispensable necessity. We now adjourned to our kitchen, and observed with pleasure the preparations for an excellent repast. On one side of the fire was a turnspit, which my wife had contrived by driving two forked pieces of wood into the ground, and placing a long even stick, sharpened at one end, across them. By this invention she was enabled to roast fish, or other food, with the help of little Francis, who was intrusted with the care of turning it round from time to time. On the occasion of our return, she had prepared us the treat of a goose, the fat of which ran down into some oyster-shells placed there to serve the purpose of a dripping-pan. There was, besides, a dish of fish, which the little ones had caught; and the iron pot was upon the fire, provided with a good soup, the odour of which increased our appetite. By the side of these most exhilarating preparations stood one of the casks which we had recovered from the sea, the head of which my wife had knocked out, so that it exposed to our view a cargo of the finest sort of Dutch cheeses, contained in round tins.

We seated ourselves on the ground: my wife had placed each article of the repast in one of our new dishes, the neat appearance of which exceeded all our expectations. My sons had not patience to wait, but had broken the cocoa-nuts, and already convinced themselves of their delicious flavour; and then they fell to making spoons with the fragments of the shells.

The boys were preparing to break some more of the nuts with the hatchet, after having drawn out the milk through the three little holes, when I pronounced the word *halt*, and bade them bring me a saw;—the thought had struck me, that by dividing the nuts carefully with this instrument, the two halves, when scooped, would remain in the form of tea-cups or basins already made to our hands. Jack, who was on every occasion the most active, brought me the saw. I performed my undertaking in the best manner I could, and in a short time each of us was provided with a convenient receptacle for food.

By the time we had finished our meal, the sun was retiring from our view; and recollecting how quickly the night would fall upon us, we were in great haste to regain our place of rest. My wife had considerately collected a tenfold quantity of dry grass, which she had spread in the tent, so that we anticipated with joy the prospect of stretching our limbs on a substance somewhat approaching to the quality of mattresses, while, the night before, our bodies seemed to touch the ground. Our flock of fowls placed themselves as they had done the preceding evening: we said our prayers, and, with an improved serenity of mind, lay down in the tent, taking the young monkey with us, who was become the little favourite of all. We all lay down upon the grass, in the order of the night before, myself remaining last to fasten the sail-cloth in front of the tent; when, heartily fatigued by the exertions of the day, I, as well as the rest, soon fell into a profound and refreshing sleep.

But I had no long enjoyed this pleasing state, when I was awakened by the motion of the fowls on the ridge of the tent, and by a violent barking of our vigilant safeguards, the dogs. I was instantly on my legs: my wife and Fritz, who had also been alarmed, got up also: we each took a gun, and sallied forth.

The dogs continued barking with the same violence, and at intervals even howled. We had not proceeded many steps from the tent, when, to our surprise, we perceived by the light of the moon a terrible combat. At least a dozen of jackals had surrounded our brave dogs, who defended themselves with the stoutest courage. Already the fierce champions had laid three or four of their adversaries on the ground, while those which remained began a timid kind of moan, as if imploring pity and forbearance. Meanwhile they did not the less endeavour to entangle and surprise the dogs, thus thrown off their guard, and so secure to themselves the advantage. But our watchful combatants were not so easily deceived: they took good care not to let the enemy approach them too nearly.

I, for my part, had apprehended something worse than jackals.— "We shall soon manage to set these gentlemen at rest," said I. "Let us fire both together, my boy; but let us take care how we aim, for fear of killing the dogs; mind how you fire, that you may not miss, and I shall do the same." We fired, and two of the intruders fell instantly dead upon the sands. The others made their escape; but we perceived it was with great difficulty, in consequence, no doubt, of being wounded. Turk and Flora afterwards pursued them, and put the finishing stroke to what we had begun; and thus the battle ended.

The body of one of the jackals was left on the rock, by the side of the tent in which were the little sleepers, who had not once awaked during the whole of the scene which had been passing. Having, therefore, nothing further to prevent us, we lay down by their side till day began to break, and till the cocks, with their shrill morning salutation, awoke us both. The children being still asleep, this afforded us an excellent opportunity to consult together respecting the plan we should pursue for the ensuing day.

CHAPTER V

Return to the Wreck

I BROKE a silence of some moments, with observing to my wife that I could not but view with alarm the many cares and exertions to be made:—"In the first place, a journey to the vessel. This is of absolute necessity; at least, if we would not be deprived of the cattle and other useful things, all of which from moment to moment we risk losing by the first heavy sea. What ought we to resolve upon? For example, should not our very first endeavour be the contriving a better sort of habitation, and a more secure retreat from wild beasts, also a separate place for our provisions? I own I am at a loss what to begin first."

"All will fall into the right order by degrees," observed
my wife; "patience and regularity in our plans will go as far
as actual labour. I cannot, I confess, help shuddering at the
thought of this voyage to the vessel; but if you judge it to be
of absolute necessity, it cannot be undertaken too soon. In
the meanwhile, nothing that is immediately under my own
care shall stand still, I promise you. Let us not be over-
anxious about to-morrow: sufficient unto the day is the evil
thereof. These were the words of the true Friend of man-
kind, and let us use so wise a counsel for our own benefit."

"I will follow your advice," said I, "and without further
loss of time. You shall stay here with the three youngest
boys; and Fritz, being so much stronger and more intelligent
than the others, shall accompany me in the undertaking."

At this moment I started from my bed, crying out loudly
and briskly, "Get up, children, get up; it is almost light, and
we have some important projects for to-day; it would be a
shame to suffer the sun to find us still sleeping, we who are
to be the founders of a new colony!"

At these words Fritz sprang nimbly out of the tent, while
the young ones began to gape and rub their eyes, to get rid
of their sleepiness. Fritz ran to visit his jackal, which during
the night had become cold and perfectly stiff. He fixed him
upon his legs, and placed him like a sentinel at the entrance
of the tent, joyously anticipating the wonder and exclamations of his brothers at so unexpected an appearance. But
no sooner had the dogs caught sight of him, than they began
a howl, and set themselves in motion to fall upon him
instantly, thinking he was alive. Fritz had enough to do to
restrain them, and succeeded only by dint of coaxing and
perseverance.

In the meantime, their barking had awaked the younger
boys, and they ran out of the tent, curious to know what
could be the occasion. Jack was the first who appeared, with
the young monkey on his shoulders; but when the little
creature perceived the jackal, he sprang away in terror, and
hid himself at the furthest extremity of the grass which
composed our bed, and covered himself with it so completely, that scarcely could the tip of his nose be seen.

The children were much surprised at the sight of a yellow-
coloured animal standing without motion at the entrance of
the tent.—"Oh, heavens!" exclaimed Francis, stepping back

a few paces for fear, "it is a wolf!"—"No, no," said Jack, going near the jackal, and taking one of his paws, "it is a yellow dog, and he is dead; he does not move at all."—"It is neither a dog nor a wolf," interrupted Ernest in a consequential tone: "do you not see that it is the golden fox?" —"Best of all, most learned professor!" now exclaimed Fritz. "So you can tell an agouti when you see him, but you cannot tell a jackal; for jackal is the creature you see before you, and I killed him myself in the night."

Ernest.—In the night, you say, Fritz? In your sleep, I suppose——

Fritz.—No, Mr. Ernest; not in my sleep, as you so good-naturedly suppose, but broad awake, and on the watch to protect you from wild beasts! But I cannot wonder at this mistake in one who does not know the difference between a jackal and a golden fox!

Ernest.—You would not have known it either, if papa had not told you——

"Come, come, my lads, I will have no disputes," interrupted I. "Fritz, you are to blame in ridiculing your brother for the mistake he made. Ernest, you are also to blame for indulging that little peevishness of yours. But as to the animal, you all are right and all are wrong; for he partakes at once of the nature of the dog, the wolf, and the fox." The boys in an instant became friends; and then followed questions, answers, and wonder in abundance.—"And now, my boys, let me remind you, that he who begins the day without first addressing the Almighty ought to expect neither success nor safety in his undertakings. Let us therefore acquit ourselves of this duty before we engage in other occupations."

Having finished our prayers, the next thing thought of was breakfast; for the appetites of young boys open with their eyes. To-day their mother had nothing to give them for their morning meal but some biscuit, which was so hard and dry, that it was with difficulty we could swallow it. Fritz asked for a piece of cheese to eat with it, and Ernest cast some searching looks on the second cask we had drawn out of the sea, to discover whether it also contained Dutch cheese. In a minute he came up to us, joy sparkling in his eyes. "Father," said he, "if we had but a little butter spread upon our biscuit, do you not think it would improve it?"

"That indeed it would; but—*if*—*if*; these never-ending *ifs* are but a poor dependence. For my part, I had rather eat a bit of cheese with my biscuit at once, than think of *ifs*, which bring us so meagre a harvest."

Ernest.—Perhaps, though, the *ifs* may be found to be worth something, if we were to knock out the head of this cask.

Father.—What cask, my boy? and what are you talking of?

Ernest.—I am talking of this cask, which is filled with excellent salt butter. I made a little opening in it with a knife; and see, I got out enough to spread nicely upon this piece of biscuit.

"That glutton instinct of yours for once is of some general use," answered I. "But now let us profit by the event. Who will have some butter on his biscuit?" The boys surrounded the cask in a moment, while I was in some perplexity as to the best method of getting at the contents. Fritz was for taking off the topmost hoop, and thus loosening one of the ends. But this I objected to, observing that the great heat of the sun would not fail to melt the butter, which would then run out, and be wasted. The idea occurred to me, that I would make a hole in the bottom of the cask, sufficiently large to take out a small quantity of butter at a time; and I set about manufacturing a little wooden shovel to use for the purpose. All this succeeded vastly well, and we sat down to breakfast, some biscuits and a cocoa-nut shell full of salt butter being placed upon the ground, round which we all assembled. We toasted our biscuit, and, while it was hot, applied the butter, and contrived to make a hearty breakfast.

"One of the things we must not forget to look for in the vessel," said Fritz, "is a spiked collar or two for our dogs, as a protection to them should they again be called upon to defend themselves from wild beasts, which I fear will probably be the case."

"Oh!" said Jack, "I can make spiked collars, if my mother will give me a little help."

"That I will, most readily, my boy; for I should like to see what new fancy has come into your head," cried she.

"Yes, yes," pursued I, "as many new inventions as you please; you cannot better employ your time; and if you produce something useful, you will be rewarded with the commendations of all. But now for work. You, Mr. Fritz, who, from your superior age and discretion, enjoy the high honour of being my privy-counsellor, must make haste and get yourself ready, and we will undertake to-day our voyage to the vessel, to bring away whatever may be possible. You younger boys will remain here, under the wing of your kind mother: I hope I need not mention, that I rely on your perfect obedience to her will, and general good behaviour."

While Fritz was getting the boat ready, I looked about for a pole, and tied a piece of white linen to the end of it: this I drove into the ground, in a place where it would be visible from the vessel; and I concerted with my wife, that in case of any accident that should require my prompt assistance, they should take down the pole and fire a gun three times as a signal of distress, in consequence of which I would immediately turn back. But I gave her notice, that there being so many things to accomplish on board the vessel, it was probable that we should not, otherwise, return at night; in which case I, on my part, also promised to make signals.

We embarked in silence, casting anxious looks on the beloved objects we were quitting. Fritz rowed steadily, and I did my best to second his endeavours, by rowing from time to time, on my part, with the oar which served me for a rudder. When we had gone some distance, I remarked a current which was visible a long way. To take advantage of this current, and to husband our strength by means of it, was my first care. Little as I knew of the management of sea affairs, I succeeded in keeping our boat in the direction in which it ran, by which means we were drawn gently on, till at length the gradual diminution of its force obliged us again to have recourse to our oars; but our arms having now rested for some time, we were ready for new exertions. A little afterwards we found ourselves safely arrived at the cleft of the vessel, and fastened our boat securely to one of its timbers.

Fritz the first thing went to the main deck, where he found all the animals we had left on board assembled. I followed him, well pleased to observe the generous impatience he showed to relieve the wants of the poor abandoned creatures, who, one and all, now saluted us by the sounds natural to their species. We examined the food and water of the animals, taking away what was half spoiled, and adding a fresh supply, that no anxiety on their account might interrupt our enterprise. Nor did we neglect the care of renewing our own strength by a plentiful repast.

While we were seated, and appeasing the calls of hunger, Fritz and I consulted what should be our first occupation; when, to my surprise, the advice he gave was, that we should contrive a sail for our boat.—"In the name of Heaven," cried I, "what makes you think of this at so critical a moment, when we have so many things of indispensable necessity to arrange?"—"True, father," said Fritz; "but let me confess that I found it very difficult to row for so long a time, though I assure you I did my best, and did not spare my strength. I observed that, though the wind blew strong against us, the current still carried us on. Now, as the current will be of no use in our way back, I was thinking that we might make the wind supply its place. Our boat will be very heavy when we have loaded it with all the things we mean to take away, and I am afraid I shall not be strong enough to row to land; so do you not think that a sail would be a good thing just now?"

"Ah—ha, Mr. Fritz! You wish to spare yourself a little trouble, do you? But seriously, I perceive much good sense in your argument, and feel obliged to my privy-counsellor for his good advice. The best thing we can do is to take care and not overload the boat, and thus avoid the danger of sinking, or of being obliged to throw some of our stores overboard. We will, however, set to work upon your sail; it will give us a little trouble. But come, let us begin."

I assisted Fritz to carry a pole strong enough for a mast, and another not so thick for a sailyard. I directed him to make a hole in a plank with a chisel, large enough for the mast to stand upright in it. I then went to the sail-room, and cut a large sail down to a triangular shape: I made holes along the edges, and passed cords through them. We then got a pulley, and with this and some cords, and some contrivance in the management of our materials, we produced a sail.

"But now Father," said Fritz, "As you have eased me of the labour of rowing, it is *my* turn to take care of *you*. I am thinking to make you a better contrived rudder; one that would enable you to steer with greater ease and greater safety."—"Your thought would be a very good one," said I, "But that I am unwilling to lose the advantage of being able to proceed this way and that, without being obliged to veer.

I shall therefore fix our oars in such a manner as to enable me to steer the raft from either end." Accordingly I fixed bits of wood to the stem and stern of the machine, in the nature of grooves, which were calculated to spare us a great deal of trouble.

During these exertions the day advanced, and I saw that we should be obliged to pass the night in our tubs without having made much progress in out task of emptying the vessel.

We employed the remnant of the day in emptying the tubs of the useless ballasts of stones, and putting in their place what would be of service, such as nails, pieces of cloth, and different kinds of utensils, ect., etc. The Vandals themselves could not have made a more complete pillage than we had done. The prospect before us of an entire solitude made us devote out attention to the securing as much powder and shot as we could, as a means of catching animals for food, and of defending ourselves against wild beasts to the latest moment possible. Utensils for every kind of workmanship, of which there was a large provision in the ship were also of incalculable value to us.

The vessel, which was now a wreck, had been sent out as a preparation for the establishment of a colony in the South Seas, and had been provided with a variety of stores not commonly included in the loading of a ship. Among the rest, care had been taken to have on board considerable numbers of European cattle: but so long a voyage had proved unfavourable to the oxen and the horses, the greatest part of which had died, and the others were in so bad a condition, that it had been found necessary to destroy them. The quantity of useful things which presented themselves in the store-chambers made it difficult for me to select among them, and I much regretted that circumstances compelled me to leave some of them behind. Fritz, however, already meditated a second visit; but we took good care not to lose the present occasion for securing knives and forks, and spoons, and a complete assortment of kitchen utensils. In the captain's cabin we found some services of silver, dishes and plates of high-wrought metal, and a little chest filled with bottles of many sorts of excellent wine. Each of these we put into our boat. We next descended to the kitchen, which we stripped of gridirons, kettles, pots of all kinds, a small roasting-jack, etc. Our last prize was a chest of choice eatables, intended for the table of the officers, containing Westphalia hams, Bologna sausages, and other savoury food. I took good care not to forget some little sacks of maize, of wheat, and other grain, and some potatoes. We next added such implements for husbandry as we could find; shovels, hoes, spades, rakes, harrows, etc. Fritz reminded me that we had found sleeping on the ground both cold and hard, and prevailed upon me to increase our cargo by some hammocks, and a certain number of blankets; and as guns had hitherto been the source of his pleasures, he added such as he could find of a particular costliness or structure, together with some sabres and clasp-knives. The last articles we took were a barrel of sulphur, a quantity of ropes, some small string, and a large roll of sail-cloth. The vessel appeared to us to be in so wretched a condition, that the least tempest must make her go to pieces. It was then quite uncertain whether we should be able to approach her any more.

Our cargo was so large, that the tubs were filled to the very brim, and no inch of the boat's room was lost. The first and last of the tubs were reserved for Fritz and me to seat ourselves in and row the boat, which sank so low in the water, that if the sea had not been quite calm, we should have been obliged to ease her of some of the loading: we, however, used the precaution of putting on our swimming-jackets, for fear of any misfortune.

It will easily be imagined that the day had been laboriously employed. Night suddenly surprised us, and we lost all hope of returning to our family the same evening. A large blazing fire on the shore soon after greeted our sight,—the signal agreed upon for assuring us that all was well, and to bid us close our eyes in peace. We returned the compliment, by tying four lanterns, with lights in them, to our mast-head. This was answered, on their part, by the firing of two guns; so that both parties had reason to be satisfied and easy.

CHAPTER VI
A Troop of Animals in Cork Jackets

EARLY the next morning, though it was scarcely light, I mounted the vessel, hoping to gain a sight of our beloved companions through a telescope. Fritz prepared a substantial breakfast of biscuit and ham; but, before we sat down, we recollected that in the captain's cabin we had seen a telescope of a much superior size and power, and we speedily conveyed it to the deck. While this was doing, the brightness of the day had come on. I fixed my eye to the glass, and discovered my wife coming out of the tent, and looking attentively towards the vessel, and at the same moment perceived the motion of the flag upon the shore. A load of anxiety was thus taken from my heart; for I had the certainty that all were in good health, and had escaped the dangers of the night.—"Now that I have had a sight of your mother," said I to Fritz, "my next concern is for the animals on board; let us endeavour to save the lives of some of them at least, and to take them with us."

"Would it be possible to make a raft, to get them all upon it, and in this way get them to shore?" asked Fritz.

"But what a difficulty in making it! and how could we induce a cow, an ass, and a sow, either to get upon a raft, or, when there, to remain motionless and quiet? The sheep and goats one might perhaps find means to remove, they being of a more docile temper: but for the larger animals, I am at a loss how to proceed."

"My advice, father, is to tie a long rope round the sow's neck, and throw her without ceremony into the sea: her immense bulk will be sure to sustain her above water; and we can draw her after the boat."

"Your idea is excellent: but unfortunately it is of no use but for the pig; and she is the one I care the least about preserving."

"Then here is another idea, father: let us tie a swimming-jacket round the body of each animal, and contrive to throw one and all into the water; you will see that they will swim like fish, and we can draw them after us in the same manner."

"Right, very right, my boy; your invention is admirable: let us therefore not lose a moment in making the experiment."

We hastened to the execution of our design: we fixed a jacket on one of the lambs, and threw it into the sea; and full of anxious curiosity, I followed the poor beast with my eyes. He sank at first, and I thought him drowned; but he soon reappeared, shaking the water from his head, and in a few seconds he had learned completely the art of swimming. After another interval, we observed that he appeared fatigued, gave up his efforts, and suffered himself to be borne along by the course of the water, which sustained and conducted him to our complete satisfaction.— "Victory!" exclaimed I, hugging my boy with delight: "these useful animals are all our own; let us lose not a moment in adopting the same means with those that remain; but take care not to lose our little lamb." Fritz now would have jumped into the water to follow the poor creature, who was still floating safely on the surface; but I stopped him till I had seen him tie on a swimming-jacket. He took with him a rope, first making a slip-knot in it, and soon overtaking the lamb, threw it round his neck, and drew him back to our boat: and then took him out of the water.

We next got four small water-butts. I emptied them, and then carefully closed them again. I united them with a large piece of sail-cloth, nailing one end to each cask. I strengthened this with a second piece of sail-cloth, and this contrivance I destined to support the cow and the ass, two casks to each, the animal being placed in the middle, with a cask on either side. I added a thong of leather, stretching from the casks across the breast and haunches of the animal, to make the whole secure; and thus, in less than an hour, both my cow and my ass were equipped for swimming.

It was next the turn of the smaller animals: of these, the

sow gave us the most trouble: we were first obliged to put a muzzle on her to prevent her biting; and then we tied a large piece of cork under her body. The sheep and goats were more accommodating, and we had soon accoutred them for our adventure. And now we had succeeded in assembling our whole company on the deck, in readiness for the voyage: we tied a cord to either the horns or the neck of of each animal, and to the other end of the cord a piece of wood similar to the mode used for making nets, that it might be easy for us to take hold of the ropes, and so draw the animal to us if it should be necessary. We began our experiment with the ass, by conducting him as near as possible to the brink of the vessel, and then suddenly shoving him off. He fell into the water, and for a moment disappeared; but we soon saw him rise, and in the action of swimming between his two barrels, with a grace which really merited our commendation.

Next came the cow's turn: and as she was infinitely more valuable than the ass, my fears increased in due proportion. The ass had swum so courageously, that he was already at a considerable distance from the vessel, so that there was sufficient room for our experiment on the cow. We had more difficulty in pushing her overboard; but she reached the water in as much safety as the ass had done before; she did not sink so low in it, and was no less perfectly sustained by the empty barrels; and she made her way with gravity, and, if I may so express it, a sort of dignified composure. According to this method we proceeded with our whole troop, throwing them one by one into the water, where by and by they appeared in a group floating at their ease, and seemingly well content. The sow was the only exception: she became quite furious, set up a loud squalling, and struggled with so much violence in the water, that she was carried to a considerable distance, but fortunately in a direction towards the landing-place we had in view. We had now not a moment to lose. Our last act was to put on our cork jackets; and then we descended without accident through the cleft, took our station in the boat, and were soon in the midst of our troop of quadrupeds. We carefully gathered all the floating bits of wood, and fastened them to the stern of the machine, and thus drew them after us. When everything was adjusted, and our company in order, we hoisted our sail,

which, soon filling with a favourable wind, bore us towards
the land.

Proud of the success of so extraordinary a feat, we were
in high spirits, and seated ourselves in the tubs, where we
made an excellent dinner. I was occupied in thinking of
those I had left on land, when a sudden exclamation from
Fritz filled me with alarm.—"Oh, heavens!" cried he, "we
are lost! a fish of an enormous size is coming up to the
boat."—"And why lost?" said I, half angry, and yet half
partaking of his fright. "Be ready with your gun, and the
moment he is close upon us we will fire upon him." He had
nearly reached the boat, and with the rapidity of lightning
had seized the foremost sheep: at this instant Fritz aimed his
fire so skilfully, that the balls of the gun were lodged in the
head of the monster, which was an enormous shark. The
fish half turned himself round in the water and hurried off
to sea, leaving us to observe the lustrous smoothness of his
belly, and that as he proceeded he stained the water red,
which convinced us he had been severely wounded.

The animal being now out of sight, and our fears appeased, I resumed the rudder; and as the wind drove us
straight towards the bay, I took down the sail, and continued rowing till we reached a convenient spot for our cattle
to land. I had then only to untie the end of the cords from
the boat, and they stepped contentedly on shore. Our voyage thus happily concluded, we followed their example.

Ernest and Jack now ran to the boat, and began to shout
their admiration of the mast, the sail, and the flag, desiring
their brother to explain to them how all the things they saw
had been effected, and what he himself did of them. In the
meantime we began to unpack our cargo, while Jack stole
aside and amused himself with the animals, took off the
jackets from the sheep and goats, bursting from time to
time into shouts of laughter at the ridiculous figure of the
ass, who stood before them adorned with his two casks and
his swimming apparatus, and braying loud enough to make
us deaf.

By and by I perceived, with surprise, that Jack had round
his waist a belt of metal covered with yellow skin, in which
were fixed two pistols. "In the name of Heaven," exclaimed
I, "where did you procure this curious costume, which gives
you the look of a smuggler?"

"From my own manufactory," replied he; "and if you cast your eyes upon the dogs, you will see more of my specimens."

Accordingly I looked at them, and perceived that each had on a collar similar to the belt round Jack's waist, with, however, the exception of the collars being armed with nails, the points of which were outwards, and exhibited a formidable appearance. "And is it you, Mr. Jack," cried I, "who have invented and executed these collars and your belt?"

"Yes, father, they are indeed my invention, with a little of my mother's assistance when it was necessary to use the needle."

"But where did you get the leather and the thread and the needle?"

"Fritz's jackal furnished the first," answered my wife; "and as to the last, a good mother of a family is always provided with them. Then have I not an enchanted bag, from which I draw out such articles as I stand in need of? So if you have a particular fancy for anything, you have only to acquaint me with it." I tenderly embraced her, to express my thanks for this effort to amuse by so agreeable a raillery, and Jack too came in for his share both of the caresses and our hearty commendations.

Perceiving that no preparations were making for supper, I told Fritz to bring us the Westphalia ham. The eyes of all were now fixed upon me with astonishment, believing that I could only be in jest; when Fritz returned, displaying with exultation a large ham, which we had begun to cut in the morning. "A ham!" cried one and all; "a ham! and ready dressed! What a nice supper we shall have!" said they, clapping their hands to give a hearty welcome to the bearer of so fine a treat.—"It comes quite in the nick of time too," interrupted I; "for, to judge by appearances, a certain careful steward I could name seems to have intended to send us supperless to bed, little thinking, I suppose, that a long voyage by water is apt to increase the appetite."

"I will tell you presently," replied my wife, "what it was that prevented me from providing a supper for you all at an early hour: your ham, however, makes you ample amends; and I have something in my hand with which I shall make a pretty side-dish; in the twinkling of an eye you shall see it make its entrance." She now showed us about a dozen of turtles' eggs, and then hurried away to make an omelette of some of them.

"Look, father," said Ernest, "if they are not the very same which Robinson Crusoe found in his island! See, they are like white balls, covered with a skin like wetted parchment! We found them upon the sands along the shore."

"Your account is perfectly just, my dear boy," said I: "by what means did you make so useful a discovery?"—"Oh, that is part of our history," interrupted my wife; "for I also have a history to relate, when you will be so good as to listen to it."

"Hasten then, my love, and get your pretty side-dish ready, and we will have the history for the dessert. In the meantime I will relieve the cow and the ass from their jackets. Come along, boys, and give me your help."—I got up, and they all followed me gaily to the shore. We were not long in effecting our purpose with the cow and the ass, who were animals of a quiet and kind temper; but when it was the sow's turn, our success was neither so easy nor so certain; for no sooner had we untied the rope than she escaped from us, and ran so fast that none of us could catch her. The idea occurred to Ernest of sending the two dogs after her, who caught at her ears, and sent her back, while we were half deafened with the hideous noise she made; at last she suffered us to take off her cork jacket. We now laid the accoutrements across the ass's back, and returned to the kitchen; our slothful Ernest highly delighted that we were likely in future to have our loads carried by a servant.

In the meanwhile, the kind mother had prepared the omelette, and spread a tablecloth on the end of the cask of butter, upon which she had placed some of the plates and silver spoons we had brought from the ship. The ham was in the middle, and the omelette and the cheese opposite to each other; and altogether made a figure not to be despised by the inhabitants of a desert island. By and by the two dogs, the fowls, the pigeons, the sheep, and the goats had all assembled round us, which gave us something like the air of sovereigns of the country.

When we had finished our repast, I bade Fritz present our company with a bottle of Canary wine, which we had brought from the captain's cabin, and I desired my wife to indulge us with the promised history.

CHAPTER VII

Second Journey of Discovery Performed by the Mother of the Family

YOU pretend," said my wife, with a little malicious smile, "to be curious about my history, yet you have not let me speak a single word in all this time: but the longer a torrent is pent up, the longer it flows when once let loose. Now, then, that you are in the humour to listen, I shall give vent to a certain little movement of vanity which is fluttering at my heart. Not, however, to intrude too long upon your patience, we will skip the first day of your absence, in the course of which nothing new took place. But this morning, when I was made happy by the sight of your signal, and had set up mine in return, I looked about, before the boys were up, in hopes to find a shady place where we might now and then retire from the heat of the sun; but I found not a single tree. This made me reflect a little seriously on our situation. It will be impossible, said I to myself, to remain in this place with no shelter but a miserable tent, under which the heat is even more excessive than without. Courage, then! pursued I; my husband and my eldest son are at this moment employed for the general good; why should not I be active and enterprising also? why not undertake, with my youngest sons, to do something that shall add some one comfort to our existence? I will pass over with them to the other side of the river, and with my own eyes examine the country respecting which my husband and Fritz have related such wonders. I will try to find out some well shaded agreeable spot, in which we may all be settled.

"I assembled the boys round me, and informed them of

55

my plans for an excursion; and you may believe I heard nothing like a dissenting voice. They lost not a moment in preparing themselves; they examined their arms, their game-bags, looked out the best clasp-knives, and cheerfully undertook to carry the provision-bags; while I, for my share, was loaded with a large flask of water and a hatchet, for which I thought it likely we might find a use. I also took the light gun which belongs to Ernest, and gave him in return a carbine, which might be loaded with several balls at once. We took some refreshment, and then sallied forth, attended by the two dogs for our escort. We arrived at the place at which you had crossed the river, and succeeded in passing over, though not without difficulty. After having filled my flask with river water, we proceeded on our way till we had reached to the top of the hill which you described to us as so enchanting, and where I partook of the pleasure you had experienced.

"In casting my eyes over the vast extent before me, I had observed a small wood of the most inviting aspect. I had so long sighed for a little shade, that I resolved to bend our course towards it; for this, however, it was necessary to go a long way through a strong kind of grass, which reached above the heads of the little boys; an obstacle which, on trial, we found too difficult to overcome. We therefore resolved to walk along the river, and turn at last upon the wood. We found traces of your footsteps, and took care to follow them till we had come to a place which seemed to lead directly to it; but here again we were interrupted by the height and thickness of the grass, which nothing but the most exhausting endeavours could have enabled us to get through.

"On a sudden we perceived a large bird rising from the thickest part of the grass, and mounting in the air. Each of the boys prepared to fire, but before they could be ready, the bird was out of the reach of shot. Ernest was bitterly disappointed, and instantly exchanged the gun for the carbine I had given him, crying, 'What a pity! If I had but had the lightest gun! if the bird had not got away so fast, I would lay any wager I should have killed him.'

" 'The mischief was, no doubt, that you did not let him know beforehand that it was your pleasure he should wait till you could be quite ready,' observed I, laughing.

" 'But, mother, how could I possibly suppose that the bird could fly away in less than the twinkling of an eye? Ah, if one would but come at this very moment!'

" 'A good sportsman, Ernest, always holds himself in readiness, this being, as I understand, one of his great arts; but as the opportunity is gone, let us look for the place in the grass from which he mounted; we may judge at least of his size by the mark he will have left there.' The boys all scampered away to the place, when suddenly a second bird, exactly like the first, except that he was a little larger, rushed out with a great noise and mounted above their heads.

"The boys remained stupid with astonishment, following him with their eyes and open mouths without speaking a word, while for my own part I could not help laughing heartily. 'Oh! such fine sportsmen as we have here!' cried I: 'they will never let us be in want of game, I plainly perceive. *Ah! if one would but come at this very moment!*' We now minutely examined the place from which the birds had mounted, and found a kind of large nest formed of dry plants, of clumsy workmanship; the nest was empty, with the exception of some broken shells of eggs. I inferred from this that their young had lately been hatched; and observing at this moment a rustling motion among some plants of shorter growth, at some distance from the spot on which we stood, I concluded that the young covey were scampering away in that direction; but as the motion soon ceased, we had no longer a guide to conduct us to their retreat.

"We next reached a little wood. A prodigious quantity of unknown birds were skipping and warbling on the branches of the trees, without betraying the least alarm at our vicinity. The boys wanted to fire on them; but this I absolutely forbade, and with the less scruple, as the trees were of so enormous a height as to be out of gun-shot reach. No, my dear husband, you cannot possibly form an idea of the trees we now beheld! You must somehow have missed this wood; or so extraordinary a sight could not have escaped your observation. What appeared to us at a distance to be a wood was only a group of about fourteen of them, the trunks of which seemed to be supported in their upright position by arches on each side, these arches being formed by the roots of the tree.

"Jack climbed with considerable trouble upon one of these arch-formed roots, and with a pack-thread in his hand measured the actual circumference of the tree itself. He found that it measured more than fifteen braches.[1] I made thirty-two steps in going round one of those giant productions at the roots; and its height from the ground to the place where the branches begin to shoot may be about thirty-six braches. The twigs of the tree are strong and thick; its leaves moderately large in size, and bearing some resemblance to the hazel tree of Europe; but I was unable to discover that it bore any fruit. The large breadth of shade which presented itself seemed to invite us to make this spot the place of our repose: and my predilection for it grew so strong that I resolved to go no further, but to enjoy its delicious coolness till it should be time to return. I sat down in this verdant elysium with my three sons around me. We took out our provision-bags: a charming stream, formed to increase the coolness and beauty of the scene, flowed at our feet, and supplied us with a fresh and salutary beverage. It occurred to me, that if we could but contrive a kind of tent that could be fixed in one of the trees, we might safely come and make our abode here. I had found nothing in any other direction that suited us so well in every respect; and I resolved to look no further. When we had shared our dinner among us, and well rested from our fatigue, we set out on our return, again keeping close to the river, half expecting to see along the shore some of the pieces or other vestiges of the vessel, which the waves might have washed up.

"As I expected, we found there pieces of timber, poles, large and small chests, and other articles, which I knew had come from the vessel. None of us, however, were strong enough to bring them away; we therefore contented ourselves with dragging all we could reach to the dry sands, beyond the reach of the waves at high water.

"We now suddenly cast our eyes on Flora, whom we perceived employed in turning over a round substance she had found in the sands, some pieces of which she swallowed from time to time. Ernest also perceived her motions, and did us the favour, with his usual composure, to pronounce just these words:—'They are turtles' eggs.' We found it

---

[1] The brache is equal to twenty-two inches and a half.

difficult to make Flora leave the eggs, to which she had taken a great fancy. At length, however, we succeeded in collecting near two dozen of them, which we secured in our provision-bags. When we had concluded this affair, we by accident cast our eyes upon the sea, and to our astonishment perceived a sail, which seemed to be joyfully approaching towards the land. I knew not what to imagine; but Ernest exclaimed that it was you and Fritz; and we soon had the happiness of being convinced that it was indeed our well-beloved! We ran eagerly towards the river, and soon arrived at the place of your landing, when we had nothing further to do but to throw ourselves into your arms!"

CHAPTER VIII
Construction of a Bridge

WHEN my wife and I awaked the next morning, we resumed the question of our change of abode. I observed to her that it was a matter of difficulty, and that we might have reason to repent such a step. "My own opinion is," said I, "that we had better remain here, where Providence seems to have conducted us; the place is favourable to our personal safety, and is near the vessel, from which we may continue to enrich ourselves: we are on all sides protected by the rocks; it is an asylum inaccessible but by sea, or by the passage of the river, which is not easily accomplished. Let us then have patience yet a little longer at least, till we have got all that can be removed, or that would be useful to us, from the ship."

My wife replied, that the intense heat of the sands was insupportable; that by remaining, we lost all hope of procuring fruits of any kind, and must live on oysters, or on wild birds.

"As for the safety you boast of," pursued she, "the rocks did not prevent our receiving a visit from the jackals; nor is it improbable that tigers or other animals might follow their example. Lastly, as to the treasures we might continue to draw from the vessel, I renounce them with all my heart. We are already in possession of provisions and other useful things: and, to say the truth, my heart is always filled with distressing apprehensions, when you and Fritz are exposed to the danger of that perfidious element the sea."

"We will then think seriously of the matter; but let us have a well-digested scheme of operation before we leave this spot for your favourite wood. First, we must contrive a store-house among the rocks for our provisions and other things, and to which, in case of invasion in the wood, we can retreat and defend ourselves. This agreed, the next thing is to throw a bridge across the river, if we are to pass it with all our family and baggage."

"A bridge!" exclaimed my wife: "can you possibly think of such a thing? If we stay while you build a bridge, we may consider ourselves as fixed for life. Why should we not cross the river as we did before? The ass and the cow will carry all we possess upon their backs."

"But do you recollect, that to keep what they carry dry, they must not perform their journey as they did from the vessel? For this reason, then, if for no other, we must contrive a bridge. We shall want also some sacks and baskets to contain our different matters; you may therefore set about making these, and I will undertake the bridge, which, the more I consider, the more I find to be of indispensable necessity."

Thus, then, we decided the important question of removing to a new abode; after which we fixed upon a plan of labour for the day, and then awaked the boys. Their delight on hearing of our project may easily be conceived, but they expressed their fear that it would be a long while before a bridge could be built.

We now began to look about for breakfast. My wife undertook to milk the cow, and afterwards gave some of the milk to each of the children: with a part of what remained she made a sort of sop with biscuits, and the rest she put into one of the flasks, to accompany us in our expedition. During this time, I was preparing the boat for another journey to the vessel, to bring away a sufficient quantity of planks and timbers for the bridge. After breakfast we set out; and now I took with me Ernest as well as Fritz, that we might accomplish our object in a shorter time.

We rowed stoutly till we reached the current, which soon drew us on beyond the bay; but scarcely had we passed a little islet, lying to one side of us, than we perceived a prodigious quantity of sea-gulls and other birds. I had a curiosity to discover what could be the reason of such an assemblage of these creatures. I steered for the spot; but finding that the boat made but little way, I hoisted my sail.

I approached near enough to step upon the land, and after bringing the boat to an anchor with a heavy stone, we stole softly up to the birds. We soon perceived that the object which attracted them was in reality an enormous fish, which had been thrown there by the sea. So eagerly were they occupied with the feast, that not one of them attempted to fly off. We observed with astonishment the extreme voracity of this plumed group: each bird was so intent upon its prey that we might have killed great numbers of them with our sticks alone. Fritz did not cease to express his wonder at the monstrous size of the animal, and asked me by what means it could have got there?

"I believe," answered I, "you were yourself the means; there is every appearance that it is the very shark you wounded yesterday. See, here are the two balls which you discharged at its head."

"Yes, yes, it is the very same," said my young hero, skipping about for joy: "I well remember I had two balls in my gun, and here they are, lodged in its head."

Ernest drew out the iron ramrod from his gun, and by striking with it to right and left among the birds, soon dispersed them. Fritz and I then advanced and cut several long strips of the skin from the head of the shark, with which we were proceeding to our boat, when I observed, lying on the ground, some planks and timbers which had recently been cast by the sea on this little island. On measuring the longest, we perceived they would answer our purpose; and with the assistance of the crow and a lever which we had brought with us, found means to get them

into the boat, and thus spare ourselves the trouble of proceeding to the vessel. With great exertion of our strength,
we contrived to bind the timbers together, with the planks
upon them, in the manner of a raft, and tied them to the
end of the boat; so that, through this adventure, we were
ready to return in four hours from the time of departure,
and might boast of having done a good day's work.

We were once more landed safely on our shore, but no
one of our family appeared. We called to them as loud as
we could, which was answered by the same sounds in return, and in a few minutes my wife appeared between her
two little boys returning from the river, a rising piece of
ground having concealed her from our sight: each carried a
handkerchief in hand, which appeared filled with some new
prize: and little Francis had a small fishing-net formed like a
bag and strung upon a stick, which he carried on his shoulder. No sooner did they hear our voice, than they flew to
meet us, surprised at our quick return. Jack reached us
before the rest; and his first act was to open the handkerchief he held, and pour out a large number of lobsters at our
feet: their mother and little Francis produced each as many
more, forming all together a prodigious heap, and all alive;
so that we were sure of excellent dinners for some days at
least.

After we had given an account of our voyage, my wife set
about dressing some of the lobsters, and in the meantime
Fritz and I employed ourselves in untying the raft of timbers
and planks, and in moving them from the boat. I then
imitated the example of the Laplanders, in harnessing their
reindeer for drawing their sledges. Instead of traces, halters,
etc., I put a piece of rope, with a running knot at the end,
round the neck of the ass, and passed the other end between
its legs, to which I tied the piece of wood which I wished to
be removed. The cow was harnessed in the same manner,
and we were thus enabled to carry our materials, piece by
piece, to the spot which had been chosen at the river as the
most eligible for our bridge. It was a place where the shore
on each side was steep, and of equal height; there was even
on our side an old trunk of a tree lying on the ground, which
I foresaw would have its use.

"Now then, boys," said I, "the first thing is to see if our
timbers are long enough to reach to the other side: by my

eye, I should think they are; but if I had a surveyor's plane, we might be quite sure, instead of working at a venture."

"But my mother has some balls of packthread, with which she measured the height of the giant tree," interrupted Ernest, "and nothing would be more easy than to tie a stone to the end of one of them, and throw it to the other side of the river; then we could draw it to the very brink, and thus obtain the exact length that would be required for our timbers."

"Your idea is excellent," cried I; "run quickly and fetch the packthread." He returned without loss of time; the stone was tied to its end, and thrown across as we had planned; we drew it gently back to the river edge, marking the place where the bridge was to rest: we next measured the string, and found that the distance from one side to the other was eighteen feet. It appeared to me, that to give a sufficient solidity to the timbers, I must allow three feet of extra length at each end for fixing them, making therefore in all twenty-four; and I was fortunate enough to find that many of those we had brought did not fall short of this length. There now remained the difficulty of carrying one end across the stream; but we determined to discuss this part of the subject while we ate our dinner, which had been waiting for us more than an hour.

We hurried through our meal, each being deeply interested in the work we were about to undertake, and thinking only of the part which might be assigned him towards the execution of the *Nonsuch*; for this, for mutual encouragement, was the name we gave our bridge, even before it was in existence.

Having consulted as to the means of laying our timbers across the river, the first thing I did was to attach one of them to the trunk of the tree, of which I have already spoken, by a strong cord, long enough to turn freely round the trunk; I then fastened a second cord to the other end of the timber, and tying a stone to its extremity, flung it to the opposite bank. I next passed the river as I had done before, furnished with a pulley, which I secured to a tree: I passed my second cord through the pulley, and recrossing the river with this cord in my hand, I contrived to harness the ass and cow to the end of the cord. I next drove the animals from the bank of the river: they resisted at first, but I made them go by force of drawing. I first fixed one end of the beam firmly to the trunk of the tree, and then they drew along the other end, so as gradually to advance over the river: presently, to my great joy, I saw it touch the other side, and at length become fixed and firm by its own weight. In a moment Fritz and Jack leaped upon the timber, and, in spite of my paternal fears, crossed the stream with a joyful step upon this narrow but effective bridge.

The first timber being thus laid, the difficulty was considerably diminished; a second and a third were fixed in succession, and with the greatest ease. Fritz and I, standing on opposite sides of the river, placed them at such distances from each other as was necessary to form a broad and handsome bridge: what now remained to be done was to lay some short planks across them quite close to each other, which we executed so expeditiously, that our construction was completed in a much shorter time than I should have imagined possible. Our labour, however, had occasioned us so much fatigue, that we found ourselves unable for that day to enter upon new exertions; and the evening beginning to set in, we returned to our home, where we partook heartily of an excellent supper, and went to bed.

CHAPTER IX
Change of Abode

AS soon as we were up and had breakfasted the next morning, I assembled all the members of my family together, to take with them a solemn farewell of this our first place of reception from the awful disaster of the shipwreck. I directed my sons to assemble our whole flock of animals, and to leave the ass and the cow to me, that I might load

them with the sacks which my wife had made; I had filled
these, and made a slit longways in the middle of each, and
to each side of the slits I tied several long pieces of cord,
which crossing each other, and being again brought round
and fastened, served to hold the sacks firmly on the back of
the animal. We next began to put together all the things we
should stand most in need of for the two or three first days
in our new abode: working implements, kitchen utensils, the
captain's service of plate, and a small provision of butter,
etc., etc. I put these articles into the two ends of each sack,
taking care that the sides should be equally heavy, and then
fastened them on. I afterwards added our hammocks to
complete the load, and we were about to begin to march,
when my wife stopped me.—"We must not," said she, "leave
our fowls behind, for fear they should become the prey of
the jackals. We must contrive a place for them among the
luggage, and also one for our little Francis, who cannot walk
so far, and would interrupt our speed. There is also my
enchanted bag, which I recommend to your particular care,"
said she, smiling, "for who can tell what may yet pop out of
it for your good pleasure?"

I now placed the child on the ass's back, fixing the enchanted bag in such a way as to support him, and I tied
them together with so many cords, that the animal might
even have galloped without danger of his falling off.

We packed and placed in the tent everything we were to
leave, and for greater security, fastened down the ends of
the sail-cloth, at the entrance, by driving stakes through
them into the ground. We ranged a number of vessels, both
full and empty, round the tent, to serve as a rampart, and
thus we confided to the protection of Heaven our remaining
treasures. At length, we set ourselves in motion: each of us,
great and small, carried a gun upon his shoulder, and a
game-bag at his back. My wife led the way with her eldest
son, the cow and the ass immediately behind them; the
goats, conducted by Jack, came next; the little monkey was
seated on the back of his nurse, and made a thousand
grimaces. After the goats came Ernest, conducting the sheep,
while I, in my capacity of general superintendent, followed
behind, and brought up the rear; the dogs for the most part
pranced backwards and forwards, like adjutants to a troop
of soldiers. Our march was slow, and there was something

solemn and patriarchal in the spectacle we exhibited; I fancied we must resemble our forefathers journeying in the deserts, accompanied by their families and their possessions.

On the other side of the river we experienced an inconvenience wholly unexpected. The tempting aspect of the grass, which grew here in profusion, drew off our animals, who strayed from us to feed upon it; so that, without the dogs, we should not have been able to bring them back to the line of our procession. The active creatures were of great use to us on this occasion; and when everything was restored to proper order, we were able to continue our journey. For fear, however, of a similar occurrence, I directed our march to the left, along the seaside, where the produce of the soil was not of a quality to attract them.

But scarcely had we advanced a few steps on the sands, when our two dogs, which had strayed behind among the grass, set up a sort of howl, as if engaged in an encounter with some formidable animal. Fritz in an instant raised his gun to his cheek, and was ready to fire; Ernest, always somewhat timid, drew back to his mother's side; Jack ran bravely after Fritz with his gun upon his shoulder; while I, fearing the dogs might be attacked by some dangerous wild beast, prepared myself to advance to their assistance. But youth is always full of ardour: and in spite of my exhortations to proceed with caution, the boys, eager for the event, made but three jumps to the place from which the noise proceeded. In an instant Jack had turned to meet me, clapping his hands, and calling out, "Come quickly, father, come quickly, here is a monstrous porcupine!"

I soon reached the spot, and perceived that it was really as he said, bating a little exaggeration. The dogs were running to and fro with bleeding noses about the animal; and when they approached too near him, he made a frightful noise, and pierced them with his quills so deeply and suddenly that the pain the wounds occasioned made them howl violently.

While we were looking on, Jack determined on an attack, which succeeded well. He took one of the pistols which he carried in his belt, and aimed it so exactly at the head of the porcupine, that he fell dead the instant he fired, and before we had a notion of what he was about. We now all got round the extraordinary animal, on whom nature has bestowed a strong defence by arming his body all over with long spears. The boys were at a loss what means to use for carrying away his carcass. They thought of dragging it along the ground; but as often as they attempted to take hold, there was nothing but squalling, and running to show the marks made by his quills on their hands.—"We must leave him behind," said they, "but it is a great pity."

While the boys were talking, my wife and I had hastened to relieve the dogs, by examining the wounds which had been inflicted by the quills. Fritz had run on before with his gun, hoping he should meet with some animal of prey. We followed him at our leisure, taking care not to expose our health by unnecessary fatigue; till at last, without further accident or adventure, we arrived at the place of the giant trees. Such indeed we found them, and our astonishment exceeded all description.—"Good heavens! what trees! what a height! what trunks! I never heard of any so prodigious!" exclaimed one and all.—"Nothing can be more rational than your admiration," answered I, measuring them with my eyes as I spoke. "I must confess I had not myself formed an idea of the reality. To you be all the honour, my dear wife, of the discovery of this agreeable abode, in which we shall enjoy so many comforts and advantages. The great point we have to gain is the fixing a tent large enough to receive us all in one of these trees, by which means we shall be perfectly secure from the invasion of wild beasts. I defy even one of the bears, who are so famous for mounting trees, to climb up by a trunk so immense, and so destitute of branches."

We began now to release our animals from their burdens, having first thrown our own on the grass. We next used the precaution of tying their two fore-legs together with a cord, that they might not go far away or lose themselves. We restored the fowls to liberty; and then seating ourselves upon the grass, we held a family council on the subject of our future establishment. I was myself somewhat uneasy on the question of our safety during the ensuing night; for I was ignorant of the nature of the extensive country I beheld around me, and what chance there might be of our being attacked by different kinds of wild beasts. I accordingly observed to my wife, that I would make an endeavour for us all to sleep in the tree that very night. While I was deliberating with her on the subject, Fritz had stolen away to a short

distance, and we heard the report of a gun. This would have
alarmed me, if at the same moment we had not recognized
Fritz's voice crying out, "I touched him! I touched him!"
and in a moment we saw him running towards us, holding a
dead animal of uncommon beauty by the paws.—"Father,
father, look, here is a superb tiger-cat," said he, proudly
raising it in the air, to show it to the best advantage.—"Bravo!
bravo!" cried I: "bravo, Nimrod the undaunted! Your exploit will call forth the gratitude of our cocks, hens, and
pigeons, for you have rendered them what they cannot fail
to think an important service. If you had not killed this
animal, he would no doubt have demolished in one night
our whole stock of poultry. One idea occurs to me: skin the
animal carefully, so as not to injure it, particularly the parts
which cover the fore-legs and the tail. You may then make
yourself a belt with it, like your brother Jack's. The odd
pieces will serve to make some cases to contain our utensils
for the table, such as knives, forks and spoons. Go then,
boy, and put away its head, and we will see how to set about
preparing the skin."

The boys left me no moment of repose till I had shown
them how to take off the skins of the animals without
tearing them. In the meanwhile Ernest looked about for a
flat stone as a sort of foundation for a fireplace, and little
Francis collected some pieces of dry wood for his mother to
light a fire. Ernest was not long in finding what he wanted,
and then he ran to join us, and give us his assistance, or
rather to reason, right or wrong, on the subject of skinning
animals; and then on that of trees, making various com-
ments and inquiries respecting the real name of those we
intended to inhabit.—"It is my opinion," said he, "that they
are, really and simply, enormously large hazel trees; see if
the leaf is not of exactly the same form."—"But that is no
proof," interrupted I; "for many trees bear leaves of the
same shape, but nevertheless are of different kinds."

Presently little Francis came running, with his mouth
crammed full of something, and calling out, "Mamma,
mamma! I have found a nice fruit to eat, and I have brought
you home some of it!"

"Little glutton!" replied his mother, quite alarmed, "what
have you got there? For Heaven's sake, do not swallow, in
this imprudent manner, the first thing that falls in your way;

for by this means you may be poisoned, and then you would die." She made him open his mouth, and took out with her finger what he was eating with so keen a relish. With some difficulty she drew out the remains of a fig.—"A fig!" exclaimed I: "where did you get this fig?"

Francis.—I got it among the grass, papa; and there are a great many more. I thought it must be good to eat, for the fowls and the pigeons, and even the pig, came to the place, and ate them in large quantities.

Father.—"You see then, my dear," said I to my wife, "that our beautiful trees are fig-trees, at least the kind which are thus named at the Antilles." I took this occasion to give the boys another lesson on the necessity of being cautious, and never to venture on tasting anything they met with, till they had seen it eaten by birds and monkeys. At the word monkeys, they all ran to visit the little orphan, whom they found seated on the root of a tree, and examining with the oddest grimaces the half-skinned tiger-cat, which lay near him. Francis offered him a fig, which he first turned round and round, then smelled at it, and concluded eating it voraciously.—"Bravo! bravo! Mr. Monkey," exclaimed the boys, clapping their hands; "so then these figs are good to eat!"

In the meanwhile my wife had been busy in making a fire, putting on the pot, and preparing for our dinner. The tiger-cat was bestowed upon the dogs, who waited impatiently to receive it. While our dinner was dressing, I employed my time in making some packing-needles with some of the quills of the porcupine, which the boys had contrived to draw from his skin, and bring home. I put the point of a large nail into the fire till it was red-hot; then taking hold of it with some wet linen in my hand, by way of guard, I with great ease perforated the thick end of the quills with it. I had soon the pleasure of presenting my wife with a large packet of long, stout needles, which were the more valuable in her estimation as she had formed the intention of contriving some better harness for our animals, and had been perplexed how to set about it without some larger needles.

I had singled out the highest fig-tree; and while we were waiting for dinner, I made the boys try how high they could throw a stick or stone into it. I also tried myself; but the lowest branches were so far from the ground, that none of

us could touch them. I perceived, therefore, that we should
want some new inventions for fastening the ends of my
ladder to them. I allowed a short pause to my imagination,
during which I assisted Jack and Fritz in carrying the skin of
the tiger-cat to a near rivulet, where we confined it under
water with some large stones. After this we returned and
dined heartily on some slices of ham and bread and cheese,
under the shade of our favourite trees.

CHAPTER X

Construction of a Ladder

OUR repast ended, I observed to my wife that we should
be obliged to pass the night on the ground. I desired
her to begin preparing the harness for the animals, that they
might go to the seashore, and fetch pieces of wood, or other
articles which might be useful to us. I, in the meantime, set
about suspending our hammocks to some of the arched
roots of the trees. I next spread a piece of sail-cloth large
enough to cover them, to preserve us from the dew, and
from the insects. I then hastened with the two eldest boys to
the seashore, to choose out such pieces of wood as were
most proper for the steps of my ladder. Ernest was so lucky
as to discover some bamboo canes in a sort of bog. I took
them out, and, with his assistance, completely cleared them
from the dirt; and stripping off their leaves, I found, to my
great joy, that they were precisely what I wanted. I then
instantly began to cut them with my hatchet, in pieces of
four or five feet long; the boys bound them together in
faggots, and we prepared to return with them to our place
of abode. I next secured some of the straight and most
slender of the stalks, to make some arrows with, of which I

knew I should stand in need. At some distance from the place where we stood, I perceived a sort of thicket, in which I hoped to find some young pliant twigs, which I thought might also be useful to me: we proceeded to the spot; but apprehending it might be the retreat of some dangerous reptile or animal, we held our guns in readiness. Flora, who had accompanied us, went before. We had hardly reached the thicket before she made several jumps, and threw herself furiously into the middle of the bushes; when a troop of large-sized flamingoes sprang out, and with a loud rustling noise mounted into the air. Fritz fired, when two of the birds fell among the bushes: one of them was quite dead; the other was only slightly wounded in the wing, and finding that he could not fly, he ran so fast towards the water, that we were afraid he would escape us. Fritz, in the joy of his heart, plunged up to his knees in the water, to pick up the flamingo he had killed, and with great difficulty was able to get out again; while I, warned by his example, proceeded more cautiously in my pursuit of the wounded bird. Flora came to my assistance, and running on before, caught hold of the flamingo, and held him fast till I reached the spot, and took him into my protection. All this was effected with considerable trouble; for the bird made a stout resistance, flapping its wing with violence for some time. But at last I succeeded in securing him.

Fritz was not long in extricating himself from the swamp; he now appeared holding the dead flamingo by the feet: but I had more trouble in the care of mine, as I had a great desire to preserve him alive. I had tied his feet and his wings with my handkerchief; notwithstanding which, he still continued to flutter about to a distressing degree, and tried to make his escape. I held the flamingo under my left arm, and my gun in my right hand. I made the best jumps I was able to get to the boys, but the risk of sinking every moment in the mud, which was extremely deep, and from which it would have been difficult to release me.

I now selected some of the oldest of the stalks of bamboo, and cut from them their hard pointed ends, to serve for the tips of my arrows. Lastly, I looked for two of the longest canes, which I cut, for the purpose of measuring the height of our giant tree, about which I felt so deep an interest.

When I told my sons the use I intended to make of the two
longest canes, they indulged themselves in a hearty laugh at
me, and maintained that, though I should lay ten such canes
up the trunk of the tree, the last would not reach even the
lowest branch. I requested they would oblige me by having
a little patience. We now thought of returning. Ernest took
the charge of the canes; Fritz carried the dead flamingo, and
I resumed the care of the living one.

We at length arrived once more at our giant trees, and
were received with a thousand expressions of interest and
kindness. All were delighted at the sight of our new cap-
tures. My wife, with her usual anxiety about the means for
subsisting, asked where we should get food enough for all
the animals we brought home?—"You should consider,"
said I, "that some of them feed us, instead of being fed; and
the one we have now brought need not give you much
uneasiness, if, as I hope, he proves able to find food for
himself." I now began to examine his wound, and found
that only one wing was injured by the ball, but that the
other had also been slightly wounded by the dog laying hold
of him. I applied some ointment to both, which seemed
immediately to ease the pain. I next tied him by one of his
legs, with a long string, to a stake I had driven into the
ground, quite near to the river, that he might go in and
wash himself when he pleased.

In the meantime, my little railers had tied the two longest
canes together, and were endeavouring to measure the tree
with them; but when they found that they reached no further than the top of the arch formed by the roots, they all
burst into immoderate fits of laughter, assuring me, that if I
wished to measure the tree, I must think of some other
means. I however sobered them a little by re-recalling to
Fritz's memory some lessons in land-surveying he had received in Europe, and that the measure of the highest mountains, and their distance from each other, may be ascertained
by the application of triangles and supposed lines. I instantly
proceeded to this kind of operation, fixing my canes in the
ground, and making use of some string, which Fritz guided
according to my directions. I found that the height of the
lower branches of our tree was forty feet; a particular I was
obliged scrupulously to ascertain before I could determine
the length of my ladder. I now set Fritz and Ernest to work,

to measure our stock of thick ropes, of which I wanted no less than eighty feet for the two sides of the ladder; the two youngest I employed in collecting all the small string we had used for measuring, and carrying it to their mother. For my part, I sat down on the grass, and began to make some arrows with a piece of the bamboo, and the short sharp points of the canes I had taken such pains to secure. As the arrows were hollow, I filled them with moist sand, to give them a little weight; and lastly, I tipped them with a bit of feather from the flamingo, to make them fly straight.

Just at this moment Fritz joined us, having finished measuring the ropes: he brought me the welcome tidings, that our stock, in all, was about five hundred fathoms, which I knew to be more than sufficient for my ladder. I now tied the end of a ball of strong thread to an arrow, and fixing it to the bow, I shot it off in such a direction as to make the arrow pass over one of the largest branches of the tree, and fall again to the ground. By this method I lodged my thread securely, while I had the command of the end and the ball below. It was now easy to tie a piece of rope to the end of the thread, and draw it upwards, till the knot should reach the same branch. Having thus made quite sure of being able to raise my ladder, we all set to work with increased zeal and confidence. The first thing I did was to cut a length of about one hundred feet from my parcel of ropes, an inch thick; this I divided into two equal parts, which I stretched along on the ground in two parallel lines, at the distance of a foot from each other. I then directed Fritz to cut portions of sugar-cane, each two feet in length. Ernest handed them to me, one after another; and as I received them, I inserted them into my cords at the distance of twelve inches respectively, fixing them with knots in the cord, while Jack, by my order, drove into each a long nail at the two extremities, to hinder it from slipping out again. Thus, in a very short time, I had formed a ladder of forty rounds in length, and, in point of execution, firm and compact, and which we all beheld with a sort of joyful astonishment. I now tied it with strong knots to the end of the rope which hung from the tree, and pulled it by the other, till our ladder reached the branch, and seemed to rest so well upon it, that the joyous exclamations of the boys and my wife resounded from all sides. All the boys wished to be the first to ascend upon it;

but I decided that it should be Jack, he being the nimblest and of the lightest figure among them. Accordingly, I and his brothers held the ends of the rope and of the ladder with all our strength, while our young adventurer tripped up the rounds with perfect ease, and presently took his post upon the branch; but I observed that he had not strength enough to tie the rope firmly to the tree. Fritz now interfered, assuring me that he could ascend as safely as his brother; but as he was much heavier, I was not altogether without apprehension. I fastened the end of the ladder with forked stakes to the ground, and then gave him instructions how to step in such a way as to divide his weight, by occupying four rounds of the ladder at the same time with his feet and hands. It was not long before we saw him side by side with Jack, forty feet above our heads, and both saluting us with cries of exultation. Fritz set to work to fasten the ladder, by passing the rope round and round the branch; and this he performed with so much skill and intelligence, that I felt sufficient reliance to determine me to ascend myself, and well conclude the business he had begun. But first I tied a large pulley to the end of the rope, and carried it with me. When I was at the top, I fastened the pulley to a branch which was within my reach, that by this means I might be able the next day to draw up the planks and timbers I might want for building my aërial castle. I executed all this by the light of the moon, and felt the satisfaction of having done a good day's work. I now gently descended my rope ladder, and joined my wife and children.

My wife presented me with the day's work she had performed: it was some traces, and a breast leather each for the cow and the ass. I promised her, as a reward for her zeal and exertion, that we should all be completely settled in the tree the following day, and we then assembled to supper.

CHAPTER XI
The Settling in the Giant Tree

THE next morning we took our breakfast, and fell to work. My wife, having finished her daily occupation of milking the cow, and preparing the breakfast, set off with Ernest, Jack and Francis, attended by the ass, to the sea-shore: they had no doubt of finding some more pieces of wood, and they thought it would be prudent to replenish our exhausted store. In her absence, I ascended the tree with Fritz, and made the necessary preparations for my undertaking, for which I found it in every respect convenient; for the branches grew close to each other, and in an exactly horizontal direction. Such as grew in a manner to obstruct my design, I cut off either with the saw or hatchet, leaving none but what presented me with a sort of foundation for my work. I left those which spread themselves evenly upon the trunk, and had the largest circuit, as a support for my floor. Above these, at the height of forty-six feet, I found others, upon which to suspend our hammocks; and higher still, there was a further series of branches, destined to receive the roof of my tent, which for the present was to be formed of nothing more than a large surface of sail-cloth.

The progress of these preparations was considerably slow. It was necessary to raise certain beams to this height of forty feet, that were too heavy for my wife and her little assistants to lift from the ground. I had, however, the resource of my pulley, which served to excellent purpose, and Fritz and I contrived to draw them up to the elevation of the tent, one by one. When I had already placed two beams upon the

75

branches, I hastened to fix my planks upon them; and I made my floor double, that it might have sufficient solidity if the beams should be warped from their places. I then formed a wall of staves of wood like a park-paling, all round for safety. This operation, and a third journey to the sea-shore to collect the timber necessary, filled our morning so completely, that not one of us had thought about dinner. For this once we contented ourselves with a bit of ham and some milk, which we ate, and returned to finish our aërial palace, which began to make an imposing appearance. We unhooked our hammocks from the projecting roots, and by means of my pulley contrived to hoist them up the tree. The sail-cloth roof was supported by the thick branches above; and as it was of great compass, and hung down on every side, the idea occurred to me of nailing it to the paling on two sides, thus getting not only a roof, but two walls also; the immense trunk of the tree forming a third side, while in the fourth was the entrance to our apartment: and in this I left a large aperture, both as a means of seeing what passed without, and admitting a current of air to cool us in this burning temperature. The hammocks were soon hung on the branches, and everything was ready for our reception that very evening. Well satisfied with the execution of my plan, I descended with Fritz, who had assisted me through-out the whole; and as the day was not far advanced, and I observed we had still some planks remaining, we set about contriving a large table, to be placed between the roots of the tree, and surrounded with benches; and this place we said should be called our dining-parlour.

Exhausted by the fatigues of the day, I threw myself on a bank, and my wife having seated herself near me, I thanked her for the tender care she was ever imposing on herself; and then I observed to her, that the many blessings we enjoyed led the thoughts naturally to the beneficent Giver of them all; and to-morrow being a Sabbath day, we would rest from work, in obedience to His command, and other-wise keep it holy. We now assembled round our table to supper, my wife holding in her hand an earthen pot, which we had before observed upon the fire, and the contents of which we were all curious to be informed of. She took off the cover, and with a fork drew out of it the flamingo which Fritz had killed. She informed us that she had preferred

dressing it this way to roasting, because Ernest had assured
her that it was an old bird, which would prove hard and
tough, and advised her to improve it by stewing. We rallied
our glutton boy on this foible of his character, and his
brothers gave him the name of the *cook*. We, however, had
soon reason to know that he had conferred upon us an
important obligation; for the bird, which, roasted, we perhaps should not have been able to touch, now appeared
excellent, and was eaten up to the very bones.

The boys now, by my direction, lighted one of the heaps
of wood. I tied long ropes loosely round the necks of our
dogs, purposing to mount to our tent with the ends in my
hand, that I might be able to let them lose upon the enemy
at the first barking I should hear. Every one was eager to
retire to rest, and the signal for ascending the ladder was
given. The three eldest boys were up in an instant; then
came their mother's turn, who proceeded slowly and cautiously, and arrived in perfect safety. My own ascension was
last, and the most difficult; for I carried little Francis on my
back, and the end of the ladder had been loosened at the
bottom, that I might be able to draw it up in the tent during
the night; every step, therefore, was made with the greatest
difficulty, in consequence of its swinging motion. At last,
however, I got to the top, and drew the ladder after me. It
appeared to them that we were in one of the strong castles
of the ancient cavaliers, in which, when the drawbridge is
raised, the inhabitants are secured from every attack of the
enemy. Notwithstanding this apparent safety, I kept our
guns in readiness for whatever event might require their
use. We now abandoned ourselves to repose; our hearts
experienced a full tranquility; and the fatigue we had all
undergone induced so sound a sleep, that daylight shone full
in the front of our habitation before our eyes had opened.

CHAPTER XII

The Sabbath and the Parable

THE next morning we descended the ladder, and break-fasted on warm milk: we served the animals also with their meal and then we all sat down on the tender grass; the boys full of impatient curiosity; their mother absorbed in silent reflection; while I was penetrated with the most lively desire to impress upon the young minds of my children a subject I considered of the highest importance for their well-being, both in this world and in that which is to come.

All now standing up, I repeated aloud the church service, which I knew by heart, and we sang some verses from the hundred-and-nineteenth Psalm, which the boys had before learned; after which we sat down, and I began as follows:—

"My dear children, there was once a Great King, whose kingdom was called The Country of Light and Reality, because the purest and softest light of the sun reigned there continually, which caused the inhabitants to be in a perpetual state of activity. On the farthest borders of this kingdom, northward, there was another country which also belonged to the Great King, and the immense extent of which was unknown to all but himself. From time immemorial, a plan the most exact of this country had been preserved in the royal archives. The second kingdom was called The Kingdom of Obscurity, or of Night, because everything in it was gloomy and inactive.

"In the most fertile and agreeable part of his empire of Reality, this great King had a residence called the Heavenly City, in which he lived and kept his court, which was the most brilliant that the imagination can form an idea of.

Millions of guards, and servants high in dignity, remained for ever round him, and a still larger number held themselves in readiness to receive his commands. All were happy to be admitted into his presence: their faces shone with the mildest joy: there was but one heart and one soul among them: the sentiment of paternal concord so united these beings, that no envy or jealousy ever rose among them. Among the rest of the inhabitants of the Heavenly City, there were some less close in their attendance upon the Great King, but they were all virtuous, all happy, all had been enriched by the beneficence of the monarch, and, what is of still higher price, had received constant marks of his paternal care; for his subjects were all equal in his eyes, and he loved them, and treated them as if they had been his children.

"The Great King had, besides the two kingdoms I have been describing, an uninhabited island of considerable extent: it was his wish to people and cultivate this island, for all within it was a kind of chaos: he destined it to be for some years the abode of such future citizens as he intended to receive finally into his residence, to which only such of his subjects were admitted as had rendered themselves worthy by their conduct. This island was called Earthly Abode: he who should have passed some time in it, and by his virtue, his application to labour, and the cultivation of the land, should have rendered himself worthy of reward, was afterwards to be received into the Heavenly City, and made one of its happy inhabitants.

"To effect this end, the Great King caused a fleet to be equipped, which was to transport the new colonists to this island. These he chose from the kingdom of Night, and for his first gift bestowed upon them the enjoyment of light, and the view of the lovely face of Nature, of which they had been deprived in their gloomy and unknown abode. It will easily be imagined that they arrived joyful and happy, at least they became so when they had been for a short time accustomed to the multitude of new objects which struck their feeble sight. The island was rich and fertile when cultivated. The beneficent King provided each individual who was disembarked upon it with all the things he could want in the time he had fixed for their stay in it, and all the means for obtaining the certainty of being admitted as citi-

zens of his magnificent abode, when they should leave the
Earthly Island. All that was required to entitle them to this
benefit was that they should occupy themselves unceasingly
in useful labour, and strictly obey the commands of the
Great King, which he made known to them. He sent to
them his only son, who addressed them from his father in
the following terms:—

"My dear children, I have called you from the kingdom of
Night and Insensibility, to render you happy by the gifts of
life, of sentiment, and of activity. But your happiness for
the most part will depend upon yourselves. You will be
happy if you wish to be so. If such is your sincere desire,
you must never forget that I am your good King, your
tender father; and you must faithfully fulfil my will in the
cultivation of the country I have confided to your care. Each
of you shall receive, on his arriving at the island, the portion
of land which I intended for him; and my further commands
respecting your conduct will be soon communicated to you.
I shall send you wise and learned men, who will explain to
you my commands; and that you may of yourselves seek
after the light necessary for your welfare, and remember my
laws at every instant of your lives, it is my will that each
father of a family shall keep an exact copy of them in his
house, and read them daily to all the persons who belong to
him. Further, each first day of the week I require to be
devoted to my service. In each colony, all the people shall
assemble together as brothers in one place, where shall be
read and explained to them the laws contained in my archives. The rest of this day shall be employed in making
serious reflections on the duties and destination of the colonists, and on the best means to fulfil the same.

" 'He who, in his Earthly Abode, shall most strictly have
observed my will, who shall have best fulfilled the duties of
a brother towards his fellow-inhabitants, who shall have
preserved his land in the best order, and shall show the
largest produce from it, shall be recompensed for his deeds,
and shall become an inhabitant of my magnificent residence
in the Heavenly City. But the neglectful and the idle man,
and the wicked man, who shall have spent their time in
interrupting the useful labours of others, shall be condemned
to pass their lives in slavery, or, according to the degree of

their wickedness, shall be condemned to live in subterraneous mines, in the bowels of the earth.'

"All the colonists were well satisfied with the discourse of the Great King, and made him the most sacred promises. After a short time allowed for repose from the fatigue of the voyage, a portion of land, and the proper instruments for labour, were distributed to each of the strangers. They received also seeds, and useful plants, and young trees, for producing them refreshing fruits. Each was then left at liberty to act as he pleased, and increase the value of what was confided to his care. But what happened? After some time, each followed the suggestions of his fancy: one planted his land with arbours, flowery banks, and sweet-smelling shrubs; all pleasing to the sight, but which brought forth nothing. Another planted wild apple-trees, instead of the good fruit, as the Great King had commanded; contenting himself with giving high-sounding names to the worthless fruit he had caused to be brought forth. A third had indeed sown good grain; but not knowing how to distinguish the tares that grew up along with it, he pulled up the good plants before they were mature, and left only the tares in his ground. But the greater part let their land lie fallow, and bestowed no labour upon it, having spoiled their implements, or lost their seed, either from negligence or idleness, or liking better to amuse themselves than to labour.

"From habit they continued to celebrate the first day of the week, but by far the smallest part of it was consecrated to the honour of the Great King. Great numbers of them dispensed with going to the general assembly, either from idleness, or to employ themselves in occupations which had been expressly forbidden. By far the greater part of the people considered this day of repose as intended for pleasure, and thought of nothing but adorning and amusing themselves as soon as daylight appeared. The Great King, however, observed unalterably the laws he had laid down. From time to time, some frigates appeared on their coasts, each bearing the name of some disastrous malady; and these were followed by a large ship of the line, named the Grave, on board of which, the admiral, whose name was Death, caused his flag of two colours, green and black, to be constantly floating in the air. He showed the colonists, according to the situation in which he found them, either the smiling colour of Hope, or the gloomy colour of Despair.

"This fleet always arrived without being announced, and seldom gave any pleasure to the inhabitants. The admiral sent the captains of his frigates to seize the persons he was ordered to bring back with him. Many who had not the smallest inclination were suddenly embarked, while others who had prepared everything for the harvest, and whose land was in the best condition, were also seized. But these last took their departure cheerfully, and without alarm; well knowing that nothing but happiness awaited them. It was those who were conscious they had neglected to cultivate their land, who felt the most regret. It was even necessary to employ force to bring them under subjection. When the fleet was ready for departure, the admiral sailed for the port of the Royal Residence; and the Great King, who was present on their arrival, executed with strict justice both the rewards and punishments which had been promised to them. All the excuses alleged by those who had been idle, were of no avail. They were sent to the mines and to the galleys, while those who had obeyed the Great King, and well cultivated their land, were admitted into the Heavenly City, clothed in robes of brilliant colours, one exceeding the other according to the degree of merit.—Here, my dear children, ends my parable. May you have thoroughly understood its meaning, and may you reap the advantage it is capable of affording you! Make it the subject of your reflections the whole of this day."

I then put different questions to my little congregation, and explained what they had not perfectly comprehended; and, after a short review of the principal parts of my discourse, I concluded by a moral application.

"Human creatures," said I, "are the colonists of God; we are required to perform the business of probation for a certain period, and, sooner or later, are destined to be taken hence. Our final destination is Heaven, and a perfect happiness with the spirits of just men made perfect, and in the presence of the bountiful Father of us all. The piece of land entrusted to each is the soul; and according as he cultivates and ennobles it, or neglects or depraves it, will be his future reward or punishment. For ourselves, one and all, we will adopt the model of the good and zealous labourers;

and should our exertions be a little painful, we shall have adorned our souls with all that is good, just and praiseworthy. Thus, when death, which cannot fail to come at last, shall summon us, we may follow him with joy to the throne of the Good and Great King, to hear him pronounce these sweet and consoling words: 'O good and faithful servant! thou hast been tried and found faithful in many things; enter thou into the joy of thy Lord.' "—With these words, and a short prayer of benediction, I concluded the solemnity of our Sunday.

The next morning the boys assembled round me with a petition that I would show them how to use arrows. We accordingly sat down on the grass; I took out my knife, and, with the remains of a bamboo cane, began to make a bow. I was well satisfied to observe them one and all take a fancy to shooting with an arrow, having been desirous to accustom them to this exercise, which constituted the principal defence of the warriors of old, and might possibly become our only means of protection and subsistence: our provision of powder must at last be exhausted; we might even, from moment to moment, be deprived of it by accident; it therefore was of the utmost importance to us to acquire some other means of killing animals, or attacking our enemies.

While I was silently reflecting on the subject, employed in finishing a bow, Ernest, who had been observing me for some time, slipped suddenly away; and Fritz coming up at the same moment, with the wetted skin of the tiger-cat in his hand, I paid no attention to the circumstance. I began my instructions to my eldest boy respecting the trade of a tanner. I told him the method of getting rid of the fat of the skin, by rubbing it over with sand, and placing it in running water till it had no longer any appearance of flesh, or any smell; next to rub it with soft butter, to make it supple, and then to stretch the skin in different directions; and also to make use of some eggs in the operation, if his mother could spare them. "You will not at first produce such excellent workmanship as I have seen of this kind from England; but with a little patience, regretting neither your time nor your labour, you will have completed some decent-looking cases, which will give you the more pleasure, from being the work of your own hands."

At this moment we heard the firing of a gun, which

proceeded from our tent in the tree, and two birds at the same time fell dead at our feet. We were at one surprised and alarmed, and all eyes were turned upward to the place. There we saw Ernest standing outside the tent, a gun in his hand, and heard him triumphantly exclaiming, "Catch them! Catch them there! I have hit them; and you see I did not run away for nothing." He descended the ladder joyfully, and ran with Francis to take up the two birds; while Fritz and Jack mounted to our castle, hoping to meet with the same luck.

One of the dead birds proved to be a sort of thrush, and the other was a very small kind of pigeon, very fat, and of a delicious taste. We now observed for the first time that the wild figs began to ripen, and that they attracted these birds. I foresaw, in consequence, that we were about to have our table furnished with a dish which even a nobleman might envy us. I gave the boys leave to kill as many of them as they liked. I knew that, half-roasted, and put into barrels with melted butter thrown over them, they would keep a long time, and might prove an excellent resource. My wife set about stripping off the feathers of the birds, to dress them for our dinner. I seated myself by her side, and proceeded in my work of arrow-making.

Thus finished another day. Supper ended, and prayers said, we ascended the ladder in procession; and each got into his hammock to taste the sweets of a tranquil sleep.

CHAPTER XIII

Conversation, and a Walk

JACK had finished the trial of his arrows: they flew to admiration; and he practised his new art incessantly. Little Francis waited with impatience for the moment when he should try also, and followed with his eyes every stroke I made. But when I had finished my bow, and prepared some little arrows for him, I must next undertake to make him a quiver. I took some bark from the branch of a tree, which came off in a round form; and folding the edges over each other, I stuck them together with some glue produced from our soup-cakes. I next stuck on a round piece to serve for the bottom; and then tied to it a loop of string which I hung round his neck. He put his arrows into it: and, quite happy, took his bow in his hand, and ran to try his skill by the side of his brother. Fritz had also cleaned and prepared his materials for the cases, when his mother summoned us to dinner. We cheerfully placed ourselves under the shade of our tree, round the table I had manufactured. At the end of the repast, I made the following proposition to the boys, which I was sure would give them pleasure.

"What think you, my good friends," said I, "of giving a name to the place of our abode, and to the different parts of the country which are known to us? I do not mean a general name to the whole islands, but to the objects we are most concerned with."

They all exclaimed, joyfully, that the idea was excellent.

Father.—We shall naturally begin with the bay by which we entered this country. What shall we call it? What say you, Fritz? You must speak first, for you are eldest.

Fritz.—Let us call it *Oyster Bay*: you remember what quantity of oysters we found in it.

Jack.—Oh, no; let it rather be called *Lobster Bay*: for you cannot have forgotten what a large one it was that caught hold of my leg, and which I carried home to you.

My Wife.—My advice would be, that, out of gratitude to God, who conducted us hither in safety, we ought to call it *Providence Bay*, or the *Bay of Safety*.

Father.—These words are both appropriate and sonorous, and please me extremely. But what name shall we give to the spot where we first set up our tent?

Fritz.—Let us simply call it *Tent House*.

Father.—That will do very well. And the little islet at the entrance of *Providence Bay*, in which we found so many planks and beams that enabled us to make our bridge, how shall it be named?

Ernest.—It may be called *Sea-Gull Island*, or *Shark Island*; for it was here we saw those animals.

Father.—I am for the last of these names, *Shark Island*; for it was the shark that was the cause of the sea-gulls being there; and thus we shall also have a means of commemorating the courage and the triumph of Fritz, who killed the monster.

Jack.—For the same reason, we will call the marsh, in which you cut the canes for our arrows, *Flamingo Marsh*.

Father.—Quite right, I think. But now comes the great question: What name shall we give to our present abode?

Ernest.—It ought to be called simply *Tree Castle*.

Fritz.—No, no, that will not do at all; that is the same as if, when we wanted to name a town, we called it *The Town*. Let us invent a more noble name.

Jack.—Yes, so we will. I say *Fig Town*.

Fritz.—Ha, ha, ha! a noble name, it must be confessed! Let us call it the *Eagle's Nest*, which I am sure has a much better sound. Besides, our habitation in the tree is really much more like a nest than a town, and the eagle cannot but ennoble it, since he is the king of birds.

Father.—Will you let me decide the question for you? I think our abode should be called *The Falcon's Nest*; for you are not arrived at the dignity of eagles, but are, too truly, poor simple birds of prey: and like the falcon, you also are, I trust, obedient, docile, active and courageous. Ernest can have no objection to this; for, as he knows, falcons make their nests in large trees.

All exclaimed, clapping their hands, "Yes, yes; we will have it *The Falcon's Nest*! the sound is quite chivalrous; so health to *Falcon's Nest Castle*!" cried they, all looking up to the tree, and making low bows. I poured out a small quantity of sweet wine, and presented it to each, to solemnize our baptism. "Now then," said I, "for the promontory, where Fritz and I in vain wearied our eyes in search of our companions of the vessel;—I think it may properly be called *Cape Disappointment*."

All.—Yes, this is excellent. And the river with the bridge——

Father.—If you wish to commemorate one of the greatest events of our history, it ought to be called *The Jackal's River*; for these animals crossed it when they came and attacked us, and it was there that one of them was killed. The bridge I should name *Family Bridge*, because we were all employed in its construction, and all crossed it together on our way to this place. Let me ask you all, if it will not be a great pleasure to converse about the country we inhabit, now that we have instituted names as if everything belonged to us?

Ernest.—It will be just as if we had farms and country houses, all dependent upon our castle.

In this pleasing kind of chat, the time of dinner passed agreeably away. We settled the basis of a geography of this our new country; and amused ourselves with saying it must go by the first post to Europe.

As the evening advanced, and the intense heat of the day began to diminish, I invited all my family to take a walk. "Leave your work for this time, my boys," said I, "and let us make a short excursion; let us seek, in the beautiful face of nature, the traces of the wisdom and goodness of the Creator. Which way shall we direct our steps?"

Fritz.—Let us go to Tent House, father; we are in want of powder and shot for the little consumers of our figs; nor must we miss our dinner for to-morrow, or forget that we are to secure a supply for winter.

My Wife.—I too vote for Tent House; my butter is nearly gone, for Fritz took an unreasonable share for his new trade of tanning.

Father.—To Tent House, then, we will go; but we will not take our accustomed road along the seashore, but rather vary our pleasure, by trying to explore some other way. We will keep along our own little stream as far as the wall of rocks; it will be easy for us to cross it by jumping from stone to stone, and so to get to Tent House: we will return with our provisions by the road of Family Bridge, and along the seashore. This new route may possibly furnish some additional discoveries.

My idea was highly applauded, and all was soon arranged for our setting out. Our route along the stream was at first extremely agreeable, being sheltered by the shade of large trees, while the ground under our feet was a short and soft kind of grass. To prolong the pleasure of our walk, we proceeded slowly, amusing ourselves with looking about us to the right and left; the eldest boys made frequent escapes on before, so that we sometimes lost sight of them. In this manner we reached the end of the wood; but the country now appearing to be less open, we thought it would be prudent to bring our whole company together.

On looking forward, we saw the boys approaching us full gallop, and this time, for a wonder, the grave Ernest was first. He reached me panting for breath, and so full of joy and eagerness that he could not pronounce a single word distinctly: the rest soon came up, and our expedition was resumed.

CHAPTER XIV

Continuation of Preceding Chapter—Discoveries

CONVERSING on different subjects, we reached the long chain of rocks, over which our pretty Falcon's Stream made its escape in a cascade, delighting at once the eye and the ear in its progress. We thus reached Jackal's River, and from thence proceeded to Tent House, having with difficulty pushed through the high grass which presented itself. Our fatigue, however, was relieved by the beauty of the scenery around: on the right hand was a boundless sea: on the left, the island, with the bay by which it was accessible, and the chain of rocks, forming altogether an assemblage of the picturesque, equal to what the liveliest fancy could desire. We distinguished different families of grasses, many of them of the thorn-leaved species, and stronger than those cultivated in the green-houses of Europe. There was also in abundance the Indian fig, with its large broad leaf; aloes of different forms and colours; the superb prickly candle, or cactus, bearing straight stalks, taller than a man, and crowned with long straight branches, forming a sort of star; while that which pleased us best, and which was found there in great abundance, was the king of fruits, both for figure and relish, the crowned pineapple, of which we all partook with avidity.

Soon after, I was fortunate enough to discover among the multitude of plants which grew either at the foot or in the clefts of the rocks, the karata, many of which were now in blossom. As I was acquainted with the properties of this useful plant, the pith of which is used for tinder by the negroes, who also make a strong kind of thread from the fibres of its leaves, I was not less satisfied with this discovery than I had been with any we had previously made. Wishing to exhibit one of its uses to my children, I desired Ernest to take out my flint and steel.

I took a dried stalk of the tree, stripped off the bark, and there appeared a kind of dry spongy substance, which I laid upon the flint; and then striking it with a steel, it instantly caught fire. The boys looked on with astonishment, and soon began to caper about, exclaiming, "Long live the tinder-tree!"

"Here then," said I, "we have an article of greater usefulness than if it served merely to gratify the appetite. Your mother will next inform us what materials she will use for sewing your clothes, when her provision of thread from the enchanted bag is exhausted."

My Wife.—I have long been uneasy upon this very subject, and would willingly exchange our greatest luxury for some hemp or flax.

Father.—And your wish shall be accomplished. If you examine, you will find some excellent thread under the leaves of this extraordinary plant, where all-provident nature has placed a storehouse of this valuable article, though the lengths of thread will be found not longer than the leaf. I accordingly drew out of one of the leaves a strong piece of thread of a red colour, which I gave to my wife. "How fortunate it is for us," said she, "that you have had the habit of reading and of study! None of us would have had a thought about this plant, or have conceived that it could be of any use:—but will it not be difficult to draw out the lengths of thread through the prickles that surround them?"

Father.—Not in the least; we shall put the leaves to dry, either in the sun, or by a gentle fire. The useless part of the leaf will then separate by being beaten, and the mass of thread will remain.

Fritz.—I see clearly, father, that we ought not to trust to
appearances; but one may, I suppose, assert that there are
no good qualities in the prickly plants, which are growing
here in all directions, and wounding the persons who go
near them: of what use can they possibly be?

Father.—The greatest part of these possess medicinal vir-
tues; great use is made in pharmacy of the aloe, which
produces such abundance of beautiful flowers: in green-
houses in Europe some have been seen to bear more than
three thousand blossoms. But look—here, too, is the Indian
fig, or prickly pear, a vegetable of no common interest; it
grows in the poorest soils, and, as you see, upon the rocks:
the poorer the soil, the more luxuriant and succulent its
leaves. I should be tempted to believe that it was nourished
by the air rather than by the earth. The plant bears a kind of
fig, which is said to be sweet and palatable when ripened in
its native sun, and it is a salutary and refreshing food. This,
then, is another plant of great utility. I next instructed them
how to gather this prickly fruit without injury to their fingers. I threw up a stone, and brought down a fig, which I
caught upon my hat; I cut off one end, and was thus enabled
to hold it on a knife while I peeled off the skin. I then
resigned it to the curiosity of my young companions.

In the meantime, I perceived Ernest holding a leaf upon
the end of his knife, turning it about in all directions, and
bringing it close to his eye with a look of curious inquiry.—"I
wish I could know," said at length our young observer,
"what little animals these are on the leaf, which feed so
eagerly upon it, and are of quite a scarlet colour."

Father.—Ha, ha! this too will perhaps turn out a new
discovery, and an additional source of usefulness. Let me
look at your leaf: I will wager that it is the insect called the
cochineal.

Jack.—The cochineal! what a droll name! What is the
cochineal, father?

Father.—It is an insect of the kind called *suckers*, or
kermes. It lives by sucking the juice of the leaves of the
Indian fig, which, no doubt, is the cause of its beautiful
colour, so much esteemed in dyeing; for nothing else produces so fine a scarlet.

We reached Jackal's River, which we crossed, stepping
with great care from stone to stone, and shortly arrived at

THE SWISS FAMILY ROBINSON

our old habitation, where we found everything as we had left it; and each went in pursuit of what he intended to take away. Fritz loaded himself with powder and shot: I and my wife and Francis employed ourselves in filling our pot with butter. Ernest and Jack looked about for the geese and ducks; but as they were become somewhat savage, the boys could not succeed in catching one of them. The idea then occurred to Ernest of taking a small bit of cheese, and tying it to the end of a piece of string, and holding it to float in the water. The voracious animals hastened eagerly to seize it. In this way Ernest drew them towards him, one by one, with the cheese in its mouth, till he had caught the whole: each bird was then tied in a pocket-handkerchief, leaving the head at liberty, and fastened one to each game-bag, so that all had a share in carrying them.

We now set out loaded on our return. The ducks and geese, with their heads and necks stretching out at our shoulders, cackling with all their might, gave us a truly singular and ludicrous appearance; and we could not help laughing immoderately as we passed the bridge, one after another, accoutred in so strange a fashion. Our mutual jokes, and the general good humour which prevailed, served to shorten the length of the walk, and none complained of fatigue, till seated under our tree at Falcon's Stream.

CHAPTER XV

Hopes of a Sledge—Some Short Lessons in Useful Things

I HAD observed along the shore many pieces of wood, of which I thought I could make a kind of conveyance for our cask of butter and other provisions from Tent House to Falcon's Stream, and had secretly determined to go early the next morning, before my family should be awake, to the spot. I had fixed upon Ernest for my assistant, thinking that his indolent temper required to be stimulated to exertion. I made him feel as a great favour the preference I gave him, and he promised to be ready at a very early hour.

At the first dawn of morning I quietly awoke Ernest. He got up, and we descended the ladder without being perceived by the rest, who continued to sleep soundly. We roused the ass, and I made him draw some large branches of a tree, which I wanted for my undertaking.

We were not long in finding the pieces of wood, and set to work to cut them the proper length, and we then laid them cross-ways on the branches, which we thus converted into a kind of vehicle. We added to the load a little chest, which we found half-buried in the sands, quite close to the waves, and then we set out on our return to Falcon's Stream. When we reached our abode, the chest we had brought was soon opened by a strong hatchet; for all were eager to see what was within. It contained only some sailors' dresses and some linen, and both were wet with the sea.

We then sat down tranquilly to breakfast; and I next inspected the booty of the young sportsmen, who had shot, in all, no less than fifty ortolans and thrushes, and had used so large a quantity of powder and shot, that when they were about to resume their sport, my wife and I stopped them, recommending a more frugal use of those valuable materials. I taught them how to make some snares, to be suspended from the branches of the fig-tree, and advised them to use the thread of the karata, which is as strong as horsehair, for the purpose.

Jack, who had got up into the tree, and had suspended some of the snares to the branches, came down again to bring us the acceptable intelligence that our pigeons had made a sort of nest there of some dry grass, and that it already contained several eggs. I therefore forbade the boys from firing any more in the tree, for fear of alarming or wounding these gentle creatures. I also directed that the snares should be frequently examined, to see that the pigeons were not caught in them, as they might be strangled in their efforts to get loose.

Meanwhile the boys and I had been busily employed: our

work was completed. Two bent pieces of wood, the segments of a circle, which I fixed in their places by a straight piece of wood placed across, and firmly fixed to the bent pieces in the middle and at the rear, formed the outline of my machine. I then fastened two ropes in front; and here was a sledge as perfect as could be desired. As I had not raised my eyes from my work, I did not know what my wife and the two youngest boys had been about. On looking up, I perceived that they had been stripping off the feathers from a quantity of birds which the boys had killed, and that they afterwards spitted them on an officer's sword, which Fritz had fancied and brought from the ship, and which my wife had turned into this useful kitchen utensil. I approved of the idea; but I blamed her profusion in dressing more birds at once than we could eat. She reminded me that I had myself advised her to half-roast the birds before putting them into the butter, to be preserved for future use. She was in hopes, she said, that as I had now a sledge, I should not fail of going to Tent House after dinner to fetch the cask of butter, and in the meanwhile she was endeavouring to be ready with the birds. I had no objection to this, and determined on going to Tent House the same day, requesting my wife to hasten the dinner for that purpose. She replied that this was already her intention, as she also had a little project in her head, which I should be informed of at my return. I, for my part, had one too, which was to refresh myself, after the heat and fatigue of my laborious occupations, by a plunge into the sea. I wished that Ernest, who was to accompany me, should bathe also; while Fritz was to remain at home for the protection of the family.

CHAPTER XVI
Bathing, Fishing and a Kangaroo

WE had harnessed the ass and the cow to our sledge; and, resting our guns upon our shoulders, began our journey. We bade adieu to our companions, and put our animals in motion. We took the road by the seashore, where the sands afforded better travelling for our vehicle than the thick wild grass. We reached Family Bridge, on Jackal's River, and arrived at Tent House without either obstacle or adventure, and unharnessed the animals to let them graze, while we set to work to load the sledge with the cask of butter, the cask of cheese, a small barrel of gunpowder, different instruments, small ball and some shot. These exertions had so occupied our thoughts, that it was late when we first observed that our animals, attracted by the excellent quality of the grass on the other side of the river, had repassed the bridge, and wandered so far as to be out of sight. I was in hopes they would be easily found, and directed Ernest to go with Flora and bring them back, intending in the meantime to look for a convenient place on the other side of Tent House to bathe in. In a short time I found myself at the extremity of Providence Bay, which ended, as I now perceived, in a marsh, producing some fine bulrushes; and further on was a chain of steep rocks, advancing somewhat into the sea, and forming a kind of creek, as if expressly contrived for bathing.

I desired Ernest to fill a small bag with some of the salt he had formerly observed here, and then to empty it into the large one for the ass to carry; and to take care to fill equally on each side. "During this time I will take the refreshment of bathing; and then it will be your turn to bathe, and mine to take care of the animals."

I returned to the rocks, and was not disappointed in my expectation of an enjoyment the most delicious. When I had dressed myself, I returned to Ernest to see if his work had advanced: presently I heard his voice calling out, "Father, father, a fish! a fish of monstrous size! Run quickly, father: I can hardly hold him; he is eating up the string of my line!" I ran to the place from which the voice proceeded, and found Ernest lying along the ground on his face, upon the extremity of a point of land, and pulling in his line, to which a large fish was hanging, and struggling to get loose. I ran hastily and snatched the rod out of his hand, for I feared the weight and activity of the fish might pull him into the water. I gave the line length, to calm the fish, and then contrived to draw him gently along into a shallow, from which he could no longer escape, and thus he was effectually secured. We examined him thoroughly, and he appeared to weigh not less than fifteen pounds; so that our capture was magnificent, and would afford the greatest pleasure to our good steward of provisions at Falcon's Stream.

While Ernest went to the rocks and bathed, I had time to fill some more bags with salt. We then harnessed and loaded our animals, and resumed the road to Falcon's Stream.

When we had proceeded about half way, Flora, who was before us, suddenly sprang off, and by her barking gave notice that she scented some game. We soon after saw her pursuing an animal which seemed endeavouring to escape, and made the most extraordinary jumps imaginable. The dog continued to follow; the creature, in trying to avoid him, passed within gun-shot of the place where I stood. I fired, but its flight was so rapid that I did not hit. Ernest, who was at a small distant behind, hearing the report of my gun, prepared his own, and fired it off at the instant the singular animal was passing near him, seeking to hide itself among the tall herbage just by: he had fired so skilfully that the animal fell dead at the same instant. I ran with extreme curiosity to ascertain what kind of quadruped it might be. It was as large as a sheep, with the tail resembling that of a tiger; but its snout and hair were like those of a mouse, and its teeth were like a hare's, but much larger; the fore-legs resembled those of the squirrel, and were extremely short;

but to make up for this, its hind-legs were as long as a pair of stilts, and of a form strikingly singular. We examined the creature a long time in silence. I could not be sure that I had ever seen an engraving or description of it in any natural history, or book of travels. Ernest at length, clapping his hands together, joyously exclaimed, "And have I really killed this wonderful animal? What do you think is its name, father? I would give all the world to know."

Father.—And so would I, my boy; but I am as ignorant as you. One thing, however, is certain, that this is your lucky day. Let us again examine this interesting stranger, that we may be certain to what family of quadrupeds it belongs: this will perhaps throw a light upon its name.

Ernest.—I think it can hardly be named a quadruped; for the little fore-legs look much more like hands, as is the case with monkeys.

Father.—They are notwithstanding legs, I can assure you. Let us look for its name among the animals who give suck: on this point we cannot be mistaken. Now let us examine its teeth.

Ernest.—Here are the four incisory teeth, like the squirrel.

Father.—Thus we see that it belongs to the order of Nibblers. Now let us look for some names of animals of this kind.

Ernest.—Besides squirrels, I recollect only mice, marmots, hares, beavers, porcupines, and jumpers.

Father.—Jumpers! That short word furnishes the necessary clue; the animal is completely formed like the jerboa, or jumping hare, except that it is twice the size of those of which I have read a description. . . . Wait a moment—an idea strikes me: I will wager that our animal is one of the large jumpers, called kangaroos. To the best of my knowledge, this animal has never been seen but on the coast of New Holland, where it was first observed by the celebrated navigator, Captain Cook. You may then be highly flattered with your adventure of killing an animal at once so rare and so remarkable. But now let us see how we shall manage to drag him to the sledge. Ernest requested that I would rather assist him to carry it, as he was afraid of spoiling its beautiful mouse-coloured skin by dragging it on the ground. I therefore tied the fore-legs of the kangaroo together; and by means of two canes, we, with considerable trouble, contrived to carry it to the sledge, upon which it was securely fastened.

We at length arrived happily, though somewhat late, at Falcon's Stream, having heard from a great distance the salutations of our family. We concluded the day with our ordinary occupations. I gave some salt to each of our animals, to whom it was an acceptable treat. We then skinned our kangaroo, and put it carefully aside till the next day, when we intended to cut it to pieces, and lay such parts in salt as we could not immediately consume. We made an excellent supper of our little fish, to which we added some vegetables; nor were our faithful companions Turk and Flora neglected. The labours of the day had more than usually disposed us all to seek repose; we therefore said our prayers at an early hour, mounted our ladder, and were soon asleep.

CHAPTER XVII
More Stores from the Wreck

I ROSE with the first crowing of the cock, descended the ladder, and set about skinning the kangaroo, taking care not to deface its beautiful smooth coat; but I advanced so slowly in the business, that my family were assembled about me, and calling out Famine! before I had finished my work. Breakfast over, I ordered Fritz to get ready for Tent House, where we should prepare the boat, and again proceed to the vessel.

We took Ernest and Jack a little way with us, and then I sent them back with a message to their mother, which I had not the resolution to deliver myself—that we might be forced to pass the night on board the vessel and not return till the evening of the following day. It was most essential to get out of it, if yet afloat, all that could be saved, as a moment might complete its destruction.

We got into the boat, and, gaining the current, quickly cleared Safety Bay, and reached the vessel, whose open side offered us an ample space to get on board. When we had fastened our boat, our first care was to select fit materials to construct a raft. Our boat of staves had neither room nor solidity enough to carry a considerable burden; we therefore looked about, and found a sufficient number of water-casks, which appeared to me proper for my new enterprise. We emptied them, replaced the bungs carefully, and threw the casks overboard, after securing them with ropes and cramps, so as to keep them together at the vessel's side: this completed, we placed a sufficient number of planks upon them to form a firm and commodious platform, or deck, to which we added a gunwale of a foot in depth all round, to secure the lading. Thus we contrived a handsome raft, in which we could stow thrice as much as in our boat. This laborious task had taken up the whole day; we scarcely allowed ourselves a minute to eat some cold meat we had provided, that we might not lose any time in looking for the provisions on board the vessel. In the evening, Fritz and I were so weary, that it would have been impossible for us to row back to land; so having taken all due precaution in case of a storm, we lay down in the captain's cabin, on a good elastic mattress, which induced such sound repose, that our prudent design to watch in turn, for fear of accident, was forgotten, and we both slept heavily, side by side, till broad daylight opened our eyes. We rose, and actively set to work to load our raft.

We began with stripping the cabin of its doors and windows, with their appendages; next we secured the carpenter's and gunner's chests, containing all their tools and implements: those we could remove with levers and rollers were put entire upon the raft, and we took out of the others what rendered them too heavy. One of the captain's chests was filled with costly articles, which, no doubt, he meant to dispose of to the opulent planters of Port Jackson, or among the savages. In the collection were several gold and silver watches, snuff-boxes of all descriptions, buckles, shirt-buttons, necklaces, rings; in short, an abundance of all the trifles of European luxury. But the discovery that delighted me most was a chest containing some dozens of young plants of every species of European fruits, which had been carefully packed in moss for transportation. I perceived pear, plum, almond, peach, apple, apricot, chestnut trees, and vine shoots. We discovered a number of bars of iron, and large pigs of lead, grinding-stones, cart-wheels ready for mounting, a complete set of farrier's instruments, tongs, shovels, ploughshares, rolls of iron and copper wire, sacks full of maize, pease, oats, vetches, and even a little handmill. The vessel had been freighted with everything likely to be useful in an infant colony so distant. We found a saw-mill in a separated state, but each piece numbered, and so accurately fitted that nothing was easier than to put it together for use.

We with difficulty and hard labour finished our loading, having added a large fishing-net, quite new, and the vessel's great compass. With the net, Fritz found two harpoons and a rope-windlass, such as they use in the whale-fishery. He asked me to let him place the harpoons, tied to the end of the rope, over the bow of our tub-boat, and thus be in readiness in case of seeing any large fish; and I indulged him in his fancy.

Having completely executed our undertaking, we stepped into the tub-boat, and pushed out for the current, drawing our raft triumphantly after us with a stout rope, which we had been careful to fasten securely at its head.

CHAPTER XVIII
The Tortoise Harnessed

THE wind was favourable, and briskly swelled our sail. The sea was calm, and we advanced at a considerable rate. Fritz had for some time fixed his eyes on something of a large size which was floating on the water, and he now desired me to take the glass, and see what it could be. I

soon perceived that it was a tortoise, which had fallen asleep
in the sun on the surface of the water. No sooner had Fritz
learned this, than he entreated me to steer softly within
view of so extraordinary a creature. I readily consented; but
as his back was towards me, and the sail between us, I did
not observe his motions, till a violent jerk of the boat, a
sudden turning of the windlass, and then a second jerk,
accompanied by a rapid motion of the boat, gave me the
necessary explanation. "For Heaven's sake, what are you
about, Fritz?" exclaimed I, somewhat alarmed.

"I have caught him!—I touched him!" cried Fritz, without
hearing one word I had been saying.—"The tortoise is ours;
it cannot escape, father! Is not this, then, a valuable prize,
for it will furnish dinners for us all for many weeks?"

I soon perceived that the harpoon had caught the animal,
which, feeling itself wounded, thus agitated the vessel in its
endeavours to get away. I quickly pulled down the sail, and
seizing a hatchet, sprang to the boat's head to cut the rope,
and let the harpoon and the tortoise go; but Fritz caught
hold of my arm, conjuring me to wait a moment, and not so
hastily bring upon him the mortification of losing, at one
stroke, the harpoon, the rope, and the tortoise: he proposed
watching himself, with the hatchet in his hand, to cut the
rope suddenly should any sign of danger appear; and I
yielded to his entreaties.

Thus, then, drawn along by the tortoise, we proceeded
with a hazardous rapidity. I soon observed that the creature
was making for the sea; I therefore again hoisted the sail;
and as the wind was to the land, and very brisk, the tortoise
found resistance of no avail; he accordingly fell into the
track of the current, and drew us straight towards our usual
place of landing, and, by good fortune, without striking
upon any of the rocks. We, however, did not disembark
without one difficult adventure. The state of the tide was
such as to throw us upon a sand-bank; we were at this time
within gun-shot of the shore; the boat, though driven with
violence, remained upright in the sand. I stepped into the
water, which did not reach far above my knees, for the
purpose of conferring upon our conductor his just reward
for the alarm he had caused us, when he suddenly gave a
plunge, and then disappeared. Following the rope, I presently saw the tortoise stretched at length at the bottom of

the water, where it was so shallow that I soon found means to put an end to his pain, by cutting off his head with the hatchet. Being now near Tent House, Fritz gave a halloo, and fired a gun, to apprise our relatives that we were not only arrived, but arrived in triumph. This soon produced the desired effect: the mother and her three young ones soon appeared, running toward us; upon which Fritz jumped out of the boat, placed the head of our sea-prize on the muzzle of his gun, and walked to shore, which I reached at the same moment.

I requested my wife to go with two of the younger boys to Falcon's Stream, and fetch the sledge and the beasts of burden, that we might see at least a part of our booty from the ship put safely under shelter the same evening. A tempest, or even the tide, might sweep away the whole during the night. We took every precaution in our power against the latter danger, by fixing the boat and the raft, now, at the time of its reflux, as securely as we could without an anchor.

While we were employed on this scheme, the sledge arrived, and we placed the tortoise upon it, and also some articles of light weight, such as mattresses, pieces of linen, etc. Our first concern, on reaching our abode, was the tortoise, which we immediately turned on his back, that we might strip off his shell, and make use of some of the flesh while it was fresh. Taking my hatchet, I separated the upper and under shell all round, which were joined together by cartilages. The upper shell of the tortoise is extremely convex; the under, on the contrary, is nearly flat. I cut away as much of the flesh of the animal as was sufficient for a meal, and laid the rest carefully on the under shell, which served as a dish, recommending to my wife to cook what I had cut off, on the other shell, with no other seasoning than a little salt, and pledged myself that she would produce a luxurious dish.

Fritz.—I thought, father, of cleaning the shell thoroughly, and fixing it by the side of our river, and keeping it always full of pure water for my mother's use, when she has to wash the linen, or cook our victuals.

Father.—Excellent, excellent, my boy! all honour to the founder of the *pure water-tub*! This is what I call *thinking for the general good*. And we will take care to execute the idea as soon as we can prepare some clay, as a solid foundation for its bottom.

Ernest.—When the water-tub is complete, I will put some roots I have found to soak a little in it, for they are now extremely dry. I do not exactly know what they are: they look something like the radish, or horse-radish; but the plant from which I took them was almost the size of a bush.

Father.—If my suspicion is right, you have made a beneficial discovery, which, with the assistance of our own wild roots, may furnish us the means of existence as long as we may remain in this island! I think your roots are *manioc*, of which the natives of the West Indies make a sort of bread or cake which they call *cassava*. But we must first carry the production through a certain preparation, without which it possesses pernicious properties. Try to find the same place, and bring a sufficient quantity for our first experiment.

We had finished unloading the sledge, and I bade the three eldest boys accompany me to fetch another load before it should be dark. Having reached the raft, we took from it as many effects as the sledge could hold, or the animals draw along. One object of my attention was to secure two chests which contained the clothes of my family. I reckoned also on finding in one of the chests some books on interesting subjects, and principally a large handsomely printed Bible. I added to these, four cart-wheels and a hand-mill for grinding; which, now that we had discovered the manioc, I considered of signal importance. These and a few other articles completed our present load.

On our return to Falcon's Nest, we found my wife looking anxiously for our arrival, and ready with the welcome she had promised of an ample and agreeable repast. Before she had well examined our new stores, she drew me, with one of her sweetest smiles, by the arm. "Step this way," said she, and leading to the shade of a tree,—"this is the work I performed in your absence," pointing to a large cask half sunk in the ground, and the rest covered over with branches of trees. She then applied a small corkscrew to the side, and filling the shell of a cocoa-nut with the contents, presented it to me. I found the liquor equal to the best canary I had ever tasted. "How then," said I, "have you performed this new miracle? I cannot believe the enchanted bag produced it." "Not exactly," replied she; "for this time it was an obliging white wave which threw it on shore. I took a little ramble in your absence yesterday, to see what I could find, and well my trouble was rewarded! The boys ran for the sledge, and had but little difficulty in getting the cask to Falcon's Stream, where we dug this place in the earth to keep it cool."

My wife now proposed that all should be regaled with some of the delicious beverage. My own share so invigorated me, that I found myself able to complete my day's work, by drawing up the mattresses we had brought from the ship, to our chamber in the tree, by means of a pulley. When I had laid them along to advantage, they looked so inviting that I could scarcely resist my desire of at once committing myself to the kind relief they seemed to offer to my exhausted strength.

But now the savoury smell of the tortoise laid claim to my attention. I hastened down, and we all partook heartily of the luxurious treat. We returned thanks to God, and speedily retired to taste the blessing of sound repose upon the said mattresses.

CHAPTER XIX

Another Trip to the Wreck—Baking

AFTER breakfast the next morning we returned to the seaside to complete the unloading of the raft, that it might be ready for sea on the flowing of the tide. We were not long in taking two cargoes to Falcon's Stream. At our last trip the water was nearly up to our craft. I sent back my wife and the boys, and remained with Fritz till we were quite afloat; when observing Jack still loitering near, I guessed at his wish, and consented to his embarking with us. Shortly after, the tide was high enough for us to row off. Instead of

steering for Safety Bay to moor our vessels there securely, I
was tempted by a fresh sea-breeze to go out again to the
wreck; but it was too late to undertake much, and I was
unwilling to cause my dear partner uneasiness by passing
another night on board. I therefore determined to bring
away only what could be obtained with ease and speed: we
searched hastily through the ship for any trifling articles that
might be readily removed. Jack was up and down everywhere, at a loss what to select; and when I saw him again,
he drew a wheelbarrow after him, shouting that he had
found a vehicle for carrying our wild roots.

But Fritz next disclosed still better news, which was, that
he had discovered, behind the bulkhead amidship, a pinnace
(i.e. a small craft, the fore part of which is square), taken to
pieces, with all its appurtenances, and even two small guns
for its defence. This intelligence so delighted me, that I
quitted everything else to run to the bulkhead, when I was
convinced of the truth of the lad's assertion: but I instantly
perceived that to put it together, and launch it, would be an
Herculean task. I collected various utensils, a copper boiler,
some plates of iron, tobacco-graters, two grinding-stones, a
small barrel of gunpowder, and another full of flints, which
I much valued. Jack's barrow was not forgotten; two more
were afterwards found and added, with straps belonging to
them. All these articles were hurried into the boat, and we
re-embarked with speed, to avoid the land wind that rises in
the evening.

Arrived at Falcon's Stream, my wife exhibited a good
store of tuberous roots, which she had got in during our
absence, and a quantity of the roots I had taken for manioc,
and in which I was not mistaken.

"But now," said I, "for some supper and repose; and if
my little workmen should be industriously inclined tomor-
row, I shall reward them with the novelty of a new trade to
be learned." This did not fail to excite the curiosity of all;
but I kept my word, and made them wait till the following
day for the explanation I had to give.

I waked the boys very early, reminding them that I had
promised to teach them a new trade.

"What is it? What is it?" exclaimed they, all at once,
springing suddenly out of bed, and hurrying on their clothes.

Father.—It is the art of the baker, my boys. Hand me

those iron plates that we brought yesterday from the vessel,
and the tobacco-graters also, and we will make our experiment. Ernest, bring hither the roots you found; but first, my
dear, I must request you to make me a small bag of a piece
of strong wrapper cloth.

My wife set instantly to work to oblige me; but having no
great confidence in my talents for making either bread or
cakes, she first filled a copper boiler with roots, and put it
on the fire, that we might not be without something to eat at
dinner-time: in the meanwhile I spread a piece of coarse
linen on the ground, and assembled my young ones round
me: I gave each of the boys a grater, and showed him at the
same time how to rest it on the linen, and then to grate the
roots of manioc: in a short time each had produced a considerable heap of a substance somewhat resembling pollard.

By this time my wife had completed the bag. I had it well
filled with what we called our pollard, and she closed it
securely by sewing up the end. I was now to contrive a kind
of press: I cut a long, straight, stout branch, from a
neighbouring tree, and stripped it of the bark; I then placed
a plank across the table we had fixed between the arched
roots of our tree, and which was exactly the right height for
my purpose, and on this I laid the bag; I put other planks
again upon the bag, and then covered all with the large
branch, the thickest extremity of which I inserted under an
arch, while to the other, which projected beyond the planks,
I suspended all sorts of heavy substances, such as lead, our
largest hammers, and bars of iron, which, acting with great
force as a press on the bag of manioc, caused the sap it
contained to issue in streams, which flowed plentifully on
the ground.

We then opened the bag, and took out a small quantity of
the pollard, which already was dry enough: we stirred the
rest about with a stick, and then replaced it under the press.
The next thing was to fix one of our iron plates, which was
of a round form, and a little hollow, so as to rest upon two
blocks of stone at a distance from each other; under this we
lighted a large fire, and when the iron plate was completely
heated, we placed a portion of the dough upon it with a
wooden spade. As soon as the cake began to be brown
underneath, it was turned, that the other side might be
baked also.

When the cake was cold, we broke some of it into crumbs, and gave it to two of the fowls, and a larger piece to the monkey, who nibbled it with a perfect relish, making all the time a thousand grimaces, while the boys stood by envying the preference he enjoyed.

The first thing after dinner was to visit our fowls. Those which had eaten the manioc were in excellent condition, and no less so was the monkey. "Now then to the bakehouse, young ones," said I, "as fast as you can scamper." The grated manioc was soon emptied out of the bag, a large fire was quickly lighted, and I placed the boys where a flat surface had been prepared for them, and gave to each a plate of iron and the quantity of a cocoa-nut full to make a cake apiece, and they were to try who could succeed the best. They were ranged in a half circle round me, that they might observe how I proceeded, and adopt the same method for themselves. The result was not discouraging for a first experiment, though it must be confessed we were now and then so unlucky as to burn a cake; but there was not a greater number of these than served to feed the pigeons and the fowls, which hovered round us to claim their share of the treat.

The rest of the day was employed by the boys in making several turns with their wheelbarrows, and by myself in different arrangements, in which the ass and our sledge had a principal share, both being employed in drawing to Tent House the remaining articles we had brought from the ship.

CHAPTER XX
The Cracker and the Pinnace

FROM the time of discovering the pinnace, my desire of returning to the vessel grew every moment more irresistible; but one thing I saw was absolutely necessary, which was, to collect all my hands to get her out from the situation where we had found her.

After breakfast, then, we prepared for setting out. The boys were gay and on the alert, in the expectation of the pleasure that awaited them. We took with us an ample provision of boiled roots and cassave; and in addition, arms and weapons of every kind. We reached Safety Bay without any remarkable event: here we thought it prudent to put on our cork jackets; we then scattered some food for the geese and ducks which had taken up their abode there, and soon after stepped gaily into our tub-raft, at the same time fastening the new boat by a rope to her stern, so that she could be drawn along. We put out for the current, though not without considerable fear of finding that the wreck had disappeared. We soon, however, perceived that it still remained firm between the rocks.

Having got on board, all repaired, on the wings of curiosity and ardour, to that part of the vessel called the bulkhead, which contained the enviable prize, the pinnace. On further observation, it appeared to me that the plan we had formed was subject to at least two alarming difficulties; the one was the situation of the pinnace in the ship; and the other was the size and weight it would necessarily acquire when put together. The enclosure which contained the pinnace was in the interior of the ship, and timbers of prodigious bulk and weight separated it from the breach, and in this part of the deck there was not sufficient space for us to put the pinnace together, or to give her room when done. The breach also was too narrow and too irregular to admit of her being launched from this place, as we had done with our tub-raft. In short, the separate pieces of the pinnace were too heavy for the possibility of our removing them even with the assistance of our united strength. What therefore was to be done?

The cabinet which contained the pinnace was lighted by several small fissures in the timbers, which, after standing in the place a few minutes to accustom the eye, enabled one to see sufficiently to distinguish objects. I discovered, with pleasure, that all the pieces of which she was composed were so accurately arranged and numbered, that without too much presumption I might flatter myself with the hope of being able effectually to collect and put them together, if I could be allowed the necessary time, and could procure a convenient place. I therefore, in spite of every disadvantage, decided on the undertaking; and we immediately set about it. We proceeded at first so slowly as to have produced discouragement, if the desire of possessing so admirable a little vessel had not at every moment inspired us with new strength and ardour.

We passed an entire week in this arduous undertaking. I embarked every morning with my three sons, and returned every evening, and never without some small addition to our stores. We were now so accustomed to this manner of proceeding, that my wife bade us good-bye without concern, and we, on our parts, left Tent House without anxiety.

At length the pinnace was completed, and in a condition to be launched: the question now was, how to manage this remaining difficulty. She was an elegant little vessel, perfect in every part: she had a small neat deck; and her masts and sails were no less perfect than those of a little brig. It was probable she would sail well, from the lightness of her construction, and in consequence drawing but little water. We had pitched and towed all the seams, that nothing might be wanting for her complete appearance: we had even taken the pains of further embellishing, by mounting her with two small cannon of about a pound weight; and, in imitation of larger vessels, had fastened them to the deck with chains.

But in spite of the delight we felt in contemplating a work, as it were, of our own industry, the great difficulty still remained: the said commodious, charming little vessel still stood fast, enclosed within four walls: nor could I conceive a mode of getting her out. To effect a passage through the outer side of the vessel, by means of our united industry in the use of all the utensils we had secured, seemed to present a prospect of exertions beyond the reach of man, even if not attended with dangers the most alarming. We examined if it might be practicable to cut away all intervening timbers, to which, from the nature of the breach, we had easier access: but should we even succeed in this attempt, the upper timbers being, in consequence of the inclined position of the ship, on a level with the water, our labour would be unavailing: besides we had neither strength nor time for such a proceeding; from one moment to another, a storm might arise and engulf the ship, timbers, pinnace, ourselves, and all. Despairing, then, of being able to find means consistent with the sober rules of art, my impatient fancy inspired the thought of a project, which could not however be tried without hazards and dangers of a tremendous nature.

I had found on board a strong iron mortar, such as is used in kitchens. I took a thick oak plank, and nailed to different parts of it some large iron hooks: with a knife I cut a groove along the middle of the plank. I sent the boys to fetch some match-wood from the hold, and I cut a piece sufficiently long to continue burning at least two hours. I placed this train in the groove of my plank: I filled the mortar with gunpowder, and then laid the plank thus furnished upon it, having previously pitched the mortar all round; and, lastly, I made the whole fast to the spot with strong chains, crossed by means of the hooks in every direction. Thus I accomplished a sort of cracker, from which I expected to effect a happy conclusion. I hung this machine of mischief to the side of the bulkhead next to the sea, having taken previous care to choose a spot in which its action could not affect the pinnace. When the whole was arranged, I set fire to the match, the end of which projected far enough beyond the plank to allow us sufficient time to escape. I now hurried on board the raft, into which I had previously sent the boys before applying a light to the match; and who, though they had assisted in forming the cracker, had no suspicion of the use for which it was intended, believing all the while it concealed some subject of amusement for their next trip to the vessel.

On our arrival at Tent House, I immediately put the raft in a certain order, that she might be in readiness to return speedily to the wreck when the noise produced by the cracker should have informed me that my scheme had taken effect. We set busily to work in emptying her; and during the occupation, our ears were assailed with the noise of an explosion of such violence, that my wife and the boys, who were ignorant of the cause, were so dreadfully alarmed as instantly to abandon their employment. "What can it be? —what is the matter?—what can have happened?"—cried all at once. "It must be cannon. It is perhaps the captain and the ship's company who have found their way hither! Or can it be some vessel in distress? Can we go to its relief?"

The boys lost not a moment in jumping into their tubs, whither I soon followed them, after having whispered a few words to my wife, somewhat tending to explain, but still more to tranquilize her mind during the trip we had now to engage in.

We rowed out of the bay with more rapidity than on any former occasion; curiosity gave strength to our arms. When the vessel was in sight, I observed with pleasure that no change had taken place in the part of her which faced Tent House, and that no sign of smoke appeared: we advanced, therefore, in excellent spirits; but instead of rowing, as usual, straight to the breach, we proceeded round to the side, on the inside of which we had placed the cracker. The horrible scene of devastation we had caused now broke upon our sight. The greater part of the ship's side was shattered to pieces; innumerable splinters covered the surface of the water; the whole exhibited a scene of terrible destruction, in the midst of which presented itself our elegant pinnace, entirely free from injury! We entered by the new breach, and had soon reason to be assured that the pinnace had wholly escaped injury, and that the fire was entirely extinguished. The mortar, however, and pieces of the chain, had been driven forcibly into the opposite side of the enclosure.

I then examined the breach we had thus effected, and

next the pinnace. I perceived that it would be easy, with the help of the crow and the lever, to lower her into the water. In putting her together, I had used the precaution of placing her keel on rollers, that we might not experience the same difficulty as we had formerly done in launching our tub-raft. Before letting her go, however, I fastened the end of a long thick rope to her head, and the other end to the most solid part of the wreck, for fear of her being carried out too far. We put our whole ingenuity and strength to this undertaking, and soon enjoyed the pleasure of seeing our pinnace descend gracefully into the sea.

Two whole days more were spent in completely equipping and loading the beautiful little barge we had now secured. When she was ready for sailing, I found it impossible to resist the earnest importunity of the boys, who, as a recompense for the industry and discretion they had employed, claimed my permission to salute their mother, on their approach to Tent House, with two discharges of cannon. These accordingly were loaded, and the two youngest placed themselves, with a lighted match in hand, close to the touchholes, to be in readiness. Fritz stood at the mast, to manage the ropes and cables, while I took my station at the rudder. These matters being adjusted, we put off with sensations of lively joy, which was demonstrated by loud huzzas and suitable gesticulation. The wind was favourable, and so brisk that we glided with the rapidity of a bird along the mirror of the waters; and while my young ones were transported with pleasure by the velocity of the motion, I could not myself refrain from shuddering at the thought of some possible disaster.

Our old friend the tub-raft had been deeply loaded, and fastened to the pinnace, and it now followed as an accompanying boat to a superior vessel. We took down our large sail as soon as we found ourselves at the entrance of Safety Bay, to have the greater command in steering the pinnace; and soon the smaller ones were lowered one by one, that we might the more securely avoid being thrown with violence upon the rocks so prevalent along the coast: thus, proceeding at a slower rate, we had greater facilities for managing the important affair of the discharge of the cannon. Arrived within a certain distance—"*Fire!*" cried Commander Fritz. The rocks behind Tent House returned the sound. "*Fire!*"

said Fritz again. Ernest and Jack obeyed, and the echoes again majestically replied. Fritz at the same moment had discharged his two pistols, and all joined instantly in three loud huzzas.

"Welcome! welcome! dear ones," was the answer from the anxious mother, almost breathless with astonishment and joy. "Welcome!" cried also little Francis, with his feeble voice, as he stood clinging to her side, and not well knowing whether he was to be sad or merry. We now tried to push to shore with our oars in a particular direction, that we might have the protection of a projecting mass of rocks, and my wife and little Francis hastened to the spot to receive us.

Fritz now invited his mother to get on board, and gave her his assistance. When they had all stepped upon the deck, they entreated the permission to salute, by again discharging the cannon, and at the same moment to confer on the pinnace the name of their mother—*The Elizabeth*.

My wife was particularly gratified by these our late adventures; she applauded our skill and perseverance: "But," said she, "we have not, I assure you, remained idle while the rest were so actively employed for the common benefit. No, not so; little Francis and his mother found means to be doing something also, though not at this moment prepared to furnish such unquestionable proofs as you, by your salutations of cannon, etc.; but wait a little, good friends, and our proofs shall hereafter be apparent in some dishes of excellent vegetables which we shall be able to regale you with. It depends, to say the truth, only on yourselves, dear ones, to go with me and see what we have done."

We did not hesitate to comply, and jumped briskly out of the pinnace for the purpose. Taking her little coadjutor Francis by the hand, she led the way, and we followed in the gayest mood imaginable. She conducted us up an ascent of one of our rocks, and stopping at the spot where the cascade is formed from Jackal's River, she displayed to our astonished eyes a handsome kitchen-garden, laid out properly in beds and walks, and, as she told us, everywhere sowed with the seed of useful plants.

"This," said she, "is the pretty exploit we have been engaged in, if you will kindly think so of it. In this spot the earth is so light, being principally composed of decayed leaves, that Francis and I had no difficulty in working in it, and then dividing it into different compartments: one for potatoes, one for manioc, and other smaller shares for lettuces of various kinds, not forgetting to leave a due proportion to receive some plants of the sugar-cane. You, dear husband, and Fritz, will easily find means to conduct sufficient water hither from the cascade, by means of pipes of bamboo, to keep the whole in health and vigour."

I stood transported in the midst of so perfect an exhibition of the kind zeal and persevering industry of this most amiable of women! I could only exclaim, that I should never have believed in the possibility of such a labour in so short a time, and particularly with so much privacy as to leave me wholly unsuspicious of the existence of such a project.

The pinnace was anchored on the shore, and fastened with a rope, by her head, to a stake. When all our stores were disposed of, we began our journey to Falcon's Stream, but not empty-handed; we took with us everything that seemed to be absolutely wanted for comfort; and when brought together, it was really so much, that both ourselves and our beasts of burden had no easy task to perform.

CHAPTER XXI

Gymnastic Exercises—Various Discoveries—Singular Animals, etc.

I RECOMMENDED to my sons to resume the exercise of the shooting of arrows; for I had an extreme solicitude about their preserving and increasing their bodily strength and agility. On this occasion, I added the exercises of running, jumping, getting up trees, both by means of climbing by the trunk, or by a suspended rope, as sailors are obliged to do to get to the masthead. We began at first by making

knots in the rope, at a foot distance from each other; then
we reduced the number of knots, and before we left off we
contrived to succeed without any. I next taught them an
exercise of a different nature, which was to be effected by
means of two balls of lead, fastened one to each end of a
string about a fathom in length. While I was preparing this
machinery, all eyes were fixed upon me.

"I am endeavouring," said I, "to imitate the arms used by
the Patagonians, inhabitants of the most southern point of
America; but, instead of balls, which they are not able to
procure, they tie two heavy stones, one at each end of a
cord, but considerably longer than the one I am working
with: every Patagonian is armed with this simple instrument,
which they used with singular dexterity. If they desire to kill
or wound an enemy, or an animal, they fling one of the ends
of this cord at him, and begin instantly to draw it back by
the other, which they keep carefully in their hand, to be
ready for another throw, if necessary: but if they wish to
take an animal alive, and without hurting it, they possess
the singular art of throwing it in such a way as to make it
run several times round the neck of the prey, occasioning a
perplexing tightness; they then throw the second stone, and
with so certain an aim, that they scarcely ever miss their
object: the operation of the second is, the so twisting itself
about the animal as to impede his progress, even though he
were at full gallop. The stones continue turning, carrying
with them the cord: the poor animal is at length so entangled,
that he can neither advance nor retire, and thus falls a prey
to the enemy."

This description was heard with much interest by the
boys, who now all entreated I would that instant try
the effect of my own instrument upon a small trunk of
a tree which we saw at a certain distance. My throws entirely succeeded; and the string with the balls at the end so
completely surrounded the tree, that the skill of the
Patagonian huntsmen required no further illustration. Each
of the boys must then needs have a similar instrument; and
in a short time Fritz became quite an expert in the art.

The next morning, as I was dressing, I remarked from my
window in the tree, that the sea was violently agitated, and
the waves swelled with the wind. I rejoiced to find myself in
safety in my home, and that the day had not been destined

for out-of-door occupation. We now fell to a more minute examination than I had hitherto had time for, of all our various possession at Falcon's Stream. My wife showed me many things she had herself found means to add to them during my repeated absences from home: among these was a pair of young pigeons, which had been lately hatched, and were already beginning to try their wings, while their mother was again sitting on her eggs. From these we passed to the fruit trees we had laid in earth to be planted, and which were in real need of our assistance. I immediately set myself to prevent so important an injury. I had promised the boys, the evening before, to go all together to the wood of gourds, to provide ourselves with vessels of different sizes to keep our provisions in: they were enchanted with the idea, but I bargained that they must first assist me to plant all the young trees: which was no sooner said than set about.

When we had finished, the evening was too far advanced for so long a walk. By sunrise the next morning all were on foot, and we set out, full of good-humour and high spirits, from Falcon's Stream. Turning round Flamingo Marsh, we soon reached the pleasant spot which before had so delighted us. Fritz took a direction a little further from the seashore; and sending Turk into the tall grass, he followed himself, and both disappeared. Soon, eager for sport, we heard Turk barking loud; a large bird sprang up, and almost at the same moment a shot from Fritz brought it down: but though wounded it was not killed: it raised itself, and got off with incredible swiftness, not by flying, but by running. Turk followed, and seizing the bird, held it fast till Fritz came up. Now a different scene succeeded from that which took place at the capture of the flamingo. The legs of that bird are long and weak, and it was able to make but a poor resistance. The present captive was large in size, and strong; it struck the dogs, or whoever came near, with its legs, with so much force, that Fritz, who had received a blow or two, dared not again approach the enemy. Fortunately I reached the spot in time to give assistance, and was pleased to see that it was a female bustard of the largest size.

To secure the bird without injuring it, I threw my pocket-handkerchief over the head of the bustard; it could not disengage itself, and its efforts served only to entangle it the more. As it could not now see me, I got near enough to pass

a string with a running knot over its legs, which, for the
present, I drew tight, to prevent further mischief from such
powerful weapons. I gently released its wing from Turk's
mouth, and tied it, with its fellow, close to the bird's body.
In short, the bustard was our own.

As we advanced, I was frequently obliged to use the
hatchet to make a free passage for the ass in the tall grass.
The heat also increased, and we were all complaining of
thirst, when Ernest, whose discoveries were generally of a
kind to be of use, made one of a most agreeable nature. He
found a kind of hollow stalk, of some height, which grew at
the foot of trees, and entangled our feet in walking. He cut
one of them, and was surprised to see a drop of pure fresh
water issue at the place where the knife had been applied:
he showed it to us, put it to his lips, and found it pure, and
felt much regret that there was no more. I then fell to
examining the phenomenon myself, and soon perceived that
the want of air prevented a more considerable issue of
water. I made some more incisions, and presently water
flowed out as if from a small conduit. I tried the experiment
of dividing the plants longways, and they soon gave out
water enough to supply even the ass, the monkey, and the
bustard.

We were still compelled to fight our way through thick
bushes, till at length, arrived at the wood of gourds, we
were not long in finding the spot where Fritz and I had once
before enjoyed so agreeable a repose. My wife now gave us
notice that she should want some vessels to contain milk, a
large flat spoon to cut out butter by pieces, and next, some
pretty plates for serving it at table, made from the gourd
rinds.

I made the boys gather or collect the gourds, till we were
in possession of a sufficient number. We now began our
work: some had to cut; others to saw, scoop out, and model
into agreeable forms. It was a real pleasure to witness the
activity exhibited in this our manufacture of porcelain; each
tried what specimens he could present for the applause of
his companions. For my own part, I made a pretty basket,
large enough to carry eggs, with one of the gourds, leaving
an arch at the top to serve as a cover. I likewise accomplished a certain number of vessels, also with covers, fit to
hold our milk, and then some spoons to skim the cream. My

next attempt was some bottles large enough to hold fresh water, and these occasioned me more trouble than all the rest. It was necessary to empty the gourd through the small opening of the size of one's finger, which I had cut in it; I was obliged, after loosening the contents with a stick, to get them out by friction with shot and water well shaken on the inside. Lastly, to please my wife, I undertook the labour of a set of plates for her use. Fritz and Jack engaged to make hives for the bees, and nests for the pigeons and hens. For this last object they took the largest gourds, and cut a hole in front, the size of the animal for whose use it was intended. The pigeons' nests were intended to be tied to the branches of our tree; those for the hens, the geese, and the ducks, were to be placed between its roots, or on the seashore, and to represent a sort of hencoop.

Our work, added to the heat of the day, had made us all thirsty; but we found nothing on this spot like our *fountain* plants, as we had named them. The boys entreated me to go with them in different directions, and try to find some water, not daring by themselves to venture further into the wood.

Ernest with great eagerness proposed relieving me of this trouble, and putting himself in my place. It was not long before we heard him calling loudly to us, and saw him returning in great alarm.—"Run quick, father," said he, "here is an immense wild boar."

I then cried out to the boys to call the dogs quickly. "Halloo, here, Turk! Flora!" The dogs arrived full gallop. Ernest was our leader, and conducted us to the place where he saw the boar; but it was gone, and we saw nothing but a plot of roots which appeared to have been ransacked by the animal. We soon heard the cry of the dogs; for they had overtaken the runaway, and soon after the most hideous growling assailed our ears from the same quarter. We advanced with caution, holding our guns in readiness to fire together the instant the animal should be within the proper distance. Presently the spectacle of the two brave creatures attacking him on the right and left presented itself; each held one of his ears between its teeth. But it was not a boar, but our own sow which had run away and so long been lost! After the first surprise we could not resist a hearty laugh; and then we hastened to disencumber our old friend of the

teeth of her two adversaries. But here the attention of all
was attracted to a kind of small potato which we observed
lying thick on the grass around us, and which had fallen
from some trees which appeared loaded with the same production: our sow devoured them greedily, thus consoling
herself for the pain and fright the dogs had occasioned her.

The fruit was of different colours, and extremely pleasing
to the eye. Fritz expressed his apprehension that it was the
poisonous apple called the mancenilla; but the sow ate them
with so much eagerness, and the tree which bore them
having neither the form nor foliage ascribed by naturalists to
the mancenilla, that I doubted the truth of his idea. I desired my sons to put some of the fruit in their pockets, to
make an experiment with them upon the monkey. We now
again, from extreme thirst, began to recollect our want of
water, and determined to seek for some in every direction.
Jack sprang off, and sought among the rocks, hoping that he
should discover some little stream: but scarcely had he left
the wood than he bawled to us that he had found a crocodile.

"A crocodile!" cried I, with a hearty laugh; "you have a
fine imagination, my boy! Who ever saw a crocodile on such
scorching rocks as these, and with not a drop of water near?
Now, Jack, you are surely dreaming . . ."

"Not so much of a dream as you may think, father,"
answered Jack, trying to speak in a low voice; "fortunately
he is asleep; he lies here on a stone at his full length, do,
father, step here, and look at it; it does not stir in the least."

We stole softly to the place where the animal lay; but
instead of a crocodile, I saw before me a large sort of lizard,
named by naturalists *Leguana*, or *Yguana*, an animal by
nature of a mild character, and excellent as food. Instantly
all were for seizing him, and presenting so rare a prize to
their mother. Fritz was already taking aim with his gun: but
I prevented him, observing that the animal being protected
by a coat of scales, it might be difficult to destroy him, and
that he is known to be dangerous, if approached, when
angry. "Let us try," said I, "another sort of experiment; as
he is asleep, we need not be in a hurry."

I cut a stout stick from a bush, to the extremity of which I
tied a string with a running knot. I guarded my other hand
simply with a little switch, and thus with cautious steps
approached the creature. When I was very near to him, I

began to whistle a lively air, taking care to make the sounds low at first, and to increase in loudness till the lizard was awaked. The creature appeared entranced with pleasure as the sounds fell upon his ear; he raised his head to receive them still more distinctly, and looked round on all sides to discover from whence they came. I now advanced by a step at a time, without a moment's interval in the music, which fixed him like a statue to the place. At length I was near enough to reach him with my switch, with which I tickled him gently, still continuing to whistle, one after the other, the different airs I could recollect. The lizard was bewildered by the charms of the music: the attitudes he threw himself into were expressive of a delirious voluptuousness; he stretched himself at full length, made undulating motions with his long tail, threw his head about, raised it up, and by this sort of action disclosed the formidable range of his sharp-pointed teeth, which were capable of tearing us to pieces if we had excited his hostility. I dexterously seized the moment of his raising his head, to throw my noose over him. When this was accomplished, the boys drew near also, and wanted instantly to draw it tight and strangle him at once; but this I positively forbade, being unwilling to cause the poor animal so unmerited a suffering. I had used the noose only to make sure of him, in case it should happen that a milder mode of killing him, which I intended to try, failed of success, in which case I should have looked to the noose for protection; but this was rendered unnecessary. Continuing to whistle my most affecting melodies, I seized a favorable moment to plunge my switch into one of his nostrils. The blood flowed in abundance, and soon deprived him of life, without his exhibiting the least appearance of being in pain; on the contrary, to the last moment, he seemed to be still listening to the music.

We had now to consider of the best way for transporting to Falcon's Stream so large and valuable a booty. After a moment of reflection, I perceived that I had better come at once to the determination of carrying him across my shoulders; and the figure I made with so singular an animal on my back, with his tail dragging on the ground, was not the least amusing circumstance of the adventure.

We were proceeding in our return, when we distinguished the voices of my wife and little Francis calling loudly upon

my name. Our long absence had alarmed them: we had
forgotten on this occasion to give them notice of our approach by firing our gun, and they had imagined some
terrible disaster must have befallen us. We had so many
things to tell, that, till reminded by my wife, we forgot to
mention that we had failed of procuring any water. My sons
had taken out some of the unknown apples from their
pockets, and they lay on the ground by our sides. Knips
soon scented them, and came slily up and stole several, and
fell to chewing them with great eagerness. I myself threw
one or two to the bustard, who also ate them without
hesitation. Being now convinced that the apples were not of
a poisonous nature, I announced to the boys, who had
looked on with envy all the time, that they also might begin
to eat them, and I myself set the example. We found them
excellent in quality, and I began to suspect that they might
be the sort of fruit called *guava*, which is much esteemed in
such countries. This regale of the apples had in some measure relieved our thirst; but on the other hand, they had
increased our hunger; and as we had not time for preparing
a portion of the lizard, we were obliged to content ourselves
with the cold provisions we had brought with us.

We had scarcely finished, before my wife earnestly entreated we would begin our journey home, and it appeared
to me, as the evening was so far advanced, that it would be
prudent to return this once without the sledge, which was
heavy laden, and the ass could have drawn it but slowly. I
therefore determined to leave it on the spot till the following day, when I could return and fetch it, contenting myself
with loading the ass, for the present, with the bags which
contained our new sets of porcelain; the lizard, which I
feared might not keep fresh so long; and our little Francis,
who began to complain of being tired. I took these arrangements upon myself, and left to my wife and Fritz the care of
confining the bustard in such a manner that she could walk
before us without danger of escaping.

When these preparations were complete, our little caravan was put in motion, taking the direction of a straight line
to Falcon's Stream. The course of our route now lay along a
wood of majestic oaks, and the ground was covered with
acorns. My young travellers could not refrain from tasting
them; and finding them both sweet and mild to the palate, I

had the pleasure of reckoning them as a new means of support.

We arrived shortly at Falcon's Stream, and had time to employ ourselves in some trifling arrangements before it was completely dark. We concluded the exertions of the day with a plain repast, and the contriving a comfortable bed for the bustard by the side of the flamingo, and then stretched our weary limbs upon the homely couch, rendered by fatigue luxurious, in the giant tree.

CHAPTER XXII

Excursion into Unknown Tracts

MY first thought, the next morning, was to fetch the sledge from the wood. I had a double motive for leaving it there, which I had refrained from explaining to my wife, to avoid giving her uneasiness. I had formed a wish to penetrate a little farther into the land, and ascertain whether anything useful would present itself beyond the wall of rocks. I was, besides, desirous to be better acquainted with the extent, the form, and general productions of our island: I wished Fritz only, who was stronger and more courageous than his brothers, and Turk, to accompany me. We set out very early in the morning, and drove the ass before us for the purpose of drawing home the sledge.

As we were picking up some acorns, different birds of exquisite plumage flitted about us; for this once, I could not refuse Fritz the pleasure of firing upon them, that we might learn their species. He brought down three. I recognized one to be the great blue Virginia jay, and the other two were parrots. One of the two was a superb red parrot: the other was green and yellow.

We soon arrived at the guava trees, and a little after at the spot where we had left the sledge, when we found our treasures in the best possible condition; but as the morning was not far advanced, we entered upon our intended project of penetrating beyond the wall of rocks.

We pursued our way in a straight line at the foot of these massy, solid productions of nature, every moment expecting to reach their extremity, or to find some turn, or breach, or passage through them, that should conduct us into the interior of the island, if, as I presumed, it was not terminated by these rocks. We walked on, continually looking about, that nothing might escape us worthy of notice, and to anticipate and avoid such dangers as should threaten.

We next entered a pretty little grove, the trees of which were unknown to us. Their branches were loaded with large quantities of berries of an extraordinary quality, being entirely covered with a minute meal or farina. I knew of a sort of bush, the berries of which, when boiled, yield a viscous scum resembling wax: it grows in America, and is named by botanists *Myrica cerifera*, or candleberry tree; this plant resembled it much, and the discovery gave me great pleasure.

A short time after, another object presented itself with equal claims to our attention; it was the singular modes of behaviour of a kind of bird scarcely larger than a chaffinch, and clothed in feathers of a common brown colour. These birds appeared to exist as a republic, there being among them one common nest, inhabited at pleasure by all their tribes. We saw one of these nests in a tree, in a somewhat retired situation; it was formed of plaited straws and bulrushes intermixed; it enclosed great numbers of inhabitants, and was built round the trunk of a tree; it had a kind of roof formed of roots and bulrushes, carefully knit together. We observed in the sides small apertures, seemingly intended as doors and windows to each particular cell of this general receptacle; from a few of these apertures issued some small branches, which served the birds as points of rest for entering and returning: the external appearance of the whole excited the image of an immensely large open sponge.

While we were attentively examining this interesting little colony, we perceived numbers of a very small kind of parrot hovering about the nest. Their gilded green wings, and the variety of their colours, produced a beautiful effect; they seemed to be perpetually disputing with the colonists, and not infrequently endeavoured to prevent their entrance into the building; they attacked them fiercely, and even tried to peck at us, if we but advanced our hand to the structure. Fritz, who was well trained in the art of climbing trees, was earnestly desirous to take a nearer view of them, and to secure if possible a few individuals. He threw his burden down, and climbed to the nest: he then tried to introduce his hand into one of the apertures, and to seize whatever living creature it should touch in that particular cell; what he most desired, was to find a female brooding, and to carry both her and the eggs away. Several of the cells were empty, but by perseverance he found one in the situation he wished; but he received so violent a peck from an invisible bird, that his only care was now to withdraw his hand; presently, however, he ventured a second time to pass his hand into the nest, and succeeded in seizing his prey, which he laid hold of, and in spite of the bird's resistance, he drew it through the aperture, and squeezed it into the pocket of his waistcoat, and buttoning it securely, he slided down the tree, and reached the ground in safety. The signals of distress sent forth by the prisoner collected a multitude of birds from their cells, who all surrounded him, uttering loud cries, and attacking him with their beaks, till he had made good his retreat. He now released the prisoner, and we discovered him to be a beautiful green parrot,[1] which Fritz entreated he might be allowed to preserve, and make a present of to his brothers, who would make a cage to keep him in, and would then tame him and teach him to speak.

On the road home, we observed to each other, that from the circumstance of this young bird's nesting within the structure, it appeared probable that the true right of property was in this species, and that the brown-coloured birds we at first observed were intruders endeavouring to deprive them of it.

We reached a wood, the trees of which, in a small degree, resembled the wild fig-tree; at least the fruit they bore, like the fig, was round in form, and contained a soft juicy

[1] *Tuiete*. This is the smallest kind of Brazilian parrot. There is an infinite variety in their plumage.

substance full of small grains. Their height was from forty to sixty feet; the bark of the trunk was scaly, like the pineapple, and wholly bare of branches, except at the very top. The leaves of these trees are very thick; in substance tough, like leather; and their upper and under surfaces are different in colour. But what surprised us the most was a kind of gum which issued in a liquid state from the trunk of the tree, and became immediately hardened by the air. This discovery awakened Fritz's attention: in Europe he had often made use of the gum produced by cherry trees, either as a cement or varnish, in his youthful occupations: and the thought struck him, that he could do the same with what he now saw.

As he walked, he frequently looked at his gum, which he tried to soften with his breath, but without success: he now discovered a still more singular property in the substance: that of stretching on being pulled at the extremities, and, on being let go, of reducing itself instantly, by the power of an elastic principle. He was struck with surprise, and sprang towards me, repeating the experiment before my eyes, and exclaiming, "Look, father! if this is not the very thing we formerly used to rub out bad strokes in our drawings."

"Ah! what do you tell me?" cried I with joy; "such a discovery would be valuable indeed. The best thanks of all will be due to you, if it is the true *caoutchouc* tree which yields the Indian rubber. Quick, hand it here, that I may examine it."—Having satisfied myself of our good fortune, I had now to explain that caoutchouc is a kind of milky sap, which runs from its tree, in consequence of incisions made in the bark. "This liquid is received in vessels placed expressly for the purpose: it is afterwards made to take the form of dark-coloured bottles, of different sizes, such as we have seen them, in the following manner. Before the liquid has time to coagulate, some small earthen bottles are dipped into it a sufficient number of times to form the thickness required. These vessels are then hung over smoke, which completely dries them, and gives them a dark colour. The concluding part of the operation is to break the mould, and to get out the pieces by the passage of the neck, when there remains the complete form of a bottle. In the same way we may be able to make shoes and boots without seams, if we can add the assistance of earthen moulds of the size of the

leg or foot to be fitted. We must consider of some means of
restoring masses of the caoutchouc to its liquid form, for
spreading upon the moulds; and if we should not succeed,
we must endeavour to draw it in sufficient quantities, in its
liquid state, from the trees themselves."

We now began to consider how much farther we would
go: the thick bushes of bamboo, through which it was impossible to pass, seemed to furnish a natural conclusion to
our journey. We were, therefore, unable to ascertain whether
or not we should have found a passage beyond the wall of
rocks: we perceived then no better resource than to turn to
the left towards Cape Disappointment, where the luxurious
plantations of sugar-canes now again drew our attention.
That we might not return empty-handed to Falcon's Stream,
and might deserve forgiveness for so long an absence,
we each took the pains to cut a large bundle of the canes,
which we threw across the ass's back, not forgetting the
ceremony of reserving one apiece to refresh ourselves with
along the road. We soon arrived on the well-known shore of
the sea, which at length afforded an open and a shorter
path; we next reached the wood of gourds, where we found
our sledge loaded as we had left it the night before; we took
the sugar-canes from the ass, and fastened them to the
sledge, and then we harnessed the ass, and the patient
animal began to draw towards home.

CHAPTER XXIII

Useful Occupations and Labours—
Embellishments—A Painful but
Natural Sentiment

ON the following day, my wife and the boys importuned
me to begin my manufactory of candles: I therefore set
myself to recollect all I had read on the subject. I soon

perceived that I should be at a loss for a little fat to mix with the wax I had procured from the berries, for making the light burn clearer; but I was compelled to proceed without. I put as many berries into a vessel as it would contain, and set it on a moderate fire; my wife in the meantime employed herself in making some wicks with the threads of sailcloth. When we saw an oily matter, of a pleasing smell and light green colour, rise to the top of the liquid the berries had yielded, we carefully skimmed it off and put it into a separate vessel, taking care to keep it warm. We continued this process till the berries were exhausted, and had produced a considerable quantity of wax; we next dipped the wicks one by one into it, while it remained liquid, and then hung them on the bushes to harden: in a short time we dipped them again, and repeated the operation till the candles were increased to the proper size, and they were then put in a place and kept till sufficiently hardened for use. We, however, were all eager to judge of our success that very evening, by burning one of the candles, with which we were well satisfied.

Our success in this last enterprise encouraged us to think of another, the idea of which had long been cherished by our kind steward of provisions; it was to make fresh butter of the cream we every day skimmed from the milk, and which was frequently, to her great vexation, spoiled and given to the animals. The utensil we stood in need of was a churn to turn the cream in. Having earnestly applied my thoughts as to the best manner of conquering the difficulty, I suddenly recollected what I had read in a book of travels, of the method used by the Hottentots for making butter; but instead of a sheep-skin sewed together at its extremities, I emptied a large gourd, washed it clean, filled it again with cream, and stopped it close with the piece I had cut from the top. I placed my vase of cream on a piece of sail-cloth with four corners, and tied to each corner a stake: I placed one boy midway between each stake, and directed them to shake the cloth briskly, but with a steady measure, for a certain time. This exercise, which seemed like children's play, pleased them mightily, and they called it rocking the cradle. They performed their office, singing and laughing all the time, and in an hour, on taking off the cover, we had the satisfaction of seeing some excellent butter. I had now to propose to my sons a work of a more difficult nature than we had hitherto accomplished: it was the construction of a cart, for the conveyance of our effects from place to place, to supersede the sledge, which caused us so much fatigue to load and draw. I tried earnestly and long to accomplish such a machine; but it did not entirely succeed to my wishes, and I wasted in the attempt both time and timber: I however produced what from courtesy we called a cart, and it answered the purpose for which it was designed.

By this time we had nearly exhausted our stock of clothes, and we were compelled once more to have recourse to the vessel, which we knew still contained some chests fit for our use. To this motive we added an earnest desire to take another look at her, and, if practicable, to bring away a few pieces of cannon.

The first fine day I assembled my three eldest sons, and put my design into execution. We reached the wreck without any striking adventure, and found her still fixed between the rocks, but somewhat more shattered than when we had last seen her. We secured the chests of clothes, and whatever remained of ammunition stores: powder, shot, and even such pieces of cannon as we could remove, while those that were too heavy we stripped of their wheels, which might be extremely useful.

But to effect our purpose, it was necessary to spend several days in visits to the vessel, returning constantly in the evening, enriched with everything of a portable nature which the wreck contained; doors, windows, locks, bolts—nothing escaped our grasp: so that the ship was now entirely emptied, with the exception of the large cannon, and three or four immense copper caldrons. We by degrees contrived to tie the heaviest articles to two or three empty casks well pitched, which would thus be sustained above water. I supposed that the wind and tide would convey the beams and timbers ashore, and thus with little pains we should be possessed of a sufficient quantity of materials for erecting a building at some future time. When these measures were taken, I came to the resolution of blowing up the wreck, by a process similar to that which had so well succeeded with the pinnace. We accordingly prepared a cask of gunpowder, which we left on board for the purpose: we rolled it to the place most favourable for our views: we made a small opening in its side, and on quitting the vessel, we inserted a piece of match-wood, which we lighted at the last moment, as before. We then sailed with all possible expedition for Safety Bay, where we arrived in a short time.

About the time of nightfall, a majestic rolling sound like thunder, accompanied by a column of fire and smoke, announced that the ship so awfully concerned with our peculiar destiny, which had brought us to our present abode in a desert, and furnished us there with such vast supplies for general comfort, was that instant annihilated, and withdrawn for ever from the face of man! At this moment, love for the country that gave us birth, that most powerful sentiment of the human heart, sank with a new force into ours. The ship had disappeared for ever! Could we then form a hope ever to behold that country more? We had made a sort of jubilee of witnessing the spectacle: the boys had clapped their hands and skipped about in joyful expectation; but the noise was heard; the smoke and sparks were seen; and the sudden change which took place in our minds could be compared only to the rapidity of these effects of our concerted scheme against the vessel. We all observed a mournful silence, and all rose, as it were by an impulse of mutual condemnation, and took the road to Tent House.

A night's repose had in some measure relieved the melancholy of the preceding evening, and I went rather early in the morning with the boys, to make further observations as to the effects of this remarkable event. We perceived in the water, and along the shore, abundant vestiges of the departed wreck; and amongst the rest, at a certain distance, the empty casks, caldrons, and cannon, all tied together and floating in a large mass upon the water. We jumped instantly into the pinnace, with the tub-boat fastened to it, and made a way towards them through the numberless pieces of timber, etc., that intervened, and in a little time reached the object of our search, which from its great weight moved slowly upon the waves. Fritz, with his accustomed readiness, flung some rope round two four-pounders, and contrived to fasten them to our barge; after which he secured also an enormous quantity of poles, laths, and other useful articles. With this rich booty we returned to land.

We performed three more trips for the purpose of bringing away more cannon, caldrons, fragments of masts, etc., all of which we deposited for present convenience in Safety

Bay; and now began our most fatiguing operations—the removing such numerous and heavy stores from the boats to the Tent House. We separated the cannon and the caldrons from the tub-raft, and from each other, and left them in a place which was accessible for the sledge and the beasts of burden. With the help of the cow we succeeded in getting the caldrons upon the sledge, and in replacing the four wheels we had before taken from the cannon; and now found it easy to make the cow and the ass draw them.

The largest of the boilers or copper caldrons we found of the most essential use. We brought out all our barrels of gunpowder, and placed them on their ends in three separate groups, at a short distance from our tent; we dug a little ditch round the whole, to draw off the moisture from the ground, and then put one of the caldrons turned upside down upon each, which completely answered the purpose of an outhouse. The cannon were covered with sail-cloth, and upon this we laid heavy branches of trees; the larger casks of gunpowder we prudently removed under a projecting piece of rock, and covered them with planks till we should have leisure for executing the plan of an ammunition store-house, about which we had all become extremely earnest.

My wife, in taking a survey of these our labours, made the agreeable discovery that two of our ducks and one of the geese had been brooding under a large bush, and at the time were conducting their little families to the water. The news produced general rejoicings; and the sight of the little creatures so forcibly carried our thoughts to Falcon's Stream, that we all conceived the ardent desire of returning to the society of the numerous old friends we had left there. We therefore fixed the next day for our departure, and set about the necessary preparations.

CHAPTER XXIV

A New Domain—The Troop of Buffaloes—The Vanquished Hero

ON entering our plantation of fruit-trees forming the avenue to Falcon's Stream, we observed that they had not a vigorous appearance, and that they inclined to curve a little in the stalk: we therefore resolved to support them with sticks, and I proposed to walk to the vicinity of Cape Disappointment for the purpose of cutting some bamboos. I had no sooner pronounced the words, than the three eldest boys and their mother exclaimed, at once, that they would accompany me.

We accordingly fixed the following morning, and set out in full procession. For myself, I had a great desire to explore more thoroughly this part of our island. I therefore made some preparations for sleeping, should we find the day too short for all we might have to accomplish. I took the cart instead of the sledge, having fixed some planks across it for Francis and his mother to sit upon when they should be tired: I was careful to be provided with the different implements we might want; some rope machinery I had contrived for rendering the climbing of trees more easy; and lastly, some provisions, some water in a gourd-flask, and one bottle of wine from the captain's store.

It was not without much difficulty that we conducted the cart through the thick entangled bushes, the most intricate of which I everywhere cut down, and we helped to push it along with all our strength. We soon arrived at the caoutchouc, or gum-elastic trees. I thought we could not do better than to halt here, and endeavour to collect a sufficient quantity of the sap to make the different utensils and the impenetrable boots and shoes, as I had before proposed. It was with this design that I had taken care to bring with me several of the most capacious of the gourd rinds. I made deep incisions in the trunks, and fixed some large leaves of trees, partly doubled together lengthways, to the place, to serve as a sort of channel to conduct the sap to the vessels I had kept in readiness to receive it. We had not long begun this process before we perceived the sap begin to run out as white as milk, and in large drops, so that we were not without hopes, by the time of our return, to find the vessels full, and thus to have obtained a sufficient quantity of the ingredient for a first experiment.

We left the sap running, and pursued our way, which led us to the wood of cocoa-trees: from thence we passed to the left, and stopped halfway between the bamboos and the sugar-canes, intending to furnish ourselves with a provision of each. We aimed our course so judiciously, that on clearing the skirts of the wood, we found ourselves in an open plain with the sugar-cane plantations on our left, and on our right those of bamboo, interspersed with various kinds of palm-trees, and, in front, the magnificent bay formed by Cape Disappointment, which stretched far out into the sea.

The prospect that now presented itself to our view was of such exquisite beauty, that we determined to choose it for our resting-place, and to make it the central point of every excursion we should in future make; we were even more than half disposed to desert our pretty Falcon's Stream, and transport our possessions hither; a moment's reflection, however, betrayed the folly of quitting the thousand comforts we had there, with almost incredible industry, assembled; and we dismissed the thought with promising ourselves to include this ravishing spot evermore in our projects for excursions.

It was now evening; and as we had determined to pass the night in this enchanting spot, we began to think of forming some large branches of trees into a sort of hut, as is practised by the hunters in America, to shelter us from the dew and the coolness of the air. While we were thus engaged, we were suddenly roused by the loud braying of the ass, which we had left to graze at a distance but a short time before. On going to the place, we saw him throwing his head in the air, and kicking and prancing about; and while we were thinking what could be the matter, he set off at a full gallop. Unfortunately, Turk and Flora, whom we sent after him, took the fancy of entering the plantation of the sugar-canes, while the ass had preferred the direction of the bamboos on the right.

The following morning we breakfasted on some milk from the cow, some boiled roots, and a small portion of Dutch cheese, and formed, during our meal, the plan of the business for the day. It was decided that one of the boys and myself, attended by the two dogs, should seek the ass through the bamboo plantation. I took with me the agile Jack, who was almost beside himself with joy at this determination.

We soon reached the bamboo plantation, and found means to force ourselves along its intricate entanglements. After great fatigue, and when we were on the point of relinquishing all further hope, we discovered the print of the ass's hoofs on the soil, which inspired us with new ardour in the pursuit. After spending a whole hour in further endeavours, we at length, on reaching the skirts of the plantation, perceived the sea in the distance, and soon after found ourselves in an open space, which bounded the great bay. A considerable river flowed into the bay at this place, and we perceived that the ridge of rocks, which we had constantly seen, extended to the shore, and terminated in a perpendicular precipice, leaving only a narrow passage between the rocks and the river, which, during every flux of the tide, must necessarily be under water, but which at that moment was dry and passable. The probability that the ass would prefer passing by this narrow way, to the hazard of the water, determined us to follow in the same path: we had also some curiosity to ascertain what might be found on the other side of the rocks, for as yet we were ignorant whether they formed a boundary to our island, or divided it into two portions; whether we should see there land or water. We continued to advance, and at length reached a stream which issued foaming from a large mass of rock, and fell in a cascade into the river. The bed of this stream was so deep, and its course so rapid, that we were a long time finding a part where it might be most practicable for us to cross. When we had got to the other side, we found the soil again sandy, and mixed with a fertile kind of earth: in this place we no longer saw naked rock; but the print of the ass's hoofs were again visible on the ground.

By observing closely, we saw with astonishment the prints of the feet of other animals, much larger and different in many respects from those of the ass. Our curiosity was so strongly excited, that we resolved to follow the traces; and they conducted us to a plain at a great distance, which presented to our wondering eyes a terrestrial paradise. We ascended a hill, which partly concealed from our view this delicious scene, and then, with the assistance of a glass, we beheld an extensive range of country, exhibiting every kind of rural beauty, and in which a profound tranquillity had seemed to take up its abode.

By straining our eyes, however, as far as we could see, we thought we perceived at a great distance some specks upon the land, that seemed to be in motion. We hastened towards the spot; and as we drew nearer, to our inexpressible surprise, beheld a pretty numerous group of animals, which in the assemblage presented something like the outline of a troop of horses or of cows. I observed them sometimes run up to each other, and then suddenly stoop to graze. Though we had not lately met with farther traces of the ass, I was not entirely without the hope of finding him among these animals. On a nearer approach, we perceived they were wild buffaloes. My alarm was so great that I remained for a few moments fixed to the spot like a statue. By good luck the dogs were far behind us, and the buffaloes gave no sign of fear or of displeasure at our approach: they stood perfectly still, with their large round eyes fixed upon us in vacant surprise: those which were lying down got up slowly, but not one among them seemed to have any hostile disposition towards us. The circumstance of the dogs' absence was most likely, on this occasion, the means of our safety; as it was, we had time to draw back quietly, and prepare our firearms. It was not, however, my intention to make use of them in any way but for defence, being sensible that we were unequal to the encounter, and recollecting also to have read that the sound of a gun drives the buffalo to a state of desperation. I therefore thought only of retreating; and with my poor Jack, for whom I was more alarmed than for myself, was proceeding in this way, when unfortunately Turk and Flora ran up to us, and we could see were noticed by the buffaloes. The animals instantly, and all together, set up such a roar as to make our nerves tremble; they struck their horns and their hoofs upon the ground, which they tore up by pieces and scattered in the air. Our brave Turk and Flora, fearless of danger, ran, in spite of all our efforts, into the midst of them, and, according to their manner of attacking, laid hold of the ears of a young buffalo, which happened to be standing a few paces nearer to us than the rest; and, though the creature began a tremendous roar and motion with his hoofs, they held him fast, and were dragging him towards us. Our every hope seemed now to be in the chance of the terror the buffaloes would feel at the noise of our musketry, which, perhaps, for the first time would assail their organs, and most likely excite them to flight. With, I must confess, a palpitating heart and trembling hands, we fired both at the same moment: the buffaloes, terrified by the sound and by the smoke, remained for an instant motionless, as if struck by a thunderbolt, and then one and all betook themselves to flight with such incredible rapidity, that they were soon beyond the reach of our sight. We heard their loud roaring from a considerable distance, which by degrees subsided into silence, and we were left with only one of their terrific species near us; this one, a female, was no doubt the mother of the young buffalo which the dogs had seized; she had drawn near on hearing its cries, and had been wounded by our guns, but not killed; the creature was in a furious state: after a moment's pause, she took aim at the dogs, and with her head on the ground, as if to guide her by the scent, was advancing in her rage, and would have torn them to pieces, if I had not prevented her by firing upon her with my double-barrelled gun, and thus putting an end to her existence.

The young buffalo still remained a prisoner, with his ears in the mouths of the dogs, and the pain occasioned him to be so furious, that I was fearful he might do them some injury; I therefore determined to advance and give them what assistance I might find practicable. To say the truth, I scarcely knew in what way to effect this. The buffalo, though young, was strong enough to revenge himself if I were to give the dogs a sign to let go his ears. I had the power of killing him with a pistol at a stroke; but I had a great desire to preserve him alive, and to tame him, that he might be a substitute for the ass, which we had but little hope of recovering. I found myself in a perplexing state of indecision, when Jack suddenly interposed an effective means for accomplishing my wishes. He had his string with balls in his pocket; he drew it out hastily, and making a few steps backward, he threw it so skilfully as to entangle the buffalo completely, and throw him down. As I could then approach him safely, I tied his legs two and two together with a very strong cord; the dogs released his ears, and from this moment we considered the buffalo as our own.

The question was now, how we were to get the buffalo home: having reflected, I conceived that the best way would be to tie his two fore-legs together so tight that he could not run, yet loose enough for him to walk; "and," pursued I, "we will next adopt the method practised in Italy; you will think it somewhat cruel, but the success will be certain; and it shall afterwards be our study to make him amends by the kindest care and treatment. Hold you the cord which confines his legs with all your strength, that he may not be able to move." I then called Turk and Flora, and made each again take hold of the ears of the animal; I took from my pocket a sharp-pointed knife, and taking hold of the snout, I made a hole in the nostril, into which I quickly inserted a string, which I immediately tied so closely to a tree that the animal was prevented from the least motion of the head, which might have inflamed the wound and increased his pain. I drew off the dogs the moment the operation was performed. The creature, thus rendered furious, would have run away, but the stricture of the legs and the pain in the nostril prevented it. The first attempt I made to pull the cord found him docile and ready to accommodate his motions to our designs, and I perceived that we might now begin our march.

I was unwilling to leave so fine a prey as the dead buffalo behind us: I therefore, after considering what was to be done, began by cutting out the tongue, which I sprinkled with some of the salt we had in our provision-bag. I next took off the skin from the four feet, taking care not to tear it in the operation. I remembered that the Americans use these skins, which are of a soft and flexible quality, as boots and shoes, and I considered them as precious articles. I lastly cut some of the flesh of the animal with the skin on,

and salted it, and abandoned the rest to the dogs, as a
recompense for their behaviour. I then repaired to the river,
to wash myself, after which we sat down under the shade of
a large tree, and ate the rest of our provisions.

As we were not disposed to leave the spot in a hurry, I
desired Jack to take the saw and cut down a small quantity
of the reeds, which from their enormous size might be of
use to us. We set to work, but I observed that he took pains
to choose the smallest. "What shall we do," said I, "with
these small-sized reeds? You are thinking, I presume, of a
bagpipe, to announce a triumphal arrival to our companions!"

"You are mistaken, father," answered Jack; "I am thinking of some candlesticks for my mother, who will set so high
a value on them!"

"This is a good thought," said I; "I am pleased both with
the kindness and the readiness of your invention, and I will
assist you to empty the reeds without breaking them; if we
should not succeed, at least we know where to provide
ourselves with more."

We had so many and such heavy articles to remove, that I
dismissed for that day all thoughts of looking further for the
ass. I began now to think of untying the young buffalo; and
on approaching him perceived with pleasure that he was
asleep, which afforded me a proof that his wound was not
extremely painful. As I began to pull him gently with the
string, he gave a start, but he afterwards followed me without resistance.

We repassed the river in safety, and, accompanied by the
agreeable sounds of its foaming cascades, we regained the
narrow pass at the turn of the rocks. We proceeded with
caution, and when safe on the other side, we thought of
quickening our pace to arrive the sooner at the hut.

The first solicitudes about health and safety being answered, we entered upon the narrative of our adventures;
when question after question was rapidly proposed to us,
that we, on our parts, were obliged to ask for the necessary
time for our replies. All agreed that our success with the
buffalo was the most extraordinary of our achievements: all
longed for the morning, when they might take their fill of
looking at the spirited creature we had brought with us. The
day concluded with supper, and sound repose.

CHAPTER XXV

The Malabar Eagle—Sago Manufactory—Bees

MY wife next morning began the conversation. She told me that the boys had been good and diligent; that they had ascended Cape Disappointment with her, and had gathered wood, and made some torches for the night; and, what seemed almost incredible, had ventured to fell and bring down an immense palm-tree. It lay prostrate on the ground, and covered a space of at least seventy feet in length. To effect their purpose, Fritz had got up the tree with a long rope, which he fastened tight to the top of it. As soon as he had come down again, he and Ernest worked with the axe and saw to cut it through. When it was nearly divided, they carefully managed its fall with the rope, and in this manner they succeeded. Fritz was in high spirits too on another account: he brought me on his wrist a young bird of prey, of the most beauteous plumage; he had taken it from the nest in one of the rocks near Cape Disappointment. Very young as the bird was, it had already all its feathers, though they had not yet received their full colouring: it answered to the description I had read of the beautiful eagle of Malabar, and I viewed it with the admiration it was entitled to: meeting with one of these birds is thought a lucky omen; and it being neither large nor expensive in its food, I was desirous to keep it and train it like a falcon, to pursue smaller birds. Fritz had already covered its eyes, and tied a string to its foot: and I advised him to hold it often, and for a length of time, on his hand, and to tame it with hunger, as falconers do.

When all the narratives were concluded, I ordered a fire

to be lighted, and a quantity of green wood to be put on it, for the purpose of raising a thick smoke, over which I meant to hang the buffalo meat I had salted, to dry and preserve it for our future use. The young buffalo was beginning to browse, and we gave him also a little of the cow's milk; and in a few days we fed him with a heap of sliced roots, which he greedily devoured; and this led us to conclude that the pains from the wound in his nose had subsided, and that he would soon become tame.

The morning of this day was spent in again talking over our late extraordinary adventures; we left our meat suspended over the smoke of the fires during our sleep; we tied the young buffalo by the side of the cow, and were pleased to see them agree and bid fair to live in peace together. At night the dogs were set upon the watch. The time of repose elapsed so calmly that none of us awoke to keep in the torchlights, which now for the first time the industry of the boys had supplied us with, and we did not get up till after sunrise. After a moderate breakfast, I chanted the accustomed summons for our setting out; but my young ones had some projects in their heads, and neither they nor their mother were just then in the humour to obey me.

"Let us reflect a little first," said my wife: "as we had so much difficulty in felling the palm-tree, would it not be a pity to lose our labour, by leaving it in this place? Ernest assures me it is a sago-tree; if so, the pith would be an excellent ingredient for our soups. Do, my dear, examine it, and let us see if in any way we can turn it to account."

I found she was in the right; but in that case it was necessary to employ a day in the business; since to lay open from one end to the other a tree of such a length and substance, was no trivial task. I however consented; as, independent of the use of the farinaceous pith, I could, by emptying it, obtain two handsome and large troughs for the conveyance of water from Jackal's River to my wife's kitchen garden at Tent House, and thence to my new plantations of trees.

I now desired them to bring me the graters they had used for the manioc, and observed that they had to assist me in raising the palm-tree from the ground, which must be done, continued I, by fixing at each end two small cross pieces or props to support it; to split it open as it lies would be a work of too much labour: this done, I shall want several wooden wedges to keep the cleft open while I am sawing it, and afterwards a sufficient quantity of water. "There is the difficulty," said my wife; "our Falcon's Stream is too far off, and we have not yet discovered any spring in the neighbourhood of this place."

Ernest.—That is of no consequence, mother; I have seen hereabouts so great an abundance of plants which contain water, that we need not be at a loss; for they will fully supply us if I could only contrive to get vessels enough to hold it.

We now produced the enormous reeds we had brought home, which, being hollow, would answer the purpose of vessels; and as some time was required to draw off the water from such small tubes, he and Francis at once set to work: they cut a number of the plants, which they placed slantingly over the brim of a vessel, and whilst that was filling, they were preparing another. The rest of us got round the tree, and with our united strength we soon succeeded in raising the heavy trunk, and the top of it was then sawn off. We next began to split it through the whole length, and this the softness of the wood enabled us to effect with little trouble. We soon reached the pith or marrow that fills up the middle of the trunk the whole of its length. When divided, we laid one half on the ground, and we pressed the pith together with our hands, so as to make temporary room for the pith of the other half of the trunk, which rested still on the props. We wished to empty it entirely, that we might employ it as a kneading-trough, leaving merely enough of the pith at both ends to prevent a running-out; and then we proceeded to form our paste.

My young manufacturers fell joyfully to work: they brought water, and poured it gradually into the trough, whilst we mixed it with the flour. In a short time the paste appeared sufficiently fermented; I then made an aperture at the bottom of the grater on its outside, and pressed the paste strongly with my hand: the farinaceous parts passed with ease through the small holes of the grater, and the ligneous parts which did not pass were thrown aside in a heap, in the hope that mushrooms, etc., might spring from them. My boys were in readiness to receive in reed vessels what fell from the grater, and conveyed it directly to their mother, whose business was to spread out the small grains in the sun upon sail-cloth, for the purpose of drying them. Thus we procured a good supply of a wholesome and pleasant food. The paste which remained was thrown upon the mushroom-bed, and watered well to promote a fermentation.

We next employed ourselves in loading the cart with our tools and the two halves of the tree. Night coming on, we retired to our hut, where we enjoyed our usual repose, and early next morning were ready to return to Falcon's Stream. Our buffalo now commenced his service, yoked with the cow; he supplied the want of the ass, and was very tractable: it is true, I led him by the cord in his nose, and thus restrained him whenever he was disposed to deviate from his duty.

We returned the same way as we came, in order to load the cart with a provision of berries, wax and elastic gum. I sent forward Fritz and Jack as a vanguard, with one of the dogs: they were to cut an ample road through the bushes for our cart. The two water-conductors, which were very long, produced numerous difficulties, and somewhat impeded our progress. We reached the wax and gum-trees with tolerable speed, and without any accident, and halted to place our sacks of berries in the cart. The elastic gum had not yielded as much as I expected, from the too rapid thickening caused by an ardent sun. We obtained, however, about a quart, which sufficed for the experiment of the impenetrable boots I had so long desired.

We set out again, still preceded by our pioneers, who cleared the way for us through the little wood of guavas. Suddenly we heard a dreadful noise, which came from our vanguard, and beheld Fritz and Jack hastening towards us. I began now to fear a tiger or panther was near at hand, or had perhaps attacked them. Turk began to bark so frightfully, and Flora joined in so hideous a yell, that I prepared myself for a conflict. I advanced at the head of my troop to the assistance of my high-mettled dogs, who ran furiously up to a thicket, where they stopped, and with their noses to the ground, and almost breathless, strove to enter it. I had no doubt some terrible animal was lurking there; and Fritz, who had seen it through the leaves, confirmed my suspicion; he said it was about the size of the young buffalo, and that his hair was black and shaggy. I was going to fire promiscu-

ously into the thicket, when Jack, who had thrown himself
on his face on the ground to have a better view of the
animal, got up in a fit of laughter. "It is only," exclaimed
he, "our old sow, who is never tired of playing off her tricks
upon us." Half vexed, half laughing, we broke into the
midst of the thicket, where in reality we found our old
companion stretched supinely on the earth, but by no means
in a state of dreary solitude; she had round her seven little
creatures, which had been littered a few days, and were
sprawling about, contending with each other for the best
place near their mother for a hearty meal. This discovery
gave us considerable satisfaction, and we all greeted the
good matron, who seemed to recollect and welcome us with
a sociable kind of grunting, while she licked her young
without any ceremony or show of fear. And now a general
consultation took place: should this new family be left where
we found it, or conveyed to Falcon's Stream? Opinions
being at variance, it was decided that for the present the
sow and her young should keep quiet possession of their
retreat.

We then, so many adventures ended, pursued our road,
and arrived at Falcon's Stream in safety, experiencing what
is so generally true, that home is always dear and sacred to
the heart, and anticipated with delight. All was in due
order, and our animals welcomed our return in their own
jargon and manner, but which did not fail to be expressive
of their satisfaction at seeing us again. We threw them some
of the food they were most partial to, which they greedily
accepted, and then voluntarily went back to their usual
stand. It was necessary to practise a measure dictated by
prudence, which was to tie up the buffalo again, to inure it
by degrees to confinement; and the handsome Malabar eagle shared the same fate: Fritz chose to place it near the
parrot, on the root of a tree; he fastened it with a piece of
packthread, of sufficient length to allow it free motion, and
uncovered its eyes: till then the bird had been tolerably
quiet: but the instant it was restored to light it fell into a
species of rage that surprised us; it proudly raised its head,
its feathers became ruffled, and its eyeballs seemed to whirl
in their orbits, and dart out vivid lightnings. All the poultry
were terrified and fled; but the poor luckless parrot was too
near the sanguinary creature to escape. Before we were

aware of the danger, it was seized and mangled by the formidable hooked beak of the eagle. Fritz vented his anger in loud and passionate reproaches; he would have killed the murderer on the spot, had not Ernest run up and entreated him to spare its life: "Parrots," said he, "we shall find in plenty, but never perhaps so beauteous, so magnificent a bird as this eagle, which, as father observes, we may train for hawking. You may too blame only yourself for the parrot's death;—why did you uncover his eyes? I could have told you that falconers keep them covered six weeks, till they are completely tamed. But now, brother, let me have the care of him; let me manage the unruly fellow; he shall soon, in consequence of the methods I shall use, be as tractable and submissive as a new-born puppy."

Fritz refused to part with his eagle, and Ernest did not long oppose giving him the information he wanted:—"I have read," said he, "somewhere, that the Caribs puff tobacco smoke into the nostrils of the birds of prey and of the parrots they catch, until they are giddy and almost senseless; —this stupefaction over, they are no longer wild and untractable."

Fritz resolved on the experiment; he took some tobacco and a pipe, of which we had plenty in the sailors' chests, and began to smoke, at the same time gradually approaching the unruly bird. As soon as it was somewhat composed, he replaced the fillet over the eyes, and smoked close to its beak and nostrils so effectually, that it became motionless on the spot, and had the exact air of a stuffed bird. Fritz thought it dead, and was inclined to be angry with his brother; but I told him it would not hold on the perch if it were lifeless, and that its head alone was affected;—and so it proved. The favourite came to itself by degrees, and made no noise when its eyes were unbound; it looked at us with an air of surprise, but void of fury, and grew tamer and calmer every day.

We next began a business which I and my wife had been thinking of for some time: she found it difficult, and even dangerous, to ascend and descend our tree with a rope ladder. We never went there but on going to bed, and each time felt an apprehension that one of the children, who scrambled up like cats, might make a false step, and perhaps be lame for ever: bad weather might come on, and compel us for a long time together to seek an asylum in our aërial apartment, and consequently to ascend and descend oftener.

My wife had repeatedly applied to me to remedy this evil, and my own anxiety had often made me reflect if the thing were really possible. A staircase on the outside was not to be thought of; the considerable height of the tree rendered that impracticable, as I had nothing to rest it on, and should be at a loss to find beams to sustain it; but I had for some time formed the idea of constructing winding stairs within the immense trunk of the tree, if it should happen to be hollow, or I could contrive to make it so. I had heard the boys talking of a hollow in our tree, and of a swarm of bees issuing from it, and I now, therefore, went to examine whether the cavity extended to the roots, or what its circumference might be. The boys seized the idea with ardour; they sprang up, and climbed to the tops of the roots like squirrels, to strike at the trunk with axes, and to judge from the sound how far it was hollow; but they soon paid dearly for their attempt; the whole swarm of bees, alarmed at the noise made against their dwelling, issued forth, buzzing with fury, attacked the little disturbers, began to sting them, stuck to their hair and clothes, and soon put them to flight, uttering lamentable cries. My wife and I had some trouble to stop the course of their uproar, and cover their wounds with fresh earth to allay the smart. Jack, whose temper was on all occasions rash, had struck fiercely upon the bees' nest, and was most severely attacked by them than the rest: it was necessary, so serious was the injury, to cover the whole of his face with linen. The less active Ernest got up the last, and was the first to run off when he saw the consequences, and thus avoided any further injury than a sting or two; but some hours elapsed before the other boys could open their eyes, or be in the least relieved from the acute pain that had been inflicted. When they grew a little better, the desire of being revenged of the insects that had so roughly used them had the ascendant in their minds: they teased me to hasten the measures for getting everything in readiness for obtaining possession of their honey. The bees in the meantime were still buzzing furiously round the tree. I prepared tobacco, a pipe, some clay, chisels, hammers, etc. I took the large gourd long intended for a hive, and fitted a place for it, by nailing a piece of board on a branch

of the tree; I made a straw roof for the top, to screen it from
the sun and rain; and as all this took up more time than I
was aware of, we deferred the attack of the fortress to the
following day, and got ready for a sound sleep, which completed the cure of my wounded patients.

CHAPTER XXVI

Treatment of Bees—Staircase—
Training of Various Animals—
Manufactures, etc.

NEXT morning, almost before dawn, all were up and in
motion; the bees had returned to their cells, and I
stopped the passages with clay, leaving only sufficient aperture for the tube of my pipe. I then smoked as much as was
requisite to stupefy, without killing, the little warlike creatures. Not having a cap with a mask, such as bee-catchers
usually wear, nor even gloves, this precaution was necessary. At first a humming was heard in the hollow of the
tree, and a noise like the gathering tempest, which died
away by degrees. All was become calm, and I withdrew my
tube without the appearance of a single bee. Fritz had got
up by me: we then began with a chisel and a small axe to cut
out of the tree, under the bees' hole of entrance, a piece
three feet square. Before it was entirely separated, I repeated the fumigation, lest the stupefaction produced by the
first smoking should have ceased, or the noise we had been
just making revived the bees. As soon as I supposed them
lulled again, I separated from the trunk the piece I had cut
out, producing as it were the aspect of a window, through
which the inside of the tree was laid open to view; and we
were filled at once with joy and astonishment on beholding
the immense and wonderful work of this colony of insects.
There was such a stock of wax and honey, that we feared

our vessels would be insufficient to contain it. The whole interior of the tree was lined with fine honeycombs. I cut them off with care, and put them in the gourds the boys constantly supplied me with. When I had somewhat cleared the cavity, I put the upper combs, in which the bees had assembled in clusters and swarms, into the gourd which was to serve as a hive, and placed it on the plank I had purposely raised. I came down, bringing with me the rest of the honeycombs, with which I filled a small cask, previously well washed in the stream. Some I kept out for a treat at dinner; and had the barrel carefully covered with cloths and planks, that the bees, when attracted by the smell, might be unable to get at it. We assembled round the table, and regaled ourselves plentifully with the delicious treat. My wife then put by the remainder; and I proposed to my sons to go back to the tree, to prevent the bees from swarming again there on being roused from their stupor, as they would not have failed to do but for the precaution I took of placing a board at the aperture, and burning a few handfuls of tobacco on it, the smell and smoke of which drove them back whenever they attempted to return. At length they desisted, and became gradually reconciled to their new residence, where their queen no doubt had settled herself. I now advised that all should watch during the night over the whole provision of honey obtained while the bees were torpid, who, when recovered, would not fail to be troublesome, and come in legions to get back to their property; and to this end we threw ourselves on our beds, in our clothes, to take an early doze. On awakening about nightfall, we found the bees quiet in the gourd, or settled in clusters upon near branches, so we went expeditiously to business. The cask of honey was emptied into a kettle, except a few prime combs, which we kept for daily consumption; the remainder, mixed with a little water, was set over a gentle fire, and reduced to a liquid consistence, strained and squeezed through a bag, and afterwards poured back into the cask, which was left upright and uncovered all night to cool. In the morning the wax was entirely separated, and had risen to the surface in a compact and solid cake, that was easily removed: beneath was the purest, most beautiful and delicate honey that could be seen; the cask was then carefully headed again, and put into cool ground near our wine-vessels. This task accomplished, I mounted to revisit the hive, and found everything in order; the bees going forth in swarms, and returning loaded with wax, from which I judged they were forming fresh edifices in their new dwelling-place. I had been surprised that the numbers occupying the trunk of the tree should find room in the gourd, till I perceived the clusters upon the branches, and I thence concluded a young queen was among each of them. In consequence, I procured another gourd, into which I shook them, and placed it by the former; thus I had the satisfaction of obtaining at an easy rate two fine hives of bees in activity.

Soon after these operations we proceeded to examine the inside of the tree. I sounded it with a pole from the opening I had made; and a stone fastened to a string served us to sound the bottom, and thus to ascertain the height and depth of the cavity. To my great surprise, the pole penetrated without any resistance to the branches on which our dwelling rested, and the stone descended to the roots. The trunk, it appeared, had wholly lost its pith, and most of its wood internally. It seems that this species of tree, like the willow in our climates, receives nourishment through the bark; for it did not look decayed, and its far-extended branches were luxuriant and beautiful in the extreme. I determined to begin our construction in its capacious hollow that very day. The undertaking appeared at first beyond our powers; but intelligence, patience, time, and a firm resolution vanquished all obstacles.

We began to cut into the side of the tree, towards the sea, a doorway equal in dimensions to the door of the captain's cabin, which we had removed with all its framework and windows. We next cleared away from the cavity all the rotten wood, and rendered the interior even and smooth, leaving sufficient thickness for cutting out resting-places for the winding stairs, without injuring the bark. I then fixed in the centre the trunk of a tree about twenty feet in length, and a foot thick, completely stripped of its branches, in order to carry my winding staircase round it. On the outside of this trunk, and the inside of the cavity of our own tree, we formed grooves, so calculated as to correspond with the distances at which the boards were to be placed to form the stairs. These were continued till I had got to the height of the trunk round which they turned. I made two more apertures at suitable distances, and thus completely lighted the whole ascent. I also effected an opening near our room, that I might more conveniently finish the upper part of the staircase. A second trunk was fixed upon the first, and firmly sustained with screws and transverse beams. It was surrounded, like the other, with stairs cut slopingly; and thus we happily effected the stupendous undertaking of conducting it to the level of our bed-chamber. Here I made another door directly into it. To render it more solid and agreeable, I closed the spaces between the stairs with plank. I then fastened two strong ropes, the one descending the length of the central trunk, the other along the inside of our large tree, to assist in case of slipping. I fixed the sash windows taken from the captain's cabin in the apertures we had made to give light to the stairs; and I then found I could add nothing further to my design.

I have now to relate some occurrences that took place during the construction of our staircase.

A few days after the commencement of our undertaking, our brave Flora whelped us six young puppies, all healthy, and likely to live. The number was so alarming, that I was under the necessity of drowning all but a male and female to keep up the breed. A few days later, the two she-goats gave us two kids, and our ewes five lambs: so that we now saw ourselves in possession of a pretty flock.

Next to the winding stairs, my chief occupation was the management of the young buffalo, whose wound in the nose was quite healed, so that I could lead it at will with a cord or stick passed through the orifice, as the Caffrarians do. I preferred the stick, which answered the purpose of a bit, and I resolved to break in this spirited beast for riding as well as drawing. It was already used to the shafts, and very tractable in them; but I had more trouble in inuring him to a rider, and to wearing a girth, having made one out of the old buffalo's hide. I formed a sort of saddle with sail-cloth, and tacked it to the girth. Upon this I fixed a burden, which I increased progressively. I was indefatigable in the training of the animal, and soon brought it to carry, patiently, large bags of roots, salt, and other articles in the place of the ass. The monkey was his first rider, who stuck so close to the saddle, that in spite of the plunging and kicking of the buffalo, it was not thrown. Francis was then tried, as the

lightest of the family; but throughout his excursion I led the
beast with a halter, that it might not throw him off. Jack
now showed some impatience to mount the animal in his
turn. I next passed the stick through the buffalo's nose, and
tied strong packthread at each end of it, bringing them
together over the neck of the animal, and put this new-
fangled bridle into the hands of the young rider, directing
him how to use it. For a time the lad kept his saddle,
notwithstanding the unruly gestures of the creature; at length
a side jolt threw him on the sand, without his receiving
much injury. Ernest, Fritz, and lastly myself, got on succes-
sively, with more or less effect. His trotting shook us to the
very centre, the rapidity of his gallop turned us giddy, and
our lessons in horsemanship were reiterated many days before the animal was tamed, and could be ridden with either
safety or pleasure. At last, however, we succeeded without
any serious accident; and the strength and swiftness of our
saddled buffalo were prodigious. It seemed to sport with the
heaviest loads. My three eldest boys mounted it together
now and then, and it ran with them with the swiftness of
lightning.

We now began to think of manufacturing our impenetrable boots without seams, of the caoutchouc, or elastic-gum.
I began with a pair for myself; and I encouraged my children to afford a specimen of their industry, by trying to
form some flasks and cups that could not break. They began
by making some clay moulds, which they covered with layers
of gum, agreeably to the instructions I had given them. In
the meanwhile I filled a pair of stockings with sand, and
covered them with a layer of clay, which I first dried in the
shade, and afterwards in the sun. I then took a sole of
buffalo leather, well beaten, and studded round with tacks,
which served me to fix it under the foot of the stocking;
after this I poured the liquid gum into all the interstices,
which, on drying, produced a close adhesion between the
leather and stocking sole. I next proceeded to smear the
whole with a coat of resin of a tolerable thickness; and as
soon as this layer was dried on, I put on another, and so on
till I had applied a sufficiency with my brush. After this I
emptied the sand, drew out the stocking, removed the hardened clay, shook off the dust, and thus obtained a pair of
seamless boots, as finished as if made by the best English

workman, being pliant, warm, soft, smooth, and completely waterproof.

We had also been engaged in the construction of our fountain, which afforded a perpetual source of pleasure to my wife, and indeed to all of us. In the upper part of the stream we built with stakes and stones a kind of dam, that raised the water sufficiently to convey it into the palm-tree troughs; and afterwards, by means of a gentle slope, to glide on contiguous to our habitation, where it fell into the tortoiseshell basin, which we had elevated on stones to a certain height for our convenience; and it was so contrived that the redundant water passed off through a cane pipe fitted to it. I placed two sticks athwart each other for the gourds, that served as pails to rest on; and we thus produced, close to our abode, an agreeable fountain, delighting with its rill, and supplying us with a pure crystal fluid, such as we frequently could not get when we drew our water from the bed of the river, which was often encumbered with the leaves and earth fallen into it, or rendered turbid by our water-fowls.

CHAPTER XXVII

The Wild Ass—Difficulty in breaking it—The Heath Fowl's Nest

WE were scarcely up one morning, and had just got to work in putting the last hand to our winding staircase, when we heard at a distance two strange kinds of voices, that resembled the howlings of wild beasts mixed with hissings and sounds of some creature at its last gasp; and I was not without uneasiness: our dogs too pricked up their ears, and seemed to whet their teeth for a sanguinary combat with a dangerous enemy.

From their looks we judged it prudent to put ourselves in

a state of defence; we loaded our guns and pistols, placed them together within our castle in the tree, and repaired to repel vigorously any hostile attack from that quarter. The howlings having ceased an instant, I descended from our citadel, well armed, and put on our two faithful guardians their spiked collars and sideguards; I assembled our cattle about the tree to have them in sight, and I then re-ascended to look around for the enemy's approach.

At this instant the howlings were renewed, and almost close to us. Fritz got as near the spot as he could, listened attentively, and with eager looks, then threw down his gun, and burst into a loud laughter, exclaiming, "Father, it is our ass! the deserter comes back to us, chanting the hymn of return: listen! do you not hear his melodious brayings in all the varieties of the gamut?" I listened, and a fresh roar, in sounds unquestionable, raised loud peals of laughter amongst us. Shortly after we had the satisfaction of seeing among the trees our old friend Grizzle, moving towards us leisurely, and stopping now and then to browse; but, to our great joy, he was accompanied by one of his own species, of very superior beauty; and when it was nearer, I knew it to be a fine onagra, or wild ass, which I conceived a strong desire to possess, though at the same time aware of the extreme difficulty there would be in taming and rendering him subject to the use of man. Without delay I descended the ladder with Fritz, desiring his brothers to keep still; and I consulted my privy-counsellor on the means of surprising and taking the stranger captive.

I got ready, as soon as possible, a long cord with a running knot, one end of which I tied fast to the root of a tree; the noose was kept open with a little stick slightly fixed in the opening, so as to fall of itself on the cord being thrown round the neck of the animal, whose efforts to escape would draw the knot closer. I also prepared a piece of bamboo about two feet long, which I split at the bottom, and tied fast at top, to serve as nippers. Fritz attentively examined my contrivance, without seeing the use of it. Prompted by the impatience of youth, he took the ball-sling, and proposed aiming at the wild ass with it, which he said was the shortest way of proceeding. I declined adopting this Patagonian method, fearing the attempt might fail, and the beautiful creature avail itself of its natural velocity to evade us beyond recovery; I therefore told him my project of catching it in the noose, which I gave him to manage, as being nimbler and more expert than myself. The two asses drew nearer and nearer to us. Fritz, holding in his hand the open noose, moved softly on from behind the tree where we were concealed, and advanced as far as the length of the rope allowed him. The onagra started on perceiving a human figure; it sprang some paces backward, then stopped, as if to examine the unknown form; but as Fritz now remained quite still, the animal resumed its composure, and continued to browse. Soon after he approached the old ass, hoping that the confidence that would be shown by it would raise a similar feeling in the stranger; he held out a handful of oats mixed with salt. Our ass instantly ran up to take its favourite food, and greedily devoured it: this was quickly perceived by the other. It drew near, raised its head, breathed strongly, and came up so close, that Fritz, seizing the opportunity, succeeded in throwing the rope round its neck; but the motion and stroke so affrighted the beast that it instantly sprang off. It was soon checked by the cord, which, in compressing the neck, almost stopped its breath: it could go no farther, and, after many exhausting efforts, it sank panting for breath upon the ground. I hastened to loosen the cord, and prevent its being strangled. I then quickly threw our ass's halter over its head; I fixed the nose in my split cane, which I secured at the bottom with packthread. Thus I succeeded in subduing the first alarm of this wild animal, as farriers shoe a horse for the first time. I wholly removed the noose that seemed to bring the creature into a dangerous situation; I fastened the halter with two long ropes to two roots near us, on the right and left, and let the animal recover itself, noticing its actions, and devising the best way to tame it in the completest manner.

In a few moments the onagra got up again, struck furiously with its foot, and seemed resolved to free itself from all bonds; but the pain of its nose, which was grasped and violently squeezed in the bamboo, forced it to lie down again. Fritz and I now gently undid the cords, and half led, half dragged it, between two roots closely connected, to which we fastened it afresh, so as to give the least scope for motion, and thus render its escape impracticable, whilst it enabled us to approach securely, and examine the valuable capture we had made. We also guarded against master Grizzle playing truant again, and tied him fast with a new halter, confining its fore legs with a rope. I then fastened it and the wild ass side by side, and put before both plenty of good provender to solace their impatience of captivity.

We had now the additional occupation of training the onagra for our service or our pleasure, as might turn out to be most practicable: my boys exulted in the idea of riding it, and we repeatedly congratulated each other on the good fortune which had thus resulted from the flight of our ass.

During the training of the onagra, which we named *Lightfoot*, a triple brood of our hens had given us a crowd of little feathered beings; forty of these at least were chirping and hopping about us, to the great satisfaction of my wife, whose zealous care of them sometimes made me smile. Some of these we kept near us, while others were sent in small colonies to feed and breed in the desert, where we could find them as they were wanted for our use.

This increase of our poultry reminded us of an undertaking we had long ago thought of, and was not in prudence to be deferred any longer; this was the building between the roots of our great tree covered sheds for all our bipeds and quadrupeds. The rainy season, which is the winter of these countries, was drawing near; and to avoid losing most of our stock, it was requisite to shelter it.

We began by forming a kind of roof above the arched roots of our tree, and employed bamboo canes for the purpose; the longest and strongest supported the roofing in the place of columns, the smaller more closely united and composed the roof itself. I filled up the interstices with moss and clay, and I spread over the whole a thick coat of tar. By these means I formed a compact and solid covering, capable of bearing pressure. I then made a railing round it, which gave the appearance of a balcony, under which, between the roots, were various stalls, sheltered from rain and sun, that could be easily shut and separated from each other by means of planks nailed upon the roots: part of them were calculated to serve as a stable and yard, part as an eating-house, a store-room, etc., and as a hay-loft, to keep our hay and provisions dry in. This work was soon completed; but afterwards it was necessary to fill these places with stores of every kind for our supply throughout the wet season. In this

task we engaged diligently, and went daily here and there
with our cart to collect everything useful, and that might
give us employment when the weather prevented our going
far.

One evening, on our return from digging up roots, as our
cart, loaded with bags, drawn by the buffalo, ass, and cow,
was gently rolling along, seeing still a vacant place in the
vehicle, I advised my wife to go home with the two youngest
boys, whilst I went round by the wood of oaks with Ernest
and Fritz, to gather as many sweet acorns as we could find
room for. We had still some empty sacks. Ernest was accompanied by his monkey, who seldom left him; and Fritz,
horsemanlike, was on the onagra, which he had appropriated to himself, inasmuch as he had helped to take and tame
it, and indeed because he knew how to manage it better
than his brothers. Ernest was too lazy, and preferred walking at ease with the monkey on his shoulder, and the more
so because it spared him the trouble of gathering fruit.

When we reached the oaks, Lightfoot was tied to a bush,
and we set actively to work to gather the acorns that had
dropped from the trees. While all were busily employed, the
monkey quitted its master's shoulder, and skipped unperceived into an adjoining bush. It had been there some time,
when we heard on that side loud cries of birds and flapping
of wings, and this assured us a sharp conflict was going on
betwixt master Knips and the inhabitants of the bushes. I
dispatched Ernest to reconnoitre. He went stoutly towards
the place, and in an instant we heard him exclaim, "Come
quickly, father! A fine heath-fowl's nest, full of eggs."

Fritz ran up directly, and in a few moments brought out
alive the male and female heath-fowl, both very beautiful. I
was rejoiced at this discovery, and helped my son to prevent
their escape, by tying their wings and feet, and hold them
while he returned to the bush for the eggs. And now Ernest
came forward, driving the monkey before him, and carrying
his hat with the utmost care. He had stuck his girdle full of
narrow sharp-pointed leaves, in shape like a knife-blade,
which reminded me of the production named sword-grass;
but I did not pay much attention, as I was too busily engaged in our egg-hunt. On coming up to me he uncovered
his hat, and gave it me in a transport of joy, crying out,
"Here, father, are some heath-fowl's eggs. I found them in

a nest so well concealed under these long leaves, that I should not have observed them had not the hen, in defending herself against the monkey, scattered them about. I am going to take them home, they will please my mother; and these leaves will amuse Francis, for they are like swords, and he will like them for a plaything." It was now time to think of moving homeward: my two sons filled the bags with acorns, and put them on Lightfoot. Fritz mounted, Ernest carried the eggs, I took charge of the hen, and we proceeded to Falcon's Stream, followed by our train-waggon. When arrived, our first care was to examine the eggs: the female bird was too frightened and wild to sit upon them; fortunately we had a hen that was hatching: her eggs were immediately removed, and the new ones put in their place: the female heath-fowl was put into the parrot's cage, and hung up in the room, to accustom it to our society. In less than three days all the chickens were hatched; they kept close to their foster-mother, and ate greedily a mixture of sweet acorns bruised in milk, such as we gave our tame poultry. As they grew up I plucked out the large feathers of their wings, lest they should naturally take flight; but they and their real parent gradually became so domesticated, that they daily accompanied our feathered stock in search of food, and regularly came back at night to the roost I had prepared for them, and in which this little new colony of feathered beings seemed to delight.

CHAPTER XXVIII

Flax, and the Rainy Season

FRANCIS for a short time was highly amused with his sword-leaves, and then, like all children, who are soon tired of their toys, he grew weary of them, and they were thrown aside. Fritz picked up some of them that were quite soft and withered; holding up one which was pliable as a riband in his hand, "Francis," said he, "you can make whips of your sword-grass, and they will be of use in driving your goats and sheep." It had been lately decided that it should be the business of Francis to lead these to pasture. Fritz accordingly sat down to help him to divide the leaves, and afterwards plait them into whipcords. As they were working, I saw with pleasure the flexibility and strength of the bands: I examined them more closely, and found they were composed of long fibres, or filaments; and this discovery led me to surmise that this supposed sword-grass might be a very different thing, and not improbably the flax plant of New Zealand. This was a valuable discovery in our situation: I knew how much my wife wished for the production, and that it was the article she felt the most the want of; I therefore hastened to communicate the intelligence to her, and she expressed the liveliest joy. "This," said she, "is the most useful thing you have found; lose not a moment in searching for more of these leaves, and bring me the most you can of them; I will make you stockings, shirts, clothes, thread, ropes;—in short, give me flax, looms, and frames, and I shall be at no loss in the employment of it." I could not help smiling at the scope she gave to her imagination on the bare mention of flax, though so much was to be done between the gathering the leaves and having the cloth she was already sewing in idea. Fritz whispered a word in Jack's ear; both went to the stable, and, without asking my leave, one mounted Lightfoot, the other the buffalo, and galloped off towards the wood, so fast that I had no time to call them back: they were already out of sight. Their eagerness to oblige their mother in this instance pleaded their forgiveness, and I suffered them to go on without following them, purposing to proceed and bring them back if they did not soon return.

In a quarter of an hour our deserters came back; like true hussars, they had foraged the woods, and heavily loaded their cattle with the precious plant, which they threw at their mother's feet with joyful shouts. It was next proposed that all should assist her in preparations for the work she was to engage in, and previously in steeping the flax.

Next morning the ass was put to the small light car, loaded with bundles of leaves; Francis and the monkey sat on them, and the remainder of the family gaily followed with shovels and pickaxes. We stopped at Flamingo Marsh, divided our large bundles into smaller, which we placed in the water, pressing them down with stones, and leaving them in this state till it was time to remove and set them in the sun to dry, and thus render the stems soft and easy to peel.

In a fortnight we took the flax out of the water, and spread it on the grass in the sun, where it dried so rapidly that we were able to load it on our cart the same evening, and carry it to Falcon's Stream, where it was put by till we had time to make the beetles, wheels, reels, carding-combs, etc., required by our chief for the manufacture. It was thought best to reserve this task for the rainy season, and to employ the present time in collecting a competent stock of provisions for ourselves and for all the animals. Occasional slight showers, the harbingers of winter, had already come on; the temperature, which hitherto had been warm and serene, became gloomy and variable; the sky was often darkened with clouds, the stormy winds were heard, and warned us to avail ourselves of the favorable moment to get all that might be wanted ready.

Our first care was to dig up a full supply of yams and other roots for bread, with plenty of cocoa-nuts and some

bags of sweet acorns. It occurred to us, while digging, that,
the ground being thus opened and manured with the leaves
of plants, we might sow in it to advantage the remainder of
our European corn. Notwithstanding all the delicacies this
stranger land afforded us, the force of habit still caused us
to long for the bread we had been fed with from childhood.
We had not yet laid ourselves out for regular tillage, and I
was inclined to attempt the construction of a plough of some
sort as soon as we had a sufficient stock of corn for sowing.
For this time, therefore, we committed it to the earth with
little preparation: the season, however, was proper for sowing and planting, as the ensuing rain would moisten and
swell the embryo grain, which otherwise would perish in an
arid burning soil. We accordingly expedited the planting of
the various palm-trees we had discovered in our excursions
at Tent House, carefully selecting the smallest and the youngest. In the environs we formed a large handsome plantation of sugar-canes, so as to have hereafter everything useful
and agreeable around us, and thus be dispensed from the
usual toil and loss of time in procuring them.

Unfortunately, the weather changed sooner than we had
expected, and than, with all our care, we could be prepared
for: before we had completed our winter establishment, the
rain fell in such heavy torrents that I could not refrain from
painful apprehension in surmising how we should resist such
a body of water, that seemed to change the whole face of
the country into a lake.

The first thing to be done was to remove our aërial
abode, and to fix our residence at the bottom of the tree,
between the roots and under the tarred roof I had erected:
for it was no longer possible to remain above, on account of
the furious winds that threatened to bear us away, and
deluged our beds with rain through the large opening in
front, our only protection here being a piece of sail-cloth,
which was soon dripping wet and rent to pieces. In this
condition we were forced to take down our hammocks,
mattresses, and every article that could be injured by the
rain; and most fortunate did we deem ourselves in having
made the winding stairs, which sheltered us during the operation of the removal. The stairs served afterwards for a kind
of lumber-room; we kept all in it we could dispense with,
and most of our culinary vessels, which my wife fetched as

she happened to want them. Our little sheds between the roots, constructed for the poultry and the cattle, could scarcely contain us all; and the first days we passed in this manner were painfully embarrassing, crowded all together, and hardly able to move in these almost dark recesses, which the fœtid smell from the close adjoining animals rendered almost insupportable: in addition, we were half stifled with smoke whenever we kindled a fire, and drenched with rain when we opened the doors. For the first time since our disaster, we sighed for the comfortable houses of our dear country: —but what was to be done? we were not there, and losing our courage and our temper would only increase the evil. I strove to raise the spirits of my companions, and obviate some of the inconveniences. We confined our live stock to a smaller number, and gave them a freer current of air, dismissing from the stalls those animals that, from their properties, and being natives of the country, would be at no loss in providing for themselves. That we might not lose them altogether, we tied bells round their necks; Fritz and I sought and drove them in every evening when they did not spontaneously return.

As to the smoke, our only remedy was to open the door when we made a fire; and we did without fire as much as we could, living on milk and cheese, and never making one but to bake our cakes: we then used the occasion to boil a quantity of our favourite roots and salt meat enough to last us a number of days. Our dry wood was also nearly expended, and we thanked Heaven the weather was not very cold; for had this been the case, our other trials would have much increased. A more serious concern was our not having provided sufficient hay and leaves for our European cattle, which we kept housed to avoid losing them. The cow, the ass, the sheep, and the goats, the two last of which were increased in number, required a large quantity of provender, so that we were ere long forced to give them our tuberous roots and sweet acorns, which, by the bye, they found very palatable, and we remarked that they imparted a delicate flavour to their milk; the cow, the goats, and even the sheep, amply supplied us with that precious article. Milking, cleaning the animals, and preparing their food, occupied us most of the morning, after which we were usually employed in making flour of the manioc root, with which we filled the large gourds, previously placed in rows. The gloom of the atmosphere and our low windowless habitation sensibly abridged our daylight; fortunately we had laid in a huge store of candles, and felt no want of that article. When darkness obliged us to light up, we got round the table, where a large taper fixed on a gourd gave us an excellent light, which enabled my wife to pursue her occupation with the needle, while I on my part was forming a journal, and recording what the reader has perused of the narrative of our shipwreck and residence in this island, assisted from time to time by my sons and their admirable mother, who did not cease to remind me of various incidents belonging to the story. To Ernest, who wrote a fine hand, was entrusted the care of writing off my pages in a clear legible character; Fritz and Jack amused themselves by drawing from memory the plants and animals which had most struck their observation; while one and all contributed to teach little Francis to read and write. We concluded the day with a devotional reading in the Holy Bible, performed by each in turn, and we then retired to rest, happy in ourselves and in the innocent and peaceful course of our existence.

It was unanimously resolved on, however, that we would not pass another rainy season exposed to the same evils; even my gentle-tempered and most beloved consort was a little ruffled now and then with our inconvenient situation, and insisted more than any of us on the plan of building elsewhere a more spacious winter residence; she wished, however, to return to our castle in the tree every summer, and we all joined with her in that desire. The choice of a fresh abode now engrossed our attention, and Fritz in the midst of consultation came forward triumphantly with a book he had found in the bottom of our clothes chest. "Here," said he, "is our best counsellor and model, *Robinson Crusoe*; since Heaven has destined us to a similar fate, whom better can we consult? As far as I remember, he cut himself a habitation out of the solid rock: let us see how he proceeded; we will do the same, and with greater ease, for he was alone; we are six in number, and four of us able to work." This idea of Fritz was hailed by all. We assembled, and read the famous history with an ardent interest; it seemed, though so familiar, quite new to us; we entered earnestly into every detail, and derived considerable information from it, and never failed to feel lively gratitude towards God, who had rescued us all together, and not permitted one only of us to be cast, a solitary being, on the island.

Francis expressed his wish to have a *Man Friday*; Fritz thought it better to be without such a companion, and to have no savages to contend with. Jack was for the savages, warfare, and encounters. The final result of our deliberations was to go and survey the rocks round Tent House, and to examine whether any of them could be excavated for our purpose.

Our last job for the winter, undertaken at my wife's solicitation, was a beetle for her flax, and some carding combs. I filed large nails till they were even, round, and pointed; I fixed them at equal distances in a sheet of tin, and raised the side of it like a box; I then poured melted lead between the nails and the sides to give firmness to their points, which came out four inches. I nailed this tin on a board, and the machine was fit to work. My wife was impatient to use it; and the drying, peeling, and spinning her flax, became from this time a source of inexhaustible delight.

CHAPTER XXIX

Spring—Spinning—Salt Mine

I CAN hardly describe our joy, when, after many tedious and gloomy weeks of rain, the sky began to brighten, the sun to dart its benign rays on the humid earth, the winds to be lulled, and the state of the air became mild and serene. We issued from our dreary hovels with joyful shouts, and walked round our habitation breathing the enlivening balmy ether, while our eyes were regaled with the beauteous verdure beginning to shoot forth on every side.

Our summer occupations commenced by arranging and thoroughly cleaning Falcon's Nest, the order and neatness of which the rain and dead leaves blown by the wind had disturbed; in other respects, however, it was not injured, and in a few days we rendered it fit for our reception; the stairs were cleared, the rooms between the roots reoccupied, and we were left with leisure to proceed to other employments. My wife lost not a moment in resuming the process of her flax. Our sons hastened to lead the cattle to the fresh pastures; whilst it was my task to carry the bundles of flax into the open air, where, by heaping stones together, I contrived an oven sufficiently commodious to dry it well. The same evening, we all set to work to peel, and afterwards to beat it and strip off the bark; and lastly to comb it with my carding machine, which fully answered the purpose. I took this laborious task on myself, and drew out such distaffs full of long soft flax ready for spinning, that my enraptured wife ran to embrace me, to express her thankfulness, requesting me to make her a wheel without delay, that she might enter upon her favourite work.

At an early period of my life I had practised turnery for my amusement; now, however, I was unfortunately destitute of the requisite utensils; but as I had not forgotten the arrangement and component parts of a spinning-wheel and reel, I by repeated endeavours found means to accomplish those two machines to her satisfaction; and she fell so eagerly to spinning, as to allow herself no leisure even for a walk, and scarcely time to dress our dinners.

Our first visit was to Tent House, and here we found the ravages of winter more considerable than even at Falcon's Stream; the tempest and rain had beaten down the tent, carried away a part of the sail-cloth, and made such havoc among our provisions, that by far the largest portion was spotted with mildew, and the remainder could be only saved by drying it instantly. Luckily our handsome pinnace had been for the most part spared; it was still at anchor, ready to serve us in case of need; but our tub-boat was in too shattered a state to be of any further service.

In looking over the stores, we were grieved to find the

gunpowder, of which I had left three barrels in the tent, the most damaged. The contents of two were rendered wholly useless. I thought myself fortunate in finding the remaining one in tolerable condition, and derived from this great and irreparable loss a cogent motive to fix upon winter quarters where our stores, our only wealth, would not be exposed to such cruel dilapidations.

Fritz and Jack were constant in their endeavours to make me undertake the excavation of the rock, but I had no hopes of success. Robinson Crusoe found a spacious cavern that merely required arrangement: no such cavity was apparent in our rock, which bore the aspect of extreme solidity and impenetrableness; so that with our limited powers, three or four summers would scarcely suffice to execute the design. Still, the earnest desire of a more substantial habitation, to defend us from the elements, perplexed me incessantly, and I resolved to make at least the attempt of cutting out a recess that should protect the gunpowder, the most valuable of all our treasures. I accordingly set off one day, accompanied by my two boys, leaving their mother at her spinning with Ernest and Francis. We took with us pick-axes, chisels, hammers, and iron levers, to try what impression we could make on the rock. I chose a part nearly perpendicular, and much better situated than our tent: the view from it was enchanting, for it embraced the whole range of Safety Bay, the banks of Jackal's River, and Family Bridge, and many of the picturesque projections of the rocks. I marked out with charcoal the opening we wished to make, and we began the heavy toil of piercing the quarry. We made so little progress the first day, that, in spite of our courage, we were tempted to relinquish the undertaking; we persevered, however, and my hope was somewhat revived as I perceived the stone was of a softer texture as we penetrated deeper. I concluded from this, that the ardent rays of the sun striking upon the rock had hardened the external layer, and that the stone within would increase in softness as we advanced. When I had cut about a foot in depth, we could loosen it with a spade like dried mud; this determined me to proceed with double ardour, and my boys assisted me with a spirit and zeal beyond their years.

After a few days of assiduous labour, we measured the opening, and found we had already advanced seven feet into the rock. Fritz removed the fragments in a barrow, and discharged them in a line before the place, to form a sort of terrace; I applied my own labour to the upper part, to enlarge the aperture; Jack, the smallest of the three, was able to get in and cut away below. He had with him a long iron bar sharpened at the end, which he drove in with a hammer to loosen a piece at a time. Suddenly he bawled out, "It is pierced through, father! Fritz, I have pierced it through!"

"Hah, hah, Master Jack at his jokes again!—But let us hear, what have you pierced? Is it the mountain? Not peradventure your hand or foot, Jack?" cried I.

Jack.—No, no, it is the mountain (the rocks resounding with his usual shout of joy); huzza, huzza! I have pierced the mountain!

Fritz now ran to him. "Come, let us see then: it is no doubt the globe at least you have pierced," said he, in a bantering tone: "you should have pushed on your tool boldly, till you reached Europe, which they say is under our feet; I should have been glad to peep into that hole."

Jack.—Well, then, peep you may, but I hardly know what you will see; come and look how far the iron is gone in, and tell me if it is all my boasting.

"Come hither, father," said Fritz, "this is really extraordinary: his iron bar seems to have got to a hollow place; see, it can be moved in every direction." I approached, thinking the incident worth attention: I took hold of the bar, which was still in the rock, and working it about, I made a sufficient aperture for one of my sons to pass, and I observed that in reality the rubbish fell within the cavity, which I judged, from the falling of the stones, was not much deeper than the part we stood on. My two lads offered to go in together and examine it: this, however, I forbade. I even made them remove from the opening, as I smelled the foul air that issued abundantly from it, and began myself to feel giddiness in consequence of having gone too near; so that I was compelled to withdraw quickly, and inhale a purer air.

Under my direction the boys now hastened to gather some dry moss, which they made into bundles; they then struck a light and set fire to them, and threw the moss blazing into the opening; but, as I had foreseen, the fire was extinguished at the very entrance, thus proving that the air within was highly mephitic. I now saw that it was to be rarefied by another and more effectual method. I recollected that we had brought from the vessel a chest that was full of grenades, rockets, and other fireworks, which had been shipped for the purpose of making signals, as well as for amusement. I sought it hastily, and took some of these, together with an iron mortar for throwing; out of it I laid a train of gunpowder and set fire to the end, which reached to where we stood. A general explosion took place, and an awful report reverberated through the dark recess: the lighted grenades flew about on all sides like brilliant meteors, rebounding and bursting with a terrific sound. We then sent in the rockets, which had also a full effect. They hissed in the cavity like flying dragons, disclosing to our astonished view its vast extent. We beheld too, as we thought, numerous dazzling bodies that sparkled suddenly, as if by magic, and disappeared with the rapidity of lightning, leaving the place in total darkness.

After having played off our fireworks, I tried lighted straw; to our great satisfaction, the bundles thrown in were entirely consumed; we could then reasonably hope nothing was to be feared from the air; but there still remained the danger of plunging into some abyss, or of meeting with a body of water. From these considerations, I deemed it more prudent to defer our entrance into this unknown recess till we had lights to guide us through it. I dispatched Jack on the buffalo to Falcon's Stream to tell his mother and brothers of our discovery, directing him to return with them, and bring all the tapers that were left: my intention was to tie them together to the end of a stick, and proceed with it lighted to examine the cavity.

In three or four hours we saw them coming up in our car of state. I immediately lighted some of the tapers; but not together, as I had intended: I preferred each taking one in his right hand, an implement in his left, another taper in his pocket, flint and steel; and thus we entered the rock in solemn procession. The most beautiful and magnificent spectacle presented itself. The sides of the cavern sparkled like diamonds, the light from our tapers was reflected from all parts, and had the effect of a grand illumination. Innumerable crystals of every length and shape hung from the top of the vault, which, uniting with those of the sides, formed pillars, altars, entablatures, and a variety of other figures, composing the most splendid masses. We might have fancied ourselves in the palace of a fairy, or an illuminated temple.

The floor was level, covered with a white and very fine sand, as if purposely strewed, and so dry that I could not see the least mark of humidity anywhere. All this led me to hope the spot would be healthy, convenient, and eligible for our proposed residence. I now formed a particular conjecture as to the nature of the crystallizations shooting out on all sides, and especially from the arch-roof. They could scarcely be of that species of rock-crystals produced by the slow filtering of water falling in drops, and coagulating in succession, and seldom found in excavations exhibiting so dry a nature, nor even with so many of the crystals perpendicular and perfectly smooth. I was impatient to evince the truth or falsehood of this idea by an experiment, and discovered with great joy, on breaking a portion of one of them, that I was in a grotto of *sal-gem*, that is, fossil, or rock salt, found in the earth in solid crystallized masses, generally above a bed of spar or gypsum, and surrounded by layers of fossils or rock. The discovery of this fact, which no longer admitted a doubt, pleased us all exceedingly. The shape of the crystals, their little solidity, and finally their saline taste, were decisive evidences.

Many schemes were formed for converting this magnificent grotto into a convenient and agreeable mansion for our abode. We had possession of the most eligible premises: the sole business was to turn them to the best account; and how to effect this was our unceasing theme. Some voted for our immediate establishment there, but they were opposed by more sagacious counsel, and it was resolved that Falcon's Stream would still be our headquarters till the end of the year.

CHAPTER XXX

House in the Salt Rock—Turtles

THE lucky discovery of a previously existing cavern in the rock had, as must be supposed, considerably lessened our labour; excavation was no longer requisite. I had more room than was wanted for the construction of our dwelling: to render it habitable was the present object, and to do this did not seem a difficult task. The upper bed of the rock, in front of the cavern, through which my little Jack had dug so easily, was of a soft nature, and to be worked with moderate effort. I hoped also that, being now exposed to the air and heat of the sun, it would become by degrees as hard and compact as the first layer that had given me so much trouble. From this consideration I began, while it retained its soft state, to make openings for the doors and windows of the front. This I regulated by the measurement of those I had fixed in my winding stair-case, which I had removed for the purpose of placing them in our winter tenement. I had previously marked out the openings to be cut for the frames, which were received into grooves for greater convenience and solidity. I took care not to break the stone taken from the apertures, or at least to preserve it in large pieces, and these I cut with the saw and chisel into oblongs an inch and a half in thickness, to serve as tiles. I laid them in the sun, and was gratified in seeing they hardened quickly; I then removed them, and my sons placed them in order against the side of the rock, till they were wanted for our internal arrangements.

When I could enter the cavern freely with a good doorway, and it was sufficiently lighted by the windows, I erected a partition, for the distribution of our apartments and other conveniences. The extent of the place afforded ample room for my design, and even allowed me to leave several spaces in which salt and other articles could be stored. I laid out the interior in the following manner: A very considerable space was first partitioned off in two divisions; the one on the right was appropriated to our residence, that on the left was to contain the kitchen, stables, and work-room. At the end of the second division, where windows could not be placed, the cellar and storeroom were to be formed; the whole separated by partition-boards, with doors of communication, so as to give us a pleasant and comfortable abode.

The side we designed to lodge in was divided into three apartments; the first, next the door, was the bedroom for my wife and me, the second a dining-parlour, and the last a bedroom for the boys. As we had only three windows, we put one in each sleeping-room; the third was fixed in the kitchen, where my wife would often be. A grating for the present fell to the lot of our dining-room, which when too cold was to be exchanged for one of the other apartments. I contrived a good fireplace in the kitchen near the window; I pierced the rock a little above, and four planks nailed together, and passing through this opening, answered the purpose of a chimney. We made the work-room near the kitchen of sufficient dimensions for the performance of undertakings of some magnitude; it served also to keep our cart and sledge in. Lastly, the stables, which were formed into four compartments, to separate the different species of animals, occupied all the bottom of the cavern on this side; on the other were the cellar and magazine.

The long stay we made at Tent House, during these employments, furnished us an opportunity of perceiving several advantages we had not reckoned upon. Immense turtles were often seen on the shore, where they deposited their eggs in the sand, and they regaled us with a rich treat; but, extending our wishes, we thought of getting possession of the turtles themselves for livestock, and of feasting on them whenever we pleased. As soon as we saw one on the sands, one of my boys was despatched to cut off its retreat; meanwhile we approached the animal, and quietly, without doing it any injury, turned it on its back, then passed a long cord through the shell, and tied the end of it to a stake, which we

fixed close to the edge of the water. This done, we set the
prisoner on its legs again; it hastened into the sea, but could
not go beyond the end of the cord; apparently it was all the
happier, finding food with more facility along shore than out
at sea; and we enjoyed the idea of being able to take it
when wanted.

A number of sea-dogs came into Safety Bay, and ascended the river in search of prey, sporting in the water
along shore, without evincing any fear of us. The fish presented no attraction to the palate, but its skin, tanned and
dressed, makes excellent leather. I was in great need of it
for straps and harness, to make saddles for Fritz and Jack to
ride the onagra and buffalo, and in short for our own use to
cut up into soles, belts, and pantaloons, of which articles we
much wanted a fresh supply; besides, I knew the fat yielded
good lamp oil, that might be substituted for tapers in the
long evenings of winter; and that it would be further useful
in tanning and rendering the leather pliant.

At this time I likewise made some improvements in our
sledge, to facilitate the carrying of stores from Falcon's
Stream to our dwelling in the rock at Tent House. I raised it
on two beams, on axle-trees, at the extremities of which I
put on the four gun-carriage wheels I had taken off the
cannon from the vessel; by this alteration I obtained a light
and convenient vehicle, of moderate height, on which boxes
and casks could be placed. Pleased with the operations of
the week, we set out all together with cheerful hearts for
Falcon's Stream, to pass our Sunday there, and once more
offer our pious thanks to the Almighty, for all the benefits
He had bestowed upon His defenceless creatures.

CHAPTER XXXI

New Fishery—New Experiments—New Discoveries, and House

THE enterprise of our dwelling went on, sometimes as a principal, sometimes as an intermediate occupation, according to the greater or less importance of other concerns; but though we advanced thus with moderate rapidity, the progress was such as to afford the hope of our being settled within it by the time of the rainy season.

From the moment I discovered gypsum to be the basis of the crystal salt in our grotto, I foresaw some great advantages I should derive from it; but to avoid enlarging the dimensions of our house by digging further, I tried to find a place in the continuation of the rock, which I might be able to blow up. I had soon the good fortune to meet with a narrow slip between the projections of the rock, which I could easily, by the means I proposed, convert into a passage that should terminate in our work-room. I found also on the ground a quantity of fragments of gypsum, and removed a great number of them to the kitchen, where we did not fail to bake a few of the pieces at a time when we made a fire for cooking, which, thus calcined, rubbed into a powder when cold; we obtained a considerable quantity of it, which I put carefully into casks for use when the time should come for finishing the interior of our dwelling. My notion was to form the walls, for separating the apartments, of the squares of stone I had already provided, and to unite them together with a cement of this new ingredient, which would be the means, both of sparing the timber, and increasing the beauty and solidity of the work.

One day as Jack and I were walking near the mouth of

Jackal's River, we perceived immense quantities of a large fish moving slowly towards the banks. As they came nearer, I distinguished the largest to resemble sturgeons, a fish found in higher latitudes, while the smallest I pronounced to be salmon. Jack now strutted about in ecstasies. "What say you now, father?" said he; "this is nothing like your little paltry fry! A single fish of this troop would fill a tub!"—"No doubt," answered I; and with great gravity I added,—"Pr'ythee, Jack, step into the river, and fling them to me one by one, that I may take them home to salt and dry."

He looked at me for a moment with a sort of vacant doubt if I could possibly be in earnest: then seizing suddenly a new idea—"Wait a moment, father," cried he, "and I will do so": and he sprang off like lightning towards the cavern, from whence he soon returned loaded with a bow and arrows, the bladders of the sea-dogs, and a ball of string, to catch, as he assured me, every one of the fishes. I looked on with interest and curiosity to mark what was next to happen, while the animation of his countenance, the promptitude and boyish gracefulness of his motions, and the firm determination of his manner, afforded me the highest amusement. He tied the bladders round at certain distances with a long piece of string, to the end of which he fastened an arrow and a small iron hook; he placed the large ball of string in a hole in the ground at a sufficient distance from the water's edge, and then he shot off an arrow, which the next instant stuck in one of the largest fishes. My young sportsman uttered a shout of joy. At the same moment Fritz joined us, and witnessed this unexpected feat without the least symptom of jealousy. "Well done, brother Jack," cried he; "but let me, too, have my turn."—Saying this, he ran back and fetched the harpoon and the windlass, and returned to us accompanied by Ernest. We were well pleased with their opportune arrival, for the salmon Jack had pierced struggled so fiercely, that all our endeavours to hold the string were insufficient, and we dreaded at every throw to see it break, and the animal make good its escape. By degrees, however, its strength was exhausted, and, aided by Fritz and Ernest, we succeeded in drawing it to a bank, where I put an end to its existence.

This fortunate beginning of a plan for a fishery inspired us all with hope and emulation. Fritz eagerly seized his har-

poon and windlass; I, for my part, like Neptune, wielded a
trident; Ernest prepared the large fishing-rod; and Jack his
arrow, with the same apparatus as before, not forgetting the
bladders, which were so effectual in preventing the fish from
sinking when struck. We were now more than ever sensible
of our loss in the destruction of the tub-boat, with which we
could have pursued the creatures in the water, and have
been spared much pains and difficulty; but, on the other
hand, such numbers of fishes presented themselves at the
mouth of the river, that we had only to choose among them.
Jack's arrow, after missing twice, struck the third time a
large sturgeon, which was so untractable, that we had great
difficulty in securing him. I too had caught two of the same
fish, and had been obliged to go up to the middle in the
water to manage my booty. Ernest, with his rod and line
and a hook, had also taken two smaller ones. Fritz, with his
harpoon, had struck a sturgeon at least eight feet in length,
and the skill and strength of our whole company were found
necessary to conduct him safe to shore, where we harnessed
the buffalo to him with strong cords to draw him to Tent
House.

When these various concerns were complete, we began to
meditate a plan for constructing a small boat as a substitute
for the tub-raft, to come close in to shore. I had a great
desire to make it, as the savages do, of the rind of a tree;
but the difficulty was to fix on one of sufficient bulk for my
purpose; for though many were to be found in our vicinity,
yet each was on some account or other of too much value to
be spared. We therefore resolved to make a little excursion
in search of a tree of capacious dimensions, and in a situation where it was not likely to yield us fruit, to refresh us
with its shade, or to adorn the landscape round our dwelling.

We arrived at Falcon's Stream, where we intended to pass
the night. We visited the ground my wife had so plentifully
sowed with grain, which had sprung up with an almost
incredible rapidity and luxuriance, and was now nearly ready
for reaping. We cut down what was fairly ripe, bound it
together in bundles, and conveyed it to a place where it
would be secure from the attacks of more expert grain
consumers than ourselves, of which thousands hovered round
the booty. We reaped barley, wheat, rye, oats, pease, mil-
let, lentils—only a small quantity of each, it is true, but

sufficient to enable us to sow again plentifully at the proper season. The plant that had yielded the most was maize, a proof that it best loved the soil. It had already shown itself in abundance in our garden at Tent House; but here there was a surface of land, the size of an ordinary field, entirely covered with its splendid golden ears, which still more than the other plants attracted the voracity of the feathered race. The moment we drew near, a dozen at least of large bustards sprang up with a loud rustling noise, which awakened the attention of the dogs; they plunged into the thickest parts, and routed numerous flocks of birds of all kinds and sizes, who took hastily to flight. Among the fugitives were some quails, who escaped by running; and lastly some kangaroos, whose prodigious leaps enabled them to elude the pursuit of the dogs.

We were so overcome by the surprise such an assemblage of living creatures occasioned, as to forget the resource we had in our guns; we stood as it were stupid with amazements during the first moments, and before we came to ourselves, the prey was beyond our reach, and for the most part out of sight. Fritz was the first to perceive and to feel with indignation the silly part we had been playing, and to consider in what way we could repair the mischief. Without further loss of time, he took the bandage from his eagle's eyes (for the bird always accompanied him perched upon his game-bag), and showed him with his hand the bustards still flying, and at no great distance. The eagle took a rapid flight. Fritz jumped like lightning on the back of his onagra, and galloped over everything that intervened, in the direction the bird had taken, and we soon lost sight of him.

We now beheld a spectacle which in the highest degree excited our curiosity and interest: the eagle had soon his prey in view; he mounted above one of the bustards in a direct line, without losing sight of it for an instant, and then darted suddenly down; the bustards flew about in utter confusion, now seeking shelter in the bushes, then crossing each other in every direction, in the attempt to evade the common enemy; but the eagle remained steady in pursuit of the bird he had fixed upon for his prey, and disregarded all the rest: he alighted on the unlucky bustard, fixed his claws and his beak in its back, till Fritz, arriving full gallop, got down from the onagra, replaced the bandage on the eagle's eyes, seated him once more upon the game-bag, and having relieved the poor bustard from his persecutor, he shouted to us to come and witness his triumph. We ran speedily to the place.

At the conclusion of this adventure, we hastened forward to Falcon's Stream, and dressed the wounds of the bustard. We perceived with pleasure that it was a male, and foresaw the advantage of giving him for a companion to our solitary female of the same species, which was completely tamed. I threw a few more bundles of maize into the cart, and without further delay we arrived at our tree.

The rest of the day was employed in picking the grains of the different sorts of corn from the stalks; we put what we wished to keep for sowing into some gourd-shells, and the Turkey wheat was laid carefully aside in sheaves till we should have time to beat and separate it. Fritz observed that we should also want to grind it; and I reminded him of the hand-mill we had secured from our departed ally the wrecked vessel.

Fritz.—But, father, the hand-mill is so small, and so subject to be put out of order:—why should we not contrive a water-mill, as they do in Europe? We have surely rapid streams of water in abundance.

Father.—This is true; but such a mechanism is more difficult than you imagine. The wheel alone, I conceive, would be an undertaking far beyond our strength or our capacity. I am, however, well pleased with the activity and zeal which prompted your idea; and we will hereafter consider whether it may be worth while to bestow upon it further attention. We have abundance of time before us, for we shall not want a water-mill till our harvests are such as to produce plentiful crops of corn. In the meantime, let us be thinking of our proposed excursion for to-morrow; for we should set out at least by sunrise.

We began our preparations accordingly. My wife chose some hens and two fine cocks, with the intention of taking them with us, and leaving them at large to produce a colony of their species at a considerable distance from our dwelling-places. I, with the same view, visited our beasts, and selected four young pigs, four sheep, two kids, and one male of each species; our numbers having so much increased that we could well afford to spare these individuals for the exper-

iment. If we succeeded in thus accustoming them to the
natural temperature and productions of our island, we should
have eased ourselves of the burden of their support, and
should always be able to find them at pleasure.

We took this time a new direction, which was straight
forward between the rocks and the shore, that we might
make ourselves acquainted with everything contained in the
island we seemed destined for ever to inhabit. We found, as
usual, much difficulty in pushing through the tall tough
grass, and alternately through the thick prickly bushes which
everywhere obtruded themselves. We were often obliged to
turn aside, while I cut a passage with my hatchet: but these
accidents seldom failed to reward my toil by the discovery of
different small additions to our general comfort; among
others, some roots of trees curved by nature to serve both
for saddles and yokes for our beasts of burden. I took care
to secure several, and put them in the cart.

In about an hour we found ourselves at the extremity of
the wood, and a most singular phenomenon presented itself
to our view: a small plain, or rather a grove of low bushes,
to appearance almost covered with flakes of snow, lay extended before us. Suddenly a suspicion crossed my mind,
and was soon confirmed by Fritz, who had darted forward
on his onagra, and now returned with one hand filled with
tufts of a most excellent species of cotton, so that the whole
surface of low bushes was in reality a plantation of that
valuable article. The pods had burst from ripeness, and the
winds had scattered around their flaky contents; the ground
was strewed with them, they had gathered in tufts on the
bushes, and they floated gently in the air.

The joy of this discovery was almost too great for utter-
ance. We collected as much cotton as our bags would hold,
and my wife filled her pockets with the seed, to raise it in
our garden at Tent House.

It was now time to proceed: and we took a direction
towards a point of land which skirted the wood of gourds,
and being high, commanded a view of the adjacent country.
I conceived a wish to remove our establishment to the
vicinity of the cotton plantation and the gourd wood, which
furnished so many of the utensils for daily use throughout
the family. I pleased myself in idea, with the view of the
different colonies of animals I had imagined, both winged

and quadruped; and in this elevation of my fancy, I even thought it might be practicable to erect a sort of farmhouse on the soil, which we might visit occasionally, and be welcomed by the agreeable sounds of the cackling of our feathered subjects, which would so forcibly remind us of the customs of our forsaken but ever-cherished country.

We accordingly soon reached the high ground, which I found in all respects favourable to my design. My plan for a building was approved by all, and we lost no time in pitching our tent, and forming temporary accommodations for cooking our victuals. When we had refreshed ourselves with a meal, I, for my part, resolved to look about in all directions, that I might completely understand what we should have to depend upon in this place, in point of safety, salubrity, and general accommodation. I had also to find a tree that would suit for the proposed construction of a boat; and lastly, to meet, if possible, with a group of trees, at such fit distances from each other as would assist me in my plan of erecting a farmhouse. I was fortunate enough in no long time to find in this last respect exactly what I wanted, and quite near to the spot we on many accounts had felt to be so enviable. I returned to my companions, whom I found busily employed in preparing excellent beds of the cotton, upon which, at an earlier hour than usual, we all retired to rest.

CHAPTER XXXII

Completion of Two Farmhouses—A Lake—A Boat

THE trees that I had chosen for the construction of my farmhouse embellishments were for the most part one foot in diameter in the trunk; they presented the form of a tolerably regular parallelogram, with its longest side to the

sea, the length twenty-four feet, and the breadth sixteen. I
cut little hollow places or mortises in the trunks, at the
distance of ten feet, one above the other, to form two
stories. The upper one I made a few inches shorter before
than behind, that the roof might be in some degree shelving;
I then inserted beams five inches in diameter respectively in
the mortises, and thus formed the skeleton of my building.
We next nailed some laths from tree to tree, at equal distances from each other, to form the roof, and placed on
them, in mathematical order, a covering composed of pieces
of the bark of trees, cut into the shape of tiles, and in a
sloping position, for the rain to run off in the wet season. As
we had no great provision of iron nails, we used for the
purpose the strong pointed thorn of the acacia, which we had
discovered the day before. We cut down a quantity of them,
and laid them in the sun to dry, when they became as hard as
iron, and were of essential service to our undertaking.

After our next meal we resumed with ardour our undertaking of the farmhouse, which we continued without interruption for several days. We formed the walls with matted
reeds interwoven with pliant laths to the height of six feet;
the remaining space to the roof was enclosed with only a
simple grating, that the air and light might be admitted. A
door was placed in the middle of the front. We next arranged the interior with as much convenience as the short-
ness of the time and our reluctance to use all our timber
would allow; we divided it half-way up by a partition wall
into two unequal parts; the largest was intended for the
sheep and goats, and the smallest for ourselves, when we
should wish to pass a few days here. At the further end of
the stable we fixed a house for the fowls, and above it a sort
of hay-loft for the forage. Before the door of entrance we
placed two benches, contrived as well as we could of laths
and odd pieces of wood, that we might rest ourselves under
the shade of the trees, and enjoy the exquisite prospect
which presented itself on all sides. Our own apartment was
provided with a couple of the best bedsteads we could make
of twigs of trees, raised upon four legs, two feet from the
ground, and these were destined to receive our cotton mattresses. Our aim was to content ourselves for the present
with these slight hints of a dwelling, and to consider hereaf-

ter what additions either of convenience or ornament could be made, such as plastering, etc.

I had imagined we should accomplish what we wished at the farm in three or four days; but we found in the experiment that a whole week was necessary, and our victuals fell short before our work was done. We began to consider what remedy we could apply to so embarrassing a circumstance; I could not prevail upon myself to return to Falcon's Stream before I had completed my intentions at the farm, and the other objects of my journey. I had even come to the determination of erecting another building upon the site of Cape Disappointment; I therefore decided that on this trying occasion I would invest Fritz and Jack with the important mission. They were accordingly despatched to Falcon's Stream, and to Tent House, to fetch new supplies of cheese, ham, potatoes, dried fish, manioc bread, for our subsistence, and also to distribute fresh food to the numerous animals we had left there.

During the absence of our purveyors I rambled with Ernest about the neighbouring soil, to make what new discoveries I could, and to procure, if possible, additions to our store of provisions. We followed the winding of a river towards the middle of the wall of rocks: our course was interrupted by a marsh which bordered a small lake, the aspect of which was enchantingly picturesque. I perceived, with joyful surprise, that the whole surface of the swampy soil was covered with a kind of wild rice, ripe on the stalk, and which attracted the voracity of large flocks of birds. As we approached, a loud rustling was heard, and we distinguished on the wing, bustards, Canada heath-fowl, and great numbers of smaller birds. We succeeded in bringing down five or six of them; and I was pleased to remark in Ernest a justness of aim that promised well for the future.

Presently we saw Master Knips jump from Flora's back, and smell along the ground among some thick growing plants, then pluck off something with his two paws, and eat of it voraciously. We ran to the spot to see what it could be, when, to the relief of our parched palates, we found he had discovered there the largest and finest kind of strawberry, which is called in Europe the *Chili*, or *pine strawberry*.

Pursuing our way a little further along the marsh, we reached the lake, which we had descried with so much

pleasure from a distance, and whose banks, being overgrown with thick underwood, were necessarily concealed
from the momentary view we had leisure to take of surrounding objects, particularly as the lake was situated in a
deep and abrupt valley. No one who is not a native of
Switzerland can conceive the emotion which trembled at my
heart, as I contemplated this limpid, azure, undulating body
of water, the faithful miniature of so many grand originals,
which I had probably lost sight of for ever. My eyes swam
with tears! Alas! a single glance upon the surrounding picture, the different characters of the trees, the vast ocean in
the distance, destroyed the momentary illusion, and brought
back my ideas to the painful reality, that I and mine were—
strangers in a desert island!

Another sort of object now presented itself to confirm the
certainty that we were no longer inhabitants of Europe: it
was the appearance of a quantity of swans gliding over the
surface of the lake; but their colour, instead of white, like
those of our country, was a jetty black, and their plumage
had so high a gloss as to produce, reflected on the water,
the most astonishing effect. The six large feathers of the
wings of this bird are white, exhibiting a singular contrast to
the rest of the body: in other respects these birds were
remarkable, like those of Europe, for the haughty gracefulness of their motions, and the voluptuous ease of their
nature.

We now began to look for the shortest path for returning
to the farm, which we reached at the same time with Fritz
and Jack, who had well performed the object of their journey. We, on our part, produced our offering of strawberries
and our specimen of rice, which were welcomed with shouts
of pleasure and surprise. We filled the stable with forage,
laid a large provision of grain for the fowls within their
house, and began arrangements for our departure.

The following day we took a silent leave of our animals,
and directed our course towards the eminence in the vicinity
of Cape Disappointment; we ascended it, and found it in
every respect adapted to our wishes. From this eminence we
had a view over the country which surrounded Falcon's
Stream in one direction, and in others of a richly diversified
extent of landscape, comprehending sea, land, and rocks.
When we had paused for a short time upon the exhaustless

beauties of the scene, we agreed with one voice, that it should be on this spot we would build our second cottage. A spring of the clearest water issued from the soil near the summit, and flowed over its sloping side, forming agreeable cascades in its rapid course; in short, every feature of the picture contributed to form a landscape worthy the homage of a taste the most delicate and refined. I presented my children with an appropriate word.—"Let us build here," exclaimed I, "and call the spot—*Arcadia*;" to which my wife and all agreed.

We lost no time in again setting to work; our experience at the farm enabled us to proceed with incredible rapidity, and our success was in every respect more complete. The building contained a dining-room, two bed-chambers, two stables, and a store-room for preserving all kinds of provisions for man and beast. We formed the roof square, with four sloped sides, and the whole had really the appearance of an European cottage, and was finished in the short space of six days. What now remained to be done, was to fix on a tree fit for my project of a boat. After much search, I at length found one of prodigious size, and in most respects suitable to my views.

It was, however, no very encouraging prospect I had before me, being nothing less than the stripping off a piece of the bark that should be eighteen feet in length, and five in diameter; and now I found my rope ladder of signal service: we fastened it by one end to the nearest branches, and it enabled us to work with the saw as might be necessary at any height from the ground. Accordingly we cut quite round the trunk in two places, and then took a perpendicular slip from the whole length between the circles; by this means we could introduce the proper utensils for raising the rest by degrees, till it was entirely separated. We toiled with increasing anxiety, at every moment dreading that we should not be able to preserve it from breaking, or uninjured by our tools. When we had loosened about half, we supported it by means of cords and pulleys; and when all was at length detached, we let it down gently, and with joy beheld it lying safe on the grass. Our business was next to mould it to our purpose, while the substance continued moist and flexible.

The boys observed that we had now nothing more to do

than to nail a plank at each end, and our boat would be as
complete as those used by the savages; but for my own part,
I could not be contented with a mere roll of bark for a boat;
and when I reminded them of the paltry figure it would
make following the pinnace, I heard not another word about
the further pains and trouble, and they asked eagerly for my
instructions. I made them assist me to saw the bark in the
middle of the two ends, the length of several feet, these two
parts I folded over till they ended in a point; I kept them in
this form by the help of the strong glue I had before made
from fish-bladders, and pieces of wood nailed fast over the
whole. This operation tended to widen the boat in the
middle, and thus render it of too flat a form; but this we
counteracted by straining a cord all round, which again
reduced it to the due proportion, and in this state we put it
in the sun, to harden and fix.

Before our departure for Tent House, we collected several new plants for our kitchen-garden; and lastly, we made
another trip to the narrow strait at the end of the wall of
rocks, resolved to plant there a sort of fortification of trees,
which should produce the double effect of discouraging the
invasion of savages, and allowing us to keep our pigs on the
other side, and thus secure our different plantations from
the chance of injury. We accomplished all these intentions
to our entire satisfaction, and, in addition, we placed a
slight drawbridge across the river beyond the narrow pass,
which we could let down or take up at pleasure on our side.
We now hastened our return to Arcadia, and after a night's
repose we loaded the sledge with the boat and other matters, and returned to Tent House.

As soon as we had despatched some necessary affairs, we
resumed the completion of the boat: in two days she had
received the addition of a keel, a neat lining of wood, a
small flat floor, benches, a small mast and triangular sail, a
rudder, and a thick coat of pitch on the outside, so that the
first time we saw her in the water, we were all in ecstasies at
the charming appearance she made.

We had still two months in prospect before the rainy
season, and we employed them for completing our abode
the grotto, with the exception of such ornaments as we
might have time to think of during the long days of winter.
We made the internal divisions of planks and that which

separated us from the stables of stone, to protect us from the offensive smell occasioned by the animals. Our task was difficult, but from habit it became easier every day. We took care to collect or manufacture a sufficient quantity of all sorts of materials, such as beams and planks, reeds, and twigs for matting, pieces of gypsum for plaster, etc., etc. At length the time of the rainy season was near at hand, and we thought of it with pleasure, as it would put us in possession of the enjoyments we had procured by such unremitting industry and fatigue.

We plastered over the walls of the principal apartments on each side with the greatest care, finishing them by pressure with a flat smooth board, and lastly a wash of size, in the manner of the plasterers in Europe. This ornamental portion of our work amused us all so much, that we began to think we might venture a step further in European luxury, and agreed that we would attempt to make some carpets with the hair of our goats. To this effect we smoothed the ground in the rooms we intended to distinguish with great care; then spread over it some sail-cloth, which my wife had joined in breadths, and fitted exactly; we next strewed the goats' hair, mixed with wool obtained from the sheep, over the whole; on this surface we threw some hot water, in which a strong cement had been dissolved; the whole was then rolled up, and was beaten for a considerable time with hard sticks; the sail-cloth was now unrolled, and the inside again sprinkled, rolled, and beaten as before; and this process was continued till the substance had become a sort of felt, which could be separated from the sail-cloth, and was lastly put in the sun to harden. We thus produced a very tolerable substitute for that enviable article of European comfort, a carpet; of these we completed two, one for our parlour, and the other for our drawing-room, as we jocosely named them: both of which were completely fit for our reception by the time the rains had set in.

Thus, as will be perceived, we had made the first steps towards a condition of civilization; separated from society, condemned, perhaps, to pass the remainder of life in this desert island, we yet possessed the means of happiness; we had abundance of all the necessaries, and many of the comforts, desired by human beings.

CHAPTER XXXIII

Anniversary of Our Deliverance—Motives for Thankfulness

ONE morning, having arisen earlier than the rest of my young family, I occupied myself by counting up the time that had passed away since our shipwreck. I calculated the dates with the utmost exactness, and I found that the next day would be the anniversary of that event. It was just two years since the hand of God had been extended over us to save us from a watery grave. I felt my mind filled with thanksgiving, and I resolved to celebrate the day with all the pomp our situation would permit.

As I had not yet fixed upon the arrangements for our holiday, I said nothing about it to my family. Breakfast over, we proceeded to our different employments, and it was not until we were seated at supper that I announced, in a pompous manner, the holiday for the morrow.

"Be ready," said I to my sons, "to celebrate the anniversary of the morrow; let each one prepare himself as is proper for so great a day."

These last words, joined to the announcement of a holiday, surprised and overjoyed my children. Their mother was not less astonished than they were to find that they had been on the island two years.

On the morrow we rose and dressed as decently as our scanty means afforded, and proceeded to breakfast. After our daily prayer I announced to my family that the amusements of the day would conclude with the exercises which always terminated our holidays.

"You have practised for some time," said I, "in wrestling, running, slinging, and horsemanship; the time has come when you shall receive the reward for your labours. You shall this day contend, before your mother and me, and the crown shall be given to the victor. Come, champions," I added, elevating my voice, "the barrier is open, enter the lists; and you, trumpets, sound the horn of combat." As I said these last words, I turned to the little inlet where our geese and ducks were feeding, and the whole troop, frightened by my gestures, and the tone of my voice, commenced a most deafening clamour, and furnished my sons with a good joke to excite their risible faculties.

I then organized the different combats which were to take place. First came firing at a mark; the materials for this were soon arranged by fixing in the ground a rudely-shaped piece of wood, with two bits of leather at each side of the top, which we called a kangaroo. Jack did wonders, either by chance or skill: he shot away one of the ears of our pretended kangaroo! Fritz just grazed the head, and Ernest lodged his ball in the middle of the body. The three shots were all worthy of praise. Another proof of skill was then made; it consisted in firing at a ball of cork which I threw up in the air. Ernest had the advantage here: he cut the ball to pieces. Fritz also shot well, but Jack could not hit it. We then tried the same thing with pistols, shortening the distance, and again I complimented my boys upon the progress they had made since last year.

Slinging succeeded to the pistol exercise. Fritz carried off the prize. After that came archery; and here all—even little Francis—distinguished themselves. Next came the races; and I gave them for a course the distance between Family Bridge and Falcon's Nest.

"The one that arrives first," said I to the runners, who gathered about me, "will bring me, as proof of his victory, my knife, which I left on the table, under the tree." I then gave the signal, by clapping my hands three times. My three sons set out, Jack and Fritz with all the impetuosity that marked their character; on the contrary, Ernest, who never did anything without reflecting, set off slowly at first, but gradually augmented his pace. I perceived that he had his elbows pressed firmly against his body, and I augured well from this little mark of prudence.

The runners were absent about three-quarters of an hour.

Jack returned first; but he was mounted on his buffalo, and
the onagra and the ass followed him.

"How now," said I, "is this what you call racing? It was
your legs, and not those of the buffalo, that I wished to
exercise."

"Bah!" cried he, jumping from the back of his courser; "I
knew I would never get there, so I left the course; and, as
the trial of horsemanship comes next, I thought that, as I
was near Falcon's Nest, I would bring our coursers back
with me."

Fritz came next, all out of breath and covered with sweat;
but he had not the knife, and it was Ernest who brought it
me.

"How came you to have the knife," said I, "when Fritz
got here before you?"

"The thing is simple," answered Ernest; "in going, he
could not long keep up the pace he started with, and soon
stopped to breathe, while I ran on and got the knife; but in
coming back, Fritz had learned a lesson; he pressed his arms
against his sides, and held his mouth shut, as he had seen
me do, and then the victory depended upon our relative
strength: Fritz is 16, while I am but 13, and of course he
arrived first."

I praised the two boys for their skill, and declared Ernest
conqueror.

But now Jack, mounted on his buffalo, demanded that
the equestrian exercises should commence, and he be allowed to repair the injury his reputation had sustained.

"To the saddle, to the saddle, my lads," he bellowed with
all his force, "and you shall then see who can best manage a
courser; we shall then know whether you can sit your horse
as well as you can exercise your legs."

I hastened to comply with the request of the little brag-
gart: Fritz mounted his onagra, and Ernest took the ass; but
although they tried all their skill, Jack distanced them both.
I was frightened myself to see with what boldness the boy
abandoned himself to the powerful animal that bore him.
To stop, charge, and turn was but a trifle to him; a
practised groom could not have managed a thoroughbred
horse with more ease and grace than he did his bull. Just as
I had declared the contest over, and was about to proclaim
Jack victor, the little Francis rode into the arena, mounted

on his young bull "Broumm," who was not more than three or four months old; my wife had made him a saddle of kangaroo-skin, with stirrups adjusted to his little legs, and there he sat, a whip in his right hand, and the bridle of his animal in the left.

"Gentlemen," said the little cavalier, saluting us with a gracious bend, "I have not contended with you thus far in any of the exercises of the day; will you now permit Milo of Crotona to make a trial of his horsemanship before you?"

The assembly loudly applauded this little harangue, and the cavalier commenced to manœuvre his courser. The boy was more cool and calm than those of his age are apt to be. But what I admired most was the docility of the animal. My wife looked on with maternal pride to see the success of her dear pupil, and Francis was unanimously proclaimed an excellent horseman.

After the horsemanship, the swimming occupied some time; they also climbed the trees; and, after we had finished our gymnastics, I announced that the rewards would now be distributed, and that the crowns would shade the brows of the victors.

Every one hastened to the grotto, which had been lighted up with all the torches we possessed; my wife, as queen of the day, was pompously installed in an elevated seat, decorated with flowers, and I called up the laureates to receive the rewards, which their mother distributed to each one as she impressed a tender kiss upon his forehead.

Fritz—conqueror at shooting and swimming—received a superb English rifle,[1] and a hunting-knife, which he had long wished for. Ernest had for the reward of the race a splendid gold watch. Jack—the cavalier—obtained a magnificent pair of steel spurs and a whip of whalebone. Little Francis received a pair of stirrups and a box of colours as a reward for the industry he had displayed in educating his bull.

When this distribution was finished, I rose, and, turning to my wife, presented her with a beautiful English workbox, in which was contained all those little things that add so much to the comfort of an industrious woman, such as pins, needles, scissors, etc.

[1] These articles were portion of the property brought from the wreck.

"Receive," said I, "my excellent companion, also a reward; for your services and endurance during the year well deserve one, even though the tender love of myself and children may be in itself a sufficient reward."

The day was finished as it had begun—with songs and expressions of joy; we were all happy, all contented: we all enjoyed that pure felicity which a life free from reproach had given us; and we all thanked in our hearts the Lord who had been so merciful toward us.

CHAPTER XXXIV

Gourd Plantation—Monkey Root or Ginseng—Bird Snares

WE all remembered the bountiful provision we had derived from the blackbirds and ortolans that had settled upon our giant tree at Falcon's Nest the preceding year. The time had now arrived for their reappearance, and we resolved to leave the grotto, which had become our established residence, and remove nearer to the spot, where I intended to secure as many as possible of this delicious provision for the coming winter.

The provision of India-rubber which we had collected on our last excursion was exhausted; we had made waterproof boots of it, and, before I set out, I wished to give them a new coat of it. I sent Fritz and Jack to the wood of india-rubber trees, where I thought they would find, ready drawn, a sufficient quantity of the gum, as we had made large incisions in the trees, and placed calabashes under them to receive it; and as experience had taught us that the sun hardens it immediately, we had protected our calabashes from its rays, by surrounding them with green branches.

Our two messengers were lost to our view when my wife

suddenly exclaimed, "Stupid woman that I am, I have forgotten to give the boys a calabash in which they might put
the gum, for they cannot bring it home in the flat dishes we
put there. I mean to go directly, and see whether my gourds
are ripe."

I tranquillized my good wife by assuring her that they
would not be at a loss to find something; and then, returning to the last word she had spoken, asked her what she
meant by saying "my gourds."

She then informed me that she possessed a superb plantation of gourds, the seeds of which she had found among our
European grains, and which she had planted in her kitchen-
garden. She led the way there; and we found, among many
other plants, a quantity of those bottle-shaped gourds that
the peasants in our country carry to the field. Some were
ripe, some just formed, and others in full bloom. We selected the ripest, and those the form of which could be
useful to us, and we commenced to empty them out. We
made bottles, and plates, and saucers, using alternately the
knife and the saw. But Ernest, my aid and companion, had
very little taste for such work, and he could scarcely contain
his joy when he heard me say we had done enough.

We now anxiously expected our young messengers back,
for the sun had already begun to decline. Ernest kept a
good lookout on the side his brothers were expected from,
and he soon perceived them rapidly approaching, the one
mounted on the onagra, and the other on the buffalo.

"Well," said I, "have you made out well?"

"Oh, yes, very well," said Fritz, in a singular tone, as
they leaped from their coursers, and showed us what they
had brought, which consisted of a root of anise that Jack
had brought in his buffalo-pouch; a root wrapped up in
leaves, which they called "monkey root"; two calabashes of
india-rubber, and another half full of turpentine; a sack full
of wax berries, and a crane, which Fritz's eagle had killed.
But while they were exhibiting their treasures, they talked
so fast and so rambling that I was obliged to make them
preserve a little order in their recital.

Jack then commenced telling us how he had obtained the
anise and the turpentine. Of these two things, one was, at
least, superfluous; but the other might be of some advantage, as I could use it instead of oil in making my snares for

the birds. I then asked them concerning the "monkey root" they had brought; Fritz answered as follows:—

"I do not know of what importance this root may be to us; but I can assure you that it far surpasses manioc, both in smell and savour. We discovered it close by the farmhouse, where a company of monkeys were regaling themselves on it. You would have laughed to see the manner in which the ugly animals pulled out the roots. They made use of a process which the labourers of Europe had no idea of—they pulled them up by turning somersets."

"By turning somersets!" cried we; "why, how wonderful!"

"Yes, somersets," replied Fritz. "Every monkey, after having buried his teeth as far as possible in the root, turns himself violently over, backward, and repeats the exercise until his reiterated efforts have drawn the precious root from the ground."

The monkey root, or ginseng, made its appearance at supper, and was pronounced excellent; but as its aromatic nature made it more of a medicine than an article of food, I forbade its frequent use, while I enjoined my wife to plant a few roots in our garden.

The next morning I took a certain quantity of the liquid india-rubber, which I mixed with the turpentine, and placed the mixture over the fire; and, while the glue was thickening, I sent the boys into the copse to gather a quantity of little twigs which I needed. They soon brought me a large quantity, which I made them dip in the glue and fasten to the branches of the fig-trees, the fruit of which I observed was very much liked by the ortolans,[1] thrushes, and beccafigoes,[2] who frequented the place. I discovered that we had but seen the last of the season the preceding year, as at present the birds were so numerous that a blind man firing into the tree could not have failed to bring down a large number of them. The abundance of game suggested another idea to my mind; I thought that if the ortolans were so numerous during the day they would not be less so at night,

[1] *Ortolan,* not unlike the yellow-hammer.
[2] *Beccafigo,* or *Fig-eater,* about the size of a linnet; both these birds feed on fruits and berries, and are much prized for the delicacy of their flesh; a very large trade is carried on from the island of Cyprus with the former.

and I resolved to try, in imitation of the Americans in Virginia, the experiment of a hunt with torches, persuaded that it would be more expeditious and successful than taking the birds by snares.

But my boys, while employed at making the snares, had been taken in their own trap. Hands, faces and clothes were all covered with glue, and one could not touch them without getting besmeared. They were all in great consternation, and their good mother also, for she had but very little clean linen to spare them. I calmed their fears by assuring them that some ashes and water would remedy all the disorder, and wash out all the stains.

I rallied them a little on their awkwardness. "I knew very well," said I, "that my glue would trap the birds; but I had no idea it would catch little boys."

I then taught them how to avoid the inconveniences of gluing their fingers, by plunging a packet of five or six twigs, by the aid of a pair of pincers, into the glue, instead of dipping them in singly. They adopted the plan, which succeeded perfectly. When I had made a sufficient quantity, Jack and Fritz climbed into the tree, and placed the branches of fig-trees, covered with the snares, among the limbs of the tree; and it was not long before we saw the unfortunate ortolans falling to the ground in numbers, their legs and wings stuck fast in the glue. But, although the fowling was so abundant, the labour was very fatiguing, for the branches to which Fritz and Jack had to climb were as much as sixty or seventy feet from the ground. I placed a great deal of confidence in my torches, and I arranged the materials for making them, in which turpentine was a powerful auxiliary.

While I was thus occupied, Jack brought me a beautiful bird, much larger than an ortolan, which had been taken in the snare.

"I am very certain," said Ernest, who had approached, and who, with his observing eye, had already recognized the bird, "I am very sure that it is one of our European pigeons, one of the young ones from those who built their nests last year in the branches of the tree."

I took the bird from Jack's hands, and recognized with pleasure that Ernest's conjecture was true. I rubbed the ends of his wings and his feet with ashes to clean them from the glue, and I put him in a cage with the intention of adding a dove-cot to our domestic property. We captured others, and at night we had in our possession two fine pairs of wood-pigeons.

But, notwithstanding our hard labour during the day, we were not able to fill more than one barrel. I enjoined my sons to take notice of the trees on which the ortolans roosted during the night. The bark of two or three of the fig-trees which were covered with the excrements of the birds decided the matter; and, after supper, and a few minutes of rest, I commenced my preparations. These were few in number, and consisted of two or three long bamboo canes, two bags, torches of resin, and some sugar-canes. Fritz, my grand huntsman, regarded me with a look of incredulity. He could not understand how, with these strange instruments, I could realize the prodigies I prophesied.

We set out; and the night—which succeeds immediately to the day in these climates—soon overshadowed the earth. Arrived at the foot of the trees that we had chosen, I lighted up my torches, and scarcely had the flame begun to burn, than a cloud of ortolans fell down around us, and began to fly wildly around the flickering flames.

"Well, gentlemen," said I to my sons, "you see that my stratagem has proved not to be a bad idea. Now is your time; I have placed the game within your reach; you have but to extend your hand, and you are masters."

I then armed each one with a bamboo cane, and set them an example by striking right and left among the mass of ortolans. They fell as thick and fast as rain, and we soon filled two large bags. Our flambeaux, however, would only last long enough to light us back to Falcon's Nest; and as the sacks were too heavy for me alone to carry, we placed them crosswise on the bamboo poles, and thus carried them very easily.

We arrived safely at Falcon's Nest, and, before we retired to rest, looked over our game, and terminated the sufferings of those poor birds that had not been killed by the blows. The next day, every one put his hand to the work of cleaning and preparing our game—a very disagreeable, although necessary, task. We filled two barrels with ortolans, half roasted, and packed down in butter.

CHAPTER XXXV

The Dove-Cot and its Management

MY wife took care of my pigeons, and approved of the plan of a dove-cot; consequently the waggon was immediately loaded with provisions, and all that was necessary for an excursion of some days, and we set out for the grotto. As soon as we arrived, I chose that part of the rock next our grotto as the situation of our dove-cot; and as the rock, after the outside layer was pierced, became softer, we soon made an excavation ten feet high, and large enough to contain twenty pairs of pigeons; two perches ran through the whole length, and, projecting out in front, with a board nailed across, formed a platform, which we protected by a slight roof; a door with a hole to admit light closed the front; and a rope ladder suspended from one of the perches enabled us to mount up, and look after the inhabitants. It cost us several weeks of constant labour to finish the construction, fix the boards strongly in their places, cover the inside with a coat of plaster, to prevent humidity, and arrange the perches, the nests, etc.

"There is the edifice," said I to Fritz; "but where are the inhabitants? We must call into action all our knowledge to find a way to force our wild stranger pigeons to dwell in the new habitation we have provided for them; and, besides, they must not only remain themselves, but must bring their companions with them."

"It appears to me, father, that nothing short of sorcery will do it."

"Sorcery or not, difficult as it appears, I am going to try it; and I have strong hopes of succeeding, with the assis-

J. D. Wyss

tance you can afford me. It is to a pigeon merchant that I owe the secret which I am about to put into practice. I will not warrant its success, for I have never tried it; but it consists in perfuming a new dove-cot with anise. The pigeons, it is said, are so fond of the odour of this plant that they will return themselves every night to respire its perfume; and it is in this manner that they insensibly change their country life for that of the pigeon-house."

"Nothing can be easier," replied Fritz. "The plant of anise that Jack brought will do the business. We can break the seeds on a stone; and if the oil is not as pure as that of the chemists, it will not be less useful or less aromatic."

"I think as you do," I answered; "and I am very glad that I permitted Jack to plant a root that appeared to me to be so valueless."

We then proceeded to make the oil of anise. I rubbed the door of the dove-cot, the perches, and every place where the pigeons could touch either feet or wings with it. I then mixed a sort of dough with anise, salt, and clay, and, after having placed it in the middle of the dove-cot, we put in the pigeons, which we had kept in willow-baskets while their habitation was building. We shut them up, with provision for two days, and then left them to enjoy at their leisure the odour of the anise.

When our boys had returned from our kitchen-garden at the end of that time, we formally announced to them that the pigeons had taken possession of their new abode. In a moment they flew to the ladder, in eager haste to get a sight of the new inhabitants. The two windows of isin-glass which I had placed in the door were raised by the curious, and I saw with pleasure that, instead of being frightened at the new objects that surrounded them, our prisoners appeared to have become quite tame; and when I entered, they took no more notice of me than a domestic pigeon would have done.

Two days more passed away, and I became curious myself to know the result of my *sorcery*.

On the morning of the third day I awoke Fritz very early, and commanded him to rub anew with anise the door, which was made to rise up and down by means of a pulley. He did it, and we then went, without saying anything about our preparations, to awake the still sleeping family. I then announced that the day of liberty for our prisoners had arrived, and now they were to be free.

All now took their stations. I gave the cord of the door into Jack's hands; and, scarcely able to keep my countenance, I described a magic circle with a wand, and, after having murmured a pretended conjuration, I ordered Jack to pull up the cord.

The pigeons poked their heads cautiously out of the hole, then advanced on the platform, and suddenly soared up to such a height that they were lost to our sight. But in a few moments they again flew down, and settled, tranquilly, upon the platform they had just quitted.

This incident, which I did not expect, gave new proofs of my dealings in magic, and I cried out, in the most serious manner, "I knew very well, when they flew up in the clouds, that they were not lost."

"How could you possibly know that?" said Ernest.

"Because my charms have attached them to the dovecot," was my answer.

"Charms!" cried Jack; "are you, then, a sorcerer, papa?"

"Simpleton!" replied Ernest; "who ever *heard* of sorcerers?"

At that moment the pigeons, who had been quietly picking on the ground, attracted our attention. The two Molucca pigeons suddenly quitted their European brothers, and flew off in the direction of Falcon's Nest, with such rapidity that soon they were lost to our view.

"Adieu, gentlemen," cried Jack, as they darted away, taking his hat off and making a thousand faces; "adieu, a pleasant trip to you."

My wife and Francis commenced to deplore the loss of our two handsome pigeons, while I, preserving as serious a look as possible, stretched out my hands, and, turning to the direction in which the pigeons flew, I murmured, half aloud, the following words:

"Fly, little ones, fly far, far away; till to-morrow you may stay; but then, return with your companions."

I then turned toward my family, who stood stupefied with astonishment, not knowing what to make out of my serious address to the departed pigeons.

As for the other pigeons, they did not seem disposed to follow their companions, but appeared completely tamed:

they had found the dove-cot of Europe with its shelter, and there they gladly remained.

We passed the rest of the day in the neighbourhood of the dove-cot, conversing on sorcery and the question of the pigeons; we often strained our eyes in the direction of Falcon's Nest, but nothing appeared. The evening came, and the European pigeons slept alone in their palace. We supped gaily, and retired to rest in anxious expectation of the morrow, which must establish either my defeat or my triumph.

We renewed, the next day, our habitual occupations; and though I felt a little doubtful about the return of the birds, I said nothing, but anxiously awaited the evening; when, about noon, we saw Jack running furiously toward us, clapping his hands, and screaming out:

"He has returned! he has returned!"

"Who? who?" was eagerly asked.

"The blue pigeon!" he answered, "the blue pigeon! Quick! quick! come and see him!"

We ran to the dove-cot, and, besides the blue pigeon, we found with him, on one of the exterior perches of the house, his mate, whom he was endeavouring to persuade to venture into the interior. He would put in his head, and then return to her, until at last he prevailed, and we had the satisfaction of seeing her enter the pigeon-house.

My sons would have immediately closed the door, but I prevented them, saying that some time or other it must be opened; "and besides," I added, "how are the other pigeons to enter if we close the door?"

"I begin to think," said my wife, at last, "that there is something extraordinary in this; and, unless you have used some enchantment, I cannot comprehend it."

"It is chance—pure chance," interrupted Ernest.

"Chance!" replied I, laughing; "that will do very well for one time, but when the other pigeon returns this evening, with his mate, will you think *that* chance?"

"Impossible!" answered he; "the same phenomenon could not happen twice in a day."

While we were thus speaking, Fritz suddenly interrupted us: his eagle eyes had perceived the birds we were expecting.

"What do you say now, my little doctor?" said I to Ernest: "both pairs of pigeons have now returned."

"I do not know what to say," he answered seriously; "it certainly appears very extraordinary; but as for any sorcery or magic being employed, I will not believe it."

"It gives me pleasure to see that you are not credulous; but if a third pair of Molucca pigeons should visit us to-day, would you call that chance also?"

Ernest did not answer; but his silence showed that he was far from being convinced.

We returned to our occupations, leaving Francis and his mother to provide a dinner for us. We had worked about two hours, when we saw our little Francis come running towards us. When he came near he drew up his little form, and, bowing haughtily, commenced the following speech:

"Most high and mighty lords, I am here to invite you, on the part of my good mother, to come and behold the prince of pigeons, who, with his noble spouse, has come to take possession of the magnificent palace you have provided for him."

"You are welcome for your good news, Mr. Messenger," was the universal answer.

We hastened to the dove-cot, where my wife, after cautioning us to make no noise, pointed out to us two superb birds, whom those in the interior were endeavouring to persuade to enter.

"I give up," said Ernest, at last; "my little knowledge cannot comprehend it. I beg of you, papa, to explain all."

I explained to him, in detail, all that we had done. Jack laughed heartily on hearing that his plant of anise had been the charm which had so puzzled them; and I tried to persuade him to follow the example of Ernest, and not believe everything so readily.

The following days were devoted to bringing our dove-cot as near as possible to perfection; and we saw, with joy, that the new inhabitants were permanently settled, and had already begun to construct their nests. I observed among the articles they gathered for that purpose, a sort of long, grey moss, which I had seen hanging from the branches of old trees. I recognized it as being the same thing as is exported from India as a substitute for horse-hair, in the manufacture of mattresses. The Spaniards make cords also of it, which are so light that a piece twenty feet in length, if suspended from a pole, will float, like a flag, in the air.

I made this discovery known to my good wife, and one can easily imagine my news was well received; for it added another treasure to our domestic riches, and afforded promise of some fine mattresses.

We found, from time to time, in the soil of the dove-cot, nutmegs, which, doubtless, the pigeons of Molucca had brought over. We washed them, and, although they were deprived of their silky covering, we committed them to the earth, without much hope of their ever germinating.

CHAPTER XXXVI
Jack's Adventure and Narrow Escape—A Fountain

AN adventure of which Master Jack was the hero diverted the monotony of our existence, divided as it was between new constructions and provisioning our habitation for winter.

Jack had one day set off on an expedition, the intent and purpose of which nobody but himself had any knowledge of; but his absence was not long, for we soon saw him returning, covered from head to foot with a thick, black mud, and dragging after him a bundle of Spanish rushes, likewise covered with mud.

"Where have you been," said I, "to dirty yourself so?"

"In Flamingo Marsh."

"Why, what in the name of common sense were you doing there?"

"Alas!" answered the poor boy, as he heaved a deep sigh, "I wanted to get some Spanish osiers to make nests for the pigeons."

"A praiseworthy intention," said I. "It was not your fault that the enterprise did not succeed well."

"Oh, no; and if it had not been for these bundles of

rushes I should certainly have lost my life. I wanted some thin, flexible rushes; those on the borders of the swamp were too large, and I advanced farther into the marsh, jumping from hummock to hummock, until I came to a spot where the only footing was a mass of soft, black mud; my feet slipped in, and I found myself up to my knees in the compound; and, gradually sinking deeper, I commenced screaming at the top of my voice; but nobody heard me, except my jackal, who came running up to me, and tried to assist me by howling with all his might."

"But why," said Ernest, "did you not try to swim? you excel all of us in swimming."

"Fine advice, truly; I would like to see you swimming in a swamp, up to your neck in mud, and surrounded by a thick forest of willows. When I perceived that neither my cries nor those of the jackal produced any good, I endeavoured to draw myself out; for I was sinking fast, and had no time to lose. I took my knife from my pocket, and cut, from the willows that surrounded me, two large bundles, and, placing one under each arm, they served me as a sort of hold. I then exerted all my strength, and, by moving my body, my arms, and my legs, I managed to raise myself up a little. All this time my jackal stood on the edge of the marsh, howling with all his might. I whistled him to me, and, grasping hold of his tail at last, with great difficulty, I reached terra firma."

"God be praised, my poor child," said I, "that you have been preserved to us! but the risk was great, and you may thank your jackal that you are alive."

His mother hastened to wash and clean the poor adventurer: his entire suit was put to soak in the Jackal's River, and we also washed the rushes, as I intended to make use of them. In their present condition they were too long and hard, and we were obliged to cut them in several strips.

I profited by the willows that Jack had brought, to commence the construction of a machine that my wife had long expected of me, viz., a weaving-machine.

Two rushes, split lengthwise, and wound round with pack-thread, so that they would dry without bending, formed four bars to make that part of the machine called the "combs." I made my sons cut me a quantity of little pieces of wood, to make the teeth for the combs; and when I had procured these first materials for my construction, I put them aside, saying nothing to anybody concerning their destination, as I wished the machine to be a surprise to my wife, and I proved insensible to all the ridicule showered upon my little sticks, which Ernest facetiously called *tooth-picks*.

"What are you going to make with all those sticks?" asked my wife, with womanish curiosity.

"Oh, nothing but a whim of mine," I answered, laughing. "I intend to make you a superb instrument of music, such as the Hottentots have called a *gom-gom*. Let me alone, and I promise you, you shall be the first to dance to its melodious sounds."

About this time, our onagra give birth to a beautiful little ass of its species. It was received with pleasure, for it not only added to our number of useful animals, but also afforded us a courser, that in future time would make quite a figure in our cavalcades. I gave it the name of "Rapid," as I designed him particularly for the saddle; and we saw with pleasure that his limbs were all beautifully proportioned.

The approach of the rainy season and the remembrance of the trouble we had had in collecting our animals last year, induced us to invent a method to render the service less painful; it was to accustom them to return to their homes at the sound of a conch, in which I had placed a bit of wood, like a flute. The pigs were the only ones that we could not manage. They were unruly and loved their liberty too much to be confined; we willing abandoned them, as the dogs could easily bring them together if desired.

Among the embellishments and comforts with which we had surrounded our winter habitation, we yet wanted a reservoir of pure water, which we were obliged to bring from the Jackal's River. The distance was too great in winter, and I wished to remedy the inconvenience before the rains came on. I conceived the idea of bringing a stream of water from the river to the grotto, and to establish a fountain, as we had done at Falcon's Nest. Bamboo canes, fitted into one another, served us for canals; we rested them on crutches of wood and a barrel sunk in the ground performed the office of a basin.

We proposed, when time permitted us, to give to this

construction the elegance and perfection it wanted. But such as it was, it answered our purpose; and my wife assured me she was just as contented with the little fountain as if it had been built of marble, and surrounded by dolphins and naiads, spouting water from their mouths.

CHAPTER XXXVII

The Approach of Winter and Wet Season—Invention of a New Light —Literary Acquisitions

THE season of rains was fast approaching, and we used all possible expedition to get in everything necessary. The grain, the fruits of all sorts which surrounded our habitation, potatoes, rice, guavas, sweet acorns, pineapples, anise, manioc, bananas, nothing in short was forgotten. We sowed our seeds as we had done the year before, hoping that the European sorts would sprout quicker and more easily on account of the moisture of the atmosphere.

My wife made us sacks of canvas which we filled, and by the aid of our patient beasts carried to the magazines, where they were emptied into large hogsheads prepared for them. But these labours were not accomplished without much trouble; for as we had planted our corn and wheat at different times, we were obliged to choose out the ripe stalks from a whole field—a work of no small difficulty. I resolved to devise some plan for a more regular cultivation the next year. We had a pair of buffaloes for all the labour that would have to be done; and all that was required, in addition to our present stock of harness, was a double yoke, which I intended to make during our winter seclusion.

But the rains had already commenced; several times we had been visited by heavy showers, which hastened our remaining occupations. By degrees the horizon became covered with thick clouds, the winds swept fearfully along the coast, the billows rose, and for the space of fifteen days we were witnesses of a scene of whose majesty and terrific grandeur man cannot form an idea. Nature seemed overturned, the trees bent to the terrible blasts, the lightning and the thunder were mingled with the wind and the storm; in one word, it was a concert of Nature's many voices, where the deep tones of the thunder served for the bass, and harmoniously blended with the sharp whistlings of the storm. It seemed to us that the storm of last year had been nothing in comparison to it. Nevertheless, the winds began to calm, and the rain, instead of beating down upon us in torrents, began to fall with that despair-inspiring uniformity, which we felt would last for twelve long weeks. The first moments of our seclusion were sad enough, but necessity reconciled us to our situation, and we began as cheerfully as possible to arrange the interior of our subterranean habitation.

We devoted our attention first to a crowd of minor wants which we only discovered by occupation, but yet were of primary necessity. I have said that our apartments were all on one floor; but the ground had not been carefully levelled, and we set to work to fill up the cavities and cut away the projections, so as to prevent any of us from breaking our necks. The fountain I had made did not answer the purpose, and the one great necessity of a good supply of water was as yet unprovided for. We also made tables and chairs, prepared for all the exigencies of our position, and endeavoured to render our long confinement as supportable as possible. But there was yet an inconvenience. We had not imagined we wanted light. There were but three openings in the grotto, besides the door: one in the kitchen, one in the work-room, and a third in my sleeping-chamber. The boys' room, and all the rest of our habitation, was plunged in the most complete darkness. The light never penetrated into the recesses of the grotto. I discovered that three or four more windows were necessary; but they could not be made before the return of fine weather, and I devised the following remedy for the defect.

Among the bamboos that I had procured as leaders for the water, was one of great size, which I had preserved. This bamboo I found by chance was just the height of our grotto. I trimmed it, and planted it in the ground about a foot deep, surrounding it with props to make it steady. I then gave Jack a hammer, a pulley, and a rope, and, appealing to his agility, I asked him to climb the pole. In a moment he was at the top, and, after having driven the pulley into the roof of the grotto, and thrown the cord over it, he descended safely to the ground. I then suspended to one end of the cord a large lantern which we found in the ship. Francis and my wife were officially charged with its supervision, and, thanks to the thousand reflectors which lined the sides of the rock, our grotto was as light as if it had been broad day. The light was an immense benefit to us, and enabled us to carry on our different occupations with zeal and comfort.

Ernest and Francis charged themselves with the task of arranging our library, and disposing, in its different shelves, the works we had saved from the wreck. Jack aided his mother in the kitchen; and Fritz, being stronger than his brothers, assisted me in the work-room.

We arranged there, by the window, a superb English turning-lathe, with all its equipments. I had often amused myself by turning in my younger days, and I now could put my knowledge of the art to some use. We also constructed a forge; anvils were fixed in large blocks of wood, and all the tools of the wheelwright and the cooper were laid out in long array on the racks I had put up next the wall. Our shop began to assume a business-like appearance, of which I was proud; and often did I congratulate myself that I had sufficiently acquainted myself, in youth, with mechanics to prevent their being entirely new to me.

The grotto every day grew more agreeable, and we were enabled to wait without ennui for the welcome light of the sun. We had our work-room, our dining-room, and our library, where we could refresh our minds after the fatigues of the body; for the cases we had saved from the ship contained a quantity of books which had belonged to the captain and officers. Besides Bibles and books of devotion, we found works on history, botany, philosophy, voyages, and travels, some enriched with engravings, which were a real treasure to us. We had also maps, several mathematical and astronomical instruments, a portable globe—an English invention, which blew up like a balloon; but the sort of works which prevailed were grammars and dictionaries of different nations: they generally form the chief stock of ship libraries.

We all knew a little of French, for this is as much in use as German throughout Switzerland. Fritz and Ernest had commenced to learn English at Zurich, and I had myself paid some attention to the language, in order to superintend their education. I now urged them to continue their studies, as English was the language of the sea, and there were very few ships that did not contain some one who understood it. Jack, who knew nothing at all, began to pay some attention to Spanish and Italian, the pomp and melody of these two languages according with his character. As for myself, I laboured hard to master the Malay tongue; for the inspection of charts and maps convinced me that we were in the neighborhood of these people.

Our grotto grew every day so comfortable that the children could not think of any name suitable to call it by: some wanted it called The Fairy Palace, others The Resplendent Grotto; but after a long discussion, we came to the conclusion that it should be called simply "Felsenheim," or the dwelling in the rock. Time rolled away so rapidly in all these occupations, that two months of the rainy season had elapsed, and I had not yet found time to make my double yokes, or a new pair of carding-combs, that my wife had teased me for a long time.

CHAPTER XXXVIII

Close of the Rainy Season— A Whale—Coral

THE end of the month of August was marked by a renewal of the bad weather. The rain, the winds, the thunder redoubled with new fury. How happy we were in the habitation we had made. What would have become of us in our aërial palace at Falcon's Nest? and our tent, how could that have withstood the storm? But at last the weather became more settled; the clouds dissipated; the rain ceased; and we were able to venture out from our grotto, to see whether the world yet remained firm.

We promenaded upon the belt of rocks that extended all along the coast; and, as we had need of liberty and exercise, we took pleasure in scaling the highest peaks, and looking over the plain which was spread out beneath us. Fritz, always daring, and whose eye almost rivalled that of his eagle, was standing upon the peak of rocks, when he perceived, upon the little island in Flamingo Bay, a black spot, the nature and form of which he could not determine; but he thought it was a shipwrecked vessel. Ernest, who mounted after him, took it for a sea-lion, such as Admiral Anson speaks of in his voyages. I determined to go and inspect it myself. We walked down to the sea-shore, emptied the rain-water from the canoe, and all set off.

The nearer we approached, the more rapidly one conjecture followed another. At last, when we were near enough to distinguish it, what was our surprise to see an enormous whale, lying on his side upon the strand.

Being ignorant whether he was dead or sleeping, I did not think it prudent to approach without precaution; consequently we turned around and steered for the other side of the island, which consisted of nothing more than a sand-bank elevated above the waves; but a rank growth of herbs and plants covered it, and it was the resort of numbers of sea-birds, whose nests and eggs we found in abundance.

There were two roads to choose, by which to reach the whale: one by climbing over the rocks, which rendered it laborious; the other longer, but far the less fatiguing. I took the first path, and commanded the boys to take the other, as I wished to examine fully this little island, which wanted but trees to render it charming. From this elevation I could see the whole coast, from Tent House to Falcon's Nest, which spectacle made me almost forget the whale; and when I reached the side where my children were, they came running toward me, screaming with joy, and carrying their hats full of shells and coral, which they had picked up on the beach. "Look, papa," said they, "what beautiful shells we have found; what can have brought them here?"

"It is the sea, my children," I answered; "the sea has thrown them up from its abyss, and it appears to be little cause for astonishment that she should bring such frail, light things as these shells, when she has thrown upon our shores a monster whose bulk is so immense."

On the return journey I related to my sons the phenomena of the existence of coral; and, while talking, we arrived at our destination, where my wife and son were ready to receive us. She admired the beauty of our coral, but observed that it was of no use in the household affairs; and when I had told her my resolution to return to the whale that afternoon, she cheerfully declared that she would accompany me. I was enchanted at this resolution, and we hastened to prepare the necessary provisions and articles for a stay of two days; for, perhaps, we might be detained on the island, and I thought it best to make preparations accordingly.

CHAPTER XXXIX

The Wale, its dissection—Uses of the different parts of the Whale

AFTER dinner, which we partook of an hour earlier than usual, I made a search for some barrels in which to put the blubber of the whale. I did not want to take the empty barrels we had at Falcon's Nest and Felsenheim, as I knew that it would be impossible to remove the disagreeable smell of oil. My wife reminded me that we yet had four tubs in our boat, which would answer my purpose very well. I fastened them to the stern of the canoe; and, after having armed my sons with knives, and hatchets, and saws, and all the cutting-instruments I could find, we weighed anchor, and directed our course toward the island where the whale lay.

Our whale looked like those of Greenland: the back was greenish black, the stomach yellowish, the fins and tail black. I immediately measured it, and I found that it was between sixty and seventy feet long, and about forty in diameter, which is about the ordinary size of these monsters of the deep. My children were astonished at the proportions of the head, which formed a third of the whole creature; its mouth was immense; and its jaws, which were full twelve feet in length were furnished with flexible appendages called "dewlaps,"[1] and which in Europe form an article of commerce. One thing which struck Fritz was the smallness of the monster's eye, which was not larger than that of an ox; and the opening by which his immense mouth communicated with his throat, was scarcely the diameter of my arm.

Fritz and Jack entered the head of the whale, and working with the hatchet and the saw, cut out the "dewlaps," which Francis and his mother carried to the boat; we cut out more than two hundred pieces of different sizes. While this was going on, Ernest and I cut several feet deep into the fat which covered the sides of the animal; we literally swam in grease, for walls of solid fat rose on each side of us. But we were not long the only claimants for the whale. A multitude of winged robbers surrounded us, eager to associate in our work. They flew round and round our heads; then, gradually approaching, they were so bold as to snatch pieces of fat from our hands. The birds were very troublesome; but my wife having made the remark that their down would be of use to her, I knocked down some with a club, and threw them into the boat. I cut from the back of the whale a long and large band of skin, out of which I wanted to make a harness for the ass and the two buffaloes. It was a difficult task, the skin was so thick, and so hard to cut. The tubs were placed in the canoe, and we set out for the coast with the new cargo we had acquired. It was for us a precious treasure, but far from agreeably obtained.

The next morning we again embarked in the canoe; but this time Francis and his mother were left behind, as they could have been of no use in the work I intended, which was to penetrate into the interior of the whale, and, if possible, to procure some parts of its immense intestines. A fresh

[1]Whalebone.

wind was blowing, and we soon arrived at the island, which
we found covered with gulls and other marine birds, who, in
spite of the canvas with which the pieces that had been cut
from the whale were covered, had made a plentiful meal. It
was necessary to have recourse to fire-arms to drive away
this horde of pillagers.

We took care, before commencing our work, to strip off
every article of clothing, excepting our pantaloons; then,
like true butchers, we opened the animal, selected from the
mass of entrails those which would best suit our purpose; I
cut them in pieces of from six to twelve feet long, and, after
having turned them inside out, washed them, and well rubbed
them with sand; they were then placed in the boat.

We abandoned the rest of our prey to the voracious birds;
and, after having loaded our boat with a new cargo of whale
blubber, we set sail for Felsenheim.

The reason that I had taken so much trouble to obtain the
whale's intestines was, that I wished to use them as vessels
to contain the oil.

When we arrived at home, we found my wife anxiously
expecting us; but the sight of our greasy habiliments almost
frightened her, and she anticipated the labour of washing
them with no very pleasurable sensations; but I consoled her
by promising miracles from the rich treasures of whale oil,
and the entrails we had brought home. We washed ourselves completely, and, after an entire change of clothing,
set out for Felsenheim.

CHAPTER XL

The Boat-propeller or Rowing Machine—A Turtle Drive

THE day had scarcely dawned when we were all up and ready for work. The four tubs of fat were raised from the ground, and, a strong pressure being applied, we squeezed out as much of the oil as possible; and as this was the finest and purest, we filled one or two of the entrails with it.

The rest was emptied into a large iron kettle, and, a slow fire being applied, it was soon reduced to a liquid state. A large iron spoon, which we had saved from the wreck, and which had been originally intended for the sugar factory, served us to empty the oil into the entrails from the kettle. All these works were carried on at a distance from Felsenheim, as we did not wish to perfume the air around our habitation with the fœtid odour of whale oil.

While we were occupied in our manufacture of oil, my wife made me a proposition which met my hearty approbation: it was to establish a new colony on the island of the whale. "We will put some fowls there," said she; "they will be safe from their two great plagues, the monkeys and the jackals."

I liked the project of my wife very much; and the children were so enchanted that they wanted to start immediately, and put it into execution. But it was now too late, and I calmed their ardour by mentioning an idea I had conceived of fitting a propeller machine to the canoe.

"Oh," cried Jack, "the canoe will go along without any rowing; how fine it will be!"

"Stop, stop," said I; "not so fast. All that I can do will be to save your arms some labour, and quicken our speed."

I immediately commenced the work. All my materials consisted of the wheel of a smoke-jack and an iron-toothed axle upon which it turned. The machine that I constructed was not a masterpiece of execution; but it answered the purpose very well. A handle attached to the wheel put the machine in motion, and two large flat pieces of whalebone, nailed together in the form of a cross, and fixed at each end of the axle, resembled the wheels of a steamboat. When the handle was turned, the wings of whalebone beat against the surface of the water, and drove the canoe forward. Its velocity was in proportion to the power imparted to the wheel.

I will not attempt to describe the transports of joy that my children evinced when they saw the canoe gliding over the surface of the water. I was astonished myself at the rapidity of our course. We had scarcely touched the land, when every one was in the boat, and begging me to make an excursion to the island of the whale. But the day was too far advanced to admit of such a thing, and I promised them that we would make, on the morrow, a grand trial of our vessel by an excursion, by sea, to the farmhouse at Prospect Hill, for the purpose of inspecting our colony there.

My proposition was well received, and we immediately began to prepare our arms and provisions, so that we could start early on the morrow.

At the first dawning of the day everybody was ready. We did not forget provisions; and my wife put up, in a double envelope of fresh leaves, a piece of the whale's tongue, which, by the recommendation of doctor Ernest, she had cooked and spiced as a delicate viand.

We gaily quitted the shore, and the strong current of the Jackal's River soon brought us into the sea; the breeze was good, and everything promised a favourable sail. We soon perceived Shark Island, the bank of sand where the whale had been stranded; and so well did our machine work, that in a short time we found ourselves in sight of Prospect Hill. I had kept at some distance from the coast, as I was afraid that there might be some hidden rocks inshore, which might destroy our frail bark.

When we had arrived opposite the "Wood of Monkeys," I ran the boat into a little creek, and landed, to replenish our stock of cocoa-nuts. It was with feelings of the keenest pleasure that we heard the crowing of the cocks through the woods, announcing the neighbourhood of the farmhouse. We re-embarked and rapidly neared Prospect Hill, and could plainly distinguish the bleating of our little herd. We landed, and directed our course toward the farmhouse.

Everything was in order; but what greatly astonished us was the wildness of the sheep and goats, who fled on all sides at our approach. My sons began to run after them; but as the long-bearded ladies were far more agile than they were, they soon grew tired of the chase, and, drawing from their pockets the strings with balls attached, they soon captured three or four of the fugitives. We distributed some potatoes and a handful of salt among them, in return for which they yielded us several bowls of most delicious milk.

We dined at Prospect Hill. The cold meats we had brought had composed our repast; but the whale's tongue was unanimously pronounced most detestable and only fit for a sailor. We gave it to Jack's jackal, the only one of our domestic animals who had followed us.

I left my wife to make the preparations for our departure, and started out with Fritz to gather some sugar-cane. I also dug up some roots of this precious article to plant on Whale Island.

We weighed anchor, or, at least, we pulled up the stone that secured us, and coasted along in the direction of Cape Disappointment, which I wished to double; but the cape still justified its name, and a long bank of sand stretching out prevented our progress, and we were obliged to turn back. I hoisted the sail, we redoubled our labours at the wheel, and, thanks to a little breeze that sprang up, were soon in sight of Whale Island.

On landing, my first care was to plant the roots I had brought from Prospect Hill; but my companions, on whose assistance I had counted, did not think the plantation of sufficient consequence for them, and ran off to the beach to gather shells. My good wife supplied their places, and we two began our labours. We had scarcely commenced when Jack came running up to us, all out of breath. "Papa, papa," cried he, "come here—quick, I have discovered the skeleton of a mammoth!"

I burst into a laugh, and informed my little boy that his skeleton was nothing more than the carcass of our whale.

"No, no," replied he; "they are not fish bones, but those of some immense animal; and, besides, they lie a great deal farther up on the sand than the whale did."

Jack implored and entreated so earnestly that I consented at last to go; but another voice soon stopped my progress.

"Run, run—this way," screamed Fritz, from some distance, waving his hand to hasten my arrival. "Quick—a monstrous turtle that we are not strong enough to turn." I caught up two handspikes and ran, as fast as possible, to the spot, where I found Ernest struggling with a monstrous turtle, which he held by one leg, but which, despite all his efforts, had reached the border of the sea. I arrived just in time; and, throwing one of the spikes to Fritz, we were able to turn the enormous animal on its back.

It really was of prodigious size, about eight feet and a half in length, and could not possibly weigh less than five hundred pounds. I did not know how we should be able to carry it away; however, the position in which we had placed it gave us time for reflection.

But Jack had not forgotten his mammoth, and continued teasing me to go and see it. I soon perceived that it really was our whale; but the birds of prey had not left a morsel of flesh on the bones, which had blanched in the sun. I showed him our footprints in the sand, and some morsels of whale-bone which we had forgotten.

"Can we not," said Fritz, in considering the skeleton of a whale, "draw from this mountain of bones some utility?"

"I do not know," said I, "what use we can make of them; the Hollanders make palings of them, and also rustic chairs, which produce a fine effect; and we will one day, when we have leisure, make a philosophical chair for our museum." Discussing in this manner, we arrived at our plantation. I perceived that it was too late to finish our work that night. We buried the roots, yet unplanted, in the ground, and deferred till another day this important occupation. The giant turtle was now our grand object: I brought the boat round to where he lay extended on his back, and, forming a circle around him, we debated as to the means of transporting him.

"Zounds! gentlemen," said I, striking my forehead, "we need not embarrass ourselves *much*; instead of carrying this monster, let him conduct *us* back to Felsenheim. A turtle

makes an excellent equipage on the sea: Fritz and I have
tried the experiment."

My idea was a happy one, and every one was glad. I
commenced by emptying out the barrel of water we had
brought; then, turning the turtle over on his feet, we fastened the barrel to his back, so that it was impossible for
him to sink and draw us with him; a cord, passed through a
hole which we broke in the upper shell, served me for reins;
and without losing time we all embarked for home. I placed
myself in the prow of the canoe, with a hatchet to cut the
cord in case of need.

Our course was accomplished rapidly and safely: a hand-
spike that I held in my hand served me for a whip, and a
blow well applied would rectify any deviation from the
track. Master Ernest, the professor, compared us to Neptune gliding over the waves drawn by dolphins.

We arrived safely at Felsenheim, and our first care was to
secure our turtle, and to replace the empty barrel by strong
ropes. But as we could not keep him long in this way, we
finished his life the next morning, and his enormous shell
was destined to serve as a basin to our fountain in the
grotto. The work cost some trouble and time, as it was very
difficult to detach the flesh from the shell. It was a superb
piece of meat, full six feet by three, and afforded us material for many a delicious pot of soup. We inquired into all
our works on natural history, and we came to the conclusion
(the professor and I) that our turtle was the giant green
turtle, the largest of all.

CHAPTER XLI

Weaving Machine—Basket making —The Alarm—A Dangerous Visitor —The Ass Falls a Victim

WE had had so much trouble in harvesting our crops the last season that we had resolved, instead of trusting them to the ground without any order or regularity, to prepare a field which could receive them all at the same time, and where they could ripen together. But as our animals were not yet sufficiently accustomed to the yoke to warrant our undertaking the task, I was obliged to defer it till some future period.

In the meantime, I employed myself in constructing a weaving-machine for my wife: our garments had become so tattered and torn that the machine was of incalculable benefit to us. It was neither perfect nor handsome, and nothing more could be expected. As we had none of the wheat flour that the weavers use to make paste, which they employ in hardening the warp, and preventing the threads from tangling, I substituted the glue of fish; and I may confess, without self-praise, that my composition was better than that of the weavers, for the fish-glue preserves a humidity that the ordinary glue does not, and by employing it one can weave in a dry situation, instead of descending into cellars, where the weavers from time immemorial have been obliged to confine themselves. From this fish-glue I also made window-panes, not well calculated, it is true, for windows exposed to the rain; but they answered for ours, which, on account of their deep embrasures, were protected from storm.

These two successes encouraged me, and I resolved to try my hand at another thing, or, to speak poetically, "add another flower to my wreath." My little cavaliers had long

tormented me to make them saddles and bridles, and our
beasts had need of yokes and other harness. I commenced
my work and established myself as saddler; kangaroos and
sea-dogs furnished me with the necessary leather, and I used
for wadding the moss that the Molucca pigeons had discovered to us. But as this moss would have matted together,
and grown hard under the rider, I employed my sons in
twisting it into cords, in which state it was left some time,
and then untwisted; by that means we obtained frizzed hair,
as elastic as that of horses. In a short time we had saddles
and stirrups, bits and bridles, yokes and collars, each adapted
to the strength of the animal for which it was intended.

But this sedentary course of life did not suit the restless
minds of my young people, and they earnestly begged me to
take them hunting in the country. I put the matter off, and
took in hand another sort of work, the want of which we felt
sensibly. I speak of the making of baskets, a number of
which articles we needed to carry our rice, roots, grain, etc.
Our first attempts were clumsy enough, and we reserved
them for our potato baskets. We gradually improved, and
when I thought we were skilful enough, I ventured to use
those Spanish rushes that had cost Jack so dear, and we
made a number of fine baskets; they were not as finished
workmanship as more skilful hands would have effected, but
they were light and strong, and that was all we cared for.

My sons had made a large basket to put manioc roots in,
and, in a fit of mischief, Jack and Ernest had passed a
bamboo cane through the handles, and, putting little Francis
in the basket, set off on a full run, while the poor fellow
endeavoured in vain to stop them.

Fritz, who had been looking at them, turned to me,
saying, "An idea has struck me, papa; why cannot we make
a litter of rushes for mamma, and then she will be able to
accompany us in our distant excursions?"

"Really," I replied, "a litter would be much more convenient than the back of the ass, and much easier than the
cart: we will try what can be done."

My children were delighted at the plan; but my wife
laughingly observed, "that she would make but a poor
figure seated in a wicker basket."

"Never fear," said I, "we will make you a fine palanquin
such as are used in Persia and Hindostan."

We immediately put the design into execution: the buffalo and the bull were brought out; two poles, which supported a large basket, were suspended by cords on each side, and Ernest jumped in to make the first trial. Jack mounted Storm, who was placed at the head, and Francis Broumm, who supported the hinder part, and they set off. The first steps answered admirably; the basket, balanced between the poles, resembled a luxurious carriage on its springs of steel. But it was not exactly a pleasant carriage-drive that Ernest enjoyed; for, at a given signal agreed on by his coachmen, they whipped up their beasts, and set off at full gallop, subjecting Ernest to a punishment as novel as it was ridiculous, which consisted in forcing him to perform a sort of *basket-dance* at each jump of his conductors. The fun was violent, but it was harmless, and we could not help laughing to see the phlegmatic Ernest so tossed about.

We then all returned to our basket-making; but we had scarcely recommenced, when Fritz, whose eagle eye was always making discoveries, suddenly started up as if frightened at a cloud of dust which had arisen on the other side of the river, in the direction of Falcon's Nest.

"There is some large animal there," said he, "to judge from the dust it has raised; besides, it is plainly coming in this direction."

"I cannot imagine what it is," I answered; "our large animals are in the stable, resting themselves after the experiment of the palanquin."

"Probably two or three sheep, or, perhaps, our sow, frolicking in the sand," observed my wife.

"No, no," replied Fritz, quickly; "it is some singular animal: I can perceive its movements: it rolls and unrolls itself alternately; I can see the rings of which it is formed. See, it is raising itself up, and looks like a huge mast in the dust; it advances—stops—marches on; but I cannot distinguish either feet or legs."

I ran for the spy-glass we had saved from the wreck, and directed it toward the dust.

"I can see it plainly," said Fritz; "it has a greenish-coloured body. What do you think of it, papa?"

"That we must fly as fast as possible, and entrench ourselves in the grotto."

"What do you think it is?"

"A serpent—a huge serpent, advancing directly for us."

"Shall I run for the guns, to be ready to receive him?"

"Not here. The serpent is too powerful to permit of our attacking him, unless we are ourselves in a place of safety."

We hastened to gain the interior of the grotto, and prepared to receive our enemy. It was a boa-constrictor, and he advanced so quickly that it was too late to take up the boards on Family Bridge.

We watched all his movements, and saw him stretching out his enormous length along the bank of the river. From time to time the reptile would raise up the forepart of his body twenty feet from the ground, and turn his head gently from right to left, as if seeking for his prey, while he darted a triple-barbed tongue from his half-open jaws. He crossed the bridge, and directed his course straight for the grotto: we had barricaded the door and the windows as well as we were able, and ascended into the dove-cot, to which we had made an interior entrance; we passed our muskets through the holes in the door, and waited silently for the enemy—it was the silence of terror.

But the boa, in advancing, had perceived the traces of man's handiwork, and he came on hesitatingly, until at last he stopped, about thirty paces directly in front of our position. He had scarcely advanced thus far when Ernest, more through fear than through any war-like ardour, discharged his gun, and thus gave a false signal. Jack and Francis followed his example; and my wife, whom the danger had rendered bold, also discharged her gun.

The monster raised his head; but either because none of the shots had touched him, or because the scales of his skin were impenetrable to balls, he appeared to have received no wound. Fritz and I then fired, but without any effect, and the serpent glided away with inconceivable rapidity toward the marsh which our ducks and geese inhabited, and disappeared in the rushes.

The neighbourhood of the boa threw me into the most uneviable state of mind; for I could think of no way to rid ourselves of him, and our united forces were as nothing against such an enemy. I expressly commanded my whole family to remain in the grotto, and forbade them opening the door without my permission.

The fear of our terrible neighbour kept us shut up three

days in our retreat—three long days of anguish and alarm—
during which time I suffered no one to break the rule I had
established; the interior service of the grotto was the only
consideration that could induce me to break it, and even
then I allowed no one to go beyond the reservoir of the
fountain.

The monster had given us no signs of his presence, and
we would have supposed him departed, either by traversing
the marsh, or by some unknown passage in the rock, if the
agitation which reigned among our aquatic animals had not
assured us of his presence. Every evening the whole colony
of ducks and geese would direct their course to the bay,
making a terrible noise, and sail away for Whale Island,
where they found a safe asylum.

My embarrassment daily increased; and the immovability
of the enemy rendered our position very painful. I was
afraid that a direct attack might cost us the lives of one or
more of our little family. Our dogs could do nothing against
such a foe; and to have exposed any one of our beasts of
burden would have been certain destruction to it. On the
other hand, our provisions daily diminished, as the season
was not yet far enough advanced for us to have laid in any
winter stores. In a word, we were in a most deplorable
situation, when heaven came to our aid. The instrument that
effected our deliverance was our poor old jackass, the companion of our wanderings, and faithful servant.

The fodder that we happened to have in the grotto had
diminished frightfully: it was necessary to nourish the cow,
as she contributed in great part to our subsistence, and some
must be taken from the other animals. In this dilemma I
resolved to set them at liberty, and let them provide for
their own nourishment. As inconvenient as this measure
was, it was better than to see us all dying of hunger, shut up
in the grotto. I thought that if we could get them on the
other side of the river they would find a plentiful supply of
food, and be in safety as long as the boa remained buried in
the rushes. I was afraid to cross Family Bridge, lest I should
arouse the monster, and I decided to ford at the spot where
our first crossing was made. My plan was to attach the
animals together. Fritz, mounted on his onagra, would direct the front of the procession, while I would take care that
the marsh was effected in good order. I recommended to my

son, at the first sign of the serpent's presence, to fly, as fast as his beast would carry him, to Falcon's Nest. As to our animals, I left to Providence the care of watching over and saving them. For my part, I proposed to post myself on a rock that overlooked the marsh, and in case of an attack on the part of the serpent, retreat to the grotto, where a well-directed discharge of firearms would rid us of him.

I then loaded all our arms; my sons were placed as videttes in the dove-cot, with orders to observe the movements of the enemy, while Fritz and I arranged our beasts as aforesaid. But a little misunderstanding put an end to all my plans. My wife, who had charge of the door, did not wait for the signal, and opened it before the animals were attached together. The ass, who had grown very lively, considering his age, by his three days' rest and good feed, no sooner saw a ray of light than he shot out of the door like an arrow, and was away in the open plain before we could stop him. It was a comical sight to see him kicking his heels in the air; and Fritz would have mounted his onagra, and ridden out after him, but I restrained him, and contented myself by trying every manner of persuasion to induce the poor animal to come back. We called him by his name; we made use of our cow-horn; but all was useless—the unruly fellow exulted in his liberty, and, as if urged on by some fatality, he advanced direct to the marsh. But what horror froze our veins when, suddenly, we saw the horrid serpent emerging from the rushes! He elevated his head about ten feet from the ground, darted out his forked tongue, and crawled swiftly on toward the ass. The poor fellow soon saw his danger, and began to run, braying with all his might; but neither his cries nor his legs could save him from his terrible enemy, and in a moment he was seized, enveloped, and crushed in the monstrous rings that the serpent threw around him.

My wife and sons uttered a cry of terror, and we fled in haste to the grotto, from whence we could view the horrible combat between the boa and the ass. My children wanted to fire, and deliver, said they, the poor jackass; but I forbade them to do it.

"What can you do," said I, "with firearms? The boa is too much occupied with his prey to abandon it, and, besides, if you wound him, perhaps we may become the vic-

tims of his fury." The loss of our ass was great, it was true,
but I hoped that it would save us from a greater.

The boa proceeded with horrible avidity to his repast.
The ass was dead; we had heard his last bray stifled by the
pressure of the boa, and we could now distinctly hear the
cracking of his bones. The monster, to give himself more
power, had wound his tail about a piece of rock, which gave
it the force of a lever. When the monster judged his preparation sufficient, he commenced to swallow the prey he had
secured. We observed that as he advanced the animal lost
his strength; and when all had been swallowed he remained
perfectly torpid and insensible.

I saw that the time had now arrived, and I exclaimed,
"Now, my children, now the serpent is in our power!"

I then set out from the grotto, carrying my loaded gun in
my hand; Fritz followed close by my side; Jack came next,
but the more timid Ernest lingered behind. On approaching
the reptile, I found that my suppositions were right, and
that it was the giant boa of the naturalists. The serpent raised
its head, and darting on me a look of powerless anger, again
let it fall.

Fritz and I fired together, and both our shots entered the
skull of the animal; but they did not produce death, and the
eyes of the serpent sparkled with rage. We advanced nearer,
and, firing our pistols directly through the eye, we saw its
rings contract, a slight quiver ran through its body, and it
lay dead upon the sand before us, stretched out like the
mast of a ship.

CHAPTER XLII

Discovery of a Crystal Grotto— Further Exploration

WE had nothing more to fear from the neighbourhood of the boa; but I was afraid it might have either left its mate (it was a female) behind it, or else a nest of little ones, which in time would spread terror through the land. I resolved, in consequence, to undertake two expeditions—the one through the marsh, the other toward Falcon's Nest, through the passage in the rock, where I supposed the boa had got through.

We set out loaded with our hunting equipage. We carried, besides our arms, some boards, and the bladders of sea-dogs, to sustain us on the water if necessary. The boards we wanted to assist us in our march; for, by placing one before the other, and taking them up, we made a solid walk of wood. This was a great convenience, and enabled us to search the marsh thoroughly. We easily recognized traces of the boa; the rushes were bent down where it had passed through, and there were deep spiral impressions in the wet ground where it had rested its enormous rings. But we discovered nothing that induced us to believe that the boa had a companion: we found neither eggs, nor little ones— nothing but a nest of dried rushes, and I did not think that the boa had constructed even that. Arrived at the end of the marsh, we made an interesting discovery; it was that of a new grotto, which opened out of the rock, and out of which flowed a little stream that passed on among the rushes of the marsh.

The grotto was hung with stalactites, which rose in immense columns on each side, as if to sustain the vault, and formed themselves into singular and beautiful designs. We remained some time in admiration of this miracle of nature, and as we walked on, I remarked that the ground upon which we trod was composed of an extremely fine and white sort of earth, which, after examining it, I recognized as being "fullers' clay." I immediately gathered some handfuls, and carefully placed them in my pocket-handkerchief.

"Here," said I to my sons, who were regarding me with astonishment, "here is a discovery that will be very welcome to your mother; and henceforth, if we bring her dirty clothes, we will bring her something to wash them with, for here is soap."

"I thought," said Ernest, "that soap was the result of human industry, and not a production of the earth."

"You thought right; the soap that is ordinarily used is composed of a certain salt, the acidity of which is corrected by the addition of grease and so forth, which weakens its power greatly. But this fabrication is tedious and costly, and men have been so fortunate as to find a sort of earth in which is united certain qualities of the soap; it is this we have found, and it is called 'fullers' clay,' because it is used to clean woollen goods."

We had approached the source of the spring while conversing; and Fritz, who was a little in advance, cried out that the rock had a large opening on one side. We ran forward, and soon found ourselves in a new cavern. We fired off a pistol, and we were able to judge by the echo that the grotto extended to a great distance. We then lighted two candles, with which our knapsacks were provided; they burned without obstacle, and the pure light assured us of the salubrity of the air. Having left the others behind, Fritz and I continued to advance, when suddenly we saw our torches reflected from every side of the rock.

"Ah, papa," cried Fritz, in a transport of joy, "see! see! a salt grotto! look at the enormous blocks of salt lying at our feet."

"You are very much mistaken, indeed," I answered; "these masses are not salt; if they were, the water which drips from the rock would have melted them long ago; instead of salt it is crystal: we are really in a palace of rock-crystal."

"Better yet—a palace of crystal! what an immense treasure for us!"

"Yes; such a treasure as the gold mine was to Robinson Crusoe."

When we reappeared at the entrance of the grotto, we found Jack alone. He conducted us to the border of the swamp, where we found Ernest tranquilly employed in making a rush basket such as fishermen use, consisting of a frame of long stalks, terminated at the end by a funnel, through which the fish passed, but could not return.

"Quick, quick!" he cried, when he saw us approaching, "I have killed a young boa."

We had been talking so much of serpents, etc., that the poor boy had mistaken a superb eel, four feet in length, for a snake; he had walked straight up to it, hit it two or three blows on the head with his gun, with as much courage as would have sufficed to kill a dozen boas.

The examination that I made of the snake humbled the pride of the victor; but the eel was a great treat for us, and we returned home to Felsenheim.

I had as yet only half accomplished my design, and there remained all the country about the farmhouse yet unexplored; and besides, I wished, if it were possible, by fortifying the passages in the rock, to keep out all such visitors as the one we had lately received. I made sure, before we set out, against any accident that might happen: we took plenty of provisions, arms, vessels of all sorts, torches to scare away all intruders on our night encampments, in short, everything that would render our excursion safer and less disagreeable.

We advanced in good order along the avenue of Falcon's Nest, and discovered the marks of the boa's progress half effaced by the wind. We found everything in good order at the Nest; the harvest and the fruit-trees gave promise of an abundant crop. The goats and sheep received us joyfully, and came up of their own accord to receive some salt we threw them in passing. We did not stop, as the Lake farmhouse was the object of our expedition; and we wished to arrive as soon as possible, in order to gather, before night, cotton enough to make some pillows and mattresses that might render our slumbers more agreeable.

The farther we advanced, the fewer traces we found of the serpent. We could not see a single monkey in the cocoawood; and the crowing of our cocks, mingled with the bleating of our herds, gave promise of good order at the farmhouse; and we were not disappointed. As soon as we arrived, our good housekeeper set about procuring us some dinner, while we went to gather the cotton.

After dinner I announced that we would immediately commence our search, and we divided into three parties, each one charged to explore a part of the country. Ernest and his mother had, for their division, the guard of the provisions and the collection of all the ripe blades in the rice-field; to defend them we left our brave dog Billy. Fritz and Jack, accompanied by Turk and the jackal, took the right bank of the lake, while I followed the left, with Francis, and his two young dogs. It was the first time that the little fellow had shared in any of our expeditions, or had had a gun entrusted to him; he marched along with his head up, and as proud as a new-made officer; and he burned with ardour to make trial of his new weapon. But the noise of our steps among the dried rushes frightened only some herons, and they flew so suddenly and quickly that it was impossible to shoot them. Francis began to grow despairing at his ill success, when suddenly we found ourselves in presence of an innumerable quantity of wild geese and black swans, which covered the waters in all directions. Frank was just about to fire into the mass, when suddenly a sort of deep, prolonged cry, like a bellow, issued from the middle of the rushes. We stopped, astonished, and a second after the cry was repeated.

"I am sure," said Francis, "that it is the little onagra."

"Impossible," said I; "he would not leave his mother; and, besides, we must have heard him as he passed along. It is more likely to be a swamp-bird, called a bittern."

I called the dogs to my side, and, setting them in the rushes, presently heard the report of Francis's gun. But, instead of firing in the air, he had discharged his gun right into the thickest part of the rushes, and I saw the birds that the dogs had disturbed flying away safe and sound.

"You awkward fellow," said I; "you have let your game escape you."

"On the contrary, papa, I have him! I have him!" repeated he, with passionate emotion. "Look!"

So saying, he pulled out of the rushes an animal resembling an agouti, and which the little hunter had already christened by that name.

I examined it with attention, and discovered that there was much difference between it and the agouti.

This one was about two feet in length, had incisor teeth like the rabbit, webbed feet, long snout, but no tail at all.

"You have killed a rare and curious beast," said I to my little boy. "It is an inhabitant of South America, of the same family as the agouti and peccaries, but much rarer. It is a cabiai, and what is more, a cabiai of the largest size."

"And what sort of an animal is this cabiai? I have never heard of him before."

"Oh, yes; you heard him bray just now; for it was his cry that I attributed to the bittern. This animal profits by the darkness of night to provide his food: he runs fast, can swim well, and has the power of remaining a long time under water; he eats seated on his hind legs; and as to his cry, it sounds exactly like the braying of an ass."

But it was now time to return home, and Francis rejoiced at the prospect of his triumph over his brothers. He took up his cabiai, threw it over his shoulder, and although I saw that it was much too heavy for him, I thought I would let him have the merit of the whole affair.

We found, on returning, Master Ernest tranquilly seated on the bank of the river, and surrounded by a prodigious number of enormous rats which he had killed. The phlegmatic philosopher then recounted to us the history of this massacre.

"We were occupied," said he, "my mother and I, in collecting the ripe rice-blades, when I discovered, at a little distance, a sort of high, solid causeway, which looked like a road constructed in the middle of the swamp. I immediately set off to discover what it was, and Master Knips with me. But we had scarcely advanced one step when he darted from my side in pursuit of an animal that quickly disappeared in a sort of hole bored in the causeway. I remarked, on advancing, that the two sides of the bank were pierced all along with these holes, all of the same form and size. I was curious to know what they contained, and I introduced into the opening a long bamboo cane that I had in my hand. I had scarcely drawn it out when there issued forth a legion of animals similar to the first. Knips ran after them; but the

rice grew so thick that he could not get along. An idea then
occurred to me to place my rice-sack over the hole. I did so;
and beating the top of the causeway with a stick, a great
number ran into the sack. I then began to beat the bag with
my stick, so as to kill the prisoners. But imagine my surprise
when I found myself assailed by a whole army of rats who
emerged from every side, and began to run up my pantaloons. Knips made most desperate attempts. I could do
nothing with my stick, and I cannot tell what might have
happened if Billy had not heard my voice, and come to my
assistance. He rushed bravely upon the army of rats, and
made so terrible a slaughter that the enemy fled in terror.
Those that you behold fell victims to my stick and the formidable teeth of Billy; the rest of the army took refuge in their
holes."

The narration of Ernest excited my curiosity, and I wished
to see for myself the causeway with its inhabitants, and I
recognized a series of works similar to those of the beaver,
with the single difference, that they were not so extensive. I
made my sons observe the conformity that existed between
these animals and the beaver of the north; both had the
same membrane at the feet to facilitate swimming; both had
the flat tail, and both were provided with two little bags of
musk.

Fritz and Jack returned during these conversations; they
brought back a ruffled moor-hen and a nest of eggs: we
placed them under one of our hens that happened to be
sitting at the time. We then all united around a savoury
mess of rice that my good wife had prepared. She had
cooked a small piece of the cabiai; but it was detestable, and
we abandoned it to our dogs, who would not taste the flesh
of the rats on account of the smell of musk.

The repast was a merry one. We were all delighted to
have found no traces of the boa; and my mischievous boys
showered a flood of epigrams upon the "Conqueror of Rats,"
as they called poor Ernest.

The conversation naturally turned upon what we should
do with our rat-skins; and it was determined upon to make a
carpet of them, to preserve the floor of our house dry. Our
first care was to clean them with sand and ashes, as we were
accustomed to do.

Presently Jack and Francis ran to their knapsacks.

"Look here, sir!" said the youngest, as he threw some pine cones before the philosopher.

"Look here, sir!" said Jack, placing on the table some little shining apples, of a pale green, which exhaled a strong odour of cinnamon.

A general cry of admiration greeted them.

"Stop!" cried I. "Before tasting this fruit, Master Knips must undergo the customary trial, for I am afraid these are the fruit of the manchineel tree; and the manchineel apples produce most terrible colics."

I then opened one of the fruit, and discovered that I had been deceived by the appearance. The manchineel apple has a nut, and these had very small seeds, like the common apple. While I was showing this difference to my children, Master Knips snatched one of the apples from the table and commenced to eat it, smacking his lips as if it were something excellent. This determined the matter. I distributed the fruit, and on tasting them we declared them most excellent. Fritz wished to know their name.

"They are," said I, "cinnamon apples; I think you gathered them from a low shrub; did you not, Jack?"

"Oh, yes, yes—shrub—cinnamon. I am falling asleep," stammered out the stupid fellow.

I then gave the signal for retiring. We took all necessary precautions for safety during the night, and we sought, on our mattresses of cotton, the repose that the fatigues of the day had rendered necessary.

CHAPTER XLIII

The Pig Hunt—The Supply—The Otaheitan Roast—Ham Smoking

THE next morning, at break of day, we renewed our search. We directed our course to the sugar-cane plantation, where I had built a hut of branches, but we found it all blown down; and setting up our tent, we resolved to pass the forenoon there.

While my wife was making preparations for dinner, we explored the sugar-canes, as I thought it would be a natural retreat for the serpents, if there yet remained any in this part of the country. Happily, our investigation was without any result; and we were turning to quit the sugar-canes, when suddenly our dogs began to bark, as if they had taken some dangerous animal. We could perceive nothing; but as it was not prudent to venture among the canes, I ordered my sons to direct their course toward the plain, and we soon found ourselves clear of the canes. At the same time there emerged from them a troop of pigs of quite respectable size and strength. I at first thought it was the young family of our old sow; but their number, the grey colour of their skin, and the singular manner in which they walked, soon banished that idea. They trotted one after the other with a precision and regularity that would have done honour to a troop on parade. I took good aim, fired both barrels of my gun, and two of the animals fell. The loss did not seem to make much impression on the rest of the troop, who trotted on as before. It was a singular spectacle to see the whole family marching along the borders of the sugar-canes, with an imperturbable tranquillity; every one followed exactly in his place, without any pushing for precedence; and, on examining them more closely, we found that there was but one footstep in the sand, so regularly did they march.

But Jack and Fritz, who were a little in advance, could not let them pass unheeded. Bang, bang, went their pistols, and two more animals bit the dust; the dogs also had their part in the victory, and each one strangled a victim.

I immediately recognized them as being a sort of hog, and as I knew that one part, if not immediately removed, would render the meat uneatable, I immediately set about the operation, and my sons gladly aided me, so rejoiced were they at such a splendid booty; for we had six pigs, each, on an average, three feet in length.

While we were thus occupied, I heard the reports of two other guns in the distance; I conjectured them to have come from Ernest and Francis, who had overtaken the pigs. I was right; and Ernest, who soon returned with the waggon for which I had sent Fritz, confirmed me in my conjecture. We thus had in possession three more pigs, for Billy had also done his duty.

The arrival of the doctor naturally provoked a discussion on the name of our game. Fritz thought that these were the Otaheitan pigs of which Captain Cook speaks. Ernest was of another opinion, and maintained that they were peccaries. This animal is very common in Guiana and South America. Before loading the waggon we resolved to clean our game to diminish the weight. Although we worked as diligently as possible, the work was not yet finished at dinner-time, and we were glad to find in the sugar-cane a cordial that refreshed and nourished us. We set out for the tent; but my boys were so proud of our chase that they determined to convert our convoy into a triumphal march: they cut some green boughs and decorated our equipage; they adorned their caps and guns with flowers, and we made our entrance chanting a song of victory.

"You have kept me waiting long enough, gentlemen," said my wife; "your dinner is all spoiled; but, bless me! what a quantity of meat! Why should you abuse the provision nature has so liberally provided by killing more than we require?"

We justified ourselves as well as we were able, and my children offered their mother the sugar-canes they had brought home.

Fritz proposed to regale the family with an Otaheitan roast. We received his proposition, but it was put off till the morrow, as the preparation of our pigs precluded all thoughts of anything else.

I sent the two smaller boys to gather a quantity of green branches and leaves, with which to smoke our pork, and we then set to work. Ernest skinned the pigs. Fritz and I cut them up, and my wife salted the pieces. I piled the hams all together, so that the salt would penetrate every part, and we also poured salted water over them and allowed them to remain until the hut for smoking was constructed. As for the heads and bones, they were abandoned to the dogs.

The next morning, Fritz recalled to my memory the promise I had made to allow him to serve us for dinner an Otaheitan roast. He began by digging a deep trench; he then took the pig he had reserved for the purpose, washed it with care, rubbed the interior with salt, and filled it with a sort of stuffing made of meat, potatoes, and different roots.

When the trench was full of combustibles, Fritz set it on fire, and from time to time the boys threw in, by the direction of their elder brother, a quantity of pebbles, which soon became red hot.

My wife observed all these particulars with a look of incredulity.

"Beautiful cookery you will make," said she, "with an entire pig, some ashes, and a hole in the ground—delicious eating I do not doubt!"

Nevertheless, notwithstanding her sarcasms, she could not help giving the boys some advice, and she aided Fritz in giving his pig the graceful turn that roast pigs should always have to taste good.

When these preparations were finished, our cook-in-chief enveloped his "roast" in leaves and pieces of bark; a hole was made in the burning cinders large enough to receive it, and it was then covered with red-hot stones, and the hole filled up with earth to prevent the air from penetrating.

Fritz let his "roast" cook for about two hours; and it was not without astonishment that, after having taken off the triple layer of earth, cinders, and stones, the most delicious odour saluted our olfactories. I scarcely expected anything eatable, and we had before us meat cooked to a nicety, combined with a spicy perfume that would have done honour to a Parisian cook. Fritz triumphed: his good mother avowed that she was conquered, and every one proceeded, without delay, to prove the pig. Some ashes which had fallen on it were carefully removed, and the meat was pronounced delicious.

During the three days while our meat was being smoked, I had every day, with my sons, explored the country. These excursions discovered to us no traces of the boa; but they very seldom ended without our bringing home some little addition to our comforts and luxuries.

One day we directed our course toward the wood of bamboo, and returned home loaded with cups of all dimensions, formed from rushes, which we sawed apart at every knot; some of them were very large, twenty inches in diameter. We also made another discovery the same day: it was that each knot of the rushes distilled a sugary matter which crystallized in the sun, and resembled candied sugar. These rushes also furnished us a quantity of long, strong thorns, which filled the place of nails admirably.

We also made an excursion to Prospect Hill; but we found every thing there in the greatest disorder: the walls of the farmhouse were pulled down, and the cattle gone. The monkeys had passed that way, and left unequivocal traces of their progress.

We then surrounded the hut, where our hams were suspended, with a rampart of earth, and fortified it with branches and stones, so as effectually to keep out all intruders; and we arranged everything so that we might be ready to set off on the morning of the fourth day, and commence our explorations beyond the defile that had been the barrier between the district we had inhabited for nearly three years, and an unknown land, which we had but once entered, and then were nearly destroyed by a troop of buffaloes.

CHAPTER XLIV

Excursion into the Savanna—Two Horsemen—The Ostrich Hunt— The Nest—The Land Turtles

WE began our march at daylight, and, after having journeyed on for about two hours, I gave the signal for a halt, as about gunshot from the defile which separated the two countries appeared to me to be a favourable spot for our encampment. It was situated on an elevated point that commanded a far extended prospect, and was defended on one side by a thick pine forest.

Fritz wanted me, before quitting the place, to leave, as a mark of our passage, a fortress, after the manner of the Kamschatkans, which is simply composed of some boards, elevated by stones at each corner, to a height sufficient to keep out all savage animals. Before commencing this work, we made an investigation of the forest round about; but we discovered nothing but two "margays," or wild cats, who fled into the forest before we could level a gun at them.

The rest of the morning was devoted to the fortification of our encampment. We then dined; but the heat was so powerful that we were obliged to postpone our excursion into the savanna until the morrow.

Nothing troubled the repose of the night. We were up at daylight, and in a few moments our preparations were complete. I took with me my three eldest sons, as I wished to be in force on entering into a country as yet unknown. Francis remained with his mother to take care of the baggage; and, after breakfast, we packed some provisions, and took leave of our good mother, who saw us depart without uneasiness.

We passed through the defile, at the extremity of which we had erected a palisade of bamboo and thorny palm; but it had all been torn down, and we could easily trace on the sand the spiral imprints of the boa, clearly demonstrating that he had come from savanna through this passage. I intended to erect a solid rampart here, that should be proof against the attack of any animal; but I was obliged to defer the execution of the plan until some other time.

We had now ventured into a country we had entered but once before. Jack recognized the place where we had taken the buffalo; the river which divided the plain was bordered by a rich line of vegetation. We followed its course for some time, and arrived at the grotto where my son had taken the young jackal; but the farther we advanced vegetation disappeared, and we soon found ourselves in the middle of an immense plain, only bounded by the horizon. The sun beat right down on our heads, the sand burned our feet—in one word, it was a desert—a desert without a single tree—a desert of sand, the only green things being a few withered geraniums and some sort of grass that contrasted strangely with the aridity of the soil. On crossing the river, we had filled our gourds with fresh water, but the sun had heated it so that we could not drink it, and we were obliged to throw it away.

After two hours of painful journeying we arrived at the foot of a hill that we had perceived afar off: it was a rock that elevated itself in the middle of the desert, and afforded us a refuge against the rays of the sun. We were too fatigued to climb the rock and reconnoitre the country: we could scarcely stand against the overpowering rays of the sun, and our dogs were as tired as ourselves; we were isolated in the middle of the desert, and could see the river in the distance, like a silver thread, winding through its green banks. It was like the Nile, beheld from a mountain under the burning sun of Nubia.

We had scarcely been seated five minutes when Master Knips, who had accompanied us, suddenly disappeared over the rock, having probably scented some brother monkeys in the neighbourhood; our dogs, also, and the jackal deserted us; but we were too tired to call them back.

I brought out some morsels of sugar-cane and distributed them among the boys, for our thirst was terrible. This refreshment restored our appetites, and some rounds of roast peccary furnished us with an excellent repast.

Suddenly Fritz, whose excellent sight was always making discoveries, cried out,

"What do I see! There are two horsemen galloping up towards us. There, a third has joined them—doubtless they are Arabs of the desert."

"Arabs!" said Ernest! "Bedouins you mean."

"Bedouins are but one division of the great family of Arabs, and your brother was right," said I; "but take my spy-glass, Fritz; your news astonishes me."

"Oh, I see now a number of waggons loaded with hay; but they are so distant I can scarcely distinguish anything; something extraordinary is certainly going on."

"Let me have the glass," cried Jack, impatiently; and he declared he saw a crowd of cavaliers who carried little lances, with banners at the point.

"Come, give me the glass now," said I; "your imaginations are too poetic to be relied upon."

I applied the glass to my eye, and, after having looked some time attentively—

"Well," said I to Jack, "your Arabs, your cavaliers with lances, your hay-carts, what do you think they have been transformed into?"

"Camelopards, perhaps."

"No; although not a bad idea, yet they are ostriches, and chance has thrown a splendid chase into our hands; and if you will take my advice, we will not let these beautiful inhabitants of the desert pass us by without measuring our strength with theirs."

The ostriches were rapidly approaching, and it was time to think of some mode of capturing them. It seemed to me that the best way would be to wait until they came up, and then attack them by surprise. I ordered Fritz and Jack to go in search of the dogs, whilst Ernest and I sought some shelter to conceal us from the ostriches. We threw ourselves down behind some large tufts of a plant that grew among the rocks, and which I recognized as the euphorbia, commonly called wolf's milk, and the juice of which is one of the most active poisons in the world.

Jack and Fritz now returned with our faithful companions, whom, from their wet skins, we easily judged to have been taking a bath somewhere.

The ostriches were now within eyesight, and I could distinguish that the family was composed of three females and a male, who was easily recognized by the long white feathers of his tail. We crouched closer to the ground, and held our dogs close to our sides, for fear lest their impatience should defeat our stratagem.

I now perceived that the ostriches were aware of our presence—they appeared to hesitate in their march; but, as we remained immovable, they at last seemed reassured, and were advancing directly to us, when our dogs, whom we could not keep quiet, suddenly sprang out upon them. Away went the timid birds, with a rapidity that can be compared to nothing else but the wind driving before it a bundle of feathers. Their feet did not appear to touch the ground, their half-extended wings had the appearance of sails, and the wind greatly accelerated their velocity. I then ordered Fritz to unhood his eagle; he did so, and the noble bird soon lit upon the head of the male ostrich, and, attacking his eyes, brought him to the ground. The dogs and the jackal ran up, and when we arrived the gigantic bird was just expiring under the numerous wounds that the ferocious animals had inflicted.

We were greatly disappointed at this issue of our chase; but, as the evil was without remedy, we contented ourselves with preserving the lifeless corpse. The eagle and jackal were immediately taken away, as being the most ferocious. We then deprived the unfortunate animal of the white plumes in the tail, and we placed them proudly in our hats. The rich and sumptuous feathers contrasted strangely with our old worn-out beavers; but they were an excellent protection against the rays of the sun.

"What a pity," said Fritz, as we examined the gigantic proportions of the bird, "what a pity to have put such a magnificent bird to death!—how beautiful it would have looked stalking among our domestic animals!"

While we were talking, Jack and Ernest, who had followed the jackal, made some great discovery, and we soon saw them waving their plumed hats in the air, and shouting to us to hurry on.

"A nest!" they cried, "an ostrich's nest!—Quick—quick!"

We hurried on, and found the two boys standing over a large ostrich-nest—if we can dignify a hole dug in the ground by the name of nest—in which were symmetrically arranged from twenty-five to thirty eggs, each as large as a child's head.

My sons wanted to carry away the ostrich-eggs; they would hatch them, they said, by exposing them in the daytime to the rays of the sun, and wrapping them up as warm as possible at night.

I observed to Fritz, who made the proposal, that each of these eggs weighed about three pounds, and the whole number about one hundred pounds, and that, having neither equipage nor beast, it would be impossible to transport them across a desert, through which we could hardly drag our arms and knapsacks; besides, I doubted whether artificial heat could replace the natural influence. But the children had got the idea into their heads, and they agreed that each one should take one egg, which he should carry in his pocket-handkerchief. The little boys soon repented of their agreement, and they changed their burden from hand to hand, with all the signs of ennui and fatigue. I came to their assistance, and advised them to cut some branches from a low sort of pine that grew about the rocks, and make a basket to carry their eggs, as the Dutch milk-women carry their milk-pots. My plan succeeded admirably, and my boys began their march without the slightest complaint.

We then arrived at the borders of a swamp that seemed to be formed by the confluence of several springs that flowed from the rocks; we could trace the marks of the dogs and the monkey, and recognized this as the place where they had wet themselves. We could perceive, in the distance, troops of buffaloes, monkeys, and antelopes, but so far from us that we took no further notice of them; nothing, however, indicated to us the presence of a boa, or that such animals resided here. We halted at this marsh, and refreshed ourselves with some provisions; and then, filling our empty gourds with water, prepared to depart, when we perceived the jackal had made a discovery. It was a round object which he had dug out of the sand with his paws; it resembled a mass of moist earth, and I threw it into the water to clean it, when, what was my astonishment to see it move! I took it out, and, on examining it, discovered it to be a turtle of the smallest kind, scarcely as large as an apple.

"How is this?" said Fritz. "I thought that turtles inhabited the sea only."

"Who knows?" said Ernest; "perhaps there has been a shower of turtles here, as the Romans formerly had a shower of frogs."

"Stop there," said I to the philosopher; "your irony does not show your learning. Perhaps you do not know that there are land as well as sea-turtles. They are not only found in swamps, but even in gardens, where they subsist on snails, caterpillars, and all sorts of insects."

"Well, then," replied Ernest, "let us carry some home to mamma. She would like them to put in her garden; we will also put one in our cabinet of natural history."

CHAPTER XLV

Bears! Bears!—Narrow Escape— The Combat—Discovery of Porcelain Earth

WE quitted the borders of the swamp; but, instead of directing our steps through the desert, we followed a little stream of water that led us to the rock where we had reposed on our first excursion into the savanna. It was a delicious route in comparison with our painful journey of the morning. We found trees, grass—in short, it was a little oasis in the desert, and we named it "Green Valley."

We were yet distant about half an hour's journey from the jackal's grotto; Jack and Fritz had stopped a moment to adjust their burdens, and I also stopped with them, while Ernest marched forward, followed by Folb.

"The philosopher is in a hurry to get home," said Jack, laughing; "he runs that he may be rested first."

But scarcely had the fellow finished his sentence, when we heard a cry of distress; it was the voice of Ernest, followed by two terrible howls, mingled with the barking of the dog. A moment after, Ernest reappeared; he was run-

ning at full speed, his face deadly pale, and he cried out in a
voice stifled with fear—

"Bears! bears! they are following me"; and the poor boy
fell into my arms more dead than alive. I had not time to
reassure him, and I felt myself seized with a sudden shiver,
as an enormous bear appeared, immediately followed by a
second.

"Courage, children," was all I could say. I seized my gun,
and prepared to receive the enemy. Fritz did the same; and,
with a courage and coolness far above his years, he took his
place by my side. Jack also took his gun, but remained in
the rear; while Ernest, who had no arms—for in his fright
he had let his gun fall—took to his heels and ran away.

But our dogs were already at the attack, and they had
commenced to measure themselves with their terrible adversaries. We fired together; and, although our shots did not
bring down the enemy, they nevertheless told well: one of
the bears had a jaw broken, the other a shoulder fractured.
But the combat was not yet finished: they were only par-
tially disabled. Our faithful servants did prodigies of valour;
they fought most desperately, rolling in the dust with their
enemies, while their blood poured in streams on the sand.
We would have fired again, but we were afraid that we
should kill the dogs, it being impossible, during the chang-
ing contest, to take any aim. We resolved to advance nearer,
and, at about four paces from the bears, we discharged our
pistols direct at their heads. The huge animals gave a groan
that caused us to shudder, and then fell back motionless on
the sand.

It was too late to meddle with the animals, and we took
the precaution, before leaving, to draw the two carcasses
into the jackal's cave, and cover them with thorn-bushes, to
keep off all carnivorous beasts and birds of prey; we also
buried our ostrich-eggs in the sand, as their weight retarded
our march greatly, and we could leave them here until
the morrow.

The sun was set when we rejoined my dear companion
and our little Francis. A good fire and a well-cooked supper
refreshed our weary bodies, and my little heroes commenced
a long narration of the exploits of the day, Master Jack
making up for the small share he had had in our victory by
boasting and swaggering enough for all.

My wife and Francis had not been idle during our absence; they had discovered on the banks of a stream a sort of greasy, white earth, which appeared to me to be fine pipeclay. They had also collected water enough for the use of our domestic animals, and, by the force of industry and perseverance, had amassed, at the entrance of the defile, a quantity of materials necessary for my projected fortification.

I thanked my good wife for the pains she had taken. We then lighted a large fire to guard us through the night, and our dogs, whose wounds my wife had washed and dressed with fresh butter, lay down beside it. I wished, before retiring for the night, to make a trial of the earth my wife had found, for I suspected that it was porcelain. I made two roughly-shaped bowls from it, and threw them into a furnace of hot cinders, and we then all retired to the tent, where sweet sleep soon sealed our eyelids. The next morning it required a strong effort to tear us from our beds, so wearied out had we been the preceding day. I found my two bowls hardened by the heat; they were, as I supposed, porcelain, rather coarse-grained, but well enough for our purposes. We breakfasted in haste; the beasts were harnessed to the cart, and, after a pleasant little ride, we arrived safe and sound at the cavern of the bears.

CHAPTER XLVI

Preparation of the Bears' Flesh— Cups out of Ostrich Eggs— Angora Rabbits and Antelopes

WE devoted a whole day to the preparation of the bears' flesh. After having skinned them with the utmost care and precaution, I cut off the hams, and then divided the rest of the meat into long strips, about an inch in thickness, and we exposed the whole to a good current of smoke, as the

ancient buccaneers used to do. The grease was collected in
bamboo canes, and carefully preserved; for, besides its use
in the kitchen, my wife said it was excellent on bread in lieu
of butter. We had about a hundred pounds of fat, together
with that which the peccaries had afforded us a few days
before; we abandoned the carcasses to our dogs, and they,
aided by the birds of prey, soon picked the bones so clean,
that there remained nothing but two perfectly white, dry
skeletons, which we carried home with us for our museum.
As for the skins, they were carefully washed with salt water,
and rubbed with sand and ashes; and although our talents in
the art of currying were poor enough, we rendered the skins
sufficiently soft for all purposes.

Our labours had been too peaceful for the restless, turbu-
lent character of my boys. I could see that they were tired
and fretful, and I thought that the best plan would be to
diversify our work with some amusement. I proposed to
them to make an excursion alone in the desert; my proposition, as one may suppose, was joyfully received, and the
perspective of an unchecked course rallied the flagging spirits of my little companions. Ernest refused to accompany
them, preferring to remain at home with us. On the other
hand, Francis was so eager to accompany his brothers, that I
at last permitted him to go.

My wife and I resumed our domestic labours, and Ernest,
tranquilly seated on the sand, occupied himself in making
cups from ostrich eggs; for we had discovered, by putting
our eggs into hot water, that the principle of life was exhausted. Ernest had read of a plan somewhere to separate
the eggs by surrounding them with a string steeped in strong
vinegar. The action of the acid on the lime contained in the
shell forms a circular line, which gradually eats through; but
the lining membrane of the egg was so hard, that it was
necessary to cut it with a knife; it had all the elasticity of
parchment.

We soon quitted this occupation to undertake another.
While examining a small cavern which we had discovered
near the tent, I found several minerals, among others, a
piece of amianth, known as being incombustible; and also a
superb block of talc, as transparent as glass, and which I
resolved to fashion into window panes. Ernest aided me as
much as he was able, and we soon detached a splendid

piece, about two feet in length, and the same in thickness. My wife, who received everything that could recall Europe to her mind with pleasure, was overjoyed at our new discovery, especially when I informed her that this mineral could be divided into leaves no thicker than paper.

We had been thus occupied the best part of the day, and, as evening approached, we gathered around our hearth, where our good housewife was cooking two bear's paws, which had been well soaked in brine, and the smell of which, as it escaped from the pot, promised us a delicious supper; and we sat down to while away the time in conversation until our huntsmen returned. We did not wait long, for the galloping of their steeds was soon heard, and in another moment they were at our sides.

Jack and Francis each carried a little kid on his back, with the feet tied together, and the game-bag of Fritz appeared to me to be pretty full.

"A fine chase, papa!" cried Jack. "Storm carried me through the desert like a flash of lightning. Fritz has two magnificent Angora rabbits in his pouch, and also a complaisant cuckoo, who led us to one of the finest hives I have ever seen; we shall be able to get plenty of honey."

"Jack has not told all," said Fritz: "we have taken a whole troop of antelopes prisoners, and have driven them into our domains, where we can hunt them and tame them just when we please."

Turning towards Jack, whose face seemed very much swollen, I said, "What is the matter with your cheeks? have your adventures been dangerous in any way?"

Fritz interrupted his answer, and began the following narration.

"After quitting you, we took the direction of the valley and, finding a narrow place where two or three trees had fallen down, we took advantage of this natural bridge, and crossed to the other side of the river. We rode on some time without perceiving anything, our coursers going at full speed, and the sun not being high enough to be unpleasant. At last we discovered, in the distance, two herds of small animals, of what kind we could not distinguish, but I thought they were either antelopes or gazelles. Our first care was to call our dogs together, and keep them close by our sides, as we knew the animals were more afraid of them than of us. I then divided my forces: I gave Francis the line of the river as his position; Jack occupied the middle, while I, mounted on the onagra, sustained the right wing, and endeavoured to drive the animals to the centre. We effected this movement, and one of the herds passed the river as quietly as if the act had been voluntary. The other herd did not seem to perceive us until we were close to them, when suddenly they raised themselves from the grass where they had been lying, and, stretching out their long necks and little heads, surmounted by short, pointed ears, set off at full speed; and now our chase commenced. We urged our coursers onward, and, giving our dogs their liberty, we soon forced the entire troop over the river, and drove them into the defile which separated us from the savanna. After we had secured them in our dominions, the next thing was to keep them there. Several plans were proposed, but at last the following was chosen. We stretched a long cord from one side of the defile to the other, and fastened to it every light thing we could find, the continual motion of which frightened the animals away whenever they approached it; the ostrich-plumes in our hats, our handkerchiefs, etc., furnished us with materials."

"Admirable!" said I, as the boy stopped as if to see how his stratagem was received, "admirable! The only thing is, in the night it cannot be seen; but it truly was a bright thought for such a boy. But about the rabbits," added I, "what do you intend to do with them? If they should happen to get in your mother's vegetable garden, there would not be much of it left."

"No, no; but I thought that one of our two islands would make a good home for them: for instance, Shark Island would make a magnificent warren, and furnish us many a good dish, and fine furs to make caps out of."

"But how did you come to take them alive?"

"The honour of the capture is due to my eagle; he pounced down upon a troop of rabbits that were flying before us, and carried off two in his talons. I rescued them before he had injured them, and he consoled himself by killing another, which he soon devoured."

I could see that Jack was watching every opportunity to put in a word, and I laughingly requested the poor fellow to speak.

"In my turn!" said he, "in my turn! I galloped on with

Francis while Fritz was chasing the rabbits; the dogs followed us, and suddenly we saw them jump forward, and run after two little animals about the size of a hare, that fled with incredible rapidity. Away we all went, and, after a hot chase of a quarter of an hour, we captured the two fugitives. There they are," continued the young narrator, throwing down before us two beautiful little animals; "I think they are young fawns."

"And I think," said I, "that they are antelopes."

"Well, whatever they may be," continued Jack, "our dogs behaved admirably, and so, I can say, did their masters. But that was nothing to what happened afterwards. We had scarcely commenced our progress when a sort of cuckoo began to fly before us, singing away as if to defy us. I had already levelled my gun, when Fritz requested me to recollect that it was loaded with ball, and that I should only waste the charge. I accordingly slung my gun on my back, and we rode on, the cuckoo flying on before us, when suddenly he stopped just over a bees' nest, artfully concealed in the ground. We now held a council of war about the nest, and discussed the plan of attack. Francis begged to be excused, recalling to our memories the former attack at Falcon's Nest. Fritz was willing to do all the advising part, but would rather leave the execution to somebody else; so you see, at last, the whole affair devolved upon me. Armed with some sulphur matches that I found in my knapsack, I advanced and tried to suffocate the bees by throwing the lighted matches down the hole, when suddenly a rumbling noise was heard, and, in a second, a swarm of bees emerged, attacking me on all sides. My hands and face were violently treated, and it was with the greatest difficulty that I mounted my buffalo and rode away, bearing with me the honourable marks of the conflict. I could scarcely believe," said Jack, as he finished his recital, "that so small an animal could cause so much pain."

I reflected long upon what Jack had told me concerning the strange bird that had shown them the nest of bees. I easily recognized it as being the "cuckoo-indicator" of naturalists; "But," thought I, "how, if this coast is uninhabited, could the bird have known that human beings liked honey, and would be willing to share the discovery with him? Is not such conduct a sign that we are not the first men who have

trod this soil? May not the interior of the country be inhabited?" These considerations were of the highest importance
to us, and I was convinced that it would not be prudent to
advance into the interior, unless with the greatest caution. I
also resolved to build a fortress on one side of the coast, and
I chose Shark Island as its situation, as it appeared to me
that a strong fortification that would command the coast of
Felsenheim, and fortified by our two cannons, would enable
us to defend ourselves against all attack from the interior, if
any ever took place.

CHAPTER XLVII

Ostriches Again—A Hunt and a Capture—Acquisition of Treasure —Euphorbia—Vanilla

AT the break of day I was up, and awoke my sons; our
labours were almost done—our bears' meat was smoked,
our fat all run out into bamboo vessels; and the rainy
season, which was rapidly approaching, warned us to return
to our home in the grotto. Nevertheless, I wished to make
another excursion into the desert, to see whether a second
visit to the nest of ostrich eggs would not succeed better
than the first, and I likewise wanted to gather some of the
gum of the euphorbia.

As we wished to accomplish this excursion as rapidly as
possible, it was resolved to go on horseback. We took with
us Turk and Billy, and set off, following the direction of the
Green Valley, tracing over again all the places rendered
illustrious by some remembrance of our last excursion—the
spot where we had encountered the bears, the turtle-marsh,
and, at last, the rock from which Fritz discovered the ostriches. To this rock we gave the name of "Arab's Tower,"

in allusion to the mistake he had made in thinking the ostriches to be Arabs of the desert.

Jack and Francis galloped off at full speed, and, as the plain was so level that they could not escape from my eye, I let them go on. I retained Fritz by my side to aid me in gathering the euphorbia which had congealed in the sun. I had provided myself with a vessel to put it in, and I soon filled it with the little drops of hardened gum.

This gum is one of the most violent and subtle poisons, and my son asked me why I took so much pains to collect it.

"I intend to use it," said I, "to destroy the monkeys—a cruel means, I will allow, but necessity drives us to adopt it. We can also employ the euphorbia in preparing the skins of birds and other animals; it will preserve them from corruption, and keep out all insects. To whatever use, however, we may apply it, the greatest precaution must be observed, as it is capable of producing the most dreadful results."

During our work, the two cavaliers had almost disappeared in the savanna, and it was with great difficulty that our eyes could follow them, surrounded as they were by a cloud of dust. They had passed far beyond the ostrich nest, to which we directed our course, wishing to see whether the eggs had been abandoned or not.

We had scarcely come in sight of the nest when we saw four noble ostriches rise from the sand and advance toward us. Fritz's first care was to prepare his eagle for the conflict; and, to prevent it from renewing the former scene of carnage, he fastened its beak so strongly that it was almost harmless. Our dogs were also muzzled, and we stood still, in order that we might not frighten the birds. On they came, with half-extended wings, gliding over the ground with inconceivable rapidity. They seemed to think us inanimate objects, for they came on directly for us until they had arrived within pistol-shot; they were three females and a male—the last a little in advance, with his beautiful tailfeathers floating behind him. The moment of attack was come; I seized my string with balls, and, calling up all my sleight-of-hand, I launched it against the male ostrich. Unfortunately, however, instead of catching him around the legs, as I intended, the balls of my string took a turn round his body, and I only fastened his wings to his sides. It diminished his speed somewhat, but the victory was not complete; and the frightened bird turned round, and, using his long legs, endeavoured to escape: away we dashed after him, I on the onagra, and Fritz on the colt. But we were nearly exhausted, when, happily, Jack and Francis rode up, and cut off his further retreat. Fritz then unhooded his eagle, and, pointing out the ostrich to him, he immediately pounced upon his prey; and now commenced an arduous chase. Jack and Francis on one side, and Fritz and I on the other, tormented him, and harassed him without ceasing; but the most useful combatant was the eagle. The presence of this new enemy troubled the ostrich greatly; he felt him on his head, and heard the flapping of his wings, while, on the other hand, the eagle, furious at finding his beak strongly fastened by a ligature of cotton, was so violent that, by a vigorous stroke of his wings, the ostrich fairly tottered. Jack then threw his string and balls so skilfully that the noble bird bit the sand of the desert. A cry of joy burst from the huntsmen, the eagle was recalled and hoodwinked, and we hastened to our prize in order to prevent his breaking the bonds that confined him; for he was so very violent, and struggled so vigorously, that I hardly dared to approach him. I imagined that by depriving him of light I might reduce his fury, and I threw my hunting-sack, my vest and handkerchief, over his head. I had discovered the secret: no sooner were his eyes covered than he became as quiet as a lamb. I approached, passed a large band of seadog-skin around his body, two other bands were attached as reins to each side and his legs were fastened with strong cords, long enough to allow him to walk, but which confined him sufficiently to prevent his escape.

I then attached our two coursers before and behind the ostrich with strong cords; and when all was ready, my two cavaliers jumped into their saddles, and I pulled the covering from the head of the ostrich.

The bird remained some time immovable, as if astonished at the return of light. It soon made a start; but the ropes pulled it roughly back, and it fell down on its knees; again it made the attempt, and again it was foiled. It tried to fly, but its wings were tightly fastened by the band I had passed around them: its legs were also restrained: it threw itself from side to side with the utmost violence, but the patient buffaloes did not pay the least attention to the pulling and

hauling. At last the bird appeared convinced of the inutility
of its efforts, and, submitting to its two companions, set off
with them at full gallop. They dashed gallantly on for half
an hour, until the buffalo and the bull, less accustomed to
the sands of the savanna than the ostrich, forced it to abate
its rapid pace, and adopt a slower system of movement.

While the two young cavaliers were thus occupied, Fritz
and I set out in search of the ostrich nest. The cross of
willows which we had planted in the ground near it, at our
last visit, still remained, and, as we approached, a female
bird rose up off the nest and fled rapidly away into the
desert. Her presence appeared to us a good augury, as it
assured us that the eggs still retained the principle of life. I
had taken care to bring with me a sack and a quantity of
cotton. I now took out six of the eggs, and, enveloping them
as carefully as possible in the cotton, placed them in the
sack, leaving the others in the nest, in hopes the mother
would not discover the theft.

We traversed the Green Valley without perceiving anything uncommon, and soon arrived at the tent, where Ernest and his mother received us with an astonishment they
could not find words to express.

I fastened the ostrich securely between two trees, and the
rest of the day was devoted to preparations for our departure on the morrow. We had a number of new riches to
collect, and I wished to leave nothing behind us.

The next day we set off early. The ostrich took his place
between the bull and the buffalo, as before; he was, at first,
inclined to be refractory, and threw himself from right to
left, but all in vain: his two conductors were like immovable
masses, against which all resistance was unavailing.

Fritz mounted the young colt Rapid, and I the onagra,
while Ernest directed the car, in the middle of which my
wife sat in all her majesty, among the provisions. Our march
was slow, but it was very picturesque, as may be imagined.

We halted at the entrance of the defile where my sons had
suspended the cord with the feathers attached, to keep back
the antelopes and gazelles. In the place of the cord, we
erected a solid palisade of bamboo, high enough to keep out
all animals that do not climb. We planted a row of thorn
bushes on each side, and sprinkled a layer of sand all around,
so that we could discover what sort of animals might fre-

quent it. During the construction of this fence we made a
new discovery; it was that of the Vanilla bean, which I
recognized by its brown pods and balsamic odour.

Our labours at the defile detained us a long time, and it
was night when we arrived at the cabin of the Hermitage.
We found our smoking-hut the same as before, and our
provision of peccary untouched. We lighted a fire, and,
after a frugal repast, extended ourselves on our sacks of
cotton, and courted balmy sleep.

The next day, we discovered a new treasure: our henhouse
had received an addition of twenty young chicks—the product of the eggs Jack had brought home in his hat. My wife
was enchanted at this discovery, and caught several pairs to
take home with her.

We were so anxious to return to our dear Felsenheim,
and to resume all our comforts and luxuries, that we resolved not to stop again until we arrived there. It was long
after noon when our weary journey was finished. We were
worn out with fatigue; the sun's rays had been pouring down
on our heads all day, and our strength was so exhausted we
could scarcely give our animals their evening food.

CHAPTER XLVIII

Progress in Ostrich Discipline— Efficacy of Tobacco Smoke— Hydromel—The New Hat—Pottery

THE day after our arrival at Felsenheim, my wife commenced "cleaning house." Windows were opened, beds
aired, and all swept and garnished. While she and the two
younger boys were thus employed, I, with the two elder,
unpacked and distributed the riches we had brought home.

We had tied the ostrich, at first, under a tree, and securely fastened his feet; but we changed his situation, and

tied him to one of the strong bamboo columns that supported the gallery.

We next visited the eggs, and they were, like the first, submitted to the trial of warm water. Several of them fell heavily to the bottom; but three or four moved slightly when immersed in the water, and these were carefully preserved, in order that we might try the experiment of hatching them by cotton and artificial heat. For this purpose I constructed an oven, in which I took care to maintain that degree of heat which the thermometer marked as being the natural heat of the hen.

We then installed our Angora rabbits on Shark Island; we constructed a burrow in the ground, similar to those of Europe, and, before putting them in, we combed them, and removed all the superfluous hair. We also fixed wooden combs over the entrance of each burrow, so that the rabbits, when passing in or out, would be deprived of some part of their fine wool, which I intended to manufacture into hats.

The two antelopes were also transported to Shark Island. We should have liked very much to keep these charming little creatures about us, but the fear of the dogs and beasts of prey forced us to condemn the timid creatures to confinement. In order to render their exile as agreeable as possible, I erected a hut in the middle of the island, to shelter them, and we took good care to provide them with plenty of provisions.

I wished, before the rains came on, to prepare a field to receive the seeds we had hitherto confided to the earth without any order or regularity. It was a difficult enterprise, and we felt in all its reality the force of that law which condemned man to gain his bread by the sweat of his brow. Our faithful animals were of much assistance to us; but the sun was so intense that the slightest labour utterly exhausted them. We could work but four hours in the day: two in the morning and two in the evening; we were able, however, to prepare at last about two acres of land, which would furnish us an ample harvest of maize, potatoes, and manioc-root.

During the intervals of our fatiguing field labours, we occupied ourselves by beginning the education of the ostrich. It was an enterprise as difficult as it was novel; but I had read that it could be accomplished, and I was resolved to try it.

Our pupil began by putting himself in a terrible passion; he struggled, snapped at us with his beak, and cut up all sorts of capers; but we could find no better remedy for such conduct than to treat him as we had treated Fritz's eagle, that was, by burning tobacco under his nose. This had the desired effect, and we soon saw the majestic bird totter and fall insensible to the ground. We had recourse to this plan several times. Little by little we relaxed the cord which fastened it to the bamboo post, and gave it room to wander about the doorway. A litter of rushes was provided for him; calabashes filled with sweet nuts, rice, maize, and guavas were placed every day before the animal; in a word, we neglected nothing that we thought would consort with the fellow's taste.

During three days all our cares were in vain: our choice dishes were regarded with great disdain, the beautiful captive would not eat, and it carried its obstinacy so far that at last I was seriously afraid of the consequences. At last an idea occurred to my wife, which relieved us from all embarrassment. It was to poke down the throat of the bird, willy nilly, balls of maize and butter. The ostrich made horrible faces at first, but when it got a taste of the balls, all trouble on that point was over, and the delicacies we placed before it were quickly devoured, the guavas, by the bye, being especially favoured.

The natural savageness of the bird disappeared more and more every day; it would let us approach it without striking at us, and after some days we thought we could, without much risk, unfasten it, to take a short lesson in the art of walking. We placed it between the buffalo and the bull, and put it through all the exercises of the stable—to trot, to gallop, stop short, trot again, walk slow, etc. I cannot say that the poor bird relished his first lesson very much, but the tobacco pipe and the whip were two admirable instructors, and when he was disposed to become unruly a whiff of tobacco would set all to rights.

At the end of the month its education was complete, and it had so well succeeded that I now seriously thought of making our new conquest of general usefulness. I wished it to associate with our domestic animals, to submit like them to regular movements, and to stop and march as we wished.

The first thing that was to be thought of was a bit; but how could I contrive a bit for a beak? I had never seen one, and I must confess that I felt greatly embarrassed; at last I achieved my task. I had remarked that the absence of light had a very direct influence upon the ostrich; it would stop short when blindfolded, and could not be induced to move until its eyes were uncovered. This discovery was the basis of the new invention that I constructed. I made, with the skin of a sea-dog, a sort of hood, like the one we had made for the eagle, which covered the head, being fastened about the neck. I made two openings in the side of this hood, one opposite each eye, and covered each of these holes with one of our little turtle-shells, attached to a whale-bone spring, fixed in such a manner that it would open and shut. Reins were fastened to these springs, so that, by their action, we could admit the light or shut it out, just as we pleased. When the two shells were open, the ostrich galloped straight on; when one was opened, it went in a direction corresponding with the eye that received light, and when both shells were shut, it would stop short. The most fully trained horse could not have obeyed better than our ostrich did under his novel head-dress.

My children thought that the education of our captive was now complete; but I was of a different opinion. The ostrich is a very robust animal, and capable of supporting a great deal of fatigue. I wished it to learn to carry burdens, to draw a carriage, and be adapted for horsemanship; I began, consequently, to make harness for each of these occupations. We had a great deal of difficulty in making the ostrich submit to our wishes; our hardest task was to make it submit to our mounting it; but I knew that patience and perseverance are the two first elements of success in imparting education. I was not, therefore, discouraged, and at last we had the satisfaction to see our new courser galloping between Felsenheim and Falcon's Nest with one of our young cavaliers mounted on his back.

The artificial nest of ostrich eggs, which we had enveloped in cotton, and placed in a stove, had succeeded; that is to say, out of six eggs, three had hatched. The young ostriches were the drollest-looking animals that could be imagined: they looked like ducks, mounted on long legs, and they tottered awkwardly about on their slender stilts. One died the day after its birth; the two others survived, and we endeavoured to preserve them by taking all possible care for their comfort. Maize, acorns, boiled rice, milk, and cassava, were set before them in rich profusion.

We had had nothing to drink but water since our arrival on the island, if I except the barrel of Cape wine that we had saved from the shipwreck; but that had long ago been exhausted, and I now determined to make some sort of drink for the winter.

I had often heard of the hydromel of the Russians; we had the primary material, honey, from our hives, and I determined to make the experiment. We boiled some honey in a sufficient quantity of water, and after having filled two barrels with the fluid, I threw in a large cake of sour corn bread, to make the liquor ferment; when that process was finished, we tasted it, and found it was of a pleasant flavour, agreeably acid, and a great resource for our long winter days. We placed the two tuns in our cellar, or, to speak more justly, in the hole we had dignified by that name. We then set to work and made a choicer drink than the first: to our honey and water we added nutmegs, ravensara, and, in short, a collection of all the aromatic plants we could find. This drink was reserved for extraordinary occasions, such as holiday banquets, anniversaries, etc.

When all our provisions were gathered in, and we felt sure that we could get through the winter without famine overtaking us, we commenced our manufacture of hats. It was a labour as difficult as novel for us. The first question that presented itself was the form of our hats; each one gave in his opinion, but necessity came into the council, and obliged us to give our new manufacture the form most in unison with our means of execution. It was extremely simple: I cut a wooden head, which divided into two parts, and on which we spread a thick layer of soft paste, composed of rat-skin and the glue of fishes. We let it dry, and as it took the exact impress of the mould, we obtained a sort of cap, of which my readers can form some idea of the shape.

It had cost us a great deal of trouble to produce even this ill-looking affair. My sons were scarcely less satisfied with it than I was; but our European hats were so dilapidated that it became a matter of necessity to procure something to replace them.

I now had recourse to the cochineal, and I soon gave to our beaver a beautiful brilliant purple tint. The hat looked better; I adorned it with a couple of ostrich-plumes, and it looked better still; my wife passed a ribbon round it, which she had found in her enchanted sack, and the disdain with which my poor beaver had been received, was changed into anxious requests for its possession.

But its destination had been fixed beforehand: it belonged to Francis by right, as he had lost his old hat a few days before.

Our success in the manufacture of hats emboldened us to try our hand at other things. We were much in want of kitchen utensils, and I was obliged to pass from the art of hat-making to that of potter.

I did not understand much about pottery; and what puzzled me most was the way in which the earth was to be prepared before using it; and I began my experiments with very little hope of their ever succeeding.

I constructed, in one corner of the grotto, a large stove, divided into compartments, destined to receive the different articles; earthen pipes were conducted all around, so as to equalize the heat as much as possible. These preparations occupied me a long time, as I had no idea how the thing should be done, and I can safely say I invented rather than imitated a furnace for pottery.

I next took a certain quantity of the porcelain earth, which very much resembled fine white sand. I carefully removed all foreign particles, such as bits of stone, etc., as I was afraid they would cut our hands while working the porcelain. I also mixed a quantity of the talc we had brought home for window-panes, thinking, perhaps, it would render the mixture more firm and solid. When all was well worked up together, I left it a little while to dry, while I set to work to invent a machine for turning our utensils on. The wheel of one of our cannon carriages, fixed horizontally on a pivot and surmounted by another wheel, united to it by an axle and turning with it, formed my machine. I first turned out some plates and dishes, cups and saucers, bowls, and other things. I exposed these articles to a very strong heat: a great many broke in pieces, but I completed about half. When baked they were perfectly transparent and of the most beautiful grain. My wife saw her kitchen apparatus enriched with utensils of all sorts, and, overwhelmed with joy, she promised us, in exchange, numberless good dainties, which, for want of a suitable utensil, she had hitherto been unable to make.

CHAPTER XLIX

Return of the Rainy Season—A New Want—The Cajack

THE rainy season was now rapidly approaching, and we were soon obliged to give up our excursions. The winds and the rain commenced: the sky that had so long been clear became dark with storm-clouds; terrible tempests announced the approach of winter; and we closed the door of our grotto, happy in having such a comfortable shelter.

The turning-wheel was continually in motion. We improved the quality of our fabrications more and more, and we manufactured utensils that at the outset we had despaired of ever possessing.

We had preserved the shells of the ostrich-eggs, and having divided them by means of a string steeped in vinegar, we converted the halves into elegant vases. I turned some wooden pedestals on which they were placed, and we thus obtained drinking-cups and vases for flowers in summer.

But these labours were much more interesting to me than to my young family, and I feared that the inactivity to which I saw them reduced would render them indolent. Ernest found occupation enough in his books; but his brothers never entered the library unless when driven by necessity. I felt the urgency of providing some active occupation for them, and one more to their taste than literature; but I could not think of anything, when Fritz came to my assistance.

"We have," said he, "in the person of our ostrich, a

splendid post-horse, with which to travel the highways of our kingdom; we have carts to transport our provisions; a pinnace, and a canoe, which are riding majestically at anchor in Safety Bay; but one thing is yet wanting: we have need of an equipage that will glide over the surface of the water, as the ostrich does over the sand. I have read that the Greenlanders have a sort of vessel which they call 'cajack,' and which I must have. Why cannot we construct one? We have constructed a canoe—why should we, civilized Europeans, not succeed in that which barbarous savages have attempted?"

I joyfully received the proposition of my son. The cajack, the only vessel of the Greenlander, is a sort of canoe in the form of a shell; and a piece of walrus-skin, with three or four strips of whalebone, are almost the only requisites for its construction. It is extremely light, and the navigator who has glided in it over the surface of the wave can easily carry it on his shoulder when he has arrived at land.

The strips of whalebone, bamboo-cane, and Spanish rushes, with some sea-dog skin, were the materials that we employed in making our cajack. Two arched strips of whalebone fastened at each end, and separated in the middle by a piece of bamboo fixed transversely across, formed the two sides of our canoe; other pieces of whalebone, woven in with rushes and moss, well covered with pitch, formed the skeleton.

When the skeleton was finished, and the interior covered with a coat of gum and moss, we commenced the construction of an envelope. For this I took the two entire skins of sea-calves, fastened one at each end of the canoe, and then drew them down under it, where they were strongly sewed together, and covered with a gum elastic coat, to render them impervious to water. I also cut out oars of bamboo, and fastened bladders to one end, so that they might be useful in case of accident. I also constructed, in the bow, a place to receive a sail, in case we should decide, at a future period, to put one there.

There was yet an important thing wanting in the completion of our Greenland boat: it was the equipment of him who was to manage it. I had often heard of a sort of apparel well known to those who dwell near the sea, and which consisted in enveloping a person in an airtight dress, lighter

than the volume of liquid his body displaced. I described
this apparel to my sons, narrated to them how the head of
the swimmer was covered with a hood, furnished with a pipe
intended to let in air when it was necessary to breathe under
water. My description of the costume and the air-chimney
fairly turned the boys' heads, and they would not rest, night
or day, until they persuaded me to ask their mother to
construct such a suit for them.

My good Elizabeth, to whom our desires were as laws,
kindly undertook the work; and so nimbly did her needle
ply, that in a few days she had made a complete swimming-
costume for Fritz.

A jacket of the skin of the whale's entrails, hermetically
sealed and sewed round the borders, so that the air could
not possibly escape, was furnished with a flexible pipe,
closed with a valve, so that it could be inflated or exhausted
at the pleasure of its wearer.

The winter had glided insensibly away: reading, the study
of languages, and other literary pursuits had been mingled
with our domestic avocations, and helped to render the
gloomy days we passed in the grotto more pleasant and
agreeable. But our emancipation from the grotto was approaching: the wind calmed, the sea resumed its wonted
placidity, the grass sprang up under our feet, and we revisited
Falcon's Nest, with its giant trees and its rich harvest of
springing grain.

The swimming-costume was the last thing that we had
made, and Fritz was anxious to make a trial of it; consequently, one fine afternoon, dinner over, he put on his
jacket, which was drawn close round his neck; then his
hood, with its pipe for air, was fitted to the jacket, and two
pieces of talc inserted in such a manner as to enable him to
see.

Our first movement, on seeing him thus accoutred, was to
burst into a fit of laughter; but Fritz plunged gravely into
the water, and struck out for Shark Island. We followed him
in the canoe, and arrived about the same time. We unfast-
ened his hood, and found that not a particle of water had
penetrated it; every one was rejoiced at the success of the
experiment, and we all persuaded our kind mother to make
us one each.

We then set off to explore the island, and endeavour to

discover what had become of the colony we had planted there. Our first visit was to the antelopes. They fled at our approach; but we saw with pleasure that they had devoured all the provisions we had provided them with. We strewed some rushes in their little hut, for a litter; and after renewing the stock of provisions, left the spot, so that the timid animals could return. My sons and I wandered over the island, gathering pieces of coral and beautiful shells to adorn our museum.

A second excursion to Shark Island gave us leisure to examine the different plantations we had made: they had succeeded admirably, and we found several young trees already some feet above the ground. Our rabbits had also prospered, and the family had increased to an enormous extent.

We made, too, a short excursion to Whale Island; our plantations here had also succeeded—all was prosperity around us. Our maritime possessions and those on terra firma afforded a most agreeable spectacle to the eyes of the proprietors. Abundance, richness, and a luxuriant vegetation gave promise of an excellent harvest.

One day, when I was occupied by my domestic cares in the interior of the grotto, three of my sons disappeared without saying anything; they carried with them their arms, provisions, and a number of rat-traps. The latter easily explained the secret of their expedition; they had gone for rat-skins in order to make some new hats. I wished them good luck, and thought nothing more of the matter.

Ernest, always fond of home, had remained reading in the library: my wife was occupied in the kitchen; and I resolved to imitate my sons, and attempt an excursion alone. I had need of some large blocks of wood with which to grind the grain we had gathered; but I would not cut down one of the trees around our habitation for fear of disfiguring our residence. I went to the stable for a horse; but all except the buffalo had disappeared, and I was obliged to be content with him. I soon fastened him to the sledge, and we set off in company in the direction of the Jackal's River. I took with me Folb and Braun; the faithful Billy remained with Ernest, and Turk had gone off in the morning with his young masters.

My intention in choosing the river road was that in pass-

ing I might take a look at our plantations of manioc and
potatoes which extended along its bank. I had not seen this
land, which we had prepared with a great deal of trouble,
for four months prior, and I expected to find an abundant
harvest preparing for us. Judge, then, of my surprise, on
approaching, to find the whole plantation a scene of ruin:
the roots that had just begun to sprout were all trodden
under foot, or scattered over the ground—in a word, it was
a scene of utter desolation. I thought at first that perhaps
my sons had gathered the harvest; but the prints in the
moist earth soon revealed the authors of this devastation: it
had been done either by the wild pigs, or else by the family
of our old sow.

My brave companions, Folb and Braun, had gone off in
search of the despoilers; and they soon returned, driving
before them a whole herd of pigs, at the head of which
trotted our old sow, grunting most melodiously. I was so
irritated at the unlucky animals, that almost instinctively I
raised my gun, and by a single shot brought down two
young porkers. The others took to flight, and the dogs
would have pursued them, but I called them back, and,
cutting off the heads of the two pigs, gave them to them. I
then placed the bodies on the sledge, and having marked
with a hatchet the trees I had chosen, so that I should know
them again, I set off for Felsenheim, with a saddened heart
at the devastation I had witnessed.

CHAPTER L

Return of the Boys—Their Adventures—Harvesting—Partridges and Quails

TOWARD evening we began to grow anxious about the
return of the boys, when suddenly Jack appeared in the
distance. He arrived at full gallop on his ostrich, having left

his brother far behind. He brought nothing with him, pretending that his courser would receive no other burden than himself. Fritz and Francis coming up, we discovered that each of them carried before him a sack full of game, the products of the chase, in which they had been extremely fortunate; and they had brought back with them four of those beasts whom we had christened "beasts with a bill," twenty ondatras, one monkey, a kangaroo, and two varieties of the musk-rat, which they had found in the swamp.

During supper, each one recounted his adventures, Fritz describing their passage through the valley, the attack of the ondatras and the beavers. "We also," said he, "then saw those 'beasts with a bill' coming out of the swamp to partake of a repast not intended for them. We then caught a fish or two in the lake; and relieving our dinner with a plate of ginseng cooked in the ashes, sat down to our humble meal."

"Pooh, pooh!" cried Jack the boaster; "who cares for rats and fishes? It is to my courser and me that you owe this royal prize, this noble kangaroo."

"Oh, yes," added Francis, "a prize very easy to take, as it remained quiet until you came up and shot it."

"For my part," continued Fritz, "I have brought home nothing but a plant: but it is of more value than the kangaroo. Examine these thistles, I beg of you; see their hard, sharp points. Will they not be excellent to card the hair in manufacturing our hats?"

Each one of our young adventurers had a thousand different stories to relate, each one vaunting his own prowess and extolling his share in the events of the day. I had no time to listen to their boastings, and I turned to examine the products of the expedition and determine their use. The thistles of Fritz, which I recognized as being the "carding-thistle," were received by me as a precious discovery—one more instrument added to our resources. My sons had also brought home some cuttings of sweet potatoes and cinnamon: their good mother received them with joy; and the next morning they were carefully planted in the kitchen garden.

The grain that we had sown before the rainy season, I perceived, had now come to maturity, although it was not more than five months since we had confided it to the earth. We now had our hands full of business. The herrings would soon arrive, then the sea-dogs would come; and my dear

Elizabeth lamented piteously while she enumerated all the labour we yet had to perform. There was the manioc to dig up, the potatoes to gather and sow—in short, a thousand cares to attend to, a thousand labours to undertake, that would occupy more time than the year has days.

I tranquillized my good companion as well as I was able, assuring her that the manioc would not be injured by remaining in the ground; and as to the potatoes, I informed her that she had nothing to fear for this precious fruit, as our soil was warm and sandy, and they would keep a great while in the earth.

I decided that our labours should commence with the grain, the chief and best of our resources; but wishing to effect the harvest in the shortest possible time, and with the smallest expenditure of strength, I resolved to adopt the Italian method rather than the Swiss.

I commenced by levelling a large space before the grotto, to serve as a threshing-floor. We then, after having well watered it, beat the earth for a long time with clubs. When the sun had dried it up, the operation was repeated, and we continued it until we obtained a solid, flat surface, without a crack in it, and almost as impenetrable to water as to the sun's rays.

On arriving at the field we were about to reap, my wife asked me where I would find anything with which to tie up the blades into sheaves.

"We will need nothing of the sort," said I; "everything is to be done according to the Italian method. Those people, naturally averse to labour, never use sheaves, as being too heavy to carry."

"How, then," asked Fritz, "do they manage to carry their harvest home?"

"You will soon see," said I.

At the same time I gathered up in my left hand all the stalks it could contain, and taking a long knife in my right hand, I cut off the stalks about six inches below the head. I then threw the handful into a basket. "There," said I, laughing to Fritz, "there is the first act of an Italian harvest."

My children thought it was an admirable plan; and in a short time the plain presented but an unequal surface, bristling with decapitated stalks, here and there dotted with a forgotten blade.

We now hastened to the grotto, taking with us the grain we had cut. When we arrived there, Ernest and his mother received orders to sprinkle the blades over the threshing-floor I had prepared, while my three cavaliers stood by their coursers' sides, laughing at our new invention for threshing grain.

When everything was prepared, "To the saddle!" cried I, "to the saddle!" and I told them they had nothing to do but display their horsemanship among the grain. I leave the screams, the shouts of laughter to the imagination of readers; the bull, the onagra, and the ostrich rivalled each other in swiftness; my wife, Ernest, and I, each one armed with a pitchfork, followed after them, throwing the grain under the feet of the animals.

When the grain was all threshed, we set to work to clear it of the straws and dirt that had become mixed with it. This was the most difficult and the most painful part of all the labour. We laid the grain on close hurdles, and with wooden flails we endeavoured to disengage the dirt; but this was not to be effected, except at the expense of our eyes, mouth, or nose. The poor little workmen coughed terribly, and we were obliged to desist every few moments to clear our throats.

We were several days engaged in these works, and we wished to see exactly how much we possessed. We found ourselves rich enough to defy all attacks of famine; we had sixty bushels of barley, eighty of wheat, and more than a hundred of maize, from which I concluded that the soil was more favourable to this last than to the barley and the other European grains we had sown at the same time. We had not prepared the maize as we had the other grains; but after having dried the stalks, we detached the grains by beating them with long, flexible whips; we took this care because we wanted its soft and elastic leaves to stuff our mattresses.

I had not lost sight of my intention of obtaining a second harvest before the end of the season, and we now set to work to clear our fields of the straw; but we had scarcely commenced when we beheld an innumerable swarm of quails and partridges start up from the dried stalks, where they had been enticed by the few blades of grain we had left behind. As we were unprepared for them, they all escaped, save one quail, which Fritz brought down with a stone; but the presence of these birds after the harvest was a precious discovery for following years, and we anticipated with pleasure the superb chase of quails and partridges we should have after our harvests.

When the land was all cleared I sowed it anew; but remembering what I had learned in Europe, not to exhaust the soil, I varied my original mode of operation, and contented myself by sowing, for the second crop, wheat and oats.

Our agricultural labours were scarcely finished, when the bank of herrings appeared off Safety Bay. Our winter provisions being so abundant, we did not take as many as customary of these; and we contented ourselves with preparing two barrels, one of salted and one of smoked herrings; we also preserved some of the fish alive, which we put in the Jackal's River, so that at any time we could obtain them.

CHAPTER LI

Trial of the Cajack—The Alarm— Adventure with Sea-Cows—The Drawbridge

THE trial of the cajack was a grand holiday fête; all were anxious to join in it: and when Fritz appeared, clad in his maritime costume, he was formally invited to take his place in his boat of skin. I had forgotten to say before, that the cajack was furnished with two little wheels of copper, so that it could be used as well on land as on sea. This advantage enabled my sons to arrange the ceremony with all possible pomp. Fritz was installed upon his bench, as proud as Neptune or any other marine god setting off on a distant voyage. The form of the cajack was not a bad resemblance of those immense shells that fable has assigned to the sea-

gods, as having been used for chariots. I untied the canoe
and held myself ready to start at a moment's notice, if any
real danger should threaten our Greenland sailor. When all
these precautions were taken—"To the sea!" cried I to
Fritz; "to the sea!" "Good-bye!" repeated his brothers; and
the cajack glided into the water with inconceivable rapidity.
The surface of the bay was calm and tranquil, and soon the
Greenlander was dancing gaily over the waves: then, like a
skilful actor, he began executing a series of evolutions, each
more adroit or more audacious than the other. Sometimes
he would shoot off far out of our sight; then suddenly he
would disappear in a cloud of foam, to the great terror of
his mother; in another moment we saw his head above the
floods, and an oar that he had elevated to signalize his
triumph.

The address and the audacity of our young sailor provoked, as one can easily imagine, loud and frequent applause on our part: on his part, not content with acting on
the surface of the bay, he turned his frail bark toward the
Jackal's River, and attempted to mount the current; but this
proved too strong for him, and threw him back so violently
that he disappeared from our sight. To jump into the canoe
and fly to the assistance of the poor Greenlander, was the
affair of an instant. Jack and Ernest went with me. The
wheel of the canoe appeared to us too slow; and while I
exerted all my force in turning it, my two sons took each an
oar. We scarcely touched the surface of the water, yet we
could not perceive anything; our cries had no echo but the
rocks, and our sight was lost in the foaming waves that
boiled up around us. I felt my heart beating violently, and I
had not the courage to express my uneasiness to my sons;
when suddenly, in the direction of a rock just visible through
the foam, I saw a light cloud of smoke issuing forth, and
putting my hand on my pulse, I counted its beat four times
before that smoke was followed by a report.

"He is saved!" cried I, "he is saved! Fritz is there in the
direction of the smoke: before a quarter of an hour he will
rejoin us."

I then fired my pistol, which was instantly answered by
another report in the same direction. Ernest drew out his
watch. After a hard row we perceived Fritz, and in a quarter
of an hour we reached him.

We found the young hero of the sea established on the rocks. Before him lay a walrus, or sea-cow, which he had killed with his harpoon. I commenced by reproving my son for his imprudence.

"My dear father," answered he, "it was the current that swept me away in spite of myself: my oars were like straws before the impetuosity of the Jackal's River; and I found myself thrown back into the sea, at such a distance as to lose sight of land altogether. But I had no time to fear: a company of sea-cows passed along, almost under my nose. To throw my harpoon and strike one of these animals was the work of an instant; but the wound I had inflicted was not mortal, and instead of weakening him, it seemed, on the contrary, to inspire him with new strength. He dived down; but the traces of blood he left behind, and the bladder of air fastened to the end of the rope of the harpoon, served as guides to follow him. The second time I was more successful, and I launched a second harpoon direct in his side. This last blow was decisive, and, after some struggles, the monster extended himself on this rock. Remembering our precaution with the boa, I fired two pistols at the head of the animal, and probably those were the reports you heard."

"You have achieved a truly heroic action, and the combat was a perilous one. The walrus is a redoubtable monster; and instead of flying, he would have turned upon you, and God knows, my poor child, what would have become of you if your frail boat of leather had been torn by the terrible teeth of the walrus. But, God be praised, you are safe, and that is better than the capture of ten such animals, which are not very precious game. I do not know what use this will be to us, notwithstanding it is near ten feet long."

"Well, then, if it is good for nothing," answered Fritz, "I will keep the head myself: I will prepare it and fasten it to the bow of my cajack: its long, white teeth will have a fine effect, and I will now call my cajack 'The Walrus.' "

"The teeth of the walrus," said I, "are the only things worth preserving. They are as white and hard as ivory. But make haste, for the sky gives sure token of a storm."

I wished to take Fritz and his cajack into our canoe, but he refused, and dashed on, saying he would announce our return to his mother. I let him proceed, and he soon passed us.

The storm came on quicker than I had anticipated. We had scarcely accomplished a third of our course, when the thick, black clouds that brooded over the horizon burst forth in torrents of rain. The wind, the lightning, the waves, were confounded in horrible confusion. Fritz was too far from us to allow of his joining us, and I repented of not having taken him into the boat with us. I desired Jack and Ernest to put on their swimming corsets, which we were always careful to take with us, and to lash themselves fast to the ropes of the canoe, so that they would not be carried away by the waves that occasionally broke over us.

The tempest increased, and my anxiety increased with it; the waves elevated themselves like mountains: at one moment we would be high in air, and at another precipitated to the bottom of an abyss, where it would seem we were lost for ever. But the violence of the tempest prevented its lasting a great while. The waves subsided, and after a hurricane of a quarter of an hour, the wind fell, and the storm for a time was over, although black and angry clouds rolled over our heads.

We redoubled our efforts at the oars and the wheel, and soon arrived within sight of Safety Bay. We entered the well-known harbour, and the first objects which greeted our sight were Fritz, Francis, and their mother, kneeling on the beach: they were praying for our preservation. The heart of my poor Elizabeth was almost broken with anxiety, and she needed to put all her trust in Him who alone can comfort.

We leaped from our canoe, amid the cries of joy and the embraces of the dear ones who rushed to our arms. My wife had not strength to articulate a single word of reproach for the great imprudence we had displayed: her only thought was a feeling of thankfulness to our Almighty Preserver.

We all united in prayer, and retired to the grotto, to exchange our dripping garments for dry ones.

"At last," said Fritz, who then spoke, "we are again united. I had given up all hopes of ever seeing you again, when a huge wave swept over my little barque; but I held my breath, and the wave passed on, and I found myself still alive. But it was not my exertions that brought me to the shore: there was a stronger hand than mine that sustained my cajack among the waves—the hand of God," added the young man; "and to Him have I rendered homage."

The rain had been so abundant that the Jackal's River had overflowed its banks and damaged some of our constructions, which demanded instant restoration. We therefore employed ourselves in building protections against any other storms that might visit the coast of Felsenheim. During our labours we received the visit of a superb company of salmon. We captured a number, which were salted and smoked according to the customary manner; we preserved some alive by passing a strong cord through the gills and fastening them to stakes.

We had resumed the peaceable course of our domestic avocations, when, one clear moonlight night, I was suddenly awakened by barks and cries, as if all the jackals of the country, the bears and tigers of the savanna, had made an invasion into our domain. I rose in a great fright, and arming myself with a gun, I walked to the door of the grotto, which we generally left open on account of the fresh air. Fritz had also heard the noise, and I found him half dressed, ready to face the danger.

"What do you think it is, papa?" said he; "a new invasion of jackals?"

I dissembled the real fear I entertained, and assured my son that doubtless it was our pigs, who were making us a nocturnal visit. I did not think my supposition would be true. We ran out, and found that our dogs and the jackal had captured three large hogs. Our first movement was to laugh; we tried to call off our dogs, but in vain; they had the poor pigs by the ears, and they would not let them go, and we were forced to open their mouths with our hands. The pigs never waited to see who were their liberators, but scampered away and were soon across the river.

I attributed this invasion to negligence on our part, and thought we had forgotten to take up the planks from Family Bridge; but, upon examination, I found that they had been all removed, and that the audacious pigs had come across on the beams of the bridge.

This occurrence convinced me that Family Bridge was not sufficient for our security: instead of a barrier, it was only a means of entering our domains. I had long contemplated the erection of a drawbridge, and now appeared the proper time for constructing it. To be sure, a drawbridge was not a little thing to undertake; but after having constructed two vessels, attempted and executed a thousand other things which required more skill than the simple art of carpentering, we could not recoil before the idea of constructing a drawbridge.

I understood the turning-bridges; but as I had neither vice nor windlass, I was obliged to adopt the simplest kind of drawbridge. I constructed, between two high stakes, a sweep that could be easily moved, and by the means of two ropes, a lever, and a counterpoise, we had a bridge which could be easily raised and lowered. It would only ensure us against the invasion of animals, the river being too shallow to oppose any obstacle to a more serious attack. Whatever it was, our domains were enriched with a new masterpiece, and my young people exerted themselves in a thousand gymnastic exercises about the stakes of the drawbridge: it was lowered, and raised, and for a few days it was a great source of amusement for them.

CHAPTER LII

Taming of Antelopes—Sugar Press —Combat with a Hyena—A Flying Courier—The Wild Horse and the Elephant

THE drawbridge suffered the fate of all new inventions, admiration evaporates so quickly! and at the end of several days, if any one climbed the stakes, it was that he might have the pleasure of seeing the antelopes and gazelles bounding over the plain of Falcon's Nest.

"Behold," said one, "how graceful and light those animals are! they scarcely touch the earth. What a pity we cannot tame them; or, at least, approach them without scattering the whole flock, as the wind does the dust!"

"To take them," said Ernest, "you will have to adopt the plan resorted to by the Georgians in capturing buffaloes."

"Tut, tut," said Jack, "cannot you find an example nearer home than Georgia?"

"For the world of thought," replied the professor, gravely, "there is no limitation; and it would be as well to become acquainted with the Georgian method before rejecting Georgia as being too distant."

"Well, then, doctor, give us a lesson."

The professor, who willingly forgot the sarcasms and pleasantries that were showered upon him, whenever he availed himself of an opportunity to display his scientific knowledge, now began to explain this former remark.

"In the savannas of North America, in some places beds of marl are found which contain salt, of which the animals are very fond: the buffaloes especially flock in great numbers to this luxury which Nature has provided for them. The natives of the country lie in ambush for them there, and numbers fall victims to their avidity. In the absence of salt marl," continued the professor, "we can, if we wish, prepare artificially a substitute for it, where the graceful antelopes will fall into the snare. We can, for that purpose, mix together the porcelain clay and some salt."

"Adopted! adopted!" responded all the little boys unanimously. "Long live philosopher Ernest, first professor of the academy of Falsenheim, doctor, librarian, manager of the museum, naturalist and so forth!"

To plan an excursion and ask my permission was the work of an instant, and my harebrained youngsters promised themselves so much pleasure that I had not the disposition to deny them.

"Oh do, do, papa!" was the general cry; "an excursion is much more fun that constructing bridges."

"I will make some pemmican," said Fritz; "we have bear's meat enough left for it."

"And I," said Jack, with a mysterious air, "I will take two pigeons with me. I have got an idea in my head."

"And I," added little Francis, "will take care of the coursers; and if Fritz will take my advice, he will take the cajack along—it will sail so nicely on the lake; and perhaps we can capture some of the black swans. Oh, how beautiful a pair of those swans would look in the basin of Falcon's Nest!"

The weather was calm and serene, and everything promised a pleasant excursion to the adventurers.

The making of pemmican was commenced immediately, under the inspection of Fritz. The meat was pounded and crushed, until, after two days of hard work, it was reduced to half its former size. I tasted the meat of which Fritz boasted so much, and I did not think it bad.

Baskets, sacks, and all utensils necessary for the excursion were collected together; even our old sledge was brought down, and it was mounted on cannon-wheels, and loaded with all that the young adventurers intended to carry with them. The cajack, arms, provision for the mouth and for war—nothing was forgotten; anything that came into their heads they piled on, and a caravan in the desert could not have made more preparation.

The morning of departure arrived. Every one was awake before day; and Jack, without saying a word to anybody, climbed up into the dove-cot, and took out several pairs of pigeons.

"How is this?" said I, as I saw the youngster placing his pigeons in a basket. "It appears that you gentlemen take precautions to provide a variety for yourselves. I am only afraid that those old pigeons will be pretty tough eating."

The fellow looked at me knowingly for a moment, but did not answer. When they were about to set off, I saw him conversing mysteriously with Ernest; but I could discover nothing, and I contented myself with waiting a surprise of some kind, as I knew they intended one.

At last they were ready to set out. My wife enjoined my sons to be prudent; we embraced them, and they soon disappeared in a cloud of dust, with the coursers and the sledge. Ernest alone remained with his mother and me, and we employed ourselves in constructing a sugar-cane press, which my wife had much need of. The machine, which was composed of three cylinders, placed upright, differed very little from the ordinary presses, with the exception that it was arranged so as to be moved by animals.

Meanwhile our young adventurers were pursuing their course toward the savanna. I will relate their adventures here as they were recounted to us on the return of the party.

They had passed over the tract of land that separated Family Bridge from the country which we had called Waldegg, or the Hermitage, and where they intended to pass the day, when, on approaching the farmhouse, they heard cries like that of a person in distress. It was a sort of wild, maniacal laugh; and the animals stopped in terror; the dogs barked and howled fearfully; and the ostrich, more frightened than the others, fled in the direction of the Lake of Swans with such rapidity that all the efforts of its master could not check it. The bull and the onagra trembled so violently that Fritz and his brother were obliged to dismount.

Francis seized his gun, put two pistols in his belt, called Folb and Braun, and calmly walked on in the direction of the strange laugh. He had not gone more than thirty paces when he perceived, through the bushes, an enormous hyena, who, after having killed one of our sheep, was devouring it; while ever and anon that strange laugh of joy would echo from its blood-stained lips. The presence of the little hunter did not disturb the monster in his horrid repast. While rolling his flaming eyes, he tore the poor sheep in pieces. But Francis wanted neither courage nor presence of mind: he placed himself behind a tree, and taking good aim, he discharged both barrels of his gun, and was so fortunate as to break both the forelegs and pierce the breast of the hyena. The dogs then rushed on; their terror changed into rage. The most terrible combat now ensued between them and the furious monster; growls and cries resounded through the air, and the blood flowed in torrents.

Fritz, who had succeeded in attaching the onagra and the bull to a tree, now ran up at the sound of the double explosion and the noise of the dogs. They would have fired again and terminated the combat, but the dogs were so close to the hyena that they were afraid of hitting them, so that they were obliged to await the issue of the combat. Folb took the hyena by the throat, and Braun by the muzzle, and there they held him until he dropped down dead. My sons uttered a cry of joy; and calling off the dogs, dressed the wounds they had received by rubbing them with hydromel and bears' grease, which they had brought with them to eat.

When my sons had established their tent, etc., at Waldegg, they set off with the sledge to bring the hyena thither. The following day was entirely devoted to skinning the animal and preparing the hide. While they were thus employed, we were calmly conversing under the vault of the grotto.

"I wonder where my brothers are," said Ernest. "I think we shall very soon have news from them."

"What put that idea into your head?" said his mother.

"Oh! I dreamed it," said Ernest.

"Bah! A great confidence your dreams will induce!" replied my wife.

While we were thus talking, a bird, whose genus we could not discover on account of the obscurity, fluttered in at the open door of the dove-cot.

"Shut it, shut it!" cried Ernest; "to-morrow morning we will inspect our new guest. Who knows! perhaps it is a courier from New Holland, and bears despatches under its wing from Sydney, Port Jackson and so forth."

"Why, how is it your thoughts run on despatches and news this evening, Ernest?"

"Ah, it is nothing," answered he, with indifference; "only the arrival of that pigeon recalled to my mind something I have been reading to-day, concerning the correspondence the ancient Greeks and Romans carried on by means of carrier-pigeons."

The next morning, Ernest rose before me, and paid a visit to the dove-cot; I said nothing; and after breakfast I saw him coming in, holding in his hand a piece of paper, folded and sealed like a government letter, which he presented to me on bended knees, saying as he did so, "Noble and gracious lord of these lands, I beg you to excuse the postmaster of Felsenheim for the delay that the despatches from Sydney and New Holland have experienced; the packet was retarded, and did not arrive till very late last evening."

His mother and I burst into a laugh at this ridiculous speech.

"Well," replied I, continuing the jest, "what are our subjects in Sydney and New Holland engaged in? Will the secretary open and read the despatches?"

At these words, Ernest broke the seal of the paper, and, elevating his voice, commenced—

"The Governor-General of New Holland, to the Governor of Felsenheim, Falcon's Nest, Waldegg, the Field of the Sugar-Canes, and the surrounding country.

"GREETING,

"Noble and faithful ally! We learn with displeasure that three men, whom we suppose to be part of your colony, are making inroads into our savannas, and doing much damage to the animals of the province; we have also learned that frightful hyenas have broken through the limits of our quarter, and killed many of the domestic animals of our colonists. We therefore beg you, on one part, to call back your starving huntsmen; on the other, to provide measures to purge the country of the hyenas and other ferocious beasts that infest it. Especially I pray God, my Lord Governor, that He will keep you under His holy protection.

"Done under our hand and seal at Sydney Cove, Port Jackson, the twelfth day of the eighth month of the thirty-fourth year of the colony.

"PHILIP PHILLIPSON, *Governor* "

Ernest stopped in laughter at the effect the letter produced on us. I felt that there was some mystery, and I was anxious to get at the bottom of it. Ernest enjoyed my evident embarrassment, and, jumping up and down as children do, he let fall a new paper from his pocket. I caught it up, and was going to read it, when he laid his hand on my arm, saying—

"Those also are despatches; they came from Waldegg, and, although less pompous than General Phillipson's, perhaps they are more truthful. Listen, then, to a letter from Waldegg——"

"Oh, do explain to us," said I, "this prolonged enigma. Did your brothers leave a letter before they went? Is the news of the hyena true? Did they act so rashly as to attack the animal?"

"Here is a letter from Fritz," replied Ernest; "my pigeon brought it to me last night."

He opened the paper and read the following words—

"DEAR PARENTS, and you, my good ERNEST,—I will inform you of our arrival at Waldegg; we there found a hyena, who had devoured several of our sheep. Francis alone has all the honour of having killed the monster, and he deserves much praise for his intrepidity: we have passed the whole day in preparing the skin, which is very fine, and will be very useful. The pemmican is the most detestable stuff I ever tasted. Adieu! we embrace you tenderly in spirit.

"FRITZ."

"A true hunter's letter," cried I. "But this hyena, how could it have found its way into our domains? Has the palisade been overturned?"

"We shall probably receive another letter this evening," said Ernest, "and that will give us further details of the expedition."

After dinner a new pigeon was seen to enter the dove-cot. Ernest, who had not remained quiet one moment during the day, immediately shut the door of the dove-cot, removed from the wing of the aërial messenger the despatch he had brought, and delivered it to us; it read as follows—

"The night has been fine—the weather beautiful—excursion in cajack on lake—capture of some black swans—several new animals—apparition and sudden flight of an aquatic beast, entirely unknown to us—to-morrow at Prospect Hill.

"Be of good cheer;

"Your sons,

"FRITZ, JACK, and FRANCIS."

"It is almost a telegraphic despatch," said I, laughing; "it could not be more concise. Our huntsmen would rather fire a gun than write a sentence; nevertheless, their letter tranquillizes me; but I really hope that the hyena which they killed is the only one in the country."

We received other letters at intervals; but they were so concise that I will continue here the narration the boys made on their return.

Delivered from the terrible neighbourhood of the hyena, they had undertaken to explore the marsh around the Lake of Swans. Fritz embarked in the cajack, and his brothers followed, as near as possible to him, along the shore. The black swans afforded a fine chase to our young huntsmen. A loop of wire fastened to a long bamboo was the means they employed; but they captured only three young swans, the old ones being too strong, and defending themselves with their powerful wings.

After the swans came a bird of a new kind, which, by his majestic walk and noble appearance, seemed the king of birds. The boys threw the wire loop over his head, and, drawing him to the shore, fastened his feet and wings, and laid him alongside the swans.

While they were occupied in examining their magnificent prey, which Ernest afterward pronounced to be the "heron royal," an extraordinary animal rushed out from the weeds, and passing close to their sides, struck them with terror. It was an animal about the size of a young foal, of a form like that of the rhinoceros, only it had not the horn on the nose which that animal has; the upper lip was very prominent, and the whole body of a very dark brown colour. My three huntsmen were not very distinguished naturalists, and the best name they could find for the beast was the Tapir or Anta of South America.

Fritz began to pursue it in his cajack; but the tapir swam away so rapidly that he was soon obliged to desist. During this time Jack and Francis had set out for the hut, carrying with them the black swans and the beautiful heron royal. In their way thither they encountered a flock of cranes, which hovered around their heads, uttering piercing cries. A great number were soon brought down, not by firearms, but by the bows which the boys carried. These were provided with long, triangular-pointed arrows.

Fritz, on rejoining his brothers, felt a little piqued when he perceived, from their trophies, the fine chase that they had made; and, on the other hand, his unsuccessful pursuit of the tapir made him a little ashamed. He wished to retrieve his honour and repair the damage which his reputation as a good hunter had sustained; so, calling the dogs to him, and accompanied by his eagle, he directed his course toward the wood of guavas. He had not been there more than a quarter of an hour before his dogs started a flock of the most beautiful birds Fritz had ever seen. He cast off his eagle, and while it was pursuing one, a second fell down from fright into his hands. He also captured a third, which had become entangled in a shrub. This last was a magnificent one. Its tail was more than two feet in length, and two of the feathers were longer than the others, and glowed with the most beautiful shades of gold, green, and brown, terminated at the end by a spot of black, exactly like velvet. Ernest recognized it afterward as being the Bird of Paradise, the *manu cordiata*, which is the most elegant in form and plumage of all the birds of New Holland.

Our huntsmen, after all their exertions, had acquired a most ferocious appetite; and although their repast was frugal, yet they did it ample justice. The cold meat of the peccary, guavas, cinnamon apples, and potatoes cooked in the ashes, were all devoured with thankfulness. The pemmican alone was disdained, and declared unworthy of its reputation.

And now another despatch arrived, which filled me with anxiety. It contained the following words—

"The palisade of the defile which leads to the savanna is destroyed; the sugar-canes have been all trampled down, and we have discovered large footprints, like those of the elephant, in the sand. There are also the prints of the hoofs of wild horses. Come quickly to our aid, dear parents; there is much to do for the safety of the colony. Lose not an instant, we beg of you."

I leave it to the reader to imagine the inquietude into which this letter threw me. I saddled the onagra without losing a moment, and, leaving Ernest and his mother to follow me on the next day, I set off for the defile. There was a distance of six leagues between my sons and me; but I accomplished it in three hours.

My children were surprised to see me arrive so promptly, and they received me with transports of joy. The idea I had entertained of the devastation was but faint in comparison with the reality. The sugar-canes were irretrievably lost: they had been trampled down, and the leaves torn off, by some animal that I was sure must have been an elephant. All our trouble in erecting the palisade had been wasted; the stakes had been all torn up, the trees near by deprived of their bark, the bamboos had been treated no better than the sugar-canes, and every young shrub I had planted had been torn up. I examined attentively the footprints in the sand, and was convinced that the larger ones were those of the elephant, and the smaller ones those of a hippopotamus; but I could discover no traces of the hyena. I surrounded our tent with dry branches, and amassed an abundant provision of combustibles, so that we might keep off any beasts by fires at night.

Ernest and his mother arrived after dinner, bringing with

them the waggon, the cow, the ass, and all necessary utensils for our encampment, which was likely to last a good while.

We immediately began the construction of a solid fortification across the defile, one that would effectually keep out all intruders. I will spare my readers the details of this tiresome work, which occupied us constantly for more than a month. My good Elizabeth shared in our toils, and inspired her sons with ardour and perseverance. Sometimes we would relax from our labours; Fritz would make excursions in his cajack, and the other boys would wander off, and always bring us home something useful.

CHAPTER LIII

The Redoubt—Valuable Discoveries—The Cacao Tree—The Banana—Crocodiles and Alligators—Tea Plant—Artillery and Fortification of Shark Island

OUR next labour was to construct some sort of a fort to shelter us whenever we might visit the defile. We had not strength enough to build a regular fort; and besides, our knowledge of fortification was very limited. At last Fritz thought of a plan of a Kamschatdale fort, which he had read of somewhere, and which I thought, with a little improvement, would answer admirably.

The Kamschatdale fort simply consists of four high stones, upon which are laid planks and boards, forming a platform upon which a hut of bark or branches is constructed—not a very formidable fortress certainly; but yet capable of defending us in case of an attack from wild beasts.

Instead of four stones for the foundation, we chose out

four trees to answer the same purpose. We did not cut the branches off close, but left them as rests for the beams of our platform. We surrounded our platform with a high and strong network of rushes and branches, leaving an opening for entrance; and we covered the roof with the waterproof leaves of the Talipot palm. These leaves grow so large that ten men can be covered by one of them. Our fort bore a strong resemblance to Falcon's Nest; and, surrounded as it was by green trees and flourishing verdure, it did not look much like a military construction.

To ascend to the platform, we employed one of the simplest means I could imagine: it was by a beam which descended perpendicularly to the ground, and notched deeply into steps. We also arranged this so that it could be raised and lowered at pleasure.

Fritz and Jack promised themselves wonders from our new fort, which overlooked the savanna for a great distance, and we could see the river running like a silver thread through the immense plain; and by means of spy-glasses we could discern troops of buffaloes and other animals feeding around the brink.

Our labours at the fort were diversified by some important discoveries. One day Fritz made an excursion to the river of the savanna, and found among the rich vegetation there some unknown shrubs, of which he brought me specimens to examine. One kind bore, in large clusters, a beautiful green fruit, tipped at the end with violet, and shaped like a large gherkin; the others were covered with quantities of small flowers, interspersed with large fruits like cucumbers. On examination, I recognized them as being two of the most precious productions of the tropics: the largest of the fruits was the cacao-bean, of which chocolate is made; the other was the banana, that forms an article of food for the inhabitants of several countries in America.

We tasted these far-famed fruits, but did not find them very excellent. The beans of the cacao are filled with a sort of viscous matter, like thick cream, but of an insipid taste and an odour like that of an over-ripe pear.

My wife, who had opened several bananas, sought in vain for some seeds which she might take home to plant in her kitchen-garden. I told her that the banana contained no seeds, and was always propagated from cuttings, which will easily grow if planted in rich, wet earth. My wife also wished to plant some of the cacao-beans in her garden: but she was obliged to renounce her project, as Ernest told her that unless the seeds were put in when the fruit was gathered they would be useless. It was resolved, in consequence, that Fritz should set out the next day in his cajack, and go in search of the elements necessary for the reproduction of these two precious plants. My wife never forgot her kitchen-garden; and whenever she came across a useful addition, she immediately planted a specimen there.

The next day Fritz embarked; and fearing that his cajack would not be large enough to hold the cargo he intended to bring home, he fastened a raft of rushes behind it. He was ashamed, he said, to go for some banana cuttings only, and he intended to bring home something else. We occupied ourselves during the day in preparing to set out for Felsenheim; and Fritz did not return till late in the evening, when we saw him coming toward us, the cajack and the raft loaded down to the water's edge.

"Bravo! bravo!" cried his brothers, as they saw Fritz advancing, laden with green branches. The cargo was soon unloaded, and dragged up to the hut with as much contentment as if it had been the galleons of silver that Admiral Anson captured.

Fritz now came up, holding in his hand a superb bird, the feet and wings of which he had fastened, and which he presented to us as the principal booty of the day.

It was the Sultan Cock of Buffon, the king of waterfowls, so called from its beauty of form, and the brilliancy of its plumage. I easily recognized its long red legs, and its beautiful green and violet plumage, with a red spot in the forehead. My wife wished to add it to the inhabitants of the farmyard; and as it was very gentle, it soon became as tame as the rest of our domestic fowls, who appeared jealous of the new-comer.

Fritz now recounted to us the details of the day. He informed us that he had ascended the river for a great distance, and that he had been astonished at the majestic forests which bordered it, and threw a sombre shade over its waters. He had encountered several families of turkeys, pintadoes, and peacocks, whose cries and screams imparted an air of life to the sombre river. Farther on the scene had changed: there were enormous elephants feeding along the bank, in troops of twenty or thirty; some were playing in the water, and squirting the cooling fluid over the heated bodies of their companions; tigers and panthers, too, lay sleeping in the sun, their magnificent fur contrasting strangely with the green bank upon which they reclined; but not one of these animals paid the least attention to the young navigator.

"I felt my inability and weakness," said Fritz, "on finding myself face to face with these terrible enemies; my gun, my balls, and my skill would have been of little use, and I thought I had better retrace my steps. I commenced to turn my cajack round, when what was my surprise to see, at about the distance of two gun-shots before me, a long and large mouth, armed with rows of formidable teeth, and the whole apparatus moving directly toward me. I cannot say how I found strength enough to escape, I felt so frightened at the apparition. I took a lesson then in natural history that I have no desire soon to repeat."

"What animal was it," asked Francis, "the mouth and teeth of which Fritz saw coming out of the water?"

"An alligator, probably," said Ernest; "or, if you would prefer using a name more familiar to you, a crocodile."

We finished our preparations for departure, and set off at break of day the next morning for Felsenheim. Fritz asked my permission to allow him to make the journey by water, in his cajack, and to return home by doubling Cape Disappointment. I readily consented, as the ease with which he managed his little boat gave me nothing to fear, and besides, I was anxious to know more about the cape.

We both set out at the same time, and both arrived home safely. The sailor, in doubling the cape, had made two new discoveries: among the bushes which covered the rock he remarked two shrubs, one of which was covered with very highly-scented, rose-coloured flowers, and had long, narrow leaves; the other had numerous small white flowers, and in its whole appearance very much resembled the myrtle. He brought home to us specimens of these two shrubs, one of which my wife recognized as the caper-tree, used in pickling; the other was a sort of Chinese tea-plant, which was received with marked distinction.

When we were a little rested from our fatigue, my wife recalled to mind Falcon's Nest and its aërial chateau, which we had almost forgotten since our discovery of the salt cavern.

"It is wrong," said she, "to let that beautiful habitation go to ruin. Although Felsenheim offers us a sure protection in winter, yet Falcon's Nest, with its gigantic branches and pleasant verdure, is the most agreeable habitation we could possess."

My wife spoke reasonably, and I promised her that I would do as she wished. We left Felsenheim and took up our residence in our old habitation. The roof that we had made over the roots was now plastered with gum and resin; the staircase was repaired: we substituted a bark roof for the old linen one over our chamber in the tree; we made a balcony all around it, and repaired everything, so that it was a clean, agreeable habitation.

But the embellishments at Falcon's Nest were but a prelude to more considerable and difficult works. Fritz had conceived the idea of fortifying Shark Island, and making that a sort of rallying point in case of danger. He teased me so about it, and his head was so full of plans and projects, that it was impossible to resist him, and the work was at length begun. One can easily conceive how great were the obstacles that a man and four boys had to contend with, in order to convey two cannons to the island, and level them on a platform more than fifty feet in height. It cost us immense labour even to effect the transport of the cannons. I then placed on the platform we had built a large capstan; and, to shorten the time and reduce the labour in passing round the rock, I let down a rope, made into loops, so that we could easily ascend and descend. The cannons were attached by strong ropes, and then hauled up by the capstan. This work cost us a whole day of hard labour; but at last the cannons were landed on the platform, and established with their mouths toward the sea. We placed a long pole in the rock, with a string and pulley, so that we could hoist up a flag at any time. How glad we felt when our work was done, and how proud we were of our ingenuity! When we had crowned this military construction with a flag, a cry of joy was uttered; and, as economical as I felt we must be in powder, six times we fired our cannons, and the rocks repeated the echo over a vast extent of ocean.

CHAPTER LIV

A General Review of the Colony after Ten Years of Establishment

IT is with dismay that I cast my eyes over the number of pages I have filled, and which every day grow more numerous.

Although I should like to mention the minutest details of our domestic life, yet I have some consideration for my readers, who would throw down the book in disgust and grow weary of the monotony of the design; therefore, I must content myself with merely describing our principal occupations.

Ten years have passed away since we were thrown on this coast, each year resembling the preceding one in the similarity of its works: we had our fields to sow, our harvests to gather, and our domestic cares to attend to. These formed the almost unbroken circle of our existence. My only desire is, that the end I intended in writing this journal may be fulfilled, and that my readers, if I ever have any, may learn how, with God's blessing, to provide for their necessities when thrown, as we have been, entirely on their own resources.

Providence had willed that the land of our exile should be in one of the most favoured quarters of the globe, and every day we offered up our thanks to Him for His goodness and beneficent kindness toward us.

The ten years we had passed were but years of conquest and establishment. We had constructed three habitations, built a solid wall across the defile, which would secure us against invasion from the wild beasts which infested the savanna. The part of the country in which we dwelt was defended by high mountains on one side, and the ocean on the other; we had traversed the whole extent, and rested in perfect surety that no enemy lurked within it. Our principal habitations were beautiful, commodious, and especially very healthy. Felsenheim was a safe retreat for us during the storms of winter, while Falcon's Nest was our summer residence and country villa; Waldegg, Prospect Hill, and even the establishment at the defile, were like the quiet farmhouses that the traveller finds in the mountains of our own dear Switzerland.

The remembrance of our native land is never obliterated from the mind; the love of one's birthplace is a love that survives youth, and exists in all its ardour in the bosom of the old man.

Of all our resources, the bees had prospered most; experience had taught me how to manage them, and the only trouble that I had was to provide new hives each year for the increasing swarms; and, in truth, so great was the number of our hives that they attracted a considerable flock of those birds called *merops*, or bee-eaters, who are extremely fond of these insects.

We finished the gallery which extended along the front of our grotto: a roof was made to the rock above it, and it rested on fourteen columns of light bamboo, which gave it an elegant and picturesque appearance; large pillars supported the gallery, around which twined the aromatic vines of the vanilla and the pepper, and each end of the gallery was terminated by a little cabinet with elevated roofs, having the appearance of Chinese pavilions, surrounded by flowers and foliage. A flight of steps led up into the gallery, which we had paved with a sort of stone so soft when dug out as to be cut with a chisel, but hardening rapidly in the sun.

The environs of our habitation were rich and agreeable; our plantations had perfectly succeeded; and between the grotto and the bay was a grove of trees and shrubs, planted in tasteful confusion, which gave the spot the aspect of an English garden.

Shark Island no longer was an arid bank of sand: palm and pine-apple trees had been planted everywhere, and the earth was covered with a carpet of vivid green; while far above the trees towered a staff, upon the top of which the Swiss flag floated gaily in the breeze.

Our European trees had grown with a strength and rapidity of vegetation almost incredible; but their fruits had lost their flavour; and whether because the soil or the air was unfavourable, the apples and pears became black and withered, the plums and apricots were nothing but hard kernels surrounded by a tough skin. On the other hand, the indigenous productions, multiplied a hundred-fold: the bananas, the figs, the guavas, the oranges and the citron, made our corner of the island a complete terrestrial paradise, where all the riches of vegetation were assembled. But the abundance of fruit brought on another plague: multitudes of pillagers, in the shape of birds, flocked to the spot. We kept our bird-snares always ready, and it sometimes happened that an unknown animal would be taken in the trap; for example, the great squirrel of Canada, remarkable for its beautiful tufted tail and lustrous red skin, attracted hither probably by our almonds and chestnuts; parroquets, in all their diversity of colours, would sometimes be caught; blue jays, thrushes, yellow loriots, abounded plentifully, to the great prejudice of our cherries, figs, and native grapes. Besides the birds by day, there were other destroyers by night, and we had a great deal of trouble to dislodge a nest of flying squirrels that had taken up their residence in the topmost branches of one of our finest trees.

Our beautiful flowers also attracted numerous guests: these were the humming birds; and it was one of our greatest amusements to watch these little birds flying around us, sparkling like precious stones, and hardly perceptible by the quickness of their motions; it was an amusing spectacle to see these passionate, choleric little fellows attack others twice their size, and drive them away from their nests, and at other times they would tear in pieces the unlucky flower that had deceived their expectations of a rich feast. These little scenes diverted us, and we endeavoured to induce the birds to remain in our neighbourhood by fixing little pots of honey on the branches, and planting the flowers we observed they preferred. Our cares were recompensed; several couples suspended their little nests, lined with soft cotton, to the branches of the vanilla which wound around the columns of the gallery, or on the vines of the pepper, the perfume of which is very enticing to the humming-bird.

The making of sugar was an object of our special attention, and we gradually improved our manufacture; not that I can say we crystallized it as done in the refineries, but we obtained a very satisfactory result. We had saved from the wreck of the ship many articles intended for a sugar factory; among others, three metal cylinders with which to press the sugar-cane, three great kettles to boil the liquid in, and ladles and skimmers in abundance. The press was fixed under a perpendicular screw, working in connection with the cylinders, the whole turned by a lever passed horizontally through the screw, and moved by one of our beasts of burden.

Whale Island had not been neglected: we embellished it with trees and shrubs; but it was here that we always performed our less cleanly avocations, such as the preparation of fish, the melting of fat, the tannery, and the candle-making. The materials for these works were kept under an overhanging rock, which protected them from the sun and storm.

Our cares were divided between these different establishments, without neglecting those that were more distant from us, and which we called our colonies. At Waldegg we transformed the swamp into a superb rice-field, which repaid our labour by plentiful harvests; we also planted cinnamon, which yielded us an ample return. Prospect Hill also had its share of attention; for each year, when the capers were ripe, we made an excursion thither, and gathered a large quantity, which my wife preserved in spice and vinegar; and when the tea-plant began to put forth its leaves, again we set out, and gathering enough for our use; we took it home to my wife, who, with her youngest son, occupied herself in rolling, drying, and preparing it for use.

We made, from time to time, an excursion to the defile of the savanna, so that we might see whether any elephants, or other hurtful beasts, had penetrated into our plantations. Fritz then made an excursion in his cajack up the river of the savanna, and brought back to us a rich cargo of ginseng, cacao, and bananas.

As Fritz had discovered in the woods near the defile traces of birds which, from their noise and form, he judged to be heath-cocks, we resolved one day to have a grand hunt, after the manner of the Cape colonists. For this purpose we constructed a large quadrangle of the enormous bamboo-canes I have spoken of, piled upon one another until the edifice was ten feet long and six high, and exactly resembled an enormous bird-cage; the top was covered with a lattice of canes, and the door formed of the same. To induce the birds to enter, we dug a deep ditch, which led, like a mine under a city wall, into the centre of the edifice; we covered this ditch with sticks and earth, and placed in the exterior entrance, all along the passage, different sorts of grain. We then retired, and the birds precipitated themselves on the food; the more they ate the deeper they buried themselves in the ditch, until at last, when they arrived at the end, they found themselves captured, and in vain they beat their heads against the trellis-work. We entered and soon took them all prisoners.

The family of Turk and Flora had each year been increased by a certain number of young dogs, which, notwithstanding the brilliant qualities they displayed, we were obliged to throw into the water, as to have allowed them to live would have been our own destruction. To this rule there was but one exception, and on the earnest entreaty of Jack, I permitted the canine family to retain one new member, which we called *Coco*, "because," said Jack, "the vowel *o* is the most sonorous, and will sound so fine in the forests."

The female buffalo and the cow had each year produced us a scion from their race; but we had only raised one heifer and a second bull. We had called the cow *Blanche*, on account of her pale yellow colour, and the bull *Thunder*, as his voice was so powerful. We also possessed two more asses, which we named *Arrow* and *Alert* on account of the swiftness of their course.

Our pigs were as wild as ever. The old sow had been dead many years; but she had bequeathed to her posterity a spirit of savage independence that all our exertions could not modify. Our other beasts had multiplied in the same proportion, so that we could often kill one without any fear of impoverishing ourselves. Such was the state of the colony ten years after our arrival on the coast: our resources had multiplied as our industry increased; abundance reigned around us; we were as familiar with our part of the island as a farmer with his farm. It was a perfect paradise. It would have been an Eden, but there was one great void—oh! if we could but have looked upon men, our brothers!

For ten years had we watched both by sea and land for some traces of man's existence, but all in vain; and yet we hoped on, hoped ever, and still gathered up all our treasures of cotton, and spices, and ostrich-plumes, etc., in earnest hope that some day we might again see the blessed face of man.

My sons were no longer children. Fritz had become a strong and vigorous man; although not tall, yet his limbs had been developed by exercise: he was twenty-four years of age.

Ernest was twenty-three, and although of a good constitution, he was not so strong as his brother; his reflective mind had ripened; reason now aided his studious disposition; he had conquered his habit of idleness, and was, in a word, a well-informed young man, of a sound judgment, and unquestionably the light of the family.

Jack had but little changed: he was as headlong at twenty as at ten; but he excelled in corporeal exercises.

Francis was eighteen: he was stout and tall; his character, without any predominant trait, was estimable. He was reflective, without being as deep as Ernest; agile and skilful, but without surpassing Jack or Fritz. In general my sons were good and honest men, with sound principles, and a deep sense of religion.

My dear Elizabeth had not grown very old. As for me, my hair had become whitened by age, or, to speak more justly, there were but a few scattering locks left; the heat of the climate and excessive fatigue had taken them all away, although I still felt young and vigorous.

There was one bitter, sad thought that always haunted my mind; and turning my eyes to heaven, I would often say, "My God, who didst save us from shipwreck, and hast surrounded us with so many blessings, still watch over us, I pray thee, and do not let those perish in solitude whom thy hand has saved."

CHAPTER LV

Excursion of Fritz—Startling Communication—Discovery of Pearls—Intelligence of a Fellow Creature—Fritz's Return, and Account of his Wonderful Discoveries

ONE can easily imagine that my young family was not so easy to govern now as it was during the first few years of our stay.

My children would often absent themselves whole days, hunting in the forest, or clambering over the rocks; but when they returned at evening, fatigued and wearied, if I had intended to reproach them for their wandering life, they would have so much to tell me concerning the rare and curious things that they had seen, that I never had resolution enough to scold them.

Fritz one day went off in this manner, and caused us the greatest disquietude. He had taken with him some provisions, and—as if the land was not large enough for him—also his cajack, and gone out to sea. He had set out before daylight, and night was approaching, but nothing could be seen of him. My wife was in a state of the greatest suspense; and, to alleviate her distress, I launched the canoe, and we set out for Shark Island. There, from the top of the flag-staff, we displayed our flag and fired an alarm-cannon. A few moments after, we saw a black spot in the far distance, and, by the aid of a spy-glass, we discovered our beloved Fritz. He advanced slowly toward us, beating the sea with his oars, as if his canoe was charged with a double load.

"Fire!" cried Ernest, in his capacity as commander of the fort, "fire!" and Jack touched off the cannon. We descended to the shore, and were soon in the arms of our adventurer Fritz. His boat was loaded with different things; and something heavy and dark, which looked like the head of a large animal, was towing behind.

"It appears," said I, "my dear Fritz, that your day has not been an unprofitable one; and blessed be God that He has returned you safe and sound."

"Yes," replied Fritz, "blessed be God; for, besides the booty which you see, I think I have made a discovery which is worth more to us than all the treasures of the earth."

These words, half-whispered in my ear, excited my curiosity, but I thought I would say nothing until the voyager had taken breath. When we had brought on shore his sack, filled with large oysters, as it appeared to me, and the marine monster which served as a counterpoise, we drew the little cajack, with its master seated in triumph in it, up to the grotto. The boys then returned to obtain the remainder of the cargo, while we sat down quietly in the gallery to listen to Fritz's narrative. He commenced the recital of his adventures by begging us to pardon him for running away, as he had resolved to visit the eastern part of our country, of which we as yet knew nothing.

"I had long ago intended to make this expedition," said he. "This morning, before you awoke, I softly arose and ran, as is my custom, to the borders of the sea. The weather was so beautiful, the waves so tranquil, that I could not resist the temptation. I called my eagle, and seizing a hatchet, jumped into the cajack, and falling into the current of Jackal's River, was hurried out toward the shoals where our vessel was wrecked. I directed my course toward the eastern coast, among shoals and rocks covered with the nests of sea-birds, who flew around me uttering piercing cries. Whenever the rocks offered any surface, you would see great marine monsters extended in the sun, while others were playing and bellowing frightfully in the neighbouring waters. There were sea-lions, and elephants, and walruses of all sorts, who, holding on to the rocks by their long teeth, let their hinder parts rest in the water. It seemed that this was the general rendezvous of these monsters; for I saw, in coasting along the shore, several places strewed with their bones and ivory teeth.

"I must confess," said Fritz, "that when I saw myself encompassed by these monsters, I did not feel very safe; and I endeavoured, as far as I was able, to pass through the shoals unperceived, which I effected after a hard row of an hour and a half. I stopped my course before a magnificent portico of rocks, which nature seemed to have fashioned into the most imposing forms: it was like the arch of an immense bridge, under which the sea flowed in like a canal, while the rock on each side of the entrance advanced out into the sea, like an immense promontory. I did not hesitate to enter this sombre vault, from the other extremity of which issued a feeble light. A delicious coolness filled the cavern. On all sides numbers of the little coast-swallows were flying about; and on my entrance into the cavern, a swarm of these birds surrounded me, uttering piercing cries, as if they wished to prohibit my farther approach. I tied my skiff to an angular stone in the cavern, and began to examine the inhabitants. I found I was mistaken in considering these birds swallows: they were about the size of wrens, their breast of a pure white colour, their wings of a light grey, the back of a lustrous black. Their nests appeared like those of other birds, made of feathers and dry leaves; but they were placed on a singular sort of a support, resembling a long spoon, made of greyish, polished wax. Some of these nests were empty; and having examined them with more attention, I discovered that they were made of a substance resembling fish-glue. I disengaged a few of them to bring home to you, and I now beg you will examine them, and see whether they are good for anything."

"Certainly they are, my son. If we carried on commerce with China or India, we could sell these nests for their weight in gold; for they eat them by millions, and esteem them one of the greatest delicacies."

A general cry of disgust burst forth from my wife and children, at the idea of eating birds' nests. I explained to them that the feathers and moss lining the inside were not eaten, but only the covering, which is carefully cleaned and cooked with spices, making a transparent, savoury jelly.

"I advanced boldly through the passage," said Fritz, "and came out into a magnificent bay, whose low and fertile shores stretched out into a savanna of vast extent; trees and shrubs everywhere varied the beauty of the scene: on the right, a vast mass of rocks rose up, being a prolongation of those that I had passed through; on the left rolled a calm and limpid river; and beyond this was a thick swamp, which terminated in a dense forest of cedars. While I was coasting along the shores of the bay, I perceived at the bottom of the transparent waters beds of shells resembling large oysters. 'Here,' said I to myself, 'is something that is much better than our little oysters at Felsenheim; if they taste good, I will take some home with me.' I detached some with my hook and threw them on the sand, without getting out of my canoe, and set to work to obtain more. When I returned with a new load, I found that the oysters I had first deposited on the sand were opened, and the sun had already begun to corrupt them. I took up one or two; but instead of finding the nice fat oyster I expected, I found nothing but a hard, gritty meat. In trying to detach this from the shell, I felt some little round, hard stones, like peas, under my knife; I took them out, and found them so brilliant that I filled a little box with them which I happened to have with me. Do you not think, my father," added Fritz, "that they are really pearls?"

I took the box in my hand. "They are really pearls," cried I, "oriental pearls of the greatest beauty. You have, in truth, discovered a treasure, my son, which one day will be, I hope, of immense value to us. We will pay a visit to this rich bay as soon as possible; but continue your story."

"I pursued my course," resumed Fritz, "along the coast, indented with creeks, and covered with verdure and flowers. I came up to the mouth of the river, the calm waters of which floated on tranquilly toward the sea; its surface, overgrown with aquatic plants, resembled a verdant prairie covered with different sorts of birds. I gave to this river the name of St. John, as it put me in mind of the description I had read of a river of that name in Florida. Having renewed my provision of fresh water, I then directed my course towards the other promontory, opposite the arch by which I had entered. I endeavoured to leave the bay; but the tide had risen so high that it filled the vault, and I was obliged to await its ebb. I stepped on shore, as I saw on all sides, popping up out of the water, the heads of marine animals, which appeared about the size of a calf, and they plunged and frisked about in such a manner that I was afraid they would overset my cajack; so I secured it to a point in the rock, and, taking my eagle in my hand, I stood ready to attack the first game that came near me; for I wished to procure one of the animals, which resembled a stuffed valise, as I thought its thick skin might be of use to me. A company of them soon came, plunging and diving, close to the shore. I cast off my eagle, who seized on the largest and best, and soon blinded him; I jumped on a projecting rock, and, catching hold of the animal with my boat-hook, drew it to the shore. All the others fled as if by enchantment. I had to remove the entrails of the animal, as the weight was too heavy for my little skiff; but, while I was thus occupied, a prodigious number of sea-birds clustered around me: gulls, sea-swallows, frigates, and half a dozen other kinds. They came up so close that I whirled my staff around to keep them off, and in doing so knocked down a very large bird, an albatross, I think. After this operation was finished, I fastened my sea-otter to the stern of my boat; and, taking a sack full of oysters, made preparations for my return. I soon passed through the arch, and sailed quietly along, until I saw your flag and heard the report of the cannon."

After this narrative, and while my wife and the younger boys had gone to the cajack, my son drew me aside and confided to my ear an important secret.

"A very singular circumstance," said he, "happened on my voyage. In examining the albatross which I had knocked down, judge my surprise when I saw a piece of linen around one of its feet. I untied it, and read the following words written upon it in good English: '*Save the poor shipwrecked sailor on the smoking rock.*' I cannot express to you, my father, what I felt on seeing this linen. I read and re-read the line to assure myself that it was not an optical illusion. I cried aloud to the Almighty that it might but be true. From this moment my only thought shall be to search the coast in quest of the smoking rock, to save the sufferer—my brother—my friend. Oh! once more perhaps I may see a human being. An idea occurred to me to attach the linen again to the foot of the albatross, and to write upon a second piece, which I fastened to the other foot, the following sentence in English: '*Have confidence in God: succour is near.*' If the bird returns to the place from whence it came, thought I, the person can read the answer: at all events there will be no harm in trying this experiment. The albatross had been stunned, and I poured some hydromel down its throat to reanimate it. I attached my note to its foot, and let it go, earnestly praying that its mission might be successful. The bird flew up, hesitated for a moment, and then darted rapidly away in an easterly direction, which decided me to take that route in my search. And now, my father," continued Fritz with emotion, "what do you think of this event? If we could find a new friend, a new brother—for certainly we will go in search of the stranger, oh yes, we will go—what joy! what happiness! But, alas! what despair if we should not succeed! The reason I did not communicate this to my brothers and my mother was to spare them the agonies of a hope which, after all, might never be realized."

My son pronounced these last words with sadness.

"You have acted very prudently," said I, "and I am glad that you have sufficient strength of mind to resist the temptation of immediately flying to the assistance of the sufferer. As for the result of any expedition of discovery, I cannot say much; the albatross is a traveller-bird, and it flies extremely swiftly: the linen might have been put on its foot thousands of miles from here; and even if near, perhaps years ago, and now succour may be too late. But continue to keep the secret, and I will try to imagine whether some way cannot be devised to save the poor unfortunate, if in our vicinity."

The pearls were too important an object to be forgotten, and my sons importuned me to start immediately for the newly-discovered fishery.

"Softly," said I; "before riding, you must saddle your horse; and if you wish that your enterprise should succeed, you must take with you the necessary implements. Let each one of you try to invent something useful for our purpose, and then we will start."

This proposition was received with joyous acclamations, and each member of the party set his ingenuity to work. I forged for myself two large iron rakes and two small hooks of the same metal; I fixed wooden handles to the first-named, with iron rings attached, so that I could fasten them to the boat and drag them over the banks of oysters; with the hooks I intended to loosen the oysters, which the rakes were insufficient to detach. Ernest made a sort of butterfly-net with scissors attached, intended to receive the birds' nests. Jack constructed a kind of ladder, made by piercing a long bamboo at regular distances, and fixing in sticks cross-wise; the machine looked like the stick in a parrot's cage. To the top the young man fixed a hook of iron, and a spike at the bottom, so that it should rest firmly in the rocks. Francis, very adroit in making nets, made several very strong ones to hold our oysters.

During this time, Fritz worked in silence at his cajack, endeavouring to construct a second seat in it. I alone knew his intention; but I dared not encourage him by evincing my knowledge of his object.

We next prepared our provisions for the voyage: two hams were cooked, cassava cakes, barley-bread, rice, nuts, almonds, and other dry fruits; and for drink we took a barrel of water, and one of hydromel. These stores, with our tools and finishing implements, loaded down the boat.

CHAPTER LVI

Edible Birds' Nests—Pearl-Fishery —Poor Jack is "Killed"—Discovery of Truffles

WE had spent an entire day in preparing our cargo. A fresh and favourable breeze and a slightly ruffled sea induced us to embark immediately. Francis and his mother were left to guard the shore, and we gaily put off, amid their prayers and wishes for our safe return. We took with us some of our domestics: young Knips, the successor of our good old monkey, Jack's jackal, Flora, Braun, and Folb, all found a place in the boat. Jack occupied the second seat in Fritz's cajack. Ernest and I conducted the canoe loaded with our provisions and animals.

The cajack led the way, and we followed, steering our course through the shoals and rocks with the greatest difficulty. We did not encounter any marine monsters; but the rocks were covered with the whitened bones of walruses and sea-horses, and Ernest made us stop several times, at the risk of bruising our boat against the rocks, in order that he might collect some of these osseous remains for our museum of natural history.

We soon attained the promontory, behind which, Fritz said, was the Bay of Pearls. This promontory was singular and imposing. Arch rose above arch, column above column; in a word, it resembled the front of one of those old Gothic cathedrals, embellished with a thousand grotesque carvings and antiquated decorations, with the only difference that, instead of a pavement of marble, we had the blue sea, and the columns were washed by the waves. It struck us as a temple elevated to the Eternal, in the midst of immensity. We penetrated into the vault; it was sombre and gloomy, like an old cathedral, and only lighted by a few apertures in the rock.

The noise of our oars frightened the peaceable salarganes, and they flew about in such numbers as almost to render it impossible to guide the boat; but when our eyes became habituated to the darkness, we saw with pleasure that every niche and corner was filled with their nests. These nests resembled white cups, were as transparent as horn, and filled, like the nests of other birds, with feathers, and dry sticks of some sort of perfumed wood.

The trial which we had made of this substance, after boiling it with salt and spices, convinced us that it was a delicate and wholesome food; besides, we knew how highly it was valued in China, and we were so possessed with the idea that, some day or other, a vessel would arrive on our shores, with which we could trade, that I resolved to gather a considerable number of these nests, only taking care to leave those which contained eggs or young ones. Fritz and Jack climbed like cats along the rocks and detached the nests, which they gave to Ernest and me, who placed them in a large sack we had brought. It was soon filled, and I was glad of it, as the boys were tired, and I could not bear to see them suspended on the ladder over the water.

I now gave the order for departure. Fritz had assured me

that the canal which flowed through the vault was navigable, and that by following the passage, we should soon arrive at the bay. The flood-tide carried us rapidly forward toward the other extremity of the cavern, and we could not help admiring the magnificence of the passage: the roof was covered with stalactites wrought by the hand of nature into a thousand fantastic forms. At length we issued into a beautiful bay; we were struck with surprise, and remained resting on our oars in silent admiration. The water was so calm and pure that we could see the fish far below us. I recognized the white fish, the shining scales of which are used as false pearls. I showed them to my sons; but they could not understand how a little stone would be worth so much more than the fish-scales, when the latter were full as brilliant as the former.

"It is not the object itself," said I; "it is the difficulty in procuring it which costs so much. If every river in Europe abounded in pearls, they would be worth nothing."

The day was too far advanced to commence our pearl-fishing, and we appeased our hungry stomachs with some slices of ham, fried potatoes, and some cassava cakes; and, after having lighted up fires along the coast, to keep off wild beasts, we left the dogs on shore and went on board the canoe, Knips being installed on the mast as vidette. We drew the sail over our heads, and, wrapping ourselves in our bear-skins, soon sank to rest.

We rose at daylight, and, after a frugal breakfast, commenced our labours in the pearl-fishery, and, with the aid of the rakes, hooks, nets, and poles, soon brought in a large quantity of the precious oysters: we heaped them all up in a pile on the shore, so that the heat of the sun would cause them to open.

Toward evening the coast appeared so beautiful, and the vegetation so rich and glowing, that it was impossible for us to resist the temptation of making an excursion to a little wood, where we had heard turkeys gobbling all day. Each took with him one of our faithful servants, and we separated. Ernest entered first into the wood, accompanied by Folb; Jack soon followed him, while Fritz and I remained a moment to fix our guns. A few moments after, we heard a report, then a scream from Jack, followed by another report. Fritz unhooded his eagle, I snatched up my gun, and we ran in the direction of Jack, who was screaming, "Papa! papa! quick! I am killed! quick! come!"

The poor boy had exaggerated matters a little, for he was not even wounded; but there he lay face to face with an enormous boar, with formidable tusks, who had knocked him down so rudely that he thought himself lost.

His brothers ran quickly up, and two shots well fired freed him from his terrible enemy. Ernest recounted to me the manner in which this affair happened. "I had entered into the little wood," said he, "with Folb, when suddenly the brave dog quitted me, and set off in pursuit of a wild boar, who had come out of the forest, and was sharpening his tusks against the tree with a terrible noise. At that moment Jack came up; his jackal, perceiving the boar, sprang furiously upon him, while Folb attacked him on the other side. I approached cautiously, by passing from one tree to another, until I was near enough to fire; the jackal, however, had received such a terrible blow from the boar's foot that he lay senseless on the grass. Jack then fired, but missed; and the boar, turning round, set off in pursuit of his new assailant, who fled like a Hottentot before him. Without doubt, he would have soon escaped if a projecting root had not tripped him up. Down he fell; I fired, but missed, and the boar began to butt poor Jack with his head. He, however, had not time to do him much harm, as Braun and Flora rushed in, and, seizing the animal by his ears, held him so firmly that he could not stir. Fritz's eagle now joined the fray, and, flying on the head of the boar, who fairly frothed with rage, began picking at his eyes. Fritz now fired, and hit the animal directly in the throat; it fell right across Jack's body, who could not disengage himself. I then ran up and helped him; he groaned dreadfully, and at first I thought he was seriously wounded; but I found that I was mistaken. He took Fritz's arm and walked away, while I remained by the boar. It was not without some surprise that I saw master Knips with some large black tubercles, with which the ground was covered; I gathered two or three which I put in my game-bag. Look at them."

So saying, the young naturalist presented me with six tubercles resembling potatoes, the odour of which was very penetrating. I opened one, and, having tasted it, I discovered that they were excellent truffles, of a perfumed, delicate flesh, marbled with white.

"It appears," said I to my son, congratulating him on his discovery, "that the boar, who is very fond of these things, was eating them when he was disturbed."

While talking in this way, night came on, and it was necessary to seek repose. We lighted our watch-fires, swallowed a morsel of meat, and then retired to our canoe: the dogs were again left on shore. We were soon asleep, and dreaming of the absent ones at our beloved Felsenheim.

CHAPTER LVII

Cotton Nuts—Terrific Encounter with Lion and Lioness—A Savage— Parley, and Recognition of a Friend

OUR first care, on rising the next morning, was to set about the preparation of the boar. Jack had recovered from his fear, and, accompanied by the dogs, we set out to look for the dead boar. He was enormous—between a boar and a buffalo in size, and his head was indeed frightfully large.

"I fear," said I, "that the flesh of this old African is not better than a European boar. My advice is, that instead of dragging the immense carcass away, we cut off what we want, and let the rest alone."

My sons agreed with me, and we began to cut off the hams and head of the wild boar. Some branches of trees furnished us with sleds to put the pieces on, and we made the dogs draw them to the shore.

While we were occupied in disposing of our hams, chance made known to us an important discovery. Ernest remarked on the branches we had cut to make our sleds a sort of nut; he opened one, but, instead of a kernel, it contained a beautiful fine cotton, of a deep yellow, which I recognized as being the real Nankin cotton. This cotton owes its name to a province of China, where it grows abundantly, and is cultivated with much care. We made a large provision of these nuts, and dug up two young trees to carry to Felsenheim.

Jack shrank with fright from the head of his terrible enemy, and appeared quite overjoyed that it was going to figure in our museum; but, on the observation of Ernest that it would be very difficult to prepare, and having heard that boar's head was very fine eating, we resolved to cook it with truffles, in the Otaheitan manner; consequently Fritz and Ernest set to work, and dug a deep ditch, while I cleaned the head and heated some stones. When these preparations were finished, we placed the head, stuffed with truffles, and seasoned with salt, pepper, and nutmeg, in a ditch, and covered it with red-hot stones and a thick layer of earth. While our supper was cooking, we suspended the hams over the smoke of the fire, and tranquilly sat down to talk over the events of the day, when suddenly a deep, prolonged cry rang through the forest. It was the first time we had ever heard such unearthly tones: the rocks echoed it, and we felt seized with sudden terror; the dogs and the jackal also commenced howling horribly.

"What a diabolical concert!" said Fritz, jumping up and seizing his gun; "some danger must be near. Build up the fire," continued he, "and while I try to discover the danger in my cajack, you retire to the canoe."

This plan appeared the best we could pursue, and I adopted it. We threw on the fire all the wood we could find ready cut, and, without losing time, we regained the canoe. Fritz jumped into the cajack, and was soon lost in the obscurity.

During all this time the roarings continued, and they appeared to approach nearer to us. Our dogs gathered around the fire, uttering plaintive moans. Our poor little monkey seemed to suffer painfully from fear. I imagined that it was a leopard or a panther, which had been attracted by the remains of the wild boar in the wood. My doubts did not last long, for we soon discovered by the pale light of our fires a terrible lion, considerably larger and stronger than those I had seen in the royal menageries of Europe. In two or three leaps he bounded over the space which separated the wood from the shore; he stood immovable for a moment, and then commenced lashing his flanks with his tail, and roaring furiously, every moment crouching down as if to spring on us. This frightful pantomime did not last long:

every moment he would run to the stream, lap up some water, and then return. I remarked with mortal anguish that the animal came nearer and nearer to the shore; and at length he lay crouched down, his flaming eyes fixed directly on us. Half in fear, half in despair, I raised my gun, and was about to fire, when suddenly I heard a report; the animal bounded up, gave a tremendous yell, and fell lifeless on the earth.

" 'Tis Fritz," murmured my poor Ernest, pale with terror. "O God! protect my brother."

"Yes, it is he," I cried, "our brave Fritz: he has saved us from a terrible death; let us go to him." In two strokes of the oars we were on shore; but our dogs, with an admirable instinct, began to bark terribly. I did not neglect this indication; we threw more wood on the fire, and again jumped into the boat. It was time; for scarcely were we secure, when a second enemy rushed from the forest: it was not so large as the first, but its roar was frightful. This time it was a lioness, probably the companion of the superb animal which we had just killed. How grateful I felt that both had not appeared together; what could we have done? The lioness ran straight up to the corpse of her late partner, smelled it, and licked up the blood, which had flowed from the wound; and when she was convinced that he no longer lived, she set up a howl of rage that pen could not describe; she lashed her sides and opened her enormous mouth, as if she would devour us all.

Again Fritz fired, and the shot, less fortunate than the first, only broke the shoulder of the animal. The wounded lioness commenced rolling on the sand, foaming with rage; but all three of our dogs rushed upon her. Braun and Folb seized the animal in the flanks, and Flora caught hold of the throat. Another shot would have put an end to the combat, but I was afraid of wounding the dogs; so I jumped from the boat, and, running up to the animal, who was held fast by the dogs, I plunged my hunting-knife direct to her heart: the blood spouted out, and the lioness fell; but the victory had cost us dear, for there lay our poor Flora, dead under the terrible wounds she had received from the fangs of the monster.

Fritz now ran up and threw himself into my arms, as did Ernest and poor Jack, who trembled with mortal agony. We lighted our torches, and directed our course toward the field of battle; we found poor Flora, with her teeth yet clutching the throat of her enemy, while the royal couple lay majestically extended on the sand, and we could hardly suppress a sentiment of fear which struck us as we gazed on the terrific beasts.

"What a terrible range of teeth!" said Ernest, as he raised up the head of the lion.

"Yes, and what frightful claws!" said Jack; "wouldn't they make nice holes in your skin?"

"Yes, my friends," observed I, "let us thank God that He has saved us from the danger; thank Him for the wisdom with which He has endowed men, so that they may be able to conquer such terrible beasts."

"Poor Flora!" said Fritz, as he detached the dead body of our dear dog from that of the lioness; "she has done for us to-day what our old ass did in the case of the boa. Come, Ernest, see if you cannot induce your muse to fabricate an epitaph."

"Ah! my muse, I must confess, has been too terribly frightened to make any rhymes."

"Tush! go and meditate while we dig the grave of our poor hunter, and be sure to be ready when we are done."

Flora received the honours of a funeral by torchlight; we dug a grave, and silently placed in it the remains of the faithful animal, and a flat stone served to mark her resting-place. Ernest composed the following legend, which he read to us, saying that he was too frightened for poetry, and Flora must be contented with prose:

> Here lies
> FLORA, A DOG
> remarkable
> for her courage and devotion.
> She died
> under the claws of a lion,
> on whom
> she also inflicted death.

"Admirable," said Fritz. "It must be confessed, Ernest, you write full as good prose as poetry."

At sunrise next morning we were up, and our first care was to deprive our noble prey of their superb furs. Jack wanted to make a mantle of the lion's skin, such as Hercules wore after his victory in the Nemæan forest; but I adjourned all arrangements about their appropriation till a more convenient time.

The heat of the sun had commenced to corrupt the oysters heaped upon the bank, and the effluvia which they exhaled induced us to return to Felsenheim, and early in the morning we set sail. Fritz set off before us, as if to serve as pilot; but when he had conducted us through the vault, and over the shoals, he rowed up to our canoe, and, handing me a paper, shot off again like an arrow. I opened the paper quickly, and imagine my surprise when I found that, instead of having forgotten the albatross and the smoking rock, he informed me in the letter that he was going in search of the unfortunate being! I had a thousand objections to make to this romantic project; but Fritz rowed so fast, I could barely halloo through the speaking-trumpet, "Return soon, and be prudent," before he was out of sight. We gave to the cape where he left us the name of the "Adieu Cape." We prayed that our adventurer might return safe, and I begged my rowers to redouble their endeavours, so that we could arrive early at Felsenheim, for I suspected that my good Elizabeth would be worried at our long absence of three days.

We finally arrived without accident, and the different treasures we had brought were joyfully received; the truffles, the lion-skins, the pearls, the Nankin, became the objects of a thousand questions, but they could not drive away the thoughts of Fritz; and my wife said she would willingly give up all our cargo of pearls, etc., if she could only see her beloved son.

I had not yet spoken to my wife concerning the reason of Fritz's absence, as I did not wish to give rise to hopes which were so unlikely to be realized; but now I thought that it was my duty to do so. I therefore confided to her the secret of the albatross; and the dear woman, to my surprise, was calm and resigned; she only prayed with me that he might be successful.

Five days had thus passed away and still Fritz had not returned, and his mother was so anxious and worried that I proposed to launch the pinnace and make a new excursion to the Bay of Pearls. We lost no time; the pinnace was prepared, and early the next day we bade adieu to Felsenheim, and soon were in sight of the promontory of the bay, when

suddenly the vessel ran against a black mass, and was nearly
thrown over by the shock. My wife and sons uttered a cry of
terror; but the boat soon righted, and I perceived that the
obstacle was not a point of rock, as I had thought, but a
marine monster of the family of blowers, for we soon saw
him throw up into the air two spouts of water mingled with
blood. I instantly pointed the cannons of the pinnace, and a
discharge of artillery prevented the huge monster from over-
turning us, which he certainly would have done if the blow
had not stunned him. We saw with pleasure that the waves
carried the enormous body to a sand-bank a little distance
from the shore, and there it lay like a stranded ship.

Suddenly Ernest uttered a loud scream. "A man! a savage!" said he, and he pointed out to us in the distance a sort
of canoe dancing over the waves. The person who conducted it seemed to have perceived us, for he advanced and
then made towards a projecting point, as if to communicate
his discovery to his companions. I leave our sensations to
the imagination of the reader. I had not the slightest doubt
that we had fallen in with a band of savages, and we began
to fortify our boat against their arrows, by making a bul-
wark of the stalks of maize and corn we had brought with
us. We loaded our cannons, guns, and pistols, and, everything arranged, we stood ready behind our rampart, resolved to defend it as long as we were able. We dared not
advance, for there was the savage; and Ernest, growing
tired of the pantomime, observed that, if we used the
speaking-trumpet, possibly our savage might understand some
words of the half-dozen languages we were familiar with.

The advice appeared good. I took up the speaking-trumpet
and bellowed out with all my force some words of Malay;
but still the canoe remained immovable, as if its master had
not comprehended us.

"Instead of Malay," said Jack, "suppose we try English."
So saying, he caught up the trumpet, and in his clear, loud
tone pronounced some common sailor-phrases, well known
to all who have ever been on board ship. The device succeeded, and we saw the savage advancing toward us, holding a green branch in his hand. Nearer and nearer he came,
and at last we recognized in the painted savage our own
dear Fritz.

CHAPTER LVIII

Adventures of Fritz—Sir Edward Montrose—Our Adopted Sister —Attack of Wolves—Preparations for Return

WHEN we had freed Fritz from our oft-repeated embraces, we commenced asking him all manner of questions; and, speaking all together, the poor fellow was so confused he did not know what to do. I demanded an answer on two points only—whether his excursion had been satisfactory, and why he had played this farce of dressing himself like a savage, and causing us such anxiety.

"As to the purpose of my excursion," said he, with a joy he could scarcely conceal, "I have attained it"; and the young man, as he said these words, pressed my hand, which he held in his. "As for my costume, I mistook you for a tribe of Malays, or some other nation, and, in the fear that you were enemies, I endeavoured to disguise myself by painting the upper part of my body with powder, soaked in water. The two reports of the cannon that I heard convinced me more and more that you were enemies; the Malay words that you addressed to me confirmed me, and I should still have been endeavouring to deceive you, and you would still have been in fear of me, if Jack had not bawled out those sailor-phrases in his unmistakable voice."

We all began to laugh over the farce we had been enacting; and Fritz, drawing me aside, said, in an eager, joyous tone, "I have succeeded, papa: the hand of God conducted me to the dwelling-place of the poor shipwrecked girl—for it was a woman that had written those lines. Three years has she lived on that smoking rock, all alone, destitute of everything! Can you believe it, but the poor girl has conjured me

301

not to betray her sex, except to you and my mother. I have
brought her with me: she is near by, on a little island just
beyond the Bay of Pearls; come and see her. Oh! do not say
anything to my brothers. I want to enjoy their surprise when
they find I have brought them back a sister, for I am sure
she will allow them to call her so."

I consented to the wish of my son, and, without saying
anything to the rest of the family, I ordered them to hoist
the sails, weigh anchor, and make ready to depart. Fritz,
who had changed his dress and washed off his disguise, flew
about, hastening his less eager brothers; then, jumping into
his cajack, he piloted us through the shoals and reefs that
were scattered along the coast. After an hour's sailing he
turned off, and directed his course toward a shady island not
far from the Bay of Pearls; we sailed close up to the shore,
and fastened the pinnace to the trunk of a fallen tree. Fritz,
however, was quicker than we, and he was on shore, and
had entered a little wood in the middle of the island before
we had yet landed. We followed him into the wood, and
soon found ourselves in the vicinity of a hut, built like those
of the Hottentots, with a fire burning before it, on which
some fish were cooking in a large shell. Fritz uttered a
peculiar kind of halloo, and what was our surprise to see,
descending from a large tree, a young and handsome sailor,
who, turning his timid eyes on us, stood still, as if he dared
not approach!

It was such a long time since we had seen a man—ten
years!—society had become so strange a thing to us, that
we remained stupefied; our hearts felt for the young stranger,
but our tongues remained dumb.

The silence was broken by Fritz, who, taking the young
sailor by the hand, advanced toward us. "My father, my
mother, and you, my brothers," said he, in a voice broken
by emotion, "behold a friend—a brother—that I present
you, a new companion in misfortune—Sir Edward Montrose, who, like ourselves, has been shipwrecked on the
coast."

"He is welcome among us," was the general cry; and,
approaching the young sailor, whom I easily recognized as
being a woman, and taking her by the hand, I comforted
and encouraged her, assuring the seeming man, that among
us he would always find food and sustenance; my wife and

myself would be his parents, and my sons his brothers. My
wife, moved by compassion, opened her arms, and the
young sailor rushed into them, bursting into a flood of tears,
as he thanked us for our kindness. The most lively joy now
reigned in our little circle, and his brothers poured question
after question upon Fritz, who joyfully replied, "I will tell
you all afterward; let us attend now to our new brother."
Supper was served, and my wife brought out a bottle of her
spiced hydromel to add to the feast. Everybody spoke at
once, and my sons addressed their new companion with
such vivacity as to embarrass the timid stranger: my wife
saw his distress, and, as it was late, she gave the signal for
retirement, taking the sailor with her on the pinnace where
she said she intended to provide a bed for him that would
amply console him for the uncomfortable nights he had
hitherto passed. We then separated, my wife and the stranger
retiring to the boat, while my sons and I stopped to light
and arrange our watch-fires.

The new-comer naturally became the subject of conversation, and Fritz recounted to his brothers the whole history
of the albatross. He spoke of his thoughts and actions, but
he became so excited in his narration, that he forgot himself
and the secret he had to keep. A word escaped him, and he
called the young sailor "Emily."

"Emily!—Emily!" repeated his brothers, who had begun
to doubt the mystery; "Emily!—Fritz has deceived us, and
Sir Edward is a girl!—our adopted brother turned into a
sister!"

I leave to the imagination to picture the embarrassment of
Fritz when he discovered his imprudence. In vain he endeavoured to bring back his words: it would not do, and the
girl could no longer hide her sex by the hat and pantaloons.

The next morning it was a comic sight to see the embarrassment and awkwardness with which my sons approached
one whom they had the day before embraced as a companion and a brother. My poor boys were not acquainted with
the usages of polite society and the ease it inspires, and they
appeared to a great disadvantage by the side of the beautiful
English girl. The name of sister was substituted for that of
brother, but pronounced with reserve and embarrassment.
As for Emily, she was very much astonished at the discovery
the young men had made, and she retreated, as if for

protection, to the arms of my wife; but a moment after, recovering herself, she advanced, and extending her hand to each one of the boys, gracefully demanded for the sister the friendship they had extended to the brother. Gaiety was re-established, and we sat down to breakfast, which was composed of fruits, cold meat, and chocolate of our own making, which was a great treat to my new daughter, and recalled her native land to her mind. After breakfast I proposed to weigh anchor and return to the Bay of Pearls, where the cachalot stranded on the shore offered us a magnificent prey. Arrived there, we debated in what manner we could carry away the oily substance with which the head and dorsal bone of this animal is filled. Unfortunately we had no barrels in which we could gather the precious product. Emily rescued us from our dilemma, by mentioning a process she had seen employed in India, which was, to put the half-liquid substance in wet linen bags. The idea appeared excellent, and we immediately put it into practice. I gathered all the sacks I could find, and dipping them in the sea-water, stretched them open with pieces of branches. We were two hours engaged in these preparations. The tide was not yet high enough to allow the pinnace to approach the bank, where the whale lay; but we took the canoe and the cajack and set off, leaving the two women under the safeguard of Turk, and taking with us Folb, Braun, and the jackal. The monster lay extended like a huge wall; our dogs ran up to it, and a moment after we heard some animals howling dreadfully. We hastened up, and found our brave dogs valiantly contending with a troop of black wolves, who were devouring the whale. Two of their number were already stretched on the sand, two others were yet engaged with the dogs, and the rest fled at our approach toward a little wood.

Our dogs acquitted themselves bravely: four wolves lay stretched upon the sand, but the noble animals had paid dearly for their victory; the blood streamed from all parts of their bodies, and the ears of Folb especially were dreadfully torn. Jack dressed their wounds with some hydromel, while Fritz and Francis aided me in another work. The former, after having armed his feet with cramp-irons, climbed like a cat up the back of the monster, and cut open the enormous head of the cachalot with a hatchet, and then with a ladle dipped the spermaceti out of the head, and emptied it into one of the sacks which I held ready, while Francis covered the outside with wet sand and mortar, forming a solid crust through which none of the grease could escape. Our sacks were soon full, for as fast as Fritz emptied the head the cavity was filled by a fresh supply from the backbone. The operation was very fatiguing, and I was glad when it was over. We then cut a quantity of willows, and wove them into little pointed caps, with which we covered the sacks, in order to shield them from the sun and the birds of prey, who were fast assembling in great numbers.

We now thought of returning. The tide was high, but the load was too heavy for the boat; we therefore were obliged to leave it and return to the verdant little island, which we had named "Good Rencounter," because there we had first found Emily. The appearance of the sacks ranged on the sand was very droll; they exactly resembled little Chinese with their pointed hats, and we could not help laughing heartily at the sight.

After having recounted our adventures, and shown our four fine black wolves, with their superb skins, we were invited by our dear housekeepers to sit down to an excellent dinner, enriched by a new dish—a sauce after the manner of the Caribbees, made with eggs of land-crabs, with which the island abounded. I was undecided as to what means I should adopt to transport the spermaceti to the island, for the pinnace could not approach the bank near enough, without risk of running aground, and our other boats were not large enough. Every one gave his advice; when it came to Emily's turn, she observed, in her soft, silvery tone, "If you are willing, my dear papa"—for already she had accustomed herself to address me by that endearing name—"if you are willing, while you and my brothers are engaged in that disgusting tannery, I will promise to bring over your sacks."

The next morning, before my sons were awake, Emily prepared for her expedition; she took a bladder of fresh water, a basket of provisions, and lightly descending the ladder of the pinnace, she seated herself in Fritz's cajack, untied it, and rowed off with a grace and ease that surprised me. I would have called her back, but the little vixen gaily kissed her hand, and soon was far on her way toward the bank of sand. She had chosen just the right time; the tide

was rising, and had just commenced to wet the bottom of
the sacks. The adventurous girl jumped on shore, fastened
all the sacks by cords to a rope which she had with her, and
tied the rope to the cajack, and again embarking, drew after
her all the sacks, the contents of which, being light, floated
like bladders on the water.

It was now full noon; we sat down to table, and, after
dinner, began our preparations for setting out for Felsenheim,
where we desired to instal our new companion. We packed
up everything we had, including Emily's treasures, both
those she had saved from shipwreck and those she had made
herself. Fritz had made her a box which held them all, and
they really were very curious, consisting of clothes, ornaments, domestic utensils, and all sorts of articles which she
had made in her exile, out of the scanty material she had at
her disposal.

Emily now bade adieu to the island that had received her,
and the trees that had sheltered her, during her short sojourn. We could not leave the place without giving it a
name, so we called the bay in which we anchored "Happy
Bay," in allusion to the joyful meeting we had had there.
We now took the direction of the Bay of Pearls, where we
were obliged to make a short stay before returning to
Felsenheim, to which we were impatient to introduce our
new companion.

CHAPTER LIX
The Limekiln—Fritz's Story

FRITZ, seated in his cajack, served as pilot to assist us in
penetrating safely through the rocks and shoals into the
bay, where at last we all arrived in safety. Everything was
found just as we had left it—the table and benches yet

standing, our fireplace undestroyed, and, what was more, the air was purified; and, the oysters, having all been dried up by the sun, had lost their unpleasant odour. The dead bodies of the lions and wild boar were but heaps of whitened bones, the birds of prey having completely stripped them of every particle of flesh.

We wished to go direct to Felsenheim immediately; but an unexpected discovery detained us a longer time than we intended. I had noticed among the stones which strewed the shore, a sort of rock which it appeared to me could be easily converted to lime. It was a discovery too precious to be neglected, and I resolved to establish a limekiln without delay on the beach. It did not take us long to make one to suit our purpose; but the calcination of the stones occupied us much longer, and we were obliged to sit up a great part of the night. During this time we made some barrels of pieces of pine bark, circled with strong withs of willow; a round piece of bark served for the bottom, and another for the cover. To enliven our labour, and to abridge the length of the evening, I persuaded Fritz to give us a more complete account than he had hitherto done of the manner in which he had found our new sister, and the details of his voyage. It was the best way in which to employ our remaining time, and the curiosity of my sons was so excited that they formed a circle about Fritz, who thus commenced his narration.

"You all remember," said he to his brothers, "the manner in which I left you, after having given my father a letter which contained an account of my intended excursion. The sea was calm; but I had scarcely passed the Bay of Pearls, when suddenly a violent wind arose, gradually increasing to a perfect hurricane; the rising waves, the rain, the thunder and lightning, all confounded in horrible confusion. My little bark was not strong enough to resist the tremendous sea, and all that I could do was to abandon myself to the current.

"After several hours the wind fell and the air calmed, and my canoe again found its equilibrium upon the surface of the waters. I was far from all the places that we were acquainted with; the tempest had thrown me on a coast entirely new to my eyes; the conformation of the rocks, the gigantic cliffs which seemed to lose themselves in the clouds, the vegetation, the animals I perceived on the coast, the birds which flew about me, all announced a new world. My first care was to look carefully around and see whether some light smoke did not rise behind the rocks; for, as you know, the Smoking Rock was my only thought. I could perceive nothing as yet; but full of hope, I rowed along the coast. Night came on, and I passed it in the cajack, after having made a miserable supper on pemmican.

"The next morning I continued my journey, and the farther I advanced, the more the coast appeared to change its aspect. I encountered, from time to time, majestic rivers, which flowed silently on and mingled with the sea. The mouth of one of them resembled an immense bay, and I decided to ascend it some little distance; its banks were covered with large trees, willows, and vines, so thickly woven together, that they resembled a huge mat, covered with birds, monkeys, and even squirrels.

"Toward the middle of the day the heat became so unsupportable, that it was impossible to resist the desire of seeking some shade under the trees. After being slightly refreshed, I pursued my route, and sailed on a long time without being able to land; the rivers and shores were both defended by guards I had little desire to come in contact with, for I recognized elephants, lions, panthers—in one word, a complete reunion of all the ferocious animals of creation. After travelling several leagues farther, the appearance of the coast suddenly changed, and, as if the ferocious animals had had their district marked out to them, I ceased to perceive any. The shore appeared peaceable, but desolate; the breeze which murmured among the vines, and the song of some inoffensive birds were the only noises which broke the calm stillness, and I felt reassured, and resolved to land and procure a repast. I accordingly fastened my cajack as strongly as possible, and jumped lightly to the shore; and being hungry, I lighted my fire, and began to prepare a juicy dinner from a fat goose which I had shot while landing, and a dozen of oysters.

"I rose long before daylight next morning and resumed my voyage. The country through which I now sailed was of an aspect entirely different from any I had ever yet seen. There were beautiful green plains, dotted over with clumps of towering palms; little lakes surrounded with osiers, upon the borders of which sported herds of elephants; thick tufts of cactus of all sorts, loaded with flowers and fruits, which the enormous rhinoceros seemed to devour without paying any attention to the thorns; beautiful clumps of the mimosa, the high tops of which the towering giraffe devoured with as much facility as a goat would a small shrub.

"On I sailed, and, once more seduced by the picturesque appearance of a river which lost itself in a tranquil bay, I resolved to ascend it. The water slipped gently under the prow of my little cajack—nothing appeared to indicate any danger; there were no serpents on the bank, no horrid beasts in the forests, and I floated tranquilly on, enjoying the fresh breeze and the cool shade of the overhanging trees, when suddenly there appeared before me a long throat, armed with rows of strong sharp teeth; it was distended to its full capacity as if it would take in at one mouthful myself, the cajack, and the oars. I instantly comprehended the extent of my danger, and, seizing one of the oars, I drove it with all my strength direct into the yawning mouth of the monster, who disappeared in an instant, leaving a long trace of blood behind him, showing that the wound I had made was of some importance. I did not remain long on this river; two other monsters of the same nature as the first rose up to the surface of the water. They were alligators, the most terrible kind among these animals, but whose tremendous voracity is happily balanced by a natural laziness, which retains them always near the spot where they were born. I had escaped from one danger only to fall into another. At a little distance from the River of Alligators, while coasting along a little wood, I observed that the trees were loaded with the rarest and most beautiful of birds, among which were lyras, paroquets, humming-birds, and birds of paradise —in one word, a complete assemblage of all that array of beautiful plumage which decorates the forests of the New World, and I could not resist the desire of attacking them. I landed, attached my cajack to the bank and walked up to the wood, holding my eagle unhooded in my hand. I cast him off, and he returned with a superb paroquet, whose flame-coloured feathers sparkled in the sun's rays. While I was occupied in examining him, I heard behind me a light rustling on the sand, which I though was merely caused by a little land-turtle, or some such animal, and I turned carelessly round. It was well I did so; for not twelve paces from

me there was a splendid royal tiger with open mouth,
crouched down as if about to spring upon me. I stood as if
struck with stupor; a mist came over my eyes, and scarcely
could I raise my gun, so much had horror paralysed my
strength, when suddenly my brave eagle, comprehending
my danger, flew boldly at the advancing tiger, and began to
pick at his eyes. This timely succour saved me; for it enabled me to collect my senses, and levelling my gun, I discharged its contents into the right flank of my enemy, and
then two pistol-balls lodged in the throat completed my
victory. The tiger lay dead; but alas! my victory had cost me
dear, for my poor eagle fell at the same time with his
conquered enemy, who had seized him in his claws and had
torn him in pieces. I picked him up, weeping bitterly over
my loss, and carried him to the cajack, hoping some day to
have him stuffed and placed in our museum.

"I quitted the shore with a sorrowing mind, and again I
prayed to my heavenly Father that He would give me strength
to continue my voyage. I doubled a little cape, and, suddenly, from the summit of the grey rocks which bordered
the coast, I perceived a light cloud of smoke rising in the
air. I turned my canoe in the direction of the long-sought-
for signal. The irregularities of the rocks along the coast
were the only difficulties I had to encounter, and it appeared to me that I should never get through them. At last I
landed, and, with infinite difficulty, scrambled up the rocks
until I arrived at a platform on which I perceived a human
creature. At the noise which I made in approaching, the
individual, who was arranging the fire, rose, perceived me,
uttered a cry of surprise and joy, then, joining his hands,
stood still, as if waiting for me to speak. Notwithstanding
the midshipman's dress she wore, her exclamation, and the
delicate contour of her features, convinced me that I was in
the presence of a female. I stopped about ten paces from
her, and calling to my memory all I knew of English, I said
in a subdued tone, 'I am the liberator whom God has sent
you. I have received the message of the albatross.' I must
have pronounced these words very badly, as Emily did not
at first comprehend them; I repeated them, however, and
after a few moments we understood each other well enough
to make a mutual interchange of our feelings. Gestures,
looks, accents all filled up the blank that words had left

vacant. I spoke to my new sister about the castle of Felsenheim, Falcon's Nest, our shipwreck, and ten years' sojourn on the coast, where we lived in almost European luxury; on her part, she recounted to me the history of her childhood, her shipwreck, and existence on the Island of the Smoking Rock, making a fine story for my papa to write out in the long winter evenings. Emily graciously invited me to supper, after which we passed the remainder of the night, I in my cajack, she in the branches of a tree, where she always slept from the fear of wild beasts. The next morning we again met. Emily had already prepared breakfast, which consisted of fruit and broiled fish. The repast being over, the sea looked so calm that I thought we had better start; so, after packing up all her curiosities, and putting them on board the cajack, we took our seats and set off. We sailed on a long time; but an accident happened to my little barque, and I was obliged to put in at the little island which you have called 'Good Rencounter,' in memory of our meeting; it was there I left my new-found sister, who, doubtful of her reception in a strange family, begged me to go on and ask permission of my father to bring her among them. I consented; and my canoe having been repaired, I took the well-known route home: it was then that I encountered you, and from fear that you were pirates, I disguised myself, and played you such a trick."

"Oh! I am so sorry it is done," cried Jack, as Fritz finished his story; "but you must now tell us the history of our sister."

Fritz was about to commence a new narration, of greater interest than the former, but I stopped him, and advised him to take a little rest before he talked any more.

CHAPTER LX

Emily's own Story—Return to Felsenheim with Military Honours —The Winter Season Once More

THE story of Fritz had detained us longer than I had anticipated, as upon looking at my watch, I discovered that it was midnight. The audience were not at all sleepy, however, but as we had to execute labours on the morrow, which would require strength and agility, I thought that if they sat up all night they would be over-wearied the next day; I therefore deemed it necessary to cut short the narration, deferring its completion till a more convenient time. This decision was received with a very bad grace; but it was positive, so each one sought his accustomed resting-place, either on shore or in the pinnace.

The next morning, when all the family were assembled for breakfast, the enterprise and courage of Fritz became the subject of conversation; this naturally brought on the story of last night, and I was obliged to consent that Emily's history should open the day. I wanted the dear girl herself to tell it; but she was so timid, though at the same time so lively, busied in her domestic occupations, that I could do nothing with her. Fritz was therefore entreated to act as her proxy, and resume his recital.

"As soon as I was able to understand my new sister," said he, "I asked her by what course of events she had been thrown on the desert coast where I now found her.

"She told me that she was born in India, of English parents, and that her father, after having served as major in a British regiment, obtained the command of an important English colony. The commandant, Montrose, for that was the name of Emily's father, had the misfortune to lose his wife only three years after his marriage; and, profoundly afflicted by this loss, all his affections centred in their only child. He took charge of her education, and devoted all the time he could spare from his official duties, in developing the precious qualities which nature had endowed his dear daughter with. Not content with providing her with every means for mental improvement, he endeavoured to make her a strong, healthy woman, capable of facing and resisting danger. Such was Emily's education up to the age of sixteen; she managed a fowling-piece as well as a needle, and rode as gracefully and firmly as the best cavalry officer, and shone resplendent in her father's brilliant saloons.

"Major Montrose, having been appointed colonel, was ordered to return with part of his regiment to England. This circumstance forced him to separate himself from his daughter, as naval discipline did not allow women on board a line-of-battle ship in time of war. It was arranged, however, that she should sail the same day that he did, in another ship, the captain of which was an old friend of her father's, and who would take every care of his daughter. The voyage at its commencement was prosperous and agreeable, but before many days a terrible tempest arose. The ship was thrown off her course, and a furious wind drove her down upon our rocky coast; two shallops were launched upon the angry waves, and a chance of safety offered to the shipwrecked. Emily found a place in the smallest—the captain was in the other. The storm continuing, the boats were soon separated, and the one that contained Emily was broken in pieces, and the poor girl alone, of all the crew, was fortunate enough to escape death. The waves carried her, half fainting, to the foot of the rock where I discovered her. She crawled under the shade of a projecting rock, and, sinking on the sand, slept for four-and-twenty hours. There she passed several days, abandoned to dark despair, with no nourishment but some birds' eggs, which she found on the rocks. At the end of that time, the sun reappearing and the sea growing calm, the poor castaway thought of the crew in the large shallop and, in the hope that they might see her, she resolved to establish signals of distress. As she wore a midshipman's uniform on board ship, by order of her father, she had a box in her pocket containing a flint, knife, and other articles. She picked up some pieces of wood which the sea had thrown on the sand, carried them to the summit of

the rock, and there kindled a fire, which she never allowed
to go out. You can easily imagine how drearily passed the
first days of Emily's exile; she had to contend against all the
horrors of hunger and the desert. How thankful she felt for
the semi-masculine education that her father had given her:
it had endowed her with courage and resolution far beyond
her sex. She comprehended the whole extent of her situation, and turning to heaven, she placed her trust in God and
hoped on. She built a hut, fished, hunted, tamed birds—
among others a cormorant, which she taught to catch fish—in
one word, she lived alone, with no earthly succour, for three
long dreary years."

Fritz stopped; his eyes fell upon the heroine of his story,
who could hardly conceal her embarrassment.

"My child," said I, "you are but another proof that God
never withholds His aid from those who desire it. That
which you have done for three years a poor Swiss family
have done for ten, and heavenly aid has never been with-
held from them."

I allowed some little time for commentaries on Emily's
history; but, as I had resolved that the day should be an
active one, I soon gave the signal for work. The manufacture of lime had succeeded. I submitted some pieces to the
proof of water, and found it excellent.

Toward evening the pinnace was laden with all that we
could carry away, and we talked seriously of returning to
Felsenheim. The poetic description we had given concerning
the salt grotto, and our aërial palace at Falcon's Nest, had
rendered Emily exceedingly curious to judge for herself
concerning all these wonders. The next day we weighed
anchor just as dawn was breaking; the sail of the pinnace
fluttered gaily in the fresh breeze, and Fritz's cajack, containing himself and Francis, went before us as pilots. When
we hove in sight of Prospect Hill, I proposed to stop and
take a look at the farmhouse; but Fritz and his brother
asked permission of me to go on home, so that they could
have all things prepared for us. I consented, and they set
out.

From Prospect Hill we sailed to Shark Island, where we
secured, in passing, a fine quantity of the soft wool of the
Angora rabbits. From Shark Island we directed our course
toward Felsenheim, and we could just distinguish it when a

salute of ten guns greeted our ears. This produced a very good effect, doctor Ernest only regretting that the salute was not composed of an odd number of guns. "An even number," said he, "is entirely contrary to general usage."

We returned the polite salute of our two artillerymen by a salvo of eleven guns, the execution of which was undertaken and performed by Jack and Ernest in a style that would have done honour to a practised cannoneer. Soon after we saw Fritz and Francis coming toward us in their canoe; they received us at the entrance of the bay, and followed us to the shore. They landed before us, and the moment Emily's foot touched the sand, a hurrah resounded through the air, and Fritz, springing forward, presented her his hand, like a gallant cavalier, and led her up to the portico of the grotto. There a new spectacle awaited us: a table was spread in the middle of the gallery, and loaded with all the fruits that the country produced. Bananas, figs, guavas, oranges, rose up in perfumed heaps upon flat calabashes. All the vases, cocoa-nut cups and ostrich-eggs mounted on turned wooden pedestals, urns of painted porcelain, all were filled with hydromel and milk; while a large dish of fried fish, and a huge roast turkey, stuffed with truffles, formed the solid part of the repast. A double festoon of flowers surrounded the canopy above the table, sustaining a large medallion on which was inscribed, "Welcome, fair Emily Montrose!" It was a complete holiday, and as pompous a reception as our means would allow. Emily sat down to table between my wife and myself; Ernest and Jack also took their places; while the two caterers of the feast, each with a napkin on his arm, did the honours of the table.

We passed from the table to the interior of the grotto, and our young companion had the apartment next ours for her use. She could not restrain her admiration at the effects our industry had accomplished; she was astonished that a man and four children could have effected so much. The chateau in the tree at Falcon's Nest next received a visit; it had fallen into decay, from neglect, and we passed a whole week in fitting it up. We then set out for Waldegg to gather our rice and other grains, for the season was advancing, and some violent showers already warned us to hasten our preparations for the coming winter. Emily gave proof, during these labours, of an intelligence and good will which rendered her assistance very valuable; and she inspired everybody with such zeal and industry, that when the winter set in we were all prepared for it. Ten years had accustomed us to the terrible winters, and we calmly listened to the wind and storm as it raged furiously without. We had reserved for the winter several sedentary occupations, in which our new companion proved her skill and industry; she excelled in weaving and plaiting straw, osiers, etc.; and, under her direction, we made some light straw hats for summer, some elegant baskets, and conveniently arranged game-bags. My wife was delighted with her adopted daughter, and Ernest found a companion, whose fine education rendered her a conversable and intelligent woman. In fact, Emily had become to my wife and myself a fifth child, and a beloved sister for my sons.

CHAPTER LXI

Conclusion

IT is with a thousand different sensations that I write the word *conclusion*. It recalls to my mind all that has passed. God is good! God is merciful! is the reigning sentiment in my heart: I have so many reasons for heartfelt gratitude to a gracious Providence, that I hope the reader will pardon me for the disorder in which I finish my story.

It was toward the end of the rainy season, the wind had lost its violence, and a patch of blue sky could now and then be seen; our pigeons had quitted the dove-cot, and we ourselves ventured to open the door of the grotto, and taste the fresh air.

Our first care was for our gardens, which had suffered injury; we took account of the damage as well as we were able, and then set out for our more distant possessions. Fritz and Jack proposed to make an excursion to Shark Island, to inspect our fort and colony there. I consented, and they set off in the cajack.

My sons, on their arrival, having examined the interior of the fort, and assured themselves that nothing of importance was damaged, began to look round and see if anything appeared on the horizon, but all was blank. Wishing to see whether the cannons were in good order, they began firing away, as if they had all the powder in the world at their command. But what was their astonishment and emotion when, a moment after, they heard distinctly three reports of a cannon in the distance! They could not be mistaken, for a faint light toward the east preceded each report. After a short consultation as to what should be done, the two brothers resolved to hasten home and recount their adventure to us.

We had heard the reports of the cannons they had fired, and we could not imagine why they were hurrying back so fast. I called out, as loud as I could, "Halloo, there! what is the matter?" On they came, and, jumping on shore, fell into my arms, faintly articulating, "Oh, papa, papa, did you not hear them?"

"Hear what?" said I. "We have heard nothing but the noise your waste of powder made."

"You have not heard three other reports in the distance?"

"No."

"Why, we heard them plainly and distinctly."

"It was the echo," said Ernest.

This remark nettled Jack a little, and he replied rather sharply—

"No, Mr. Doctor, it wasn't the echo; I think I have fired cannons enough in my lifetime to know whether that was an echo or not. We distinctly heard three reports of a cannon, and we are certain that some ship is sailing in this part of the world."

"If there is really a ship on our coasts," said I, "who knows whether it is manned by Europeans or by Malay pirates—who knows whether we ought to rejoice or be sorry at its presence, and that, instead of preparing for deliverance, we should not make preparations for defence?"

My first resolution was to organize a system of defence,

and provide for our safety. We watched alternately under the gallery of the grotto, so that we could be ready in case of surprise; but the night passed quietly away, and in the morning the rain commenced, and continued so violently during two long days that it was impossible for us to go out.

On the third day the sun reappeared. Fritz and Jack, full of impatience, resolved to return to Shark Island, and try a new signal. I consented; but, instead of the cajack, we took the canoe, and I went with them. On arriving at the fort we hoisted our flag, while Jack, ever impatient, loaded a cannon and fired it; but scarcely had the report died away in the distance, when we distinctly heard a louder answering report in the direction of Cape Disappointment.

Jack could not contain himself for joy. "Men, men," cried he, dancing about us; "men, papa; are you sure of it now?" And his enthusiasm communicating itself to us, we hoisted another and a larger flag on our flag-staff. Six other reports followed the first one we had heard.

Overpowered with emotion, we hastened to our boat, and were soon in the presence of the family. They had not heard the seven reports, but they had seen our two flags flying, and they were eagerly waiting for circumstantial news.

I ordered that everything in the grotto should be put in a place of safety. My three youngest sons, my wife and Emily, set off for Falcon's Nest with our cattle, and I embarked in the cajack with Fritz, to reconnoitre. It was near midday when we set out; we coasted along without discovering anything, and the illusion of the moment began to dissipate. On more calm reflection, however, the certainty that we had heard the seven reports of the cannon kept up our courage; when suddenly, on doubling a little promontory which had hitherto concealed it from us, we beheld a fine European ship majestically reposing at anchor, with a long-boat at the side, and an English flag floating at the masthead.

I seek in vain to find words that will express the sentiments which filled our souls. We elevated our hands and eyes toward heaven, and thus returned our thanks to God for His great beneficence. If I had permitted it, Fritz would have thrown himself into the sea and swum off to the ship; but I was afraid that, notwithstanding the English flag, the vessel before us might be a Malay corsair, which had assumed false colours in order to deceive other vessels. We remained at a distance, not liking to venture nearer without being more certain what it was. We could see all that was passing on board the vessel. Two tents had been raised on the shore, tables were laid for dinner, quarters of meat were roasting before blazing fires, men were running to and fro, and the whole scene had the appearance of an organized encampment. Two sentinels were on the deck of the vessel, and when they perceived us they spoke to the officer on duty who stood near, and who turned his telescope toward us.

"They are Europeans," cried Fritz; "you can easily judge from the face of the officer. Malays certainly would be more dusky than that."

Fritz's remark was true; but yet I did not like to go too near. We remained in the bay, manœuvering our canoe with all the dexterity of which we were capable. We sang a Swiss mountain song, and when we had finished I cried out through my speaking-trumpet these three words, *Englishmen, good men*! But no answer was returned: our song, our cajack, and more than all our costume, I expect, marked us for savages, from the officer making signs to us to approach, and holding up knives, scissors, and glass beads, for which the savages of the New World are generally so desirous. This mistake made us laugh; but we did not approach, as we wished to present ourselves before them in better trim. We contented ourselves with exclaiming once more, *Englishmen*, and then darted off as fast as our boat could carry us.

We passed a whole day in preparing the pinnace, and loading it with presents for the captain, as we wished him to see that those whom he had taken for savages were beings far advanced in the arts of civilization. We set off at sunrise; the weather was magnificent, and we sailed gallantly along, Fritz preceding us as pilot.

When we could clearly distinguish the ship, a sensation of vivid joy was experienced by us all: my sons were dumb with pleasure and eagerness.

"Hoist the English flag," cried I in the voice of a Stentor; and a second after, a flag similar to the one on the ship fluttered from our masthead.

If we were filled with extraordinary emotions on seeing a European ship, the English were not less astonished to see a little boat with flowing sails coming toward them. Guns

were now fired from the ship and answered from our pinnace, and joining Fritz in his cajack, we approached the
English ship to welcome the captain to our shores.

The captain received us with that frankness and cordiality
that always distinguish sailors; and conducted us to the
cabin, where a flask of Cape wine cemented the alliance
between us.

I recounted to the captain, as briefly as possible, the
history of our shipwreck, and our sojourn of ten years on
this coast. I spoke to him of Emily, and asked him if he had
ever heard of her father, Sir Edward Montrose. The captain
not only knew him, but it was a part of his instructions to
explore these latitudes, where, three years before, the ship
Dorcas, which had on board the daughter of Commander
Montrose, was supposed to have been wrecked, and to try
to discover whether any tidings of the vessel or crew could
be ascertained. In consequence, he manifested the greatest
desire to see her, and assure her that her father was alive.
He informed us that a tempest of four days' duration had
thrown him off the course which he followed for Sydney and
New Holland; and thus he had been driven on this coast,
where he had renewed his wood and water. "It was then,"
added he, "that we heard the reports of cannon, which we
answered; on the third day new discharges convinced us that
we were not alone on the coast, and we resolved to wait
until, by some means or other, we discovered who were our
companions in misfortune. But we find an organized colony,
and a maritime power, whose alliance I solicit in the name
of the sovereign of Great Britain."

This last sally made us laugh, and we cordially pressed the
hand which Captain Littleton extended to us.

The rest of the family were waiting some distance off in
the pinnace. We took leave of the captain, who, ordering
his gig to be manned, arrived on board our vessel almost as
soon as we did. We received him with every demonstration
of joy and friendship, and Emily was half wild with happiness at the sight of a fellow-countryman, and one who
brought intelligence of her father.

The captain brought with him an English family, whom
the fatigues of the passage had rendered ill, consisting of
Mr. Wolston, a distinguished machinist, his wife, and two
daughters. My wife offered Mrs. Wolston her assistance,

and promised her that her family should find every comfort and convenience at Felsenheim if they would return with us. They gladly consented, and we set out with them, taking leave of the captain, who did not like to pass the night away from his ship.

My readers can form an idea of the astonishment which was evinced by the Wolston family on seeing all our establishments. We ostentatiously pointed out to them Felsenheim with its rocky vault, the giant-tree of Falcon's Nest, Prospect Hill, and all the marvels which were comprised in our domains. A frugal repast in the evening united both families under the gallery of the grotto, and my wife prepared, in the interior, apartments and beds to receive the new-comers.

The next morning Mr. Wolston came up to me, and tenderly stretching out his hand, spoke as follows—

"Sir," said he, "I cannot express all the admiration that I feel on regarding the wonders with which you are surrounded. The hand of God has been with you, and here you live happily, far away from the strife of the world, among the works of creation, alone with your family. I came from England to seek repose: where can I find it better than here? and I shall esteem myself the happiest of men if you will allow me to establish myself in a corner of your domains."

This proposition of Mr. Wolston filled me with joy, and I immediately assured him that I would willingly share with him the half of my patriarchal empire.

Mr. Wolston hastened to communicate to his wife the success of his application, and the morning was devoted to the joy and pleasure that this news caused. But considerations of a painful nature occupied my mind: the ship which now presented itself was the second only we had seen in ten years, and probably as long a period might elapse before another appeared, should we let Captain Littleton and his ship leave us without any addition to his crew. These questions affected the dearest interests of our family. My wife did not wish to return to Europe; I was myself too much attached to my new life to leave it, and we were both at an age when hazards and dangers have no attraction, and ambition has resolved itself into a desire for repose. But our children were young, their life was but just commencing, and I did not think it right to deprive them of the advantages which civilization and a contact with the world pre-

sented; and then again, Emily, since she had heard that her
father was in England, did not conceal her desire to return;
and although we regretted losing this amiable girl, yet it was
impossible to detain her. So at last I decided to call my
children together, and ascertain their sentiments. I spoke to
them of civilized Europe, of the resources of every kind
which society offered to its members, and I asked them if
they would depart with Captain Littleton, or be content to
pass the remainder of their lives upon this coast.

Jack and Ernest declared that they would rather remain.
Ernest, the philosopher, had no need of the world to interrupt his studies; and Jack, the hunter, found the domain of
Falcon's Nest large enough for his excursions. Fritz was
silent, but I saw by his countenance that he had decided to
go. I encouraged him to speak; he confessed that he had a
great desire to return to Europe, and his younger brother,
Francis, declared that he would willingly accompany him.

Mr. Wolston also dismembered his family: he kept but
one of his daughters; the other went on to New Holland.
These family arrangements were very painful, and when
they were finished I hastened to inform the captain of the
Unicorn. He readily consented to take our three passengers.

"I resign three persons," said he, "Mr. and Mrs. Wolston
and one of their daughters; I take three more, and my
complement will not be affected."

The *Unicorn* remained eight days at anchor, and we employed them in preparing the cargo which was to be the
fortune of our voyagers on arriving in Europe. All the riches
that we had amassed—pearls, ivory, spices, furs, and all our
rare productions, were carefully packed and put on board
the ship, which we also furnished with meat and fruits.

On the eve of their departure, after having exhausted
myself in a last conversation, in which I advised my sons
always to carry out the principles in which they had been
instructed, and so to live in this world that we might, through
the merits of our Saviour, be united in the next, I gave Fritz
this narration of our shipwreck and establishment on the
desert coast, enjoining him expressly to have it published as
soon after his arrival as he possibly could; and this desire on
my part, exempt from all vanity of authorship, had for its
only object and hope that it might be useful to others as a
lesson of morality, patience, courage, perseverance, and of

Christian submission to the will of God. Perhaps some day a father may take courage from the manner in which we supported our tribulations; perhaps some young person will see, in the course of this narrative, the value of a varied education and the importance of becoming acquainted with first principles.

I have not written this as a learned man would have done, and all my results may not have been arrived at according to the correct theory; but we were in an extraordinary position, and were obliged to depend on our own resources. We placed our entire trust in the mercy of God; and He ever watched over and protected us.

We none of us slept much during the last night. At the dawn of day the cannon of the ship announced the order to go on board. We conducted our children to the shore; there they received our last embraces and benedictions.

The anchor has been weighed, the sails unfurled, the flag run up to the mast-head, and a rapid wind promises speedily to separate us from our children.

I will not attempt to paint the grief of my dear Elizabeth—it is the grief of a mother, silent and profound. Jack and Ernest are weeping bitterly, and my own grief and heartfelt sorrow is, I must confess, but badly concealed.

I finish these few lines whilst the ship's boat is waiting. My sons will thus receive my last blessing. May God ever be with you. Adieu, Europe! adieu, dear Switzerland! Never shall I see you again! May your inhabitants be always happy, pious, and free!

PENGUIN POPULAR CLASSICS

Published or forthcoming

PENGUIN POPULAR CLASSICS

PENGUIN POPULAR CLASSICS